Acclaim for the Psychic Eye Mystery Series

"Intuition tells me this book is right on target—I sense a hit!"   —Madelyn Alt, author of *Home for a Spell*

"Paranormal romance fans should turn to Victoria Laurie's Psychic Eye Mysteries. . . . These novels are superfast, easy reads, and if you like to mix a bit of witty banter with suspense and a touch of mysticism, this series is for you."
                                        —Examiner.com

"Delivers a smooth, fast-paced read. . . . Humor lightens the overall tone, while the story line captures your attention and doesn't let go until the final pages. . . . Don't miss this one."   —Monsters and Critics

"Abby Cooper is a character I hope will be around for a long time."   —Spinetingler Magazine

"Laurie's books are a delight to devour."
    —Savannah Russe, author of *Dark Night, Dark Dreams*

"Natural pacing and humor."   —*Kirkus Reviews*

"It doesn't take a crystal ball to tell it will be well worth reading."   —Mysterious Reviews

"A great new series . . . plenty of action!"
                                        —*Midwest Book Review*

"An edge-of-your-seat mystery."   —Darque Reviews

"A fabulous who-done-it."   —The Best Reviews

"Readers will understand the meaning of mission impossible when they try to put the novel down."
                                        —Genre Go Round Reviews

"Plenty of surprises and revelations in the exciting story line."   —Gumshoe

"Full of plots, subplots, mystery, and murder, yet it is all handled so deftly."   —The Mystery Reader

continued . . .

"An invigorating entry into the cozy mystery realm. . . . I cannot wait for the next book."   —Roundtable Reviews

"Victoria Laurie has crafted a fantastic tale in this latest Psychic Eye Mystery. There are few things in life that upset Abby Cooper, but ghosts and her parents feature high on her list . . . giving the reader a few real frights and a lot of laughs."   —Fresh Fiction

Acclaim for the *New York Times* Bestselling M. J. Holliday, Ghost Hunter Mysteries

"Victoria Laurie is the queen of paranormal mysteries."
    —BookReview.com

"Reminiscent of Buffy the Vampire's bunch, Laurie's enthusiastic, punchy ghost busters make this paranormal series one teens can also enjoy."   —*Publishers Weekly*

"Laurie's new paranormal series lights up the night."
    —Elaine Viets, Anthony and Agatha
    award–winning author of *Final Sail*

"Filled with laugh-out-loud moments and nail-biting, hair-raising tension, this fast-paced, action-packed ghost story will keep readers hooked from beginning to end."—Fresh Fiction

"[A] fun, suspenseful, fast-paced paranormal mystery. All the elements combine to make this entry in the Ghost Hunter series a winner."   —The Romance Readers Connection

"A lighthearted, humorous haunted hotel horror thriller kept focused by 'graveyard' serious M.J."
    —Genre Go Round Reviews

"Ms. Laurie has penned a fabulous read and packed it with ghost-hunting action at its best. With a chilling mystery, a danger-filled investigation, a bit of romance, and a wonderful dose of humor, there's little chance that readers will be able to set this book down."   —Darque Reviews

"A bewitching book blessed with many blithe spirits. Will leave you breathless."

    —Nancy Martin, author of the
    Blackbird Sisters Mysteries

The Psychic Eye Mystery Series

Abby Cooper, Psychic Eye
Better Read Than Dead
A Vision of Murder
Killer Insight
Crime Seen
Death Perception
Doom with a View
A Glimpse of Evil
Vision Impossible

The Ghost Hunter Mystery Series

What's a Ghoul to Do?
Demons Are a Ghoul's Best Friend
Ghouls Just Haunt to Have Fun
Ghouls Gone Wild
Ghouls, Ghouls, Ghouls
Ghoul Interrupted
What a Ghoul Wants

LETHAL
OUTLOOK

A Psychic Eye Mystery

Victoria Laurie

AN OBSIDIAN MYSTERY

OBSIDIAN
Published by the Penguin Group
Penguin Group (USA) Inc., 375 Hudson Street,
New York, New York 10014, USA

USA | Canada | UK | Ireland | Australia | New Zealand | India | South Africa | China

Penguin Books Ltd., Registered Offices: 80 Strand, London WC2R 0RL, England
For more information about the Pnguin Group visit penguin.com.

Published by Obsidian, an imprint of New American Library, a division of
Penguin Group (USA) Inc. First published in an Obsidian hardcover edition.

First Obsidian Mass Market Printing, June 2013
10 9 8 7 6 5 4 3 2 1

ISBN 978-0-451-41490-8

Printed in the United States of America

PUBLISHER'S NOTE
This is a work of fiction. Names, characters, places, and incidents either are the
product of the author's imagination or are used fictitiously, and any resem-
blance to actual persons, living or dead, business establishments, events, or
locales is entirely coincidental.
   The publisher does not have any control over and does not assume any responsibility for author or third-party Web sites or their content.

For all the Teekos, Cats, and Candices in my life.
Love you, my sisters!

Acknowledgments

I love writing the acknowledgments for each book. It's my chance to call out all the wonderfully special people in my life and tell them how much I love and appreciate them. Way better than a Christmas card, don't you think? ☺

So, without further ado, allow me to dive right in!

Thanks go to my wonderful and amazing editor, Mrs. Sandra Harding-Hull. You're so good to me, my friend, and I appreciate so very much how wonderful you are to work with. May the years of our continued partnership be long and prosperous!

Also, very special thanks to my fantabulous agent, Mr. Jim McCarthy. You're my brother from another mother, guy, and I hearts you huge.

Gratitude to the most amazing editorial assistant EVER! Ms. Elizabeth Bistrow is a sheer delight to work with and talk to. Girl, you always come through for me, and I appreciate it!

Must mention the fantabulous Ms. Sharon Gamboa here as well, because she works harder than anyone I know to support me and the books on the retail side.

Extended thanks to all the rest of my NAL team who time and again I'm pretty sure I test the patience of. Thank you, guys, for putting up with me—Last-minute Laurie.

Very special hugs go out to Katie Coppedge, who keeps the Web site rockin' and helps with all those newsletters! She's also, like, the nicest person on the planet and one of my very best friends, which I think helps a little.

My sister Sandy Upham, whose laugh I live to hear at least five times a week, and who constantly inspires me and feeds me fun little tidbits to use for Cat . . . who is *loosely* based on her. (Loooooosely!)

Last, please let me rattle off a few of the names in my inner circle—these are such special people, as they continually support, encourage, listen to, and, yes, even ply me with cakeballs, and they are (in no particular order): Jackie Barrett; Karen Ditmars; Leanne Tierney; Nora, Bob, Mike, and Nick Brosseau; Shannon Anderson; Hilary Laurie; my nephews, Matt and Mike Morrill; Steve McGrory; Thomas Robinson; Silas Hudson; Suzanne Parsons; Drue Rowean; Betty and Pippa Stocking; John Kwiatkowski; Juan Tamayo; Rick Michael; Molly Boyle; and Martha Bushko.

If I left anyone important out . . . apologies and cakeballs are on me. ☺

Chapter One

It was four forty-five p.m. and I was still stewing. I'd been stewing a solid nine hours now, and I was likely to continue to stew for as long as it took for me to finish working, get home, confront my fiancé, and really give him a piece of my mind.

The reason for said stew-fest was currently sitting on my desk, tucked into a beautifully polished beech-wood box, wrapped with a big red bow. It'd been waiting for me on the kitchen table with a love note and a fresh mug of coffee that morning.

Still, I shook my head at the box and grumbled anew.

The bell above the main entrance gave a jingle. "Abby?" I heard my business partner and best friend call from the tiny foyer.

"In here!"

Candice, fresh from the salon and looking more beautiful than any girl has a right to, sauntered into my office, took one look at my face, and said, "Cocktail?"

I eyed the clock and sighed. "You have no idea how much I'd like to take you up on that, but I've got a client at five and I can't leave."

Candice nodded like she already understood my woes. Coming in and sitting down across from me, she said, "Dutch?"

Huh. Lookit that. She did understand. I waved at the polished box on the edge of my desk. "He gave me an early wedding present."

Dutch and I were getting married in exactly forty-five days, which, hopefully, would give me just enough time to walk down the aisle without the assistance of a cane, a goal my physical therapist and I were intent on making.

Candice reached for the box, then hesitated. "May I?"

"Knock yourself out," I said with a sigh.

My friend carefully slid the ribbon off and lifted the catch; opening the lid and peeking inside, she whistled appreciatively. "Nice," she said.

"Nice?" I snapped. "You think it's *nice*?"

Candice's eyes darted quickly back and forth between the present and me, clearly not sure where to go with that. It didn't matter. The floodgates had opened, and out came my inner tsunami. "He gave me a *gun*, Candice! A GUN! *What* kind of a man thinks it's appropriate to give his soon-to-be bride a *lethal weapon* for a wedding gift?"

Candice smirked and ducked her chin. "A Republican?"

I narrowed my eyes suspiciously and nodded. "Yeah. And a gun-totin', NRA-lovin', small-government-supportin' one at that!" (You're probably not going to be surprised to hear that my politics lean a *weeeeeeeeensy* bit more to the left.)

Candice chuckled and lifted out the offensive object to consider it. "You know, Abs," she said in that irritatingly calm way she had, "I could totally see your point if this weren't such a sweet weapon—for you in particular." I opened my mouth to spout new protests to the contrary, but she cut me off. "Let me finish! This is a .38 Special, right?"

I clenched my jaw, rolled my eyes, sighed heavily, then nodded.

"It's the new Bodyguard Smith and Wesson, right?" Candice added. She released the chamber to check for bullets, and, finding none, closed the chamber and pointed the gun at the wall to her left.

"Yeah. So?"

Candice pushed a little knob at the top of the grip and a red dot appeared on the wall. She whistled again. "Integrated laser and a polymer grip. Sundance, this is one sweet weapon."

"You want it?"

Candice laughed lightly before tucking the gun back inside the box. "I can't think of a better weapon for you, honey."

"Candice, you're supposed to be on *my* side."

"I *am* on your side! Abs, don't you think Dutch already knows how much you hate guns?"

Recent enthusiastic history with a CIA weapons trainer aside, I had an intense dislike for guns and avoided handling them at all costs. "I seriously *do* hate them," I said.

"Exactly." Candice leaned back in her chair like I'd just made her whole case. "You make no secret about it, as Dutch well knows."

My brow furrowed. "So he gave me something he knows I'll hate just to show me how much he cares?"

Candice grinned. "No, fool. He gave you something

he knows will protect you, in spite of the fact that you hate it. And he got you a gun that's lightweight, compact, easy to load, absorbs recoil, and has an integrated laser so that even *you* couldn't possibly miss. Don't you get it, Abs?"

"I seriously don't."

Candice leaned forward to rest her elbows on my desk. "Would you say that Dutch spends a fair amount of time worrying about you?"

I scowled at Candice. She knew dang well Dutch spent much more than a "fair" amount of time worrying about me. He once dubbed me Trouble's Mecca. "Yeah. So?"

"And it's not without good reason, right?"

"It's not like I go *looking* for trouble, Candice!" I was getting a little irritated with this line of questioning.

"Of course you don't," she said calmly. "But you have to admit that your line of work has gotten you into some pretty dicey situations."

"Oh, for cripes' sake! I'm a professional psychic. Last time I checked, that wasn't one of the top ten most dangerous jobs."

"You're a professional psychic who now freelances for both the FBI and the CIA. You're also a business partner to one badass private eye," Candice said, bouncing her eyebrows.

"What's your point?"

"My point is that the panic button on your key fob and that little can of pepper spray you carry around in your purse aren't enough to protect you from the very dangerous criminals you encounter these days, toots. It's way past time you grew a pair and got yourself armed. Dutch knows you would never properly arm yourself on your own, and he likely also knows that if he just randomly brought you home a gun, you'd take it back within the hour. So instead, he's given it to you wrapped in a big red ribbon of love as a wedding present, because he's telling you he worries and he wants his wife to be safe. And to make it as painless as possible, he's gotten you a really sweet weapon tailor-made for you."

I stared hard at her, then at the box, then back at Candice. "How come you know what Dutch is thinking better than I do?"

Candice's grin widened. "Because I'm also a gun-totin', NRA-lovin', small-government-supportin' Republican, just like him."

I felt the corners of my mouth quirk too. "I'm surrounded by the enemy."

Candice leaned over the desk to squeeze my hand. "Give it time; we'll bring you around."

She then got up to walk out of the room, only to return a minute later with a white box I recognized. "These should fit," she said, opening the lid to my present and taking out the gun to load it with hollow points.

"You keep bullets in your office?"

Candice continued to load the gun without looking up. "Doesn't everyone?"

"Nooooooo," I said with a laugh. Then I started to feel like I was being handled by my business partner and fiancé. "You really don't need to do that," I told her.

Candice paused to eye me critically. "An unloaded gun does you no good, Sundance. Keep it in the box if you want, but keep it loaded."

At that moment we heard the bell above the front door give another jingle. Candice pumped the last bullet into the chamber and tucked the weapon away quickly.

"Better let you get to your client," she said, handing me my cane from where it was leaning against the wall.

I got stiffly to my feet, thanked her, and took the cane, wincing with that first step, which was always the most painful.

My body was still recovering from an awful accident I'd had several months earlier when Dutch and I had been on a mission for the CIA. The mission had ultimately been a success, but we'd both nearly died in a plane crash. We'd been incredibly lucky to survive, but I'd broken my pelvis in three places. The doctors had warned me that my recovery would be slow and often uncomfortable. I hadn't realized how much they'd sugarcoated it until I started my physical therapy. I was in near-constant pain and made progress in centimeters. There were many days, in fact, when I believed my recovery moved backward. It was one reason I was glad that my regular day job of doing psychic readings for a growing list of clients allowed me to set my own schedule, and I could take plenty of breaks and days off if needed.

I hobbled out to the waiting room and was nearly brought up short. Ms. Smith—my client—stood nervous and fidgety just inside the door. She was adorned in a large Sunday hat, red wig, Jackie O sunglasses, and bright red lipstick. Even though it was nearly eighty degrees outside, she had on a trench coat, scarf, and black leather gloves.

I wondered if she had some sort of hypersensitivity to the sun, because her only exposed skin was on her nose, mouth, and chin, but the wig was throwing me, and it was so obviously a wig. "Ms. Smith?" I asked.

Her face turned toward me, and my sixth sense picked up the waves of anxiety radiating off her. "Yes," she said; then she seemed to search for something to add but settled for, "Yes," again.

A lot of clients get very nervous when they first come to see me. So many people have a fear about what we psychics can see or predict. And the reputation for psychics as bad-news bearers is not without some merit: I've met several "professional" readers who dig deep for anything alarming they can say to their clients just to make themselves look "gifted." It irritates me no end.

"It's great to meet you," I said calmly, extending my hand. Sometimes the best way to battle someone else's fear is to simply remain as composed and professional as possible. She took my hand, pumped it once, and let go.

"We're right in here," I offered, turning to lead her down the hall, deeper in the suite of offices.

After I'd been released from the hospital, my wonderful friend and business partner had practically (literally) hauled me out of bed with the goal of finding the perfect office space in which to hang our respective shingles. While it was true that Candice and I teamed up quite often on cases she acquired, we each still retained a bit of autonomy with respect to our individual businesses.

So we needed a setting that could accommodate all three scenarios—my readings, Candice's private eye business, and the joint investigations we partnered up on.

After a week of looking (and some complaining on my part . . . cough, cough), we'd finally found a gorgeous suite of four offices and a cozy waiting area in a three-story professional building on Austin's north side. The new digs were located just off Highway 360—which was easily the most beautiful highway in all of Austin—and the road leading up to our building ascended straight into the hills, giving us spectacular views from every window.

I'd fallen in love with the space the moment I set eyes on it, and Candice and I had hung our shingles ten seconds after signing the lease. I'd finished decorating my little suite only three weeks earlier and was encouraged that my reputation and marketing efforts were starting to pay off—I had a small list of referrals, which was growing day by day. I was also kept afloat by the cold-case work I did freelancing as a consultant for the FBI. All in all, I was starting to eke out a real living again, and that felt awesome.

I led my client into the room I used exclusively for conducting my readings and felt the lovely energy of the space waft over me.

I'd had the space painted a dusky rose, the shutters were chocolate brown, and espresso high-back leather wing chairs were arranged to face each other. I'd kept the room fairly spartan, with only two accent tables, a credenza, and some choice crystals placed in small artistic clusters about the room.

Moving stiffly to my chair, I eased my way into it, much like a heavily pregnant woman. When I looked up, I caught that Ms. Smith's lips were pursed and what I could see of her brow was slightly furrowed. "Were you injured in an auto accident?" she asked.

"Yes," I lied. It was easier to tell people that Dutch and I had been in a car wreck than to tell them that the CIA had recruited us for an undercover espionage mission that had nearly ended our lives. Plus, if I told them about the mission, I'd have to kill them. (Ha, ha, ha! Yep. *Still* funny!)

"Who was at fault?" my client asked, which I thought was a very odd question.

"Uh . . ." Her question threw me, and for a minute I didn't know how to respond.

She held up her hand. "Sorry," she said, taking her seat. "Occupational hazard. The minute I hear someone's been in a car accident, I automatically ask who's to blame."

"You're an attorney," I said. That wasn't my sixth sense talking; that was just a natural assumption.

"I am. But please, don't begin telling me about my job or my future until I get a chance to tell you why I'm here."

She seemed to get all nervous and twitchy again, and for the life of me I couldn't understand the fear. So I simply motioned for her to tell me whatever she needed to before I switched on the old radar.

"I'm not here about myself," she began. "I'm here about a friend."

Ahhh . . . the old "my *friend* needs a reading" excuse. Yeah. I'd heard that one before. I barely resisted the urge to roll my eyes. "Okay," I said easily. "No worries. I can use your energy as a jumping-off point to get to your friend. Just tell me his or her name, and I'll take a look at—"

"No," Ms. Smith said—a bit too quickly, I thought. "You see, it's complicated."

Isn't it always?

"It's not really about a friend," she explained, staring at the ground as if she were laying out the pieces of whatever was troubling her. "It's about a client."

"Of mine?" I was getting lost and we'd only just started.

"No. A client who has recently retained my firm to represent them should the police get wind of certain details."

"Details?" I asked, switching on my radar because this was starting to creep me out a little.

"I'll be blunt," she said, tugging on the leather fingers of her gloves. "This client has broken the law. Several laws. And if anyone knew that I'd come to you with this, I would face immediate disbarment for breaking my firm's attorney-client privilege."

I squinted at Ms. Smith while I sifted through the ether surrounding her and listened to what she was saying. There was a whole lotta stuff in the ether to sort through. Most of the energy was heavy, and charged with a grim outlook, as if this woman carried the weight of the world with her when she'd decided to come see me.

In her energy I detected secrecy, anxiety, deception, and something that made me really take note. Violence. The woman had this lurking cloud of dark energy that hovered menacingly just behind her. I didn't think she was the source, but she knew who was, and she wasn't at all confident that she could keep this particular wolf at bay. The realization made me cold with fear for her, and I couldn't put these pieces together yet to form a more detailed picture, but whatever this woman was involved in, it was seriously dangerous.

"You're here because you're terrified," I told her. "But you're not afraid of disbarment; you're afraid of your client."

Her head jerked back a little in surprise. "You're reading me," she said—her tone accusing.

"A little," I admitted. "Ms. Smith, whoever this client of yours is, he or she cannot be trusted. Your client is dangerous—to you directly and to others. In fact," I added, following the intuitive thread, "I think this person has seriously harmed someone. I'm not even sure the victim survived."

Ms. Smith licked her lips nervously. "Yes," she said. "I know. You're right. The victim didn't survive. But no one knows that yet. The family doesn't even realize it yet. They're still hopeful she'll come home. But she won't. And I can't tell you who, or where, and I certainly can't tell you why, but I've heard a great deal about your abilities, Miss Cooper, and I was hoping you could figure out what happened to the girl and let the family know. Give them some peace. Some closure. And maybe, just maybe, you could point the police in the right direction. I'm the best defense attorney at my firm, and if I go to court with this, then of course I'll give a vigorous defense, but I'm a skillful lawyer. Skillful enough to make it look like I'm trying to keep my client out of jail without really giving it my best effort, if you know what I mean?"

I shook my head. I didn't really know what she meant, and she was apparently giving me far too much credit. "You're going to have to fill me in a little more, Ms. Smith. I'm psychic, not a mind reader."

"Watch the news," she said ominously. "You'll know it when you see it. I need you to take the case. I read up on you and discovered that you often consult with the FBI on some of their hardest cold cases. I'd recommend you to the family, of course, but I can't be linked to this. It's far too dangerous for me, and I've taken a huge risk in coming here. I'm sorry, but that's all I can say."

With that, Ms. Smith got up. "Wait!" I said, alarmed that she appeared to be leaving. She'd given me nothing, just a bunch of cryptic instructions and disjointed impressions.

"I can't answer any more of your questions, Ms. Cooper. I've already said too much. You'll have to think about everything I've told you and start from there, all right?"

I shook my head vigorously. "No," I said. "You

haven't given me anything substantial, Ms. Smith! Even the cold cases I work on for the FBI at least have a body or the name of a missing person to work from."

But it was no use. My client was already halfway out the door. Still, she did pause at the door to say over her shoulder, "I hope you'll help, but I'll understand if you can't or won't."

I sat there with my mouth agape, struggling to find the words to keep her a little longer so that I could pull more from the ether around her, but I think she was onto me, because she turned away quickly and was gone.

Chapter Two

I sat there for a bit, blinking and wondering why I always attracted Trouble with a capital *T*. I'm a good person . . . fairly good person . . . mostly . . . sometimes . . . In the grand scheme of things, I'm a relatively good person, okay?

The point is, why was *I* always the one in the middle of every big hot mess that came along?

And if you're wondering if there was any doubt in my mind as to whether Ms. Smith represented a big hot mess—allow me to clear that up right now: I knew with absolute certainty that Trouble had just come in through my door, sat down only long enough to hint at the big hot mess to come, and then left me with the impression that it was now my responsibility to clean it all up.

And that's the trouble with Trouble. It's always a pain in the asterisk.

"Candice!" I yelled.

"Yeah?" she called back.

I didn't answer. I knew if I just waited long enough, she'd come to me, which, given my physical condition, better suited the situation (and my aching hips).

Sure enough, a few seconds later she appeared in my doorway. "You okay, Sundance?"

I motioned to the chair opposite me. "Have a seat."

Once my partner had gotten comfortable, I filled her in on my mysterious client. Candice did her own blinking thing for a while before she said, "Huh."

My brow furrowed. "That's all you got? Just 'huh'?"

"It's pretty cryptic, Sundance."

I sighed. "Yeah, but there's enough there to chew on. I mean, we know that she's an attorney at a firm that's representing someone who's committed some sort of crime that may or may not have resulted in the mortal wounding of a third party, and that said attorney's client is the dangerous sort."

Candice shrugged. "Abs, three-quarters of the firms in Austin have clients like that. She didn't happen to give you the name of this mortally wounded third party, did she?"

I shook my head. "No, but she did say to watch the news."

Candice glanced at her watch. "The six o'clock news should be on in about half an hour. If we leave now, we can kill two birds with one stone."

I got stiffly to my feet. "Which two birds is that again?"

Candice ticked them off on her fingers. "Happy hour and the broadcast."

"Ah," I said, limping toward the door. "I like how you put them in order of importance."

We arrived at our favorite happy-hour bar, found a table near the TV, ordered up some nachos, and waited for the local news. Okay, so while we waited we may have downed something called a prickly pear margarita, but only because our brains needed to be properly lubricated for when the news came on and we searched the broadcast for clues about what the heck Ms. Smith was talking about.

Luck was with us; the subject of my mysterious client's visit wasn't hard to miss. It was the lead story, in fact. "The Austin Police Department needs your help locating the whereabouts of a young mother missing from her home on Austin's east side," said the news anchor.

I leaned forward and focused on the screen as the picture of a sweet-looking young woman, probably no older than thirty, flashed onto the screen. I bit my lip when I saw how flat and two-dimensional her image was. It's a weird psychic quirk of mine to be able to tell from a photograph when someone's dead, and this woman had indeed already crossed to the other side.

The coverage then shifted to a news reporter in the field. "Kendra Moreno disappeared from her home under suspicious circumstances two days ago, leaving her one-year-old son alone in his crib," the reporter began. "Her husband, Tristan Moreno, told APD detectives that he arrived home at approximately five thirty p.m. on September twenty-eighth to find no sign of his wife, and her purse, wallet, and cell phone still inside the house, while her car was missing from the garage. Also according to APD there was no sign of forced entry into the home, and the last time Kendra Moreno was heard from was earlier that morning at approximately ten a.m., when she clicked the 'like' button on one of her Facebook friend's status updates.

"Police believe the missing woman may not have left

the home willingly, but no sign of a struggle was evident. Police and the woman's family are reaching out to the community for assistance in helping to locate her. If you have any information on Kendra Moreno's whereabouts, or if you may have seen anything suspicious near the family home last Wednesday, you're asked to call the APD tip line."

The number flashed on the screen, and then the reporter signed off from her location in East Austin.

Candice swiveled in her seat to face me. "Well?"

I leaned back in my own chair so that our waiter could set down a huge plate of nachos, but truth be told, I suddenly wasn't so hungry. Once he'd left, I said, "She's dead."

Candice nodded like she had assumed as much. "Murdered?"

I sighed. "It seems like it, doesn't it? I mean, if Kendra is who Smith was talking about, then yeah, she was probably murdered."

"By the husband?" Candice asked next.

I shrugged. There'd been no photo or news footage of Kendra's husband, so it was really hard to tell. "Not sure."

Candice lifted a chip from the top of the stack and crunched on it thoughtfully. She then took a sip from the fresh margarita our waiter had just set in front of her. I watched and waited her out. For once I didn't want it to be my call.

"What do you want to do?" she asked when it was obvious I wasn't going to speak.

I threw the question back at her. "I'll go along with whatever you want to do."

Candice smiled knowingly. "Nice dodge, Sundance."

I pulled up on a chip; it came with three cheesy friends. "After the year I've had, can you blame me?"

"You want to take a pass on this one?"

"Do you?"

"No. I want to take it on."

I frowned. "Crap. I knew you'd say that."

"I have no problem investigating solo, if you want to sit this one out, Abs," she said kindly.

My frown deepened. "What if the family doesn't have the money to hire you?"

"Then I'll do it pro bono." Oh, yeah. I forgot. She didn't need the money anymore.

I still hadn't answered Candice's question, which I knew was a total dodge, but the truth was that I was tired of Trouble. I was tired of always being the one to get involved and then get hurt. I'd been beaten up but good over the years, and my broken pelvis wasn't even the worst.

"Well?" Candice said, eyeing me again. "You in? Or do you want to sit this one out?"

I shook my head no. Vigorously. "Yeah, okay," I said at the same time.

Candice laughed. "That's what I love about you, Sundance. You're a straight shooter. Never a mixed signal from you."

I smirked. "I'm in. But I'm in under protest."

"As long as you're sure," she mocked.

We ate and drank in silence for a little while, watching the weather—both of us relieved to see some rain in the forecast. It doesn't rain much down here in central Texas, and since I'd grown up in Michigan—where it rains or snows with relative frequency—it always awakens an unsettling feeling in me to go several weeks without a drop of the wet stuff.

Finally I turned to Candice and asked, "Where do we start?"

"I'll call my contact at APD and take her out for coffee." Candice had recently made friends with a beat cop. I'd met the cop. She had a definite thing for Candice, which I knew my friend must have been aware of. Candice doesn't play for the girls' team, but that doesn't mean she isn't willing to flirt with someone of the same sex to get a little intel now and then.

"You think she'll know much?" I asked. Kendra's case didn't strike me as beat-cop material.

Candice shrugged. "She might. But even if she doesn't, she should be able to hook me up with one of the detectives on the case. It never hurts to nose around."

Inwardly I disagreed; I was living proof that it definitely hurt to nose around, but I kept my thoughts to myself. "Then what?"

The corners of Candice's mouth quirked. "Careful, Sundance, or I might think you're anxious to sink your teeth into this one."

I rolled my eyes. "I'm only thinking of the family. They've gotta be crazy with worry, and it's not fair to leave them hanging."

"I agree. So let me nose around and see what I can discreetly bring up about the husband and Kendra's family, and then we'll go snoop a little, okay?"

I nodded. "Sounds like a plan."

An hour and a half later Candice dropped me off at home. The prickly pears had hit me hard, and I was already unsteady enough on my feet. I invited her in for dinner, certain that my fiancé had cooked another of his fabulous meals, but she wanted to get home to her own man candy, so I didn't push it, grateful that I had such an awesome friend. "I love you," I told her as we said goodbye.

Candice grinned. "You love prickly pear margaritas too, Sundance."

I bobbed my head up and down. "Yes. I love them too."

"Say good night, Abby," she said, waving at me to close the door of the car.

"G'night, Abby." I chuckled as I pushed on the door. It closed on my cane. "Crap on a crap heap!" I groused, wobbling unsteadily while I yanked on the cane. It came free a little too easily and I lost my balance, falling back hard against Dutch's car and setting off the alarm.

"Oopsy-doopsy," I mumbled, still struggling to get my balance.

Dutch was at the front door before I'd managed to steady myself. His raised eyebrows and stern expression were a little too judgmental for my taste. "Don't take that tone with me," I snapped, waving my cane at him.

He came down the steps, used his key fob to turn off the alarm, and leaned into the open door of Candice's car. She, of course, was laughing hysterically. "What's her poison?"

"Prickly pear margaritas," said Candice.

"How many?" he asked.

"More than one less than six," she told him. The traitor. I hated her!

"She still upset about the wedding present?" Dutch asked, reaching over to latch a hand onto my arm so I wouldn't fall over.

"Yes," Candice said, purposely withholding any information about my client and Kendra Moreno. Discreet of her. Sweet of her. I loved her.

"Okay, I've got it from here," he said, closing her door firmly and waving good-bye.

I wobbled on my feet. Damn! What was in those

prickly pears anyway? "You want to try the stairs?" Dutch asked me.

"No way, hoser," I said with a giggle. For the record, stairs suck when you've fractured your pelvis.

"I figured." Dutch sighed and reached out his arms. Lifting me easily, he proceeded to carry me up the steps.

"I luff you," I told him.

His baritone laugh rose out of his chest. "Yeah, yeah," he said. "This morning when you called, I thought you were gonna kill me, but as long as we're okay now . . ."

I leaned my head on his shoulder and sighed happily. "I luff prickly pears."

The next morning came bright and early. Too bright. Way, way, *way* too early for someone with a prickly pear hangover. Muttering a disgruntled "Mmph!" I shoved myself out of bed and fell right onto the floor. Elegant, I am not.

"Edgar?" Dutch called from the first floor. Everyone in my life seems to want to give me a nickname. I'm "Sundance" to Candice (her way of suggesting that we're the female equivalent to Butch Cassidy and the Sundance Kid), and I am "Edgar" to Dutch, who nicknamed me after the only other psychic he'd ever heard of, Edgar Cayce.

"I'm fine!" I yelled before I realized that yelling wasn't such a hot idea. I crawled to the bathroom (literally), vowing to never, ever, *ever* drink again. At least, not until I fully recovered (from my hangover).

While I was in the shower, my radar gave a little warning ping. Even through the fog of my hangover, my intuition was able to get the message through. "Shih tzu!" I hissed, hurrying to wash the suds out of my hair. I figured I had five minutes before my day got off to an even worse start.

Mindless of the pounding headache and slightly queasy feeling in my stomach, I rushed out of the shower, hardly bothering to dry off, limped painfully to the closet, threw on some jeans and the first shirt I could grab, shook some of the water from my hair, and grabbed my purse, cane, and keys before gimping as quietly as possible down the steps.

Pausing at the landing, I could hear Dutch in the kitchen. It smelled like he had cinnamon buns in the oven. "Crap on a cracker!" I whispered. I loooove cinnamon buns. I'd even eat them on a queasy stomach. But there was no time. And my escape would work only if Dutch didn't catch me sneaking out of the house.

As quietly as possible, I eased over to the door, turned the latch, and slipped outside. I managed to get down the stairs with only a few muttered expletives (swearing doesn't count if you mutter), only to realize my car wasn't in the driveway.

"Feck!" (Swearing also doesn't count if you use the slang term from a foreign country.)

Looking up and down the street nervously, I spotted a gleaming silver sedan snaking its way down the road. "Feck, feck, *feck*!" Ducking low, I turned and hobbled across the lawn as fast as I could, squatting down behind my neighbor's car just in time.

Peeking through the windows, I could see the silver Mercedes slow down and turn into our driveway. I waited with a pounding heart as my sister, Cat, chatted happily into her phone while putting the car into park and turning off the engine.

For an interminably long time she sat there, gabbing it up. I began to wonder if I could sneak off and call Candice from the corner, but just as I was getting ready to move, I saw my sister hang up and open her car door.

I hunched down again and waited, hearing her designer heels click across our driveway . . . up the steps . . . then the very faint sound of our doorbell followed by my dog Eggy's bark.

Distantly, I heard Dutch call my name. I held perfectly still.

Cat rang the bell again and muttered something herself. Eggy's bark was joined by that of our other pooch, Tuttle. Finally I heard the door open and Dutch say, "Hey, Cat. Nice to see you."

He's such a good liar.

"Morning!" my sister sang. "Is Abby up?"

"She's up. I heard her in the shower a few minutes ago. She should be down in a sec. You got more wedding stuff for her to look at?"

There was something that sounded like the shifting of papers. "Yes, I do! And I'm so glad you're still home. I've got some things for you to look over too." Cat's voice drifted merrily into the interior of our house. A moment later I heard Dutch call my name again (a bit urgently, I thought), and then the door closed and I breathed a huge sigh of relief. "That was a close one," I whispered.

"Can I help you?" asked a voice right behind me.

I let out a little "Eeek!" and stood up fast, bringing my cane around defensively. My neighbor jumped back, narrowly avoiding getting his shins whacked. "Oh, I'm so sorry, Jason!" I said, feeling my cheeks heat up when I realized who it was.

He considered me for a minute, and given the fact that my hair was now dripping onto his asphalt, I could only imagine what he might be thinking. "I gotta go to work," he said after clearing his throat.

"Sure," I said, flashing him my famous toothy grin. "I gotta get to work too." I hobbled to the end of the drive without looking back and made my way down the block. When I reached the corner, I hid behind a big cedar tree and called Candice. "You gotta come get me!"

"Morning, Sundance," she said merrily.

"Candice, I'm serious! Cat's in town again and she's at my place right now!"

"Did she come packing?"

I knew that Candice meant packing wedding ideas. It was a little joke between us. "She is locked and loaded!"

"Where are you?"

"At the end of my street." I was back to whispering just in case Cat's batlike hearing could pick up my voice. "I'm hiding behind the big cedar tree next to the stop sign."

"See you in ten minutes," Candice said.

After I hung up, I dug around in my purse for a brush and began to try to comb out the wet tangles. While I was at it, my phone went off . . . several times. I declined to answer. The first call was from Dutch. The second— my sister. The third—Dutch again. He was also the fourth, fifth, and sixth calls, but Dave—our handyman/ builder—was the seventh. I dodged his call too.

As Candice pulled up, I could only imagine the voice mails. I'd get snippy from Cat. Irritated, annoyed, then downright angry from Dutch. Dave would be his usual mellow self, but he'd leave me yet another reminder that he had cabinet, paint, tile, granite, carpet, crown molding, and fixture samples for me to look at. Who knew building a house could be fraught with *so many* decisions?

Candice hit the locks and I shuffled my butt into her

front seat quick. "Move!" I yelled even before I'd closed the door.

Candice hauled ass . . . terisk. Of course, she looked for any excuse to speed off in the shiny Porsche she drove. "Did she see you?" Candice asked as she navigated the turn (on two wheels, by the feel of it).

I waited for my stomach to move out of my throat before answering. "No. I made it out before she spotted me."

My phone went off again. It was Dutch. I set the ringer to silent.

Candice cast my phone a sideways glance. "He's gonna be super–ticked off at you for dodging her again, you know."

"Yeah, yeah." I'd rather take my lumps with Dutch than face my sister.

Now, don't get me wrong. I love Cat. If I ever got into a really bad jam, she'd be the first . . . make that the second . . . uh . . . third . . . okay, she's definitely on the list somewhere of people I'd call if I got into a jam. It's just that my sister can be . . . a bit overwhelming at times. Like right now, for instance.

See, a few months ago, when Dutch and I had come home from the hospital, I'd told Cat that we'd been in an "accident" and that we were doing just fine but that I might need a little help planning my wedding—which had also been moved up from next spring to this fall.

Cat had pounced on the idea like the feline she's nicknamed for. She'd inundated my e-mail with pictures of wedding gowns, bridesmaids' dresses, cakes, wedding bands, tuxes, DJs, photographers, flower shops, reception halls, churches, etcetera, etcetera.

I reacted as I always did when faced with something

overwhelming. I ignored it. All of it. I stopped answering her e-mails—heck, I even stopped opening them. I dodged her phone calls and texts, and then she'd started calling Candice and trying to pass messages through her. Once she found out Candice was also engaged, well, Cat just about exploded with wedding-planning glee.

Candice promptly gave me a lecture about how I needed to give my sister a lecture and rein her in. But I just figured that eventually Cat would stop.

I know, I know . . . it was one strategy I should have figured would fail. Cat amped up her efforts to get my attention by launching a satellite office for her huge marketing firm in my own backyard. One minute, Cat was firmly rooted halfway across the country in Boston, and the next moment, I started seeing ads on local cable for Wright Marketing—Cat's firm. I remember gazing at the television with a mixture of shock and horror, hoping that it was only a national ad, and I'd kept that hope alive right up to the moment a local number flashed across the screen with the added announcement that Wright Marketing was opening a brand-new location in downtown Austin.

Before I knew it, Cat was flying here about once every other week to personally oversee the new satellite office and of course to torture me.

She never told me ahead of time when she was coming. She just appeared. Like a tempest. A tiny, unruly, stubborn, irritating, wedding-planner-on-steroids tempest.

So I'd resorted to the only defense I could muster. I'd put my radar to good use by checking the ether for her energy so often that it was now on automatic pilot. And it was working, because I'd managed to dodge her the last two times she'd come to town.

Still, I knew her appearance at my door that morning meant that she wasn't about to give up and she'd probably leave a bajillion samples of stuff for me to look at—which I wouldn't—and then she'd call me the following week and leave me a message suggesting that, as I had no obvious interest in providing her with an opinion, she'd gone ahead and made all the choices for me.

Dutch and I were getting married in forty-four days, and I still had *no* idea what my wedding was going to look like. Which was fine. I only cared about the "I dos" anyway. Cat could plan the whole thing if she wanted to—which clearly she did.

The only truly unsettling thing was that for a long time I'd been having a really bad feeling about the big day. I couldn't pinpoint what it was, but I knew something was likely to blow up in my face. I think that's why I stayed out of it. If I got involved, then it'd upset me if something went crazy wrong with the caterer, or the cake, or the band, or the dress, or the photographer, or whatever could go wrong at a wedding. I figured the more removed I was, the more objective I could be when said crisis hit.

"Hey, Abs?" Candice said, pulling me out of my thoughts.

"Yeah?"

"Can you try not to drip on the leather seats?"

I draped my long, tangled hair forward over my shoulder. "Sorry. My radar warned me that Cat was coming while I was in the shower. I didn't even have time to put in conditioner."

"I can see that. And you got dressed in the dark too, I'm assuming?"

I looked down at myself. I was wearing one of Dutch's old shirts and jeans I'd last worn to paint our bedroom. "Can I borrow something from your closet?"

Candice made another turn. "Yes, ma'am," she said. "I'm having coffee with Officer Purcell in the café downstairs from my place anyway. You can clean up and put on something more appropriate at the condo."

"Will Brice be home?" Brice Harrison was Candice's fiancé and Dutch's boss. He was my boss too, but only when I was consulting for the bureau. We got along great now, but our beginning had been a little rough. Still, I really didn't want to clean up and change with my boss in the next room.

"He left early this morning," Candice told me. "He's got a meeting with Director Gaston at eleven and he wants to be prepared."

"Gaston's in town?" I adored FBI regional director Bill Gaston and considered him the smartest man in the bureau. He's Brice's boss (Dutch's boss's boss) and a real bigwig at the bureau, but he'd never put on airs with me.

"I can drop you at the office after coffee if you'd like to say hi," Candice offered.

I considered that for a few seconds. "Nah. Dutch will be there, and if he sees me, I know I'm gonna catch holy hell for sticking him with Cat." (Oops, another quarter for the swear jar.)

Candice eyed me over the rim of her sunglasses. "Can you blame him?"

I sighed. "Not really."

We got to Candice's condo and took the elevator all the way up to the thirty-eighth floor (Candice likes a view) and into her loft. I hurried into the bathroom, jumped in the shower to use her conditioner, then got ready while she brought me a few clothing selections.

I opted for a pair of black slacks and a teal sleeveless silk top with a turquoise brooch arranged decoratively at the bosom. Given the fact that I was still hobbling around with a cane, Candice let me have my pick of shoes, and I thanked my lucky stars that she was only a half size up from me. I went with a pair of strappy flat sandals that showed off a recent pedicure.

After I'd made myself presentable, we headed back down to street level and around the corner to the neighborhood café. I'd met Officer Purcell once before when she came up to the office after having had lunch with Candice. It'd been pretty obvious from that first introduction that Purcell had a crush on Candice. It'd also been pretty obvious that she considered me the competition.

I was fairly certain that Candice had filled Purcell in on the fact that she had fiancé, but for whatever reason, the officer seemed to think I was more of a threat than Brice. Maybe it was because Candice and I were business partners. Maybe because we were also best friends. Whatever the reason, I was determined to put on a good face for the meeting.

As we came closer to the café, I saw Purcell sitting outside at one of the tables. She spotted Candice and lit up like a Christmas tree. Then she spotted me and the fuse blew.

I waved enthusiastically and flashed her a big ol' smile. I'm nothing if not obnoxious. "Play nice," Candice warned out the side of her mouth.

"Don't I always?" My smile was as wide as Kansas and my wave began to take on a frantic appearance.

"No," Candice said evenly. "Which is why I'm telling you to knock it off."

I lowered my hand and a little of the toothy wattage and waited for my partner to take the lead with Purcell. "Gwen!" she said, extending her arms wide for an impromptu hug with the beat cop.

"Hey, Candy," said Purcell, squeezing back tightly. I caught her sniffing Candice's hair. (Ah, Candice Fusco, breaking hearts everywhere.)

They parted and Candice motioned to me. "You remember my partner, Abby Cooper?"

I stuck out my hand like I was drawing a trusty six-shooter. "Good morning, Officer Purcell! It's so good to see you again! I'm sorry if we kept you waiting."

Purcell barely looked at me and she gave my hand a pretty limp-wristed pump. "Hi," she said—which I thought was also a bit limp wristed.

The wattage on my smile amped back up again. "Hey, Candice, how about an espresso?" My tone was perhaps just a weeeee bit tight.

"That'd be great, Abby," Candice said stiffly, with a hint of warning in her eyes.

"I'll be back in a jiff!" I gimped quickly away. My personal tolerance for rudeness hovers just a smidge above zero. Rude, mean, or overtly cranky people set me off and often bring out my own inner snarky side. I figured the five or ten minutes it took me to get through the line and order the coffee might be just long enough to cool my jets—lest I say something I might regret.

Unfortunately, at this normally very popular café the line was nonexistent, so my cappuccino and Candice's espresso came up lickety-split.

I returned outside, juggling my cane, our drinks, and three scones (in an attempt to play nicey-nice with Officer Moody, I'd purchased her a baked good), only to find Candice and Purcell still exchanging pleasantries. Well, Candice was exchanging pleasantries. Purcell was openly flirting.

"That was fast," Candice said, and not in a way that suggested she was entirely happy about it.

"There was no line," I told her, taking my seat and vowing to eat my scone quietly. "I brought you a scone too, Officer Purcell." I placed it in front of her and tucked a folded napkin next to the wrapped bun.

"I'm on a low-carb diet," she said without even looking at the scone.

My eyes dropped to the tabletop, where I counted to ten.

Candice jumped in quickly. "The reason I called for coffee, Gwen, is that Abby and I are thinking of getting involved in a local missing-person's case."

"Oh, yeah?" she asked. "Which one?"

I glanced up to see Candice taken aback. "There's more than one?"

Purcell chuckled. "There're almost two million people in the Austin metro area, Candy. Of course there's more than one."

"Ah," Candice said. "Good point. We were thinking of looking into the Kendra Moreno case."

Purcell scoffed. "Good luck."

Candice cocked her head. "Tough case so far?"

"Word is that it's turning into one of the toughest," Purcell told her. "CSI was all over that house and found nothing—and I mean *nothing*—to indicate foul play. It's like the woman just disappeared into thin air. You ask me, she got sick of being a stay-at-home mom, planned this whole vanishing act, and split on the husband and kid."

"But why would she leave her son?" Candice pressed.

"I mean, I heard on the news that the husband found the little toddler alone in the house with no supervision. What mother would just walk out on her child like that?"

Purcell merely shrugged like she didn't know and didn't much care. Candice pushed for a little more, though. "Is there any evidence that maybe Kendra was struggling with depression or mental illness?"

"The detectives are still working through all that," Purcell said, taking a sip of her coffee. "The parents are convinced something happened to their daughter, and the husband's already lawyered up."

"The husband's already got an attorney?" I asked with a meaningful look at my partner.

Purcell kept her eyes on Candice when she answered. "Yep. Which looks a little suspicious, don't it?"

It did, but for even more reasons than Purcell currently understood.

"Who's the attorney?" Candice asked almost casually.

Purcell eyed her quizzically. "Does it matter? Defense attorneys are all scum, if you ask me."

Candice made a note in her pad before backing up the conversation with her next question. "So why do you believe Kendra planned this vanishing act and took off on her own?"

"Well, it's either one or the other, isn't it?" Purcell said. "I mean, either the husband did it and we'll have a hell of a time finding the body—if we ever do—or she ran off because she didn't want to be a mom anymore."

I was liking Purcell less and less as the conversation progressed, and I'd started by not liking her at all. Still, I kept my opinions and any further comments to myself.

Candice continued to probe for info over the course of the next ten minutes, but it was pretty evident that the officer didn't have anything significant to offer us. It was clear that we'd enter the case with very little to go on. "Can you get me a copy of the case file?" Candice asked near the end of my patience level for Purcell.

The beat cop tilted her chin back and laughed heartily. "Not likely, Candy." Candice frowned and Purcell softened. "Listen, the best I can do is give you the name of the lead detective, but I gotta be straight with you: APD ain't gonna like a private investigator with a *psychic* tagalong butting into their business."

Purcell had actually used air quotes around the word "psychic." I wanted to sock her in the nose. I felt Candice's firm hand on my wrist under the table. "I get the fact that APD, as a whole, is pretty skeptical about any intuitive insight," she said calmly. "But our track record speaks for itself, and the fact that Abby has worked for other police departments as well as the FBI and the CIA should carry some weight."

"Not around here," Purcell replied. "And not with a mandate from the DA about how no one in the department is to solicit or take info from any so-called psychics." At this point, Purcell actually looked at me. "Around here," she said, "law enforcement thinks people like you are a joke."

I could feel my face flush and my heart start to pound. For an instant I saw red and I badly wanted to unleash my temper on the woman looking at me like I was garbage. Instead I got up, gathering my coffee cup and napkin, and said, "If you'll excuse me."

I gimped my way back into the coffee shop and found a table in the corner. I sat down, turned my back to the other patrons, and worked to quell my anger and hurt feelings.

Candice found me just a few minutes later. "I'm so sorry," she said gently, taking up the seat next to me.

My eyes were brimming with tears, and I didn't know whether it was because I was mad that Purcell had hurt my feelings or because I was ticked off at a world that likely would never completely accept what I could do. There were just too many people like Purcell out there who would scoff at the very notion that I actually had a legitimate talent. "It's fine," I said, blinking furiously and donning my sunglasses so that she wouldn't see how upset I was.

"Hey," Candice said, wrapping an arm around my shoulders. "She just doesn't know how amazing you are, Abs."

I nodded and swallowed hard. "It's fine," I repeated. Candice hardly looked convinced. "Really," I said, getting up from the stool where I'd been having my little pity party and motioning for us to go.

Once we were outside walking back toward the parking garage, I took a deep, steadying breath and was able to say more than two words. "Did she give you anything more after I left?"

"Nope," Candice said. "But I sure as hell gave *her* an earful."

I stopped walking. "Wait, you what?"

"I reamed her out," Candice said, still moving.

I hobbled hastily to catch up with her. "Why would you do something like that? She was your only source at the APD and she has a gigantic crush on you! Someone like her could be a *huge* asset to you in the future. Especially if she climbs up the ranks."

Candice wrapped her arm around me again. "As long as she's such a bitch to you, Sundance, she's no good to me. There'll be other sources. And if not, well . . . as long as I've got you for a partner, why would I really need anyone else?"

My eyes welled up again, but for a completely different reason this time.

Chapter Three

After the meeting with Purcell, Candice and I drove to our office. I had a client at ten and she wanted to get to work on Kendra's case. I knew she'd want to find out who was representing Kendra's husband, but now that she'd cut ties with Purcell, I also knew that was going be a bit of a challenge. "Where're you thinking of starting?" I asked once we'd unlocked the door to our suite.

"With you," Candice said. "But I'll wait until after you're done with your client."

I eyed her curiously. "Wait, you want to start with *me*?"

Candice flipped the light switch and moved with me into my half of the office. "There's something I want to try," she explained. "You know how, when you work with the feds, you always have a file to focus on?"

"Yeah." I wondered where she was going with this.

"Well, I've watched you carefully when you work one of their cases, Sundance, and sometimes you don't even open the file. You just close your eyes, put your hand on the front cover, and start pulling relevant stuff out of the ether. It's amazing."

I blushed. Candice was at the top of my list of favorite people today. "You want me to pretend to have Kendra's case file in front of me and see what I can come up with, right?"

Candice winked. "Yep. I was thinking that I could work up a list of questions for you to help guide us through an intuitive discussion, and who knows, maybe we'll get lucky."

I considered that for about two seconds. "I think that's a *great* idea!"

"Cool. We'll meet in my office at eleven, talk until noon, then go to lunch. On me."

That gave me pause. Candice ate healthy ... like, wheat-germ-with-a-side-of-tree-bark healthy. "Are you also picking where?" I asked cautiously.

She rolled her eyes. "You can choose as long as it's not another hot dog, burger, or nacho place."

I scowled. "What's left?"

"Plenty," she said, turning on her heel to leave me to ponder the possibilities.

My client was super nervous and a little bit late, which made her energy very scattered, and it took me a minute to try to sort through it and spit out a reading that would make sense. She seemed pleased with the results, however, and I was just happy to tune in on something other than murder and mayhem for a change. She was a lovely woman, with lots of exciting things on her horizon, so I was feeling pretty good by the time we wrapped it up.

Once I'd shown her out, I moved into Candice's office. My hips were killing me and I really wanted to take a pain pill, but I didn't want to dull my sixth sense, which can happen with certain meds, so I steered clear.

I promised myself that I'd take a pain pill at lunch (and boy, did I have a great idea for where!).

"I think your limp is getting worse," Candice said, looking up from her computer to study me critically.

"I had physical therapy yesterday, remember?" The day after my physical therapy sessions was always the worst. This could be because, although I saw my therapist once or twice a week depending on my schedule, I was supposed to do some additional exercises and stretches every day. I avoided these like I did pretty much every other unpleasant thing in my life.

"It wouldn't hurt so much if you'd do your home therapy like you're supposed to," Candice remarked. She knew me pretty well.

"Did you come up with some questions for me?" I decided to change the subject before things got testy.

"Yeah, but come have a look at this first."

I moved around her desk to stand next to her and she swiveled the monitor of her computer slightly. On the screen was a grainy photo of a sizable group of women standing formally in three curved rows. The Web site indicated they were part of the Travis County Women Lawyer's Association. Candice pointed to a woman with short chestnut hair in the third row. "Who's that?" I asked.

"Chelsea Gagliano. Tristan Moreno's attorney."

"How'd you get her name?"

Candice gave me a sideways grin. "Purcell finally coughed it up after I reamed her out," she explained. "I only caught a glimpse of your client when she came in here yesterday, but this could be her, couldn't it?"

I squinted at the screen. It was really hard to tell because the photo was of a terrible quality. "Maybe," I said in a tone that suggested I definitely wasn't sure.

"Yeah, I'm not convinced either. It could have been her, but it easily could have been someone else."

Then I thought of something. "You know, she did say that her *firm* had been retained, Candice. She didn't say that she specifically had been hired to represent the murderer." In fact, she'd made sure to let me know that it was her firm that'd taken on the client and because she was the best litigator, the case might be assigned to her.

I told Candice as much, and she said, "That could have been a bit of a smoke screen, Abs."

"What do you mean?"

"Well, if I was taking a huge risk by coming to see you and putting my career on the line, I might create a little smoke so that you wouldn't look into my identity too hard, by telling you that it wasn't actually my client, but my firm's."

"That'd make her pretty crafty," I replied.

"Or a natural-born attorney," Candice countered.

She had a point there. "I think we have to assume it could be either scenario," I said after thinking about it.

Candice nodded and clicked a few keys to navigate her browser to the home page for Turner, Kramer, and Marr, attorneys at law. The photo on the home page was of a very large building, and the side menu selections indicated that these guys did it all, from divorce to personal injury, tax law, and criminal defense.

My eyes bugged. "How many attorneys at this firm?"

"Forty-two," Candice said with a sigh. "And, unfortunately, only the three male partners list their photos online."

"So we're back to square one," I said.

Candice motioned to the seat opposite her and I sat down holding in a grimace. "Not entirely. I mean, we still have your magical ability to pull all kinds of stuff out of thin air."

I laughed. "Nice way to butter me up."

"It's true," she insisted. "And as we have nothing but our suspicion that your client from yesterday was here about Kendra Moreno, I think we should go for it." Candice then placed her iPhone on the desk between us. I knew she'd want to record this. "I'm going to avoid softball questions, if that's okay with you?"

"Good," I said, loving that Candice really got how my intuition worked more like a tool than a party trick. "Bring it on, Cassidy."

"The first question I have is: What happened to Kendra Moreno on the afternoon of September twenty-eighth?"

I closed my eyes and focused on the name Kendra Moreno. Names normally don't mean anything to me, but I'd seen her picture on the news, and I'd also picked up that she was dead, so I thought I had a pretty good bead on her energy. "She never saw it coming," I whispered.

"What'd you say?" Candice asked.

I opened my eyes. "I feel like Kendra knew and trusted her killer."

"She knew her husband," Candice said. "Whether she trusted him remains to be seen."

I focused again on that feeling of betrayal. "I definitely think the killer was a male, and I definitely think he came to her house alone. I get this sense like she might have even been glad to see him, but the moment her back was turned, things got ugly . . . fast."

"So she was attacked from behind?" Candice asked.

I nodded. "Yes. I feel like it came as a quick and sudden shock to her that he would be so violent against her."

Candice's expression turned pensive.

"What?"

She sighed. "It's the fact that there was no sign of a struggle that really has me bothered. If he attacked her violently, something should have been out of place, shouldn't it? Or a fingerprint should have been left behind. I mean, if the killer showed up wearing gloves, Kendra would have sensed something was wrong. And even if he attacked her from behind—with her kid in the house, don't you think she would have put up a fight?"

I sighed. "Maybe he shoved a gun into her back," I said. "Maybe he threatened to hurt her son if she so much as flinched."

Candice's finger tapped the desktop. "Okay," she conceded. "That's a good point. What else you got?"

"I don't know. Ask me some more questions," I said, closing my eyes again. I didn't want to be led by any assumptions; I wanted to pull the answers from the ether.

"You're positive that Kendra's dead?" Candice asked.

I sighed sadly. The answer was so clear. "Yes."

"How did she die?"

I felt a slight pressure over my nose and mouth and I shuddered. That feeling always creeped me out. "She was smothered."

"Not shot or stabbed?" Candice asked.

I knew why she was asking about the manner of Kendra's death. If our theory about catching Kendra unawares from behind was correct, then the most obvious way to render someone compliant was by shoving a gun or another kind of weapon into her back. But I felt quite certain that Kendra hadn't been shot or stabbed—she'd been smothered. I said as much to Candice.

"Well, that complicates things," Candice said grimly. "If the killer had had a gun or a knife with him when he abducted her, he would have shot or stabbed her to finish her off. Smothering someone takes energy and time."

"There's more," I said feeling another series of impressions against my energy. "I think she was beaten too. Severely beaten."

"That suggests either rage or a serious psycho."

I nodded, holding my eyes closed and waiting for Candice's next question.

"Can you describe the killer?"

This was a much harder thing to extract from the ether. The violent energy of Kendra's death clouded over a lot of the details, but I was able to tweeze out some clues. "He was tall and athletic," I said.

"Why do you say athletic?" Candice asked.

I shrugged. I hadn't thought about it. The answer had just come to me. "Some things you just know," I said.

"Okay, what else?"

"He feels unassuming in some way," I told her. "Like, he may present himself as mild mannered to most people, but this guy has a crazy dark side."

"Do you think he acted alone?"

When she asked that question I got a little stumped. I wanted to say no, mostly because Ms. Smith hadn't mentioned anything about an accomplice, but I couldn't ignore that I was sensing some other energy alongside this murderer, and that energy felt distinctly female. I said as much to Candice before trying to tweeze the truth of it out, like working to unravel a tangled knot of string. "There's some sort of attachment between this man and woman," I said. "I feel like the woman is the boss; she rules the relationship in some way and he's all about acting to protect or to please her. I also feel like he has very strong romantic feelings for her, and Kendra's murder was a result of his acting to protect that romantic relationship."

I opened my eyes and looked at Candice. She was frowning. "So this female was either an acquaintance or an accomplice?"

I focused again on the energy of this couple, but it was so confusing and muddled that it was hard to make sense of it. "Yes, but I can't tell which." Then I tried to approach it from a different angle and I came across something interesting. "You know what, Candice? I feel like Kendra and this woman had some sort of connection and that there may have been some discord between the two. When I look at it from Kendra's point of view, I can definitely see some anger and maybe even some jealousy there."

"This woman is an enemy of Kendra's?" Candice asked.

I shook my head. That didn't quite fit. "No, it's more like Kendra was the enemy of this woman. It feels weirdly one-sided."

"Huh," my partner said. I knew how she felt. I was stumped too.

I opened my eyes, sat back in the chair, and rubbed my temples. "I know it doesn't make much sense."

So often the language of intuition won't translate well into actual words. Much of it is based on feelings, sensations, moods, and a deep knowing that can be very difficult to put into English. Even when I successfully could put it into words, oftentimes many of the puzzle pieces seemed to be missing and only time would work to reveal them.

"You're wincing," Candice said, eyeing me critically again.

"I've been sitting for too long. My hips are really bothering me."

Candice shut off the recorder on her phone and stood up. "Come on, partner. Let's get you something to eat."

Once in her car, I directed Candice to a row of food trailers on South Congress in downtown Austin. To her credit, she didn't protest. Much.

I figured the lunch spot was the best way to accommodate both our food preferences. Candice liked Thai, and there was an amazing Thai trailer called the Coat and Thai, and I got my meal at the Mighty Cone, which serves all its food in cute paper cones. I ordered the famous chicken sandwich with the deep-fried avocado and their amazing French fries. Candice came to the picnic table area with something that looked like it'd grown out of the vacant lot next door.

I figured between the two of us we'd balance out the food pyramid pretty well.

Candice was a little quiet during lunch, and I figured she was thinking about the case. "You looking for an angle?" I asked. I knew my partner wouldn't work on the case without at least trying to get hired by someone close to Kendra.

"Yeah," she said, taking a sip of her iced tea. "I think we should approach the husband first."

That shocked me. "The *husband*? Are you crazy? What if he's the one who killed her?" I didn't know if he'd had anything to do with it, but the guy had lawyered up pretty quick, which indicated that he was nervous about something.

Candice was unfazed by my outburst. "If we approach him and he tells us that he's not interested in hiring us, it'll give you a chance to meet him and read his energy. We'll also have more evidence that he's trying to avoid any additional scrutiny into his wife's disappearance."

"What if he says no because he doesn't have the money to pay for us?" I asked.

Candice seemed to consider that. "I'll work up a credit report on him when we get back to the office. If I discover that he's struggling financially, then we can offer to work the case either at a reduced rate or—if you're in agreement—pro bono."

"He could still say no even if he has the money because he's cheap, you know."

"He had enough to hire a lawyer," Candice countered. "And in going to him we can ask about his representation, and pin down if his attorney, Ms. Gagliano, is the same lady who came to your office the other day or if this mysterious Ms. Smith could be someone else at Gagliano's law firm."

My eyes bugged and I held up a hand in protest. "Whoa, Candice, you *can't* mention anything about his attorney to him!"

"Why not?"

"Because when Ms. Smith came to me there was this threatening energy lurking around her. I could tell she came to me at considerable risk, and if we mention her to Moreno and if he did in fact murder his wife, then he might put two and two together and go after her!"

Candice frowned. "Okay, okay," she conceded. "That's a good point. I won't mention anything to him about his legal counsel. If Moreno turns us down on our offer to investigate, we'll approach Kendra's parents. They should be able to give us plenty of access to Kendra's background along with some insight into her husband's temperament."

"You're sure you don't want to approach her folks first?"

"No. I want to give the husband a chance to show his true colors. His answer to our proposition is gonna tell us a lot, Sundance. If he stonewalls us, acts suspicious, or turns us down outright, we can go to the parents knowing we should probably keep our focus on their son-in-law."

"You think Kendra's parents will hire us?" I asked. I was used to people coming to us for our services. It felt weird going to them.

Candice smiled like I'd said something cute. "Of course they'll hire us," she said easily. "I mean, we bring the whole package, right? A PI *and* an FBI psychic? We're a dream team, Abs."

I thought she was maybe a little too confident, but I held my tongue. After lunch Candice and I got back into her car and she checked a text on her phone. "Brice wants to know if we're free to stop by the office and say hello to Director Gaston."

"Is Dutch there?" I was still nervous about getting yelled at for leaving him with Cat.

"Probably," she said, already tapping out a response.

I sighed. "I have to face the music sometime."

Candice gave me a sympathetic pat on the shoulder. "That's my girl." And we were off.

We arrived at the FBI's Austin bureau—which isn't really a normal bureau, but one devoted almost exclusively to solving cold cases—and I entered the building playing up my limp for all it was worth. Dutch could hardly yell at a cripple, right?

"May I have a word with you?" he said the second he

saw me. Unfortunately he'd been on his way out at the exact moment we were on our way in, and the three of us met in the doorway. To thwart any efforts I might make to escape, he firmly latched his hand onto my upper arm.

"Abby took a bit of a tumble this morning," Candice said quickly, moving protectively to my other side. "She seems to be okay, but she's been in some pain ever since."

I held very still, certain I'd give the ruse away if I moved.

Dutch immediately changed his demeanor. Moving his other hand to my shoulder, he stared at me with concern. "Are you okay?"

I bit my lip and managed to get my eyes to water a little. "I think so," I said in a pained whisper.

"Did you take her to the ER?" Dutch asked Candice.

"There's a doctor who works in our building," Candice lied. "He checked her out and said there didn't appear to be any broken bones, but he wants her to take it easy for a day or so."

If Dutch hadn't been watching me closely, I would have given Candice a thumbs-up. "Aw, dollface," he said to me, letting go of my shoulders to lead me by the hand. "Come on, let's get you into a chair, okay?"

Dutch moved me into the first chair he saw—which was already occupied by one of his agents, who moved only when my fiancé glared at him. I felt bad. But not bad enough to confess and face the music.

"Where did you fall?" Dutch asked as he carefully eased me into the chair and squatted down in front of me.

"At the office," I said at the same time that Candice said, "At the coffee shop."

Dutch's chin lifted and he eyed us sharply.

Uh-oh.

"At the coffee shop by our office," I said.

Dutch's eyes narrowed. He could sniff out a lie almost as well as I could.

"How'd it happen?" he asked casually. Too casually.

My mind blanked, so I looked to Candice to answer. "She—"

"Let Abby answer, please," Dutch commanded.

Candice's gaze shifted meaningfully to my cane.

"It was my cane," I told Dutch.

"Your cane?"

"Yeah. It . . . uh . . . I sort of tripped over it."

"How'd that happen?" Dutch asked, standing tall again as his hands found his hips. He knew I was lying. I knew he knew I was lying, and by the looks of it, everyone around us knew I knew he knew I was lying.

I gulped. "There was a cat," I said, "and it darted out from the alley and it bumped into my cane and I tripped over it."

"You tripped over it?" Dutch asked skeptically. "Do you mean you tripped over the cat or the cane?"

"The cat."

"What color was the cat?"

"Black." Dutch's narrowed eyes became downright squinty. "White. It was black-and-white. Also, maybe a little gray in there too, but it was hard to tell because it also had a few bald patches." My motto is: When in doubt, just keep lying. Even if you're *terrible* at it.

"Bald patches?" Dutch asked.

I gulped, wondering if I could divert him by asking for some water. "Yeah. It was obviously a stray and it probably had mange or something. Maybe one of the rats it ate gave it mange."

Standing behind Dutch, Candice ducked her chin,

covered her eyes, and shook her head. I could hardly blame her. Lying came easy for her. I think she majored in it in college.

Dutch had crossed his arms over his chest, his look darkening like a bad storm approaching. Around us several agents who'd been listening in suddenly found their computers *super* interesting.

"Is that Abigail Cooper?" I heard from the other end of the room.

I practically leaped to my feet (miraculously cured from the mangy-cat incident) and hobbled as fast as I could toward my savior. "Director Gaston!"

He held his arms out wide to me and I hugged him. "It's so good to see you!" I gushed. Not only was I happy that he'd saved me from getting a tongue-lashing from Dutch, but I was also genuinely glad to see the man who'd looked out for me nearly from the moment we'd met.

Gaston backed up but held me at arm's length, and looking me over critically he asked, "How're you recovering?"

I kept my back to Dutch. "Oh, all right, I guess. It's slow going, but I'm determined to walk down the aisle without the cane."

Gaston smiled kindly. "I'm so glad. When's the big day?"

"November fifteenth," I said. "You're coming, aren't you, sir?"

Gaston's brow rose. "Have you sent me an invitation?"

Crap on a cracker. I'd forgotten once again to send Cat the list of invitees. "They're going out next week," I promised, "and you're definitely on the list."

"Then consider me an early RSVP, Abigail. I wouldn't miss your wedding for the world."

"Hello, Director," I heard Candice say from behind me.

Gaston focused on Candice next and they exchanged pleasantries. Brice came out of his office and said his hellos. He seemed upset. Shaken even. And I was able to pick that up only from the vibe coming off him, not anything he said or did. He caught me looking at him curiously. "What?" he mouthed while Candice and Gaston chatted.

"You tell me," I whispered. "What's happened?"

Brice's forced smile vanished and he shook his head. "You'll know in a minute."

Gaston subtly laid a hand on my shoulder. "Abigail, I wonder if we might talk for a bit in private with Special Agent Harrison."

"Sure," I said. I felt my heartbeat tick up. My radar was buzzing with a forboding feeling.

"Wonderful," he said, motioning for me to enter Brice's office first. "Agent Rivers, would you also join us?"

I hustled into Brice's office and took a seat, bracing myself because the more I tried to pick up on what was at hand, the more unsettled I became. Whatever they wanted to talk about was bad. Really, *really* bad.

Brice took the chair behind his desk, Gaston sat next to me, and Dutch stood by the door, leaning against the wall. I avoided looking at him, certain I'd still catch a hint of anger in his midnight blues.

Gaston folded his hands in his lap and began. "This morning a very disturbing incident occurred in the city of College Station. Are you familiar with it?"

"The city or the incident?" I asked.

"The city."

"Yes, sir." College Station was northeast of Austin, about two hours away. "Did something happen there?"

Gaston motioned to Brice, who swiveled his computer monitor around so that it faced me. "This is a little tough to watch, Abby," he warned.

Coming from a seasoned FBI agent, that meant the image had to be awful. "Okay," I told him. "I'm braced. What is it?"

"It's a video," Gaston said, his hand again on my arm. "It was taken from a security camera inside a mall near downtown at about eleven this morning."

Gaston motioned again for Brice to play the footage.

Now, what I saw on that computer screen is the subject of an entirely different story—one that I'll go into next time—but suffice it to say the video was one of the most disturbing things I've ever had the great misfortune to witness. And trust me when I tell you that I've seen some disturbing things.

When it was over I shakily got to my feet. I felt lightheaded, nauseated, traumatized, and like I was ready to hurl all at the same time. "Excuse me," I said, hobbling out of the room as fast as my limp would allow. Dutch said my name as I passed him, but I shook my head hard and didn't even bother to look back. My breathing was coming in quick pants, and all I wanted to do was make it out of there before I lost my composure.

I limped by Candice too, and caught her concerned eye. I motioned for her to follow and felt her immediately at my side.

Behind me I heard Dutch call my name again, but I couldn't even acknowledge him; I just kept my focus on getting to the door.

Once we came into the open air of the outdoors, I

bent at the waist and took several deep breaths and noticed that I was trembling from the shock of what I'd seen. Candice wrapped an arm around me for support, which was the only thing that prevented me from blacking out. Finally I stood up tall again, and through the glass window I could see Dutch looking at me with a face full of concern. I shook my head at him, turned away, and then I burst into tears. Candice looped my arm around her shoulders and helped me to her car without a word.

She got me settled, then hurried around to her side and got in. We peeled out of the parking garage and I stared out the window, unable to stop the flood of emotion pouring out of me. After a bit I said, "Thank you."

Candice laid a gentle hand on my head. "You okay?"

"They showed me some footage of a bomb going off at a mall, Candice," I said, the tears coming back in earnest again. "It wasn't in black-and-white. It was in color. I saw . . . everything. They all died . . . they all just . . . died."

"Jesus Christ!" she hissed. "Why the hell would Brice show you that?!"

I shook my head. It hadn't been his fault, but I couldn't really form any more words because I was too overcome.

Candice continued to cast worried glances at me, and finally she picked up her cell and punched in a number. The second the other party picked up, she tore into them, and I quickly realized she was yelling at her fiancé. *"What the hell were you thinking?"* she shouted, and didn't even wait for a response. "She's so upset she can barely speak, Brice!" There was a pause then, "No! Absolutely not! I'm taking her home and you can tell Gaston, personally from me, to go feck himself!"

Candice threw the phone down and gripped the steering wheel with barely masked fury.

About then I noticed that my own cell was lighting up. It was still on silent and it appeared I'd missed more than a few calls. This call was from Dutch, as were the previous three. He'd been trying to call me from the moment I went outside, by the looks of it. I showed the display to Candice, who literally growled as I answered the line, even though I knew I wouldn't be able to say much. "I am so sorry," he said immediately. "Babe, I didn't know it would affect you like that."

Candice grabbed the phone out of my hand and gave another furious lecture to my fiancé. She then hung up on him too and threw my phone into the backseat. "Stupid men!" she yelled.

At that moment, I couldn't have agreed more.

Chapter Four

At my request, Candice drove me back to our office so that I could retrieve my car. She then followed me home and sat with me for a long while on the couch without trying to get me to talk about it.

As you can probably tell, Candice is that rare gem among friends; she's able to ferret out the truth of things without a word of explanation. Around six she asked if I'd like some dinner. I told her that I wasn't hungry, which was the truth, and a little after that I told her that I thought I'd just go upstairs and head to bed.

"Do you want me to stay here until Dutch gets home?" she asked.

I shook my head. "No. I'll be okay." Candice's frown told me she wasn't convinced. "Really," I insisted. "I pinkie swear. I'll be fine."

"Well, okay, but if you need me, Sundance, I'm only a phone call away."

"I know. And try not to worry. I just need to curl up

with the pups someplace safe for a little while." I still hadn't shaken the scene from the video. It was bothering me far more than I let on to Candice.

My friend leaned in and gave me a fierce hug. "I'll pick you up at eight tomorrow morning. We'll need to get back on the Moreno case before the trail gets too cold."

"I'll be ready," I assured her.

She left just a few minutes later, and I watched her drive away knowing I'd never find a better friend in the world. The minute her car was out of sight, I grabbed my keys and whistled to the dogs, and the three of us went for a familiar drive.

I pulled up to the almost completed house that Dutch and I would soon be calling home. The minute I put the car into park I felt myself exhale. There was something about this place that simply soothed my soul.

Dutch had purchased the property the previous April, and he'd proposed to me on the very soil that was now our breakfast nook. No wonder it was certain to become my favorite room in the house.

Eggy, Tuttle, and I all walked across the dirt path up to the front door, and I unlocked it with my key. We stepped into the quiet structure and I felt the warmth from the late afternoon sun wrap itself around me like a blanket.

I let the dogs wander around, sniffing as they went, and found my way to the back door. Opening it wide, I let in the cooler air, flipped on the outside light, and stepped out onto the spacious covered back deck. Near the fire pit sat two cushy lounge chairs, which Dutch had purchased the moment the grill went in. He and I now had dinner out here at least once a week.

The dogs found me just as I was sitting down, and I lifted them each up onto the lounge chair before tossing a cashmere throw over the three of us. It was a cool night for October in Texas. The pups curled against me and were asleep in seconds. For a very long time all I did was sit there and stare listlessly out at the view.

At the edge of our backyard, just past a very sturdy fence, was a drop of about a hundred feet to a river gorge below. The property sat on top of a peninsular bluff and the views for nearly one hundred and eighty degrees were all spectacular. From where I sat I could see lights coming up in neighborhoods twenty miles away, and there was something incredibly soothing about that.

I still saw the images from the video, however, every time I closed my eyes, and I had to work to replace them with a memory that gave me comfort. I thought of the morning that Dutch had proposed. I thought of the day I went to pick up Eggy from the breeder. I thought of playing fetch with Tuttle.

It was a technique I'd learned as a kid when my very unbalanced mother would rain down her abuse on me. Throughout all of my childhood I'd been unloved and unwanted, and my mother had taken all of her dysfunction and mental instability out on me both physically and mentally. It'd been a terrible way to grow up, but I was pretty convinced it was the impetus to developing my psychic sense.

I never knew when Clair—Mommy dearest—would flash with anger, and I had to rely heavily on my sixth sense to get me out of the house before she flew into a rage.

If I didn't escape fast enough and she caught me, I'd withdraw into myself and fill my mind with any memory that gave me comfort. It was the only reason I survived those years, I think, and the technique was a coping mechanism I was calling upon now.

After a while, and with that horrible image on the video finally outnumbered by all the sweet memories and happier thoughts I'd called upon, the knot of tension and distress inside me began to ease. I could feel myself creating some distance from it, and that helped me assess something else I hadn't even noticed was tugging away at me.

I had an intuitive feeling that I should have nothing to do with the case. It was strong and clear and very firm, and it came both from that internal compass we all rely upon as well as from my own personal crew of spirit guides. I wanted no part of the case. If Gaston asked me for help again, I'd stand up for myself and tell him no.

As justification for staying out of it, I extended my radar out into the future and could see that the case would be resolved within just a few weeks. I felt quite strongly that it would be resolved by the agents already working the case and, oddly, another woman, who in her own right had a strong sense of intuition.

"Abs?" I heard from just inside the door. Eggy, startled awake, barked and leaped off the cushion.

I turned, craning my neck to see the shadowy figure of my fiancé come out onto the stone patio to join me. "Hey," I said, filled with warmth by the sight of him. Candice might have been furious with him, but I knew he wasn't to blame.

He picked Eggy up and came to my side. After a sweet kiss he said, "I've been trying to call you all night."

Oops. I'd left my phone on the kitchen counter. And

it'd been turned to silent anyway. I had no interest in talking to anyone. "My phone's at home."

Dutch nodded and stroked my hair. "How you doin', sweethot?"

I reached up and took his hand. "Better."

"You sure?"

I kissed his hand. He was far too good to me. "I'm fine. What're you doing here, anyway?"

Dutch sat down on the other lounge chair and curled Eggy into the folds of his jacket to keep him warm. "You wouldn't answer my calls, so I called Candice, and she told me you'd gone to bed, so I figured I could sneak over here before I came home." I looked at him curiously and he added, "Sometimes after a hard day I like to come out here and hang out for a while. This place takes all the tension out of me, you know?"

I laughed. "That's what I'm doing here."

"I think we did good picking this lot," he said, leaning back with a contented sigh.

"I think *you* did good. What time is it?"

"Almost nine."

My eyes widened. I'd been there more than two and a half hours and it'd felt like only half that. "So what happened after I left?"

Dutch scratched his five-o'clock shadow and yawned. "Gaston wanted to wait until you'd gotten over your initial shock to ask you to come back and give us your impressions, and I told him to go to hell."

I eyed him sharply. "You did not!"

"I did," Dutch said. "And Brice backed me up on it too."

My jaw fell open. "What'd Gaston say?"

"Well, at first I really thought he was going to write

us both up, but when I explained that you're sensitive both in spirit and in the ability to sense the future, he kind of got it. He felt bad about showing you the video and he sent me home tonight with a personal apology from him."

"No way!"

Dutch grinned. "Way." Dutch sobered then and reached out for my hand. "I've never seen you look like that. You were so pale, you looked like a ghost. I think that video put you into a mild shock."

I remembered Candice insisting I have some Coca-Cola and a bite of a protein bar before she let me drive home from the office. I wondered if she'd thought the same thing.

"I never want to see you look like that again, Edgar."

I slid out from under the afghan, careful not to disturb Tuttle, and moved over to cuddle against Dutch on his chair. "I love you so much."

He grinned. "Rilly?"

"Rilly, rilly," I vowed.

"Then would you do me a favor?"

"Anything," I said, leaning in to kiss him affectionately.

"Anything?"

I laughed. "Yes. For getting me out of that case, I owe you, cowboy. Name it and I'll do it."

"Deal with your sister."

"Anything but that."

"Abs," Dutch growled.

"Aw, man! Dutch, come on! You know she's a nightmare!"

"Yes, Abigail, I *do* know that. I was reminded of just how much of a nightmare this morning."

"But you deal with her so much better than I do."

This wasn't actually true, but it was all I had and I was going down fighting.

"Maybe we should just elope," Dutch suggested.

I sat up and stared down at him. "That is a *genius* idea! Let's do it! Let's just run away and get married on a beach somewhere!"

Dutch's deep, rich laugh echoed out into the cool night air. "You know we can't actually do that, right?"

"Why not?"

"Well, for one thing, our friends and family would kill us. For another, your sister would never, and I do mean *never*, let us forget it."

"You're right," I groaned. The thought of facing my sister and all her decisions sent me into a good pout before I made another confession. "I've been ducking Dave too."

Dutch smirked. "Yeah. I know. He keeps calling me looking for you."

I sighed heavily. "It's all just a little too much for me right now, Dutch. I mean, the house, the wedding, and this *huge* case Candice and I just landed."

"What case?"

"It's a missing-person's case."

"Kendra Moreno?"

"Yes," I said, surprised he knew.

"I saw the news clip yesterday before you got all prickly peared on me. Is she still alive?"

"No."

"Damn," he swore, but he didn't press me for details, and I was grateful for that. "Still, you can't keep avoiding Cat and Dave, dollface. Just devote a few days to both of them and it'll all be behind you."

"I don't have a few days to spare, Dutch." I was busy with clients, cases, and physical therapy. It wasn't like I was sitting at home eating bonbons all day. And then I had an idea. "How about we agree that you take Cat and I take Dave?"

Dutch laughed like he really enjoyed that one. "How about I take something easier like world peace or global warming?"

"Oh, come on, Dutch! She's better with you than she is with me!"

"How do you figure?"

"You say yes to all her ideas. I sometimes dare to have my own opinion, and then we end up arguing."

Dutch looked affronted. "For the record, I don't just say yes to all her ideas."

"Right. Keep telling yourself that."

Dutch dug into his pocket and pulled out a coin. Flipping it into the air, he said, "Call it."

I smiled sweetly while I pointed my radar right at that shiny silver coin. He caught the quarter and slapped it onto the top of his wrist, looking up at me expectantly. "Heads," I said with a satisfied sigh. "Have a good time with Cat, cowboy."

Dutch lifted his hand to take a peek at the coin. "Damn! Best two out of three?" he asked (a bit desperately, I thought).

I moved back over to my own lounge chair. "We could do this all night, sugar, and I'd still win." For effect I tapped my temple and winked at him.

"Son of a bitch!" he swore again. "Forgot about the radar."

"It works for rock, paper, scissors too, just in case you're thinking of changing it up."

Dutch muttered under his breath and crossed his arms over his chest moodily. "Fine, I'll take Cat, but if I get *one* more call from Dave looking for you, the deal's off, got it?"

I gave him a smart salute just as my stomach growled. My appetite had returned.

Dutch's left eyebrow arched. "Didn't you eat?"

"Nope. You?"

"Nope," he said, getting up with Eggy still cuddled in his jacket. He came to my chair and offered me his hand. "Come on, hot stuff. Let's find a place that allows dogs on the patio. You can buy me dinner."

"Least I can do," I said, wincing as I got to my feet and Dutch handed me my cane. "But let's not stay out too late tonight. Candice is picking me up at eight a.m."

"No time for nooky, huh?" he asked with a bounce to his eyebrows.

I gave him a mischievous smile. "Maybe we should order dinner to go?"

Reaching for the sleepy Tuttle, Dutch winked at me and said, "Now you're talking."

Candice pulled into my driveway promptly at eight a.m. Tired as I was—Dutch and I had been up late . . . uh . . . playing Parcheesi (cough, cough)—I knew that I had to get out fast because my sister was on her way over. I could sense that her imminent arrival was just minutes away.

I felt bad about not warning Dutch, who was dragging a little himself and already on his second cup of coffee. But I was worried that if I let him know Cat was headed our way, he'd do what I was doing—bolt for them thar hills.

I knew that eventually Cat would catch up to both of us, and because of my cane, I also knew that Dutch

could easily outrun me. It wasn't that I *somewhat*
doubted he'd be true to his word and take Cat off my
hands. I *completely* doubted it. She could test the patience of a sainted saint's saintly mother.

"Hit it!" I said once I'd made it into Candice's car.

My sidekick floored it and we zoomed down the
street. "Does your sister have your new address?" she
asked me.

"You mean the one to the new house?" Candice nodded. "No. We haven't even shown her where it is yet. I
mean, you know how she can be. She'll see the house
isn't finished, and she'll start ordering us around like we
work for her, and telling the construction crew how to do
their jobs, and pretty soon we'll have a house that looks
just like one that Cat built."

"Maybe you guys should move and not tell her," Candice said seriously.

"Yeah. We've talked about that. I'm thinking of telling her the mail doesn't get delivered to our new address
and offering her a PO box instead."

Candice snickered. "Do you know she sent me so
many e-mails of all the ideas she's thinking of for your
wedding that I had to change my e-mail address?"

"I'm so sorry," I said sincerely. My sister always got
her way, mostly because she wore the opposition down
to a tired, battered nub. Well, she was Dutch's problem
now. Which reminded me . . . I picked up my phone and
sorted through the contacts to Dave's cell.

"Yo," he said by way of answer.

"It's me," I told him.

"That's funny, this doesn't sound like me."

"Ha, ha!" I said with a roll of my eyes. "Listen, when
can we get together to pick out all the deco stuff for the
house?"

"I've left you a thousand voice mails, asking you that exact question," he replied (a bit testily, I thought).

"Dude, I'm sorry, but I've been crazy busy."

"Right," he said, taking a more sympathetic tone. "I always forget that you guys are also planning a wedding. How about tonight?"

I eyed Candice. "Am I free tonight?" I whispered, remembering that I hadn't even asked her what our agenda held on the Moreno case.

"You should be," she said, weaving sharply around a car that had the audacity to travel at the posted speed limit.

"Tonight should work, Dave. I'll meet you at the house at four, okay?"

"See you then," he replied, and clicked off.

"Where're we headed again?" I asked, tucking my cell into my purse.

"We're diving right in, remember?" Candice asked. "We're on our way to see Tristan Moreno."

Then I remembered. "The husband."

"Yep."

"What're you gonna say to him when he answers the bell? I mean, how are you gonna explain why we want in on the case?"

"Don't know yet," she told me.

"Well, whatever you say, just don't mention the visit from the attorney," I reminded her.

Candice gave me a patronizing pat on the shoulder—alarming, because she was also taking a sip of coffee with her other hand while maneuvering the car with her knees. "Relax. I have no plans to mention the mysterious Ms. Smith or her possible connection to Gagliano. I figure I might say that we heard about his wife's disappearance on the news, and that your intuition has been buzzing with clues about where Kendra might be."

My brow furrowed. "But I don't know where Kendra is."

Candice looked at me sideways, still holding the cup of coffee and driving with her knees. The woman was seriously going to give me a heart attack. Or kill me in a fiery crash. "*He* doesn't know that we don't know where Kendra is," she said.

My brow dipped even lower. "Huh?"

"I've got it covered, Abs," she assured me, finally taking her hand off my shoulder and placing it lazily on the top of the steering wheel. If that was the way she was going to grip the wheel responsibly, I thought I'd prefer her knees.

Still, we managed to arrive at the Moreno residence without incident or accident (a minor miracle). It was obvious which house the Morenos lived in—it was the one with all the news crews hanging out in front. The local press had apparently settled in for the ride.

"Crap," Candice spat, pulling over and eyeing the house moodily. "I was hoping they'd all be up at College Station."

"They probably split up their reporters to cover both stories just in case something breaks." Austin was by far one of the safest cities I'd ever lived in, and with no daily murder and mayhem to report on, the news here was almost never exciting.

"Looks like they've been here awhile," I said, pointing to a few empty disposable coffee cups littering the sidewalk.

Candice frowned. "They better pick those up," she groused. Candice had no tolerance for litterbugs.

"What do we do now that the vultures have taken over?" I asked, nodding at the smattering of reporters waiting around for any signs of life from inside the

Moreno residence. I noted that every window had the blinds or curtains drawn.

Candice didn't have time to answer, because a silver Lexus came bolting down the Moreno's driveway and hit the street fast, barely avoiding a reporter stuffing a doughnut into his piehole.

Several other reporters jumped to grab their microphones and motion to their camera guys, but it was already too late, because the Lexus was roaring down the street, barely breaking for a stop sign before rounding the corner and disappearing from view. The mob of news crews scrambled to get to their vans, and almost as one they gave chase. It was sickening.

"Time for plan B," Candice said, putting her own car into drive and heading off in the opposite direction.

"The parents?"

"Yep," she said. "Nancy and Gary Woodyard. I saw them interviewed on the late news. They look like reasonable people."

The Woodyards lived not far from their daughter and son-in-law on the east side of town in a beautiful community overlooking a bucolic man-made lake. Their house had a very small front yard, a bit out of proportion for the rest of the home, which was a large contemporary structure with a mosaic pattern of dark and light sandstone set against the front and sides. Hunter green aluminum siding with coral trim gave color to the second story, and the whole thing was capped off by a silver tin roof. The effect was striking and really made the house stand out from its neighbors.

"Nice digs," I said when we'd gotten out of the car and began walking up the steps.

"Excuse me!" said a voice down the sidewalk.

"Keep walking," Candice muttered out of the side of her mouth.

I did, but I happened to glance over my shoulder at the voice. I could see a redheaded reporter I recognized from the local news hurrying toward us. "Are you friends of Kendra's?" she asked when it was clear we weren't going to respond.

Candice walked purposefully up the steps, and I was right next to her.

"Extended family?" the reporter asked next.

"Don't look and don't say a word, Abs," Candice warned softly as she pressed the bell.

"Have you heard from Kendra?" the reporter called, desperate for a quote from someone, *anyone*, that she could use on the next news broadcast. "Do you know where she is?"

Candice and I waited with our backs to the reporter, who didn't approach the house but remained on the sidewalk. I was silently cursing the Woodyards' small yard when footsteps from inside echoed through the door to us. A moment later I had the feeling that someone was peering out at us. "Who is it?" asked a woman's voice.

Candice held up her badge and her FBI ID. "Candice Fusco and Abigail Cooper, ma'am. We're consultants with the FBI and we'd like to talk with you."

As nonchalantly as I could, I turned my head a little and saw the reporter scribbling furiously onto her notepad. She'd heard Candice's every word. "Great," I muttered. When Candice looked at me I indicated the reporter. Candice eyed her too and sent the woman a dark look.

The door was opened a tiny crack and one hazel eye and part of a nose appeared. "You're with the FBI?"

"We're consultants for them," Candice corrected. I

knew even she'd be careful not to indicate that we'd actually been sent by the bureau.

The brow above the hazel eye lowered suspiciously. "You consult with them but you're not actually with them?"

I could feel Candice's energy working hard to appear pleasant and patient, but with the reporter right behind us taking notes, she'd have to be careful about what she said or it would be all over the five-o'clock news. "Are you Mrs. Woodyard?" she inquired.

"I asked my question first," the woman said stubbornly. I wondered at her attitude, but then I remembered the way the press was currently hounding Kendra's husband. Maybe they'd already tested the patience of Kendra's parents too.

"Yes, ma'am," Candice said contritely. "I'm so sorry. Abigail and I consult on a regular basis with the FBI. Abby used to work full-time at their bureau office downtown, in fact. Abs, show her your badge."

I dug through my purse and pulled up my own plastic-encased ID. I held it up to my face and smiled to mirror the photo.

The hazel eye swiveled back and forth between us. "What do you want?" she asked at last.

"We heard about your daughter's disappearance, and we'd like to offer our professional services," Candice said. When the woman showed no signs of opening the door wider than the crack, Candice added, "I promise you, ma'am, we're on the level here. May we please come in and talk to you?"

The eye stared at us for another couple of beats before finally pulling back. The door swung open to reveal a woman with gray hair, pale skin, and a blue mole on her upper lip. "I'll give you five minutes," she said curtly.

I discreetly cast Candice a look that said, "This should be fun!"

She cut me a look that said, "Behave!"

We stepped through the doorway without a word and into the foyer. In front of us was the staircase to the second floor, and to our immediate left was the dining room. The woman—whom I assumed was Kendra's mother—closed the door, locking it tightly before motioning for us to follow her. We passed a spacious study and a bathroom and finally came into a large open kitchen with dark chocolate cabinets, white marble countertops, and a central island with three counter-level chairs.

Flanking the kitchen was a cozy living room with two sofas and a large-screen TV set over the fireplace. Sitting numbly in one corner of the sofa was a sickly looking gentleman hooked up to an oxygen tank. He lifted his sad eyes to us, and I nodded and offered a polite smile. He didn't smile back.

"Gary, these two are from the FBI," said the woman. She still hadn't identified herself, but it was pretty clear that she was Mrs. Woodyard.

Candice walked across the floor right up to Kendra's father and extended her hand to him. "We're consultants at the bureau, Mr. Woodyard. We're not actually agents or here on official FBI business."

He took her hand and eyed her with interest. "You're here about Kendra?"

"Yes," Candice said. Waving her hand in my direction, she added, "This is my partner, Abigail Cooper. I'm a licensed private investigator and we saw Kendra's story on the news the other day. We felt strongly that we wanted to come to you and offer our investigative expertise."

"For a price," Mrs. Woodyard said (a bit snippily, I thought).

"Our hourly rates are quite reasonable," Candice assured her.

"The police are free," she countered, looking meanly at us. Man, this woman didn't give an inch!

Still, Candice nodded like she agreed. "Yes, they are. And if you'd like to put all your trust in them and their ability to find your daughter, then please do so."

Mrs. Woodyard shifted on her feet. She didn't appear to have a snappy comeback to that.

"May I ask how that investigation is proceeding?" Candice asked gently when the silence stretched out a bit.

"It's way past the seventy-two-hour mark," Mr. Woodyard said, his voice so forlorn that it hurt to hear it. "The detectives said that if Kendra didn't turn up within seventy-two hours, then it could mean the worst. It could mean that it wasn't her choice to leave the house that day."

"Of course it wasn't her choice, Gary!" his wife snapped. "Kendra would *never* leave Colby home alone."

Mr. Woodyard stared at the floor. Of the two, I could see he'd been the most hopeful that his daughter had somehow left her home of her own accord and might come to her senses and be back soon. I knew he would suffer a terrible blow when he discovered the truth—that she was gone for good—and sensing the illness wafting out of him as evidenced by the oxygen tank, I truly didn't look forward to that.

"We haven't heard anything from the detectives in over a day, Nancy," Mr. Woodyard said. "Maybe we should bring in some outside help."

But I could already tell that Mrs. Woodyard had

hardened to the point where she didn't want any outside help. She wanted us out of her house, and she wanted to wait for the police to tell her what had happened to her daughter. I didn't know if it was because she was cheap or just naturally suspicious of everyone and everything. I didn't really care either. She had an element of meanness about her, and I suspected that Kendra and she hadn't gotten on so well. "What're your hourly rates?" she asked, and not like she was genuinely interested, but more to appease her husband.

Candice told her, and Mrs. Woodyard reacted as if we'd said a thousand dollars a second. "That's *outrageous*!"

"It's actually below the industry standard," Candice replied calmly. "Investigating a missing person is more work than it appears. But if it would make you more comfortable, we could agree to work the case until either it's resolved to your satisfaction or we reach the end of our retainer. If it's the latter, then whatever we discover we will turn over to you and you may offer it to the police or to another PI if you wish."

I noted that Mr. Woodyard hadn't looked put off by the rate Candice had quoted. "What can you offer that the police can't?" he asked.

Candice pointed meaningfully at me. "Abby," she said. "She's an intuitive investigator with ten years' experience and dozens of solved cases to her credit. She's worked for the Royal Oak, Michigan, PD, the Denver PD, the FBI, and the CIA. Her credentials and reputation are impeccable. To my own credit, I've also had a dozen years' experience as a PI and FBI consultant. As investigators go, Mr. Woodyard, we're very good, and we wouldn't be here if we didn't know we could help you find out what happened to Kendra."

Mr. Woodyard appeared interested; however, his

wife was a whole different story. She squinted first at me, then at Candice. "Hold on," she said as she pointed at me but addressed Candice. "She's a . . . a . . . what did you say? An *intuitive* investigator? What the hell is that?"

"I'm a professional psychic, ma'am," I told her. "I've had my own private practice for over ten years, and, like Candice said, I've worked dozens of cases for various police departments and federal investigators."

Mrs. Woodyard hardly seemed impressed. In fact, she appeared downright offended. "Is this some kind of a joke?"

"No," Candice replied in that same calm manner. "Abby's the real deal, ma'am."

Mrs. Woodyard rolled her eyes and cast a meaningful look at her husband before she went over to a stack of papers about twenty pages thick. Holding them up like they were evidence in a courtroom, she said, "And these are also so-called psychics who've been sending us messages on Kendra's personal Facebook page, claiming to know where our daughter is!" Sorting through them with obvious disdain, she pulled one out of the stack and said, "This says that Kendra is in the South of France on the beach with her new lover. While this one," she growled, flipping to the next page, "says Kendra has been kidnapped by a Mexican drug lord and is being used as a sex slave!"

"Ma'am," Candice said, discreetly stepping closer to me. "I can assure you that Abby is both experienced and held in high esteem by this nation's top investigative bureaus."

Mrs. Woodyard, however, wasn't listening. Flipping to the last page, she pulled out yet another e-mail and angrily said, "This one is my personal favorite. It says that Kendra was buried alive and left in a wooded area, and that she was murdered by a man she had once trusted!"

My radar binged. A legitimate psychic actually *had* contacted the Woodyards, although perhaps that psychic's methods had been a bit too forthcoming for these two just yet.

Candice held up her hands in surrender. "Mrs. Woodyard, I'm afraid we may have gotten off on the wrong foot—"

"Thank you, but no, thank you," Mr. Woodyard cut in while he struggled to get to his feet. "We don't believe in psychics, no matter how many claims they make about who they've worked with."

I felt my spirits fall. I'd been hoping for his support at least. And that comment, "We don't believe in psychics . . . ," always cut into me like a sharp sword. It was as if someone was suggesting I didn't exist. Being psychic was so much a part of who I was that it always shocked me when people suggested it—and by extension I—wasn't real.

But then I looked into Mr. Woodyard's eyes and I saw the fear there. It wasn't fear of me; he was afraid of what I might tell him about what had happened to his daughter. He wasn't ready to hear the truth yet, and until the police had a solid lead, he could continue believing that Kendra was still alive and would return home safe and sound.

I focused on him, determined to prove to him that I wasn't a fraud and shake him out of his cloud of denial. "We understand," I said gently. "It takes a certain open-mindedness to accept that what I do is real. But, Mr. Woodyard, if I may, your doctor has some good news about that clinical trial she's been trying to get you into.

You'll be getting a call very soon from her to tell you that you've been accepted into the program, and I can tell you that you won't be given the placebo; you'll get the real deal. The experimental drugs will tackle that tumor in your right lung and shrink it down to nothing. It's the genetic engineering tied to your DNA that'll make all the difference in the drug's effectiveness. You're going to make it, sir."

The sickly man's jaw fell open slightly as he stared at me with big, wide eyes. I then wished him and his equally stunned wife a good day, turned on my heel, and headed to the door without a backward glance.

Chapter Five

"Show-off," Candice chuckled as we buckled our seat belts.

I shook my head, regretting what I'd just done inside the Woodyards' home. "I know, I know," I told her. "It would've been better to just keep my mouth shut."

Candice eyed me like I'd just said something shocking. "Are you kidding?"

"No. You're right. I was showing off a little. It just pissed me off that they were turning away legitimate help out of ignorance and fear."

"Huh," Candice said, starting the car and pulling away from the curb. "And here I thought that what'd irritated you was his comment about not believing in psychics."

In the past I *might* have shared a complaint or two (twenty) with Candice about the personal insult of that particular dig. "I may have been a little put off by that too," I admitted.

"Hey," Candice said when I took to staring out the window. "Sundance, you gave that man an amazing gift just now. Granted, you probably also should have told him about what happened to Kendra, but he looks to be a man who hasn't had his fair share of happiness in life, and he's probably way overdue for something positive. You gave him that. And you gave him a measure of hope. No one can fault you for that."

I offered her a grudging smile. "Yeah, yeah," I said, already trying to put it behind me. "Where to now?"

"Well," said Candice, taking a moment to think about it. "I doubt we can get to Moreno with all that press around, but we may try taking a more circuitous approach."

"Extended family?" I was only guessing. I was still feeling a little sluggish this morning and longed for a caffeine pick-me-up before we tackled plan C.

"Maybe we'll try extended family, or maybe we'll get lucky and find a willing partner among Kendra's friends," Candice replied cryptically. She didn't elaborate, and we drove in silence for only a few more minutes before she pulled to a stop in front of a nearby Starbucks.

I clapped with glee. "It's like you read my mind!" I hurried out of the car and gimped into the cool building. We got in line, and while we waited Candice tapped at the screen of her smart phone. I peered over her shoulder to look and saw that she was on Facebook. "Updating your status?"

"No," she said, thumbing through the screens. She didn't say anything more; in fact, she was so engrossed with her phone that I had to order for her. It got downright annoying once I paid for our drinks and moved over to a table, leaving Candice still standing next to the counter tapping at her screen.

"Yo, Cassidy!" I called to get her attention. Candice lifted a finger in one of those "hold on" moves, and I rolled my eyes and dove into my frozen caramel Frappuccino with extra whipped cream.

"Not the smartest choice for a woman a month away from fitting into her wedding dress, is it?"

I looked up. Candice had finally decided to join me. "Be nice to me or I'll have Cat swap out your bridesmaid dress for that puffy purple number with the big bow."

Candice smirked and tore open a packet of Splenda for her herbal tea. "Hey, take a look at this, Abs," she said, once she'd finished stirring. She lifted her phone so I could see the screen.

I peered down. "The Bucket List," I read. "Wasn't that a movie?"

Candice turned the screen back to her. "It was. And a good one. But this isn't related to that. It's the Web site for Kendra's business."

I blinked. "I thought she was a stay-at-home mom."

"She was. But she was also a fledgling entrepreneur." My partner scooted her chair closer to me and propped up her phone so we could read it together. "Kendra created a profile questionnaire," she explained. "Basically she set it up to ask you about thirty multiple choice questions, and after you submit the answers, the site sends you a personalized bucket list of your own."

"You got a list, didn't you?" I asked, knowing Candice too well.

She grinned. "Yeppers," she said, switching over to her e-mail. "And I have to hand it to Kendra—the site's good."

"What's in your bucket?"

Candice read a few off her list. "Snorkel the Great

Barrier Reef. Run the Boston Marathon. Learn Italian."

I cocked my head. "How do any of those things fit you?"

"Are you kidding? These are all things I've always wanted to do!"

I blinked. "Really?" Apparently, I didn't know my best friend nearly as well as I thought I did. "You want to learn Italian?"

"Brice and I were thinking of Tuscany for our honeymoon."

"Huh," I said. I hadn't even thought about our honeymoon. The CIA was paying for it, and my former handler at the agency was keeping it a well-guarded secret. I was suddenly regretting allowing him that indulgence. Maybe I wanted to go to Tuscany too.

"Anyway," Candice said, pulling me back to Kendra's Web site. "The other really cool thing about the personalized list Kendra sends you is that all the items on it have links to other sites where you can book whatever's in your bucket. And if you book something through one of those links, Kendra's site sends you a customized bucket of stuff to take along."

That intrigued me. "Like what?"

"Well," Candice said, tapping her screen again. "If I were to book a trip to the Great Barrier Reef, I'd get a snorkel, a beach towel, a mask, sunscreen, Ray-Ban sunglasses, and a book on the history of the reef and the best places along it to snorkel. All of that would show up on my doorstep in this cool big beach pail, see?" Candice swiveled her phone so I could see the screen again.

"I like it," I said, because I really *did* think it was a great idea. "So how did Kendra make money?"

"She must've had a deal worked out with all the sites

she'd linked to. It also looks like she was pulling in a little advertising cash too."

"Hey, Candice?"

"Yeah?"

"If Kendra's dead, like I suspect, who's running the site?"

Candice winked at me. "That's exactly what I wanted to know."

"You already found out, didn't you?"

She took a demure sip of her tea. "Yep. It's all there on her Web site under the 'About us' tab."

"Should I guess who it is?"

She laughed. "No, sorry, I like drawing out the suspense. Kendra built, designed, and ran the site with her best friend, Bailey Colquitt. They've been BFFs since high school."

"And we're about to go pay Bailey a visit," I said, already getting up.

"We are," Candice agreed. But then she hesitated, eyeing me in that I-have-something-to-say-to-you-that-I-don't-think-you're-gonna-like kind of way.

I sighed. "What?"

Candice tapped the side of her cup. "You know I love you, Abs, right?"

I rolled my eyes. "Oh, come on, Cassidy, just spit it out. What do you want me to do that I'm not gonna like doing?"

"It's not so much what I want you to do; it's what I don't want you to say."

I arched an eyebrow. "What don't you want me to say?"

"Anything. Or rather, say nothing."

"Shocking," I said drolly.

Candice tossed her cup in the trash and swung her

arm around my shoulders. "It's just that the Woodyards seemed to me to be pretty conservative—"

"Wow, Sherlock, nothing gets by you, does it?" (Sarcasm is my middle name . . .)

"*And,*" Candice continued like I hadn't interrupted, "I think that same conservative viewpoint may have extended to their daughter and her friends. If we go in there all psychic guns a-blazing, well, you never know who we'll turn off before we even get to ask our first question."

"Fine. Whatever," I said moodily, tossing my own empty cup in the trash. Thank God I'd had the dose of sugary, caffeine goodness, or I might've been a little more disagreeable.

"It's not you," Candice insisted.

"Yeah, yeah," I said with a wave of my hand. "I know. It's everybody else. Can we just go? I want to practice my silent treatment in the car."

The drive over was a bit chilly, and I'm not talking about the air-conditioning. I think I was ticked off because I knew darn well that Candice was right. Still, I wasn't able to let her off the hook for being the messenger—it'd been a crappy morning, and maybe the both of us needed to be miserable to get along for the rest of the day.

Still, I will give Candice a whole lot of credit, because at the end of the drive she parked in front of a set of three edgy-looking townhomes that had to be worth half a million each, and let the engine idle for a minute. "Maybe this was a bad idea," she said.

"Coming here or getting involved in the case?"

"Getting involved in this case. We're a team, Abs, and maybe if these people won't have *you*, then they won't have *us*, you know?"

I shook my head and chuckled softly. "Don't beat yourself up," I said, opening the car door. "This isn't about you—or me. It's about Kendra. And we need to remember her no matter who we end up working for. Even if none of her family or friends hire us, or help us by giving up information, we can still work this case and bring Kendra some closure by nailing her killer. That we can do just for her, okay?"

Candice squeezed my arm. "Okay, Sundance. Thanks for the reminder."

We got out of the car and headed up the walk to the middle town house, and I asked, "How'd you know where Bailey lives, anyway?"

"I had to root around a little, but I found it in tiny print at the bottom of the Bucket List."

"I guess the girls weren't making enough off the site to afford a professional office yet."

Candice shrugged. "Why would they ever need one? I mean, as long as they had enough room to prepare and send off their buckets, everything else could be run from a personal computer and a printer."

I let Candice step in front of me, and she rang the bell. The front door had an outer rim of wood, but the inner door was mostly beveled glass, and it allowed us to make out shapes inside.

We saw someone approach—a shadowy figure at first, but then she took on a clearer form. I could see a slender build and long blond hair, but once she'd pulled open the door, I couldn't help but be a little surprised; Bailey Colquitt was truly lovely. "Hello?" she said, welcoming us with a question.

Candice introduced herself formally as Candice Fusco, private investigator, then motioned to me without looking and said, "And this is my associate, Abby Cooper."

Bailey's long eyelashes fluttered while she, no doubt, tried to make sense of our appearance on her doorstep. "Ah," was all she said, while her eyes continued to bounce back and forth between Candice and me like she was watching a tennis match.

Candice decided to be helpful. "We understand that your best friend, Kendra Woodyard, is missing."

More eyelash fluttering followed by a jerky head nod.

"And my partner and I are considering taking the case," Candice added, no doubt hoping that would get the dialogue flowing.

"Uh . . . ?"

My partner and I exchanged a quick look, and I could see that Candice thought the same thing I did, namely, that Bailey Colquitt was really lucky she was pretty, because we were laying odds that she was no mental giant.

"May we come in and talk to you about Kendra?" Candice asked after an awkward silence.

Bailey's brows rose even higher on her smooth, unlined forehead, and it was like you could hear the gears in her head turning before she finally exclaimed, "Oh! Oh, yes! Please, y'all, come in."

Bailey stepped aside as we entered. The first thing I noticed were the moving boxes. They were stacked everywhere—some open and erupting with white packing paper, others closed and bulging.

Candice and I exchanged another quick look. This one said, "Innnnnteresting."

"Sorry the place is such a mess!" Bailey apologized, closing the door behind us and motioning with her hand for us to head down the hallway. "I'm in the middle of packing."

"Moving somewhere close?" Candice asked.

"Sorta," Bailey called over her shoulder as we

reached the kitchen. "We're . . . I mean, *I'm* moving closer to my folks in Dallas next month."

I kept my mouth shut but made a point to raise my brows at Candice. I knew she caught that whole "We . . . I mean I'm . . ." thing too.

Bailey indicated two seats in front of the kitchen island, and I had to move a small box to take my seat. "Can I get you something to drink?" our host asked politely. "I've got soft drinks and water and iced tea. Or if you'd like I could squeeze some lemons for lemonade. Or I could make y'all some coffee?"

That's one thing I really liked about living in the South—most everyone's got good old-fashioned manners. "Thank you," Candice said. "But we just had some coffee. I think we're fine."

Bailey nodded again and fidgeted with a dish towel on the counter. She seemed nervous to me. "Well, I'll just get myself some iced tea, then." Bailey turned away from us to get herself some refreshment, and Candice and I exchanged a whole new series of knowing looks.

Once we had Bailey's attention again, Candice got right down to business. "As I said, we're looking into the disappearance of your best friend, Kendra, and it's come to our attention that you two were in business together. Is that correct?"

Bailey took a big ol' sip of tea before she answered. It almost seemed like she was stalling. "The Bucket List was mostly Kendra's idea," Bailey told us. Right away I caught how she used the past tense, but I wasn't sure if she meant it for Kendra or the Bucket List. "She came up with it right after she saw that movie, and before I knew it she'd hired a guy to design the Web site, and then she did all the research and the marketing and stuff that she needed to do to get it off the ground. Really, it was her baby all the way."

"And yet," Candice said, pretending to refer to her notes, "according to the Web site, the headquarters for the Bucket List are located here at your house."

Bailey seemed surprised that we'd figured that out. Her fidgeting took on a whole new energy. "Well, yeah. That's true. See, Kendra was real sweet, you know? She always wanted to include me in everything she did, so she convinced me to be her business partner. I wasn't really interested in it, but she swore it'd make money, so I went along with it."

Again Bailey was using the past tense to describe her friend, and that made me wonder how she knew that Kendra was dead. I started to feel out her energy and tapped into a mix of stuff, much of it surprising.

Discreetly digging through my purse, I came up with a small notebook and began scribbling in it so I wouldn't forget anything.

"So did it?" Candice asked after jotting down her own notes.

"Did it what?" Bailey asked.

"Did the site make money?"

Bailey's face flushed. "Only a little."

Liar, I thought. I jotted that down too.

"And you're running the Bucket List while Kendra's MIA, is that right?"

Bailey squinted at her. "Huh?" she said.

"The Web site," Candice said slowly. "You're running it, while Kendra is away."

The squint deepened. "No," she said. "I'm not running it. It runs itself. Well, except for fulfilling the orders for the buckets, but most of that Kendra set up to come through a distributor so that we wouldn't get bogged down by it. Once a week I just go through the list and make sure that a bucket has been sent out for everyone who booked something on one of our links."

I scanned Bailey's energy. That part was true.

Candice made another note to herself, then asked, "When was the last time you saw Kendra, Bailey?"

Our host took another long sip of tea. "Maybe . . . two weeks ago?"

Candice cocked her head and snuck a look at me. I nodded. The last time Bailey had seen her BFF was at least two weeks before. Still, Candice pressed Bailey on that. "Two weeks? But I thought you guys were best friends. Why would you go a whole two weeks without seeing her?"

"It's not like we were tied at the hip or anything!" Bailey snapped.

Whoa. Candice had pushed a button. "Sounds like the last time you two saw each other, there might've been some friction," Candice said, taking a stab at the obvious.

Bailey's beautiful face turned down in a scowl, making it considerably less attractive. She combed her fingers through her hair nervously. I could see that she was trying to rein in her temper. "Lately we haven't been gettin' along so well."

"Why's that?" Candice asked.

Bailey rolled her eyes. "You know how it is with girlfriends. Sometimes they get along; sometimes they don't."

Candice looked down at her notes. "It sorta seems like you're not really worried about her, Bailey."

At this, Bailey's attitude changed dramatically, from petulant to distraught. "Of *course* I'm worried about her!" She put a hand to her mouth as her eyes welled up, and big wet tears began to leak down her cheeks, smudging her eye makeup. "She was my best friend, you know? What if she doesn't come back?"

For the life of me I couldn't figure this chick out. One minute she was happily talking about her BFF in the past tense like Kendra had simply moved away and didn't keep in touch much, and the next minute she was sobbing hysterically because she might never see her best friend again. None of it made sense to me.

Candice appeared puzzled too. After waiting for Bailey to dab at her eyes with the dish towel and collect herself, she said, "Do you know what might've happened to Kendra, Bailey?"

At this, Bailey only shook her head vehemently, but the lie was so evident in the ether around her that it was really hard for me to keep my mouth shut. Still, I managed, and when Candice snuck another look at me, I motioned for us to go. Bailey was clearly in no condition to continue the conversation, and I had a lot to share with Candice. I wanted to fill her in on what I'd picked up out of the ether before she pushed Bailey too far and the girl stopped talking to us.

Candice closed her notebook and stood from the chair. I did the same. "We should get out of your hair," she said to her. "Is it all right, though, to call or stop by if we find out anything about Kendra that you might be able to shed a little more light on?"

Bailey shrugged, then nodded, the tears continuing to leak down her cheeks creating black smudgy streaks from her mascara.

We thanked her for her time and waited until we were back in Candice's Porsche to talk about Bailey. "Go," Candice said the minute I'd shut the car door.

I smirked. "You don't waste time, do you?"

"Nope," she said, already flipping to a fresh page in her notebook.

I went back through my own notes to find the starting point and rattled off the tidbits I'd been able to pull out of the ether. "First, the reason Bailey is moving back to Dallas is because she's getting a divorce."

Candice's brow shot up, but otherwise she didn't look at me; she simply scribbled that down.

I went on. "And the Web site that Kendra started with her BFF is pulling in more money than 'only a little.'" I scoured my notes and found the next point, "Also, there's this really weird thing going on in her energy, and I'm sure you picked up on it with the way she spoke about Kendra in the past tense. See, I think she thinks that Kendra's gone, but I don't know that she had anything directly to do with it. She feels involved, but tangentially, and I can't figure out how."

Candice lifted her eyes to me. "She's also feeling super guilty. The fidgeting and the nervousness—that speaks of a guilty conscience."

I nodded. "Agreed. There's more to the story." I remembered that in the ether I'd felt Kendra's killer might have acted on behalf of a woman. I wondered if Bailey might have been the woman I'd felt was involved in Kendra's abduction and murder.

"What about that whole 'I haven't seen my best friend in two weeks' deal?" Candice asked next.

"That part was true," I told her. "She hasn't seen Kendra in at least that long. So again, I don't think she was present when Kendra was kidnapped and murdered, but that doesn't mean she couldn't have otherwise been involved."

Candice pointed her pen at me. "You had mentioned that yesterday when you were first focusing on Kendra."

I nodded. Candice chewed on the tip of her pen for a minute, then said, "What if Bailey hired someone to kill Kendra? Bailey's going through a divorce and she doesn't strike me as the working type."

I remembered the fine clothes, perfect hair, fresh manicure, and fit figure on Bailey. It all spoke of super–high maintenance, something most working women don't have a lot of time for. Plus, we'd visited her on a weekday, when just about everyone else was at work. Granted, she could've taken the day off to pack her stuff up, but I didn't think that was the case. "Let me guess where you're headed with this," I said to Candice. "You think that maybe she saw how much money was coming into the Web site and she decided to get greedy? Maybe she hired somebody to abduct and kill Kendra?"

"People have killed their BFFs for a whole lot less," Candice pointed out.

I sighed. "For the record, I'd never kill you over money."

The corners of Candice's mouth lifted. "Good to know." Then she seemed to linger on what I'd just said because she added, "By the way . . . where's your gun?"

That made me laugh. "At home in my closet. Where it's going to stay."

"Also good to know," my partner said. Then she motioned with her pen at my notebook. "Anything else in there you want to share?"

I looked down. "Yes and no. There's something about the argument between Bailey and Kendra that we need to focus on. Something significant sparked their fight, and my radar is suggesting that it's part of the key to unlocking this mystery."

Candice's eyes swiveled to Bailey's door. "No time like the present," she said, getting out of the car.

I had to scramble out of the car to hurry after her. By the time I caught up, Candice had already pressed the doorbell again.

Bailey answered it a bit warily. "Hey, y'all. Did you forget something?"

I had this feeling like she'd been watching us the whole time, waiting for us to leave, and she maybe didn't like so much that we'd come back to her door so soon.

"Just one more question, Bailey," Candice said. "I was wondering; that argument you and Kendra had two weeks ago—what was that about exactly?"

Bailey blushed crimson and began to twist a ring on her right hand nervously. "How exactly is that important?"

Candice smiled breezily. "It's probably not important. It's just that at this point, we don't know if Kendra disappeared on her own, or if someone else was responsible. Assuming that she went off on her own, maybe the fight you two had contributed to her leaving?"

Bailey's expression became pinched. "You think maybe she was really upset about our fight and that's why she left without telling anybody where she was going?" She practically whispered that question, and I could detect just a hint of hope there, which confused me even more.

"It's possible," Candice told her.

Bailey bit her lip, and she seemed on the verge of telling us something when her cell phone rang. We stood there patiently while she pulled it out of her purse by the door and glanced at the screen. "Sorry," she said, already shutting the door in our faces. "I gotta take this."

Candice and I stood on the step for a beat, staring at the door. "Well, that was helpful," I muttered when we both turned and headed back down the steps.

Candice growled with frustration. "Basically we learned nothing today."

I patted her on the shoulder. Candice wasn't used to her investigative efforts being wasted. She was used to asking people questions and getting results. I could already tell this case was gonna challenge her in all the wrong ways.

Chapter Six

Half an hour later I left Candice still grumbling in the confines of her office, digging into Bailey's financials and looking for proof that she'd filed for divorce.

As I had an appointment with Dave at the new house, I had the perfect excuse to quit early and boogie across town. I didn't think I'd ever been so happy to go look at tile and carpet samples in all my life.

Pulling up behind Dave's truck, I found workmen all over the dusty drive. No lawn had been planted yet—there was still too much traffic from the crew going in and out—so I had to step carefully with my cane to avoid the pitfalls of tripping over the usual trash you find at building sites.

I found Dave inside with a mug of coffee in his hand, telling a few dirty jokes to a couple of guys. When he saw me nearby with raised eyebrows, he quickly cleared his throat and shuffled away from his work crew. "Abs!" he said brightly.

"Dave," I said with a weeeeee bit less warmth.

"I didn't expect to see you here."

"We had an appointment today at four," I reminded him. "It's four."

Dave nodded. "Oh, I know we had an appointment. That's why I didn't expect to see you."

I cut him a look but had to admit that he was right. I'd blown off more appointments with him than I could count. "Yeah . . . well . . . ," was all I could think of to say in return. Rapier wit I am not.

Dave chuckled and motioned for me to follow him into the kitchen, which was quite bare and dusty. Dave pulled a large piece of plastic off the floor to get to all those samples I was going to have to decide between, and as he did so, something small and black flew off and landed right on my upper arm. In the next instant I felt a stinging sensation like nothing I've ever felt before. *"Yeeeeeow!"* I shrieked, slapping at the thing on my arm. It plopped to the floor and began to scuttle away in that really creepy way that makes your skin crawl. Except of course that my skin wasn't so much crawling as it was . . . *on fire!*

"Mother fecking fecker!" I shouted, clamping my hand over my arm and gritting my teeth hard. "What the *freaking feck* was *that*?"

Dave hurried over to me, and for a minute he didn't seem to know what to do. He still had the mug in his hand, and he sort of half turned, looking for a place to put the coffee down, then thought better of it and turned back to me, then went back to trying to figure out what to do with his coffee.

I made his mind up for him. *"Throw it down and help me!"*

Dave dropped the mug. On his foot. "Ow! Damn!" he swore when hot coffee splashed up his leg.

I made a kind of primal snarling sound, whirling around and hobbling away from him, but the pain in my arm was so intense that I couldn't use my right hand to hold my cane, and I didn't get very far before he caught up to me. "Abs!" he said, still dancing a little from his own mishap. "Let me see it!"

"Get away from me!" I blubbered through the tears that had started to fall. The pain in my arm would not subside. It stung like a thousand hornets, and I could feel a few of my fingers begin to go numb.

"Abs!" Dave tried again, clamping onto my uninjured arm and halting me. "That was a scorpion. You gotta let me take a look!"

I stopped, not because I wanted Dave to help me, but because he'd just said the word "scorpion." He could have said "rattlesnake" and I'd have been less freaked out. *"It was a what?!"*

Dave didn't answer me; he just gently turned me around and peeled my fingers off my injured arm. "Oooo," he said, wincing a little when he took a look. "He got you good."

Tears leaked out of my eyes although I tried like heck to fight them. I focused on Dave's face and waited for him to say something like, "You have five minutes to live. Any last words?"

But instead he simply pulled up a five-gallon bucket, flipped it upside down, and settled me on top of it. "Why aren't you calling nine-one-one?" I whimpered as I watched him shuffle over to a cooler.

Dave snorted. "Abs, scorpions in Texas aren't poisonous."

"How would *you* know?" I snapped. I can be a real pill when I think I'm about to die from a scorpion sting. (Okay, so I can be a real pill at other times too.)

Dave came back to me and pulled up his shirtsleeve. There were two little purple welts on his forearm. "Got stung here twice a few days ago," he told me. Then he pulled up his pant leg and pointed to another purple welt. "That one's about a week old."

I stared at his wounds in horror. "I'm getting married in less than a month and a half!" I shrieked. "I can't walk down the aisle with a big old purple welt on my arm!"

Dave lowered the leg of his jeans and stood back to regard me. Then his eyes swiveled ever so slowly to my cane on the floor at my feet. "Seems to me, you got more important things to worry about than some purple dot on your arm, Abs."

I glared hard at him. "Feck you, Dave."

He chuckled and returned to the cooler. Pulling out some ice and a leftover sandwich baggie, he came back to me with the improvised ice pack and laid it on my arm. Then he went and got another bucket, brought it over to set down beside mine, took a seat, and lifted the hand of my injured arm to rest on his shoulder. "Gotta keep it elevated," he told me.

I felt like kicking him.

"That's the spirit," he said, reading my expression with another chuckle.

"I'm glad you find this so funny," I said in a tone as cold as the ice on my arm.

"Well, Abs, if you'd have come out here three months ago like I asked you to, and picked out all your finishes, those scorpions wouldn't have been all riled up from the construction and you wouldn't have gotten stung."

"So this is *my* fault?" I screeched.

Dave winced. "No," he said patiently. "Of course not. It's mine. And the scorpion's. Feel better?"

If looks could kill, Dave would've been pushing up daisies about then, but I held my tongue and turned my eyes to the wall. After about ten minutes, I asked, "How long do we have to sit like this?"

Dave eased my hand off his shoulder and lifted the ice pack from my arm. "No swelling," he said, examining the little bump on my upper arm. "When you get home take some aspirin. Then ice it again before dinner and once more before you turn in."

I reached for my cane, noting that my arm still throbbed but not nearly as badly as before. Then I got up and eyed the floor warily. "Is this place really crawling with scorpions?" I asked meekly.

Dave shrugged. "Construction always kicks up a bunch of 'em, Abs. You wait, once we're done and we get landscaping put in, you won't notice 'em."

I leveled my gaze at him. "That's *hardly* reassuring."

Dave shrugged again and added a smile. "Welcome to Texas, darlin'. Now, you ready to pick out which paint and finishings you want?"

"No," I told him, still eyeing the floor suspiciously. I felt like at any moment one of the little buggers was going come right out and zap me again.

"No? Why not?" Dave asked.

"Because I don't think I can live here." Ignoring the perplexed look on Dave's face, I hobbled out the door without another word.

Several hours later Dutch came home to find me sitting in the dark. "You okay?" he asked when he saw me curled up on the couch with a pooch on either side and an almost totally melted ice pack on my arm.

"We have to move far, far away from here," I told him, getting right to the point.

Dutch hung there in the door with his keys for a minute. "Should I pack now, or can I sneak in some dinner?"

"I'm serious!"

Dutch closed the door and set his keys in the bowl on the side table. "So am I, Edgar," he said, moving past me into the kitchen.

I pouted on the couch for a while until I heard the sound of a cork popping free from its bottle. Scooting off the couch, I went in search of sustenance. Dutch was already pouring a second glass when I reached him, and he offered it to me the moment it was half full. I took it moodily and stood there wondering how to tell him I couldn't possibly live in a house, or a state for that matter, infested with scorpions.

Dutch picked up the other wineglass and clinked his with mine. "How was your day?" he asked (a bit drolly, I thought).

"It sucked."

He took a sip of wine and regarded me over the rim. "Wanna tell me about it?"

I pushed my shoulder forward to display my arm. "I got stung by a poisonous scorpion!"

Dutch squinted at the small red dot on my arm before taking another sip of wine. "And yet, you're miraculously still alive."

And then I knew. "Dave called you, didn't he?"

Dutch moved over to the pantry and pulled out a small Ziploc bag, which he held underneath the ice maker, waiting until the baggie was mostly full. Once he'd zipped it up, he handed it to me, pointed me toward a chair, and said, "Sit. We'll talk while I make dinner."

I gimped over to the table and took up a chair, but I found that I couldn't drink the wine and do the ice pack at the same time. Your guess which one I administered first.

"I can't live in a house with scorpions, cowboy."

Dutch began pulling out pots and pans from the cabinet, moving slowly and methodically, the way he always does in the kitchen. "Dave tells me the work crew has stirred up a few of those," he said, removing some lamb chops from the fridge before going back for more items.

I shuddered. "He's got sting marks all over his arms and legs, Dutch! I mean, it's like there's an *infestation*!"

My fiancé didn't say anything, and I couldn't believe he wasn't freaking out over this. I'd been sitting in the living room ever since I'd gotten home just thinking about those creepy crawlies, scuttling all over our floors, through our things, between our sheets (shudder, shudder). "And what about Eggy and Tuttle?" I demanded, wanting him to have some sort of alarmed reaction. "You can't expect to move them into the new house with those things crawling all over the place!"

Dutch pulled his head up out of the fridge, his arms loaded with veggies for a salad. "They're easy enough to control, Edgar. You just call an exterminator."

It was like a lightbulb went off right over my head. "An exterminator?" I asked hopefully.

"Yeah," he said, unloading the ingredients onto the counter. "Scorpions are a part of living on the west side of Austin, babe. Just about every licensed exterminator knows how to control the little critters."

I stared at him with big, wide, happy eyes for a minute. "So we don't have to move out of Texas?"

Dutch tried to hide a grin by taking a sip of his wine. "Nope."

"You'll really call an exterminator?"

At that, Dutch set his wineglass back on the counter and folded his arms over his chest. "Nope."

I shook my head a little. "Wait . . . what? Why not?"

Dutch pointed at me. "Because *you're* on house duty, sweethot. Not me. I'm on *wedding* duty. Remember?"

My shoulders slumped. "Crap on a cracker," I muttered, because I hadn't remembered. And if I called the exterminator, that'd mean I'd have to go out to the house to let him in while he did his thing, which meant that I'd have no choice but to return to the scene of the sting. "You sure you don't want to do this one teeeeeensy favor for me, sweetie?" I asked, batting my lashes at Dutch.

He laughed. But it wasn't a nice laugh. It had an edge to it. "Do you know what your sister is making me do?" he asked.

Uh-oh. I realized I'd maybe just opened up the box labeled "Pandora."

"What?"

"She's having me meet with a dance instructor. *A dance instructor!*"

My eyes bugged. "Why?" was all I thought to ask.

Dutch downed the remains of his glass before reaching for the bottle again and pouring himself an extra-generous second glass. "Because she thinks it might be *fun* to choreograph our trip down the aisle with a little dance number. *Or* she's thinking maybe the whole wedding party can do a little 'Thriller' before we cut the cake. *Or* she thinks it could be a boatload of laughs for the guests to learn the hustle. But one way or another, *your sister* is determined to bring a little Broadway to our wedding."

For several seconds Dutch and I did nothing but stare

at each other. "You're right," I finally told him. "I should call the exterminator."

Dutch lifted his glass to me. "While you're at it, see if you can find one who deals with pesky felines."

The next morning I was out of the house early. It had less to do with ducking Cat (whom, my radar suggested, was on her way over with a cache of dance CDs and chore-ography suggestions) and more to do with the fact that the case with Kendra Moreno had been niggling away at me. I felt an uneasy sense of urgency that I couldn't quite pinpoint, but I knew that I was running out of time to figure out what'd happened to her, and if Candice and I didn't solve her case quickly, something else was going to happen. Something bad.

Candice wasn't in when I got to the office, and that could've had to do with the early hour. I'd made it to the office before seven a.m.

I thought about calling my partner and asking her to come in for a little powwow, but then thought better of it, and instead, I made the trip back downstairs for a tall cup of joe before heading back to my desk to sit down with a large legal pad and a bit of determination.

There was a technique that I'd used before that I wanted to try with this case. I began by making a large circle in the middle of the legal pad and writing a question in the center: *What happened to Kendra Moreno?*

From there I drew a series of lines coming off the circle, so it looked a bit like a spider.

I sat there staring at the circle and the lines for a minute, drumming my fingers and sipping my coffee, and then, slowly at first, little facts started coming to me from out of the ether.

Kidnapped, I wrote on one line. *Murdered,* I wrote along another. Well, that much I'd already assumed.

I closed my eyes and focused on the impressions coming into my mind's eye. They felt disorderly and disconnected, but soon I began to jot down other words.

I had a sense of feeling closed in—claustrophobic—and I jotted that word on another line. Then I felt I couldn't breathe, like the air about my nose and mouth had been shut off—and I wrote down the word *Smothered.*

Other things circulated in the energy around Kendra's murder. I felt strongly that at one point her hands were tied. I knew that at some other point she'd also been beaten, but what I felt when I tripped over that clue in the ether again was that she'd also been raped.

You bastard, I thought as I penciled that in with disgust.

After I felt I had the sequence of what had happened to her in her final moments, I backed up a bit, trying to understand how Kendra had allowed herself to be taken from her home without any sign of a struggle.

As I pondered that, I felt a very sharp and incredibly quick pain in my lower back. It was so sudden and unexpected that I actually hissed and put a hand on my spine—but in an instant it was gone.

Had she been stabbed? I wondered.

The phantom pain I'd felt was at the center of my lower back, and as I analyzed exactly what I'd felt, I also experienced a slight numbing sensation in my legs.

If Kendra had been stabbed in the lower back, then it could have impacted her spinal cord, and she'd be completely vulnerable.

"But where was the blood?" I said aloud. If she'd

been stabbed, surely there would have been some trace evidence of her wound found at the scene.

I settled for creating a line that read, *Possible stabbing in lower back—spine injured to incapacitate,* and moved on.

Who was responsible? I asked next.

As I pondered that question, I silently cursed the fact that I'm one of those psychics who does not easily sense names. It's very rare for me to pull a name out of the ether, as it's simply not one of my strong suits, but that didn't mean that I couldn't try to pinpoint a suspect.

Again I had this sense of a man whom Kendra was very familiar with; someone she knew and trusted had betrayed her in the most horrendous way. Firmly attached to this man was a female who had something to do with Kendra's murder. The woman felt familiar to Kendra, and I could detect the animosity there, but what perplexed me was how one-sided the animosity was. All the hostility came from Kendra.

I rejected the notion at first, believing I'd misinterpreted the energy, but it replayed like a broken record over and over again and I couldn't make sense of it.

Even more frustrating, it felt like the key to solving the case, and the clues would line up perfectly if only I could figure out the identity of this woman and what her connection to Kendra was.

I also wanted to focus on what had become of Kendra's remains, so that's where I targeted my radar next. I had the briefest whiff of a very earthy smell—dirt, to be exact—and I quickly drew another line and wrote, *Kendra's remains have been buried.*

I refocused on that thread again, trying to get a feel for a location, and what I pulled from the ether was that she was in a shallow grave, somewhere in the woods, and on top of all that I caught another unusual smell—like wet dog.

After thinking about it for a little while, I concluded that Kendra's remains would likely be found by someone's pet at some point in the near future.

I wrote that all out on a few more lines, then sat back with a sigh.

The bell above the front door to the office gave a jingle. "Abs?" I heard Candice call.

"Morning!" I replied, wondering how she knew I was here; then I remembered that Candice usually parked next to me in the parking garage and she likely had seen my car.

A moment later my partner poked her head in. "You're in early."

I pushed my spiderweb across the desk as she came in and took a seat in front of the desk. "I've been working on the case."

Candice lifted my diagram and with her finger traced the lines I'd created. After a moment she lifted her gaze to me. "She was raped?"

I nodded soberly. "Beaten and raped before being smothered."

Candice was silent for a moment. "That's a whole lotta rage, Sundance."

"I know. We're dealing with a sick motherfecker."

A corner of Candice's mouth quirked. "Dutch lets you get away with 'fecker'?"

"He's learned to pick his battles."

"Uh-huh, and how much is in the swear jar these days?"

"About three hundred," I told her. What I didn't tell her was that I probably owed the jar at least double that.

Candice's knowing smile was just a wee bit smug for

my taste, but I decided to pick my own battles too and focused back on the diagram by tapping the paper in Candice's hand. "There are parts here that make no sense to me, and I can't find an interpretation of the little factoids I'm able to pull out of the ether that would make them line up and help us."

"What do you mean?"

"Well, this female that Kendra had some animosity toward—in a way, she feels responsible for Kendra's murder, but I can't figure out what Kendra did to spark the wrath of this duo."

"Do you think it had anything to do with her Web business?" Candice wondered.

I was silent while I considered that, trying to find the connection in the ether, but the answer eluded me. The best that I could do was say, "If it did have anything to do with the Bucket List, it was indirect." And then, the moment those words came out of my mouth, the answer was there, very clearly in my mind. "It had to do with a secret," I whispered.

"A what?"

I cleared my throat and spoke louder. "Kendra was keeping a secret, and I think she may have threatened to go public with it. That's what triggered her murder."

"What was the secret?"

I shook my head. "I have no idea."

Candice set the diagram down on the desktop and tapped her lip thoughtfully. "So we'll need to keep prying into her personal life to come up with whatever it was that Kendra knew that someone else wanted to keep quiet." After another small stretch of silence between us, she pointed to my line about where Kendra's remains were and said, "She was buried in a shallow grave?"

I nodded. "Somewhere out in the woods."

"What's this mean?" Candice asked, pointing to the line labeled, "Wet Dog."

I explained that I thought Kendra's remains would be found in the not-too-distant future by someone's dog. "Maybe a hiker will take his dog for a walk in the woods or something, and they'll stumble upon her remains."

"How soon are we talking?"

I shrugged. "Few weeks maybe?"

"That's too long to wait," Candice said softly while she studied my diagram again. "Here's a question for you, Abs: Where's her car?"

I rubbed my temples. I was starting to get a headache from focusing so long on Kendra. "Not near her," I said, "and ask me more details about it later because my head's starting to pound."

"No sweat," Candice said, but there was something bugging her, I could tell.

"What?"

Candice hesitated before she said, "Why would the killer separate Kendra from her car? I mean, he could have just as easily driven her car out into the woods and dumped both of them together. Digging a grave for her then dumping the car somewhere else seems like an awful lot of work, so why go to the trouble?"

The answer came to me quickly. "Bodies are smaller than cars, and easier to hide in the woods. Plus, you leave a body in a car, you've definitely got a murder on your hands, but if someone recovers Kendra's car soon, then there's still this question of where she might be. Or even if she could still be alive. Until you have a body, you have no hard evidence of murder."

It was Candice's turn to nod. "And you leave less trace evidence behind without a body in the trunk," she said. "This guy, whoever he is, really thought this through. And he's smart."

"Which makes him even more dangerous."

Candice didn't comment, because something else on my diagram caught her attention. "Hold on, here, Sundance—you think Kendra was stabbed in the back?"

"Oh, that I couldn't pinpoint exactly either, Candice. I know that she was taken by surprise from behind, and when I first focused on her initial attack, I felt that she thought she was in the presence of someone she trusted, turned her back to him, then was struck by something sharp from behind. The area where I think she was struck was at the small of her back, and her legs immediately went out from under her. She felt somehow incapacitated—paralyzed even—by that first blow."

Candice's brow furrowed. "But the police found no trace evidence of blood at Kendra's house."

"I know, which is why I can't say with any certainty that she was actually stabbed with a blade."

"Could it have been a shot?"

I blinked. "You mean like from a gun?"

"No. Like from a syringe. Maybe the killer stuck her with a syringe filled with a paralyzing agent."

I mulled that over for a moment. "Possibly," I said. It made sense in a way, as it would explain the lack of blood splatter found at the scene. Even if the killer had cleaned up after himself, he was likely to leave behind at least a drop or two that the CSI techs would have discovered. "The one thing I can tell you is that how Kendra was immediately incapacitated is the biggest clue in fingering her murderer," I said.

Candice cocked her head. "Say what?"

"I feel like this guy may have tried this before with

another girl," I explained, feeling out the energy as I went. "There's a pattern here."

Candice eyed me keenly before she shot out of the chair and hurried through the door. I got up a little more slowly and headed into her office, where she was already tapping on her keyboard. "I'm sending Brice an e-mail," she said without looking up. "I'm asking him to check his database for missing women who fit Kendra's profile within the past three years."

I hovered in the doorway until she was finished. When she looked up, I asked, "Now what?"

"We wait," she said.

And wait we did. An hour went by and I busied myself by playing Bejeweled Blitz on Facebook. Candice did something equally productive—she played Scrabble.

Another hour went by and we finally got an e-mail reply from Brice. "He's sent the list," she told me, pressing the print command and moving over to her printer. After looking at it, she frowned and handed it to me.

"Eight women," I read, "all reported missing from their homes in the middle of the day, but all their cases except three have been solved and the perps are either dead or in jail. Well, at least we've got three unsolved cases to possibly match to Kendra's."

"Not so fast, Sundance," Candice told me. "Look again at the location of those three unsolved."

"Two in Laredo and one in El Paso. Yeah, so?"

"Border towns," Candice said. "Kidnapping is big business these days in places like that."

"And most of the others are from high-crime cities like Houston and Dallas," I remarked. "None of them are from Austin or Travis County."

"We live in a nice safe city, Abs."

"That's probably what Kendra thought too."

Intuitively I knew that none of the names on the list from Brice were connected with Kendra's killer, but I'd felt so strongly that I'd been onto something. I just *knew* the person responsible for killing Kendra was following a pattern. And then I thought of something. "What if he recently moved here?" I said.

"Who?"

"The killer!" I was getting excited. "Can you have Brice check the national database?"

Candice's eyes widened. "Abs, that's gonna come back with literally *dozens* of names."

My shoulders sagged, and Candice took the sheet from me. "Listen," she said, "how about I have Brice run the list and we keep it handy while we work the case. We can compare any suspects we develop against the list to see if there's a match and go from there, okay?"

"Yeah. Okay. That's a good compromise. And speaking of suspects, did you get a chance to look into Kendra's BFF?"

Candice returned to her desk and motioned for me to sit too. "I did," she began, "but I didn't find much in her financials or her credit report to indicate Bailey might have been motivated to kill Kendra to gain control of the Web site and take all the profits for herself."

"What'd you come up with?" I was convinced there was some sort of Bailey connection to Kendra's disappearance, but what that was I hadn't quite figured out yet.

"Well, for starters, Bailey likes to shop. In fact, Bailey likes to shop *a lot*. But for the most part her credit is clean, and she pays the minimum on all her credit cards each month on time."

"You mean her husband pays them on time," I muttered.

Candice grinned. "Probably. Still, it appears that Bailey comes from money. Her former address before she got married puts her in the heart of some very pricey real estate. Even assuming she lived with her parents, you can't find anything in that Dallas neighborhood for under two million."

I whistled appreciatively. "There's more you found out." I was reading Candice's expression.

"Oh, yeah," she said. "We were wrong to assume that Bailey doesn't have a job besides what she earns from her half of the Web site. Mrs. Colquitt is a model for a local modeling agency here in town. And she does pretty well for herself, actually. She's not quite at six figures, but she's not far from it. Plus, I did a few calculations and made some calls last night to some of Kendra's sponsors, and according to my figures, the Web site can't be bringing in more than sixty to seventy thousand a year. Especially not in this economy."

I sighed. Why couldn't any of this be easy? "And yet," I insisted, "I still think Bailey had something to do with all this. There's a link in the ether that keeps connecting Bailey to what happened to Kendra."

"Is that thread anything your radar can pin down?" Candice asked me.

I stared at the floor for a long couple of seconds, but, try as I might, I couldn't pull the thread close enough to put words to it. "The best way I can describe it is that whatever happened to Kendra started with Bailey. Other than that, I'm sorry, but it's too nebulous for me to define."

Candice closed the lid to her laptop and rested her elbows on top of it. "Okay," she said. "We'll put Bailey on the back burner for now. If you get any more insights that point to her, we'll take another look in her direction."

"Sounds fair." I got up to stretch and relieve the pain in my hips.

"How's your physical therapy coming along?" Candice asked, obviously catching my stiff rise from the chair.

"Oh, crap!" I exclaimed, turning my wrist to check the time. I'd completely forgotten about my appointment that morning.

With a hasty wave I left Candice's office in search of my purse and keys. Even if I made every light, I'd still be ten minutes late.

An hour and a half later I walked painfully back into the office. My hips were killing me and I was grouchy after my session with my physical therapist—who'd decided to pack an hour's session into forty-five minutes.

"Hey, there, Hopalong," Candice called as I gimped past her office on the way to mine.

I muttered something (it might've contained an expletive) and kept on trucking. Just as I was about to settle into my chair, Candice appeared in my doorway. "Don't sit down," she ordered.

I stood there, half bent, ready to plop my butt into the chair, and stared at her. "I seriously need to take a load off, Cassidy."

"Then sit down in the car. I've managed to arrange a meet and greet with Tristan."

Although it sounded familiar, my brain at first had a hard time making a connection. "Who?"

"Tristan Moreno. Kendra's husband."

I rolled my eyes and eased myself into the chair— "Defiant" is my second middle name. "Can't you just go talk to him?" I asked wearily.

"Of course I could."

I exhaled happily, leaned back in the chair, and closed my eyes. "Good," I said. "Thanks, partner."

No sooner had I gotten that out than I detected a slight movement behind me, and as I snapped my eyes back open, the chair was nearly pulled out from underneath me. "Hey!" I cried when I was roughly rolled away from the desk and pushed forward toward the door at an alarming rate of speed. "What the freak are you doing, Candice?!"

"As I said," she told me, the strain of pushing my chair making her voice tight, "I *could* go talk to Tristan alone. But I'm not going to. I need that radar of yours to feel him out, Sundance, and letting you sit here and grouse about your hips all day isn't going to help anyone. Including you."

At the door Candice whipped me around and I almost flew out of the seat again. "Quit it!" I yelled, but it was no use; Candice was tugging me backward through my office door, and even though I reached out for the doorframe, she was too quick for me and all I grabbed was air.

Once we were through the door, Candice whipped me around again, and she pushed me down the short hallway at breakneck speed. *"Are you crazy?"* I shouted. "What the hell has gotten into you?"

Candice ignored me and said not a word until we reached the front lobby. She stopped only long enough to spin me around backward yet again, yank open the door, and drag me out into the hallway.

"Candice!" I cried, really alarmed now, because if I tried to launch myself out of the chair I'd most certainly hurt myself. "Quit. It!"

"Nope," she replied in that most annoying determined tone she often took with me.

"My cane!" I protested, trying to claw the air behind me. "Just let me go back and get my cane at least!"

But I'd obviously touched a nerve with my partner, who continued to propel me all the way down the hallway, right up to the elevator. Only then did she let go of my chair and step in front of me while pushing the DOWN button. "You want to walk without your cane at your wedding, Abby?" she asked as the bell above the elevator dinged and the doors opened.

I didn't say anything. I knew where this was headed.

Candice put her purse against the door to prevent it from closing, while waiting for me to answer. *"Well, do you?"* she demanded when I continued with the silent treatment.

"Yes," I said meekly.

Candice nodded, came around to the back of my chair again, and tipped the whole thing forward. I barely got my hands out in front of me before she dumped me out onto the floor. "If you truly want to walk without that cane, Sundance, then it's time to start practicing."

"Why are you being so mean to me?" I shrieked when she grabbed hold of the chair and shoved it back down the hallway away from me.

"I'm not being mean," Candice said, finally turning away from me to pick up her purse and walk casually into the elevator. Putting an arm out to hold the doors, she said, "For the past month I've barely seen any improvement from you, even though I know you're going to all your physical therapy appointments. You should've let go of that cane two weeks ago, Abs. It's time to walk, honey."

My lower lip was quivering and I was on the verge of tears again. Candice had once trained me into shape, and I'd quickly discovered that her methods were all drill with equal parts sergeant mixed in.

And I knew that this was another form of her tough-love method, but the truth was that she had really struck a nerve. I'd thought the exact same things she had about my slow recovery. I'd plateaued and wasn't making any further progress. I wanted to let go of the stupid cane so badly, but I felt too unsteady on my feet without it. But maybe she had a point. Maybe all I had to do was let go and take a chance.

"Fine," I said. If Candice believed in me, then I knew I could do it. Slowly, using the wall, I stood up straight and tall, and Candice gave me a nod of encouragement. Squaring my shoulders and fixing my gaze on her, I lifted my right leg, felt my left hip go out, splayed my arms wide for something to grab onto, and, finding nothing, went headfirst straight into the back of the elevator, striking it headfirst with a loud *whump!*

Once the stars clouding my vision cleared, I was able to make out Candice's half-amused, half-concerned face hovering above me. "Wait here," she said. "I'll be right back with your cane and an ice pack."

Chapter Seven

"Is there a bump?" I asked, holding the sad excuse for an ice pack she'd brought me to my forehead as Candice weaved her way through traffic.

"No," she said without looking.

I narrowed my eyes at her but found that hurt, so I relaxed them immediately. I now had a killer headache. Pulling down the visor, I gazed at my wound in the vanity mirror. I had a pretty good welt and a slight scratch hovering over my right eye.

"That's just great," I grumbled. "Something to go with my scorpion sting."

Candice finally decided to look guilty. "Do you want me to take you to the doctor?" she asked sweetly.

I pushed the visor back into place. "No. Thanks, though." Then I focused on our mission and asked, "How do you want play this? Did you want me to keep the psychic guns holstered?"

Candice drummed her fingers on the top of the steering wheel, and I, for one, was most relieved to see her hands actually *on* the steering wheel. "I don't think so. I'm going to say that with Mr. Moreno we should be blunt and honest."

My brows shot up (mistake!) and I put the nearly melted ice pack against my bump again. "You really want to tell him I'm your psychic sidekick?"

"Yes."

"But that shut down Kendra's parents," I said, already wondering why I was fighting her on this.

"Yes," Candice repeated before she elaborated. "Obviously, Kendra's parents didn't abduct her." I saw her eyes then dart sideways to me. "They didn't, did they?"

"I highly doubt they had anything to do with her murder." There hadn't been a hint of that in the ether.

"Right," my partner agreed, turning her gaze back to the road. "People who aren't guilty can afford to be skeptical of your abilities. People who are guilty can't."

"Ahhhh," I said. "I get it. If I go in, all psychic guns blazing, we can see how nervous or interested that makes him."

Candice pointed a finger gun at me. "Bingo," she said. "But only show off your skills if he asks for a demo, Abs. I just want to inform him about your superpowers and see what he gives up first."

"Got it."

We arrived at the Moreno residence five minutes later, and I was relieved to see the news crews had abandoned the area for the time being. Still, Candice parked down the street in front of another house and said, "Don't want some nosy reporter running my plates and leaking that Moreno is meeting with a private eye," she said. "We should try to keep as low a profile as possible for the time being."

I shrugged and got stiffly out of the car. Between my physical therapy and that stint in the elevator, it was a miracle I was still ambulatory. "You okay, Sundance?" Candice called over the top of the car. I thought it was nice that now that I'd managed to give myself a hematoma, she was finally showing some concern.

I winced and hobbled around to her side. "Ducky," I said, not really meaning it, but for the time being I thought I could suck it up.

Candice walked nice and slow, thank God, and we went up the Morenos' driveway and around to the back. "Tristan told me to come to the rear door," Candice explained. "He's stopped answering his front door altogether."

I felt a twinge of empathy for the guy. I mean, at this point we didn't really know if he had anything to do with Kendra's disappearance or not, and if he didn't have anything to do with it, then he had to be suffering not only the loss of his wife, but also all the unwanted attention and accompanying innuendo from the press corps.

Still, as we waited for him to answer Candice's knock on the back door, I worked to push that aside and gather my impressions of him with an open mind.

Tristan Moreno wasn't at all what I had expected. Tall, broad shouldered, and surprisingly handsome, he answered the door with a polite but wary smile. "Miss Fusco?"

Candice stuck out her hand. "Please, call me Candice," she said, then turned to me. "Tristan, this is my partner, Abigail Cooper."

Tristan shook my hand, and I found it warm and dry. "Please come in," he said, stepping to the side.

We entered the cozy pale blue kitchen, with white

chair-rail molding, matching white cabinets, and traver-
tine tile floors. The space was large and inviting, and the
atmosphere still had a residual warmth to it.

That, to me, was important, because so often when I
enter a home where a couple is having problems, I can
pick up on the energy of their arguments. I looked for
any telltale signs of that in the ether but felt more a
sense of neutrality in the space. If this couple argued,
they either did it quietly, or they did it in a room other
than the kitchen.

I eyed Tristan again with curiosity. Although he was
still smiling politely, I could see the slight strain about his
eyes. There was also this underlying fear that he was trying hard to conceal, and yet he wasn't nervous about
meeting us. That was evident from his dry palm and the
energy surrounding him.

He offered us a seat at the table and asked if we
wanted coffee. This time, Candice accepted and Tristan
busied himself quietly for a moment, his movements
slow, methodical, reminding me a bit of my fiancé.

When our host set down two steaming mugs and some
cream and sugar for us, Candice dove right into the interview. "As I told you on the phone, Abby and I are investigating your wife's disappearance." I noticed she distinctly
didn't mention that no one had yet hired us. *Smart,* I
thought. Better to save it till we could feel him out.

At the mention of his wife, Tristan's eyes closed
tightly for the briefest of seconds, as if hearing out loud
that Kendra had vanished hurt him deeply. "Yes," he
said, his voice never betraying what I suspected he was
feeling. "Can I ask, though, who hired you?"

Candice offered him a sly grin. He'd seen right past
her dodge. "We're working on behalf of someone concerned for your wife," she replied evasively.

Kendra's husband took a seat at the table, his expression puzzled. "I don't understand."

Candice's eyes flickered to me, and I knew she was looking for a way out of answering the question directly. "You see," she said, "my partner here is a professional intuitive. She's done work with several police departments, and she currently holds a position as a civilian profiler with the FBI here in Austin. She consults with them on some of their most difficult cases."

Tristan's gaze shifted to me, and I found only curiosity in his pale gray eyes. But then I saw something more, and those eyes narrowed and he looked more closely at me. It made me uncomfortable until he said, "You've got a welt on the top of your forehead. Did you fall or something?" His eyes then slid down to my cane, and he seemed to assume that's exactly what had happened.

I put a hand up to cover the welt. "It's nothing," I assured him. "Really, I'm fine."

Tristan got up and moved to his freezer. Pulling out a package of frozen peas, he brought them over to me along with a clean dish towel. "Here," he said.

I took them gratefully but felt my cheeks heat up with embarrassment. "Thank you. I bumped my head in the elevator right before we came here." I made sure to sneak in a dirty look at Candice, which she pretended not to see.

Tristan took his seat again and kept his focus on me. "Are you really a psychic?"

"Yes."

"Do you know what happened to my wife?" Tristan's gaze never left mine.

I cleared my throat and dropped my eyes to the table. "I think so, Mr. Moreno. Yes."

For a long moment there was only silence, and when

I glanced up again, I could see that Tristan's eyes were glistening with tears. "You think she's been murdered, don't you?"

I had the urge to look at Candice, but I resisted. My sense was that Tristan knew intuitively that his wife was dead and he was simply looking for someone to agree with him. Still, I kept my answer a bit elusive. "I can't be sure. It's only a feeling, but, to answer your question, yes, I do suspect the worst may have happened to her."

Tristan put his fist to his mouth, and he seemed to struggle mightily against a tide of emotions. There was another pause, during which no one said anything, and when Candice opened her mouth to speak, I reached out and squeezed her arm. I wanted to give Tristan a moment.

At last he got up and went to the sink. Turning the water on, he just let it run for a few seconds, and then he put his hands under the cool water before splashing a small handful onto his face.

He cleared his throat several times, then wiped his face with a paper towel and came back to the table. "Kendra would *never* have left Colby alone in the house," he said, his voice hoarse and a bit choked.

"Colby's your son?" I asked him.

Tristan nodded.

"Can you tell us what happened that day, Tristan?" Candice asked gently. "The day Kendra went missing. Can you take us through the moment you came home to find her missing?"

Tristan wiped his face again with the paper towel before speaking. "I came home around six," he said. "The first thing I noticed was that the house was dark. Kendra's always got a light on, you know; it's one of those things she does. I leave the cap off the toothpaste and

Kendra's a hog with the electricity." I saw an amused look come over Tristan's face before he seemed to remember that Kendra wouldn't be leaving the lights on ever again, and that amused expression faded away like smoke on the wind.

He took a small sip of his coffee and I saw that his hand was shaking slightly. "Anyway," he said, closing his eyes as he continued. "I came up the back stairs and I saw that the kitchen door was open, and not just a little open—wide-open. I didn't think that was weird at first. I mean, I remember wondering if Kendra hadn't noticed that it was open, and the wind blew it or something. But, what hit me right after that was that she wasn't in the kitchen and there was no dinner on the stove."

"Your wife is a good cook?" Candice asked when it appeared that Tristan was getting choked up again.

He swallowed hard and nodded. "Yeah. She loves to cook. Usually when I get home, dinner is ready and we eat a little early so that we don't keep Colby up too late."

"But that night there wasn't anything prepared on the stove?" I asked. Tristan shook his head. "What about ingredients on the counter?" I pressed. If it was obvious that Kendra was preparing dinner, then it might help us pinpoint a time when she was murdered.

But Tristan only shook his head again. "There was nothing on the counters," he said. I noticed then that Candice had discreetly set her phone down on the table, and although it was lying on its face, I suspected the phone was recording the entire conversation.

"Then what?" she asked him.

"Well, I called out to her, but she didn't answer me, and somewhere upstairs I could hear Colby crying, so I called out to Kendra a couple more times, but again she didn't answer. So on my way toward Colby's room, I passed by the front door, and something about it caught my eye and I stopped to look at it."

"What was it?" I asked.

"It was unlocked and open just a crack."

"You noticed that?" Candice asked.

Tristan gave a small nod. "Yeah. I know it's a weird thing to notice, but the dead bolt is always lined up linear, and as my eyes passed the door, I could see that it was horizontal. It was something that was out of place and made me take a pause. Neither of us ever went through the front door because it sticks a little and it's hard to close once it's been open, so we just keep it shut and locked unless we have company over or we have a package delivery or something like that."

Candice seemed to hit on that. "Were either you or your wife expecting company or a package that day?"

"No. At least, I wasn't."

Candice nodded. "Okay, so you noticed that your front door was open; then what?"

Tristan ran a hand through his hair. I thought he looked nervous about telling us the story of that day, and I wondered why the change in him, as he'd been so relaxed until now. "Well," he said, "I don't know why, but I stopped to pull the door open and look out on the front porch. I didn't see anything, but the fact that it'd been left open like that, along with the back door, and Colby upstairs crying without any sign of his mother . . . I just had this bad feeling and I remember getting this cold chill up my spine. I don't know how to explain it other than I knew things weren't okay."

"Then what?" Candice asked when Tristan paused.

He was rubbing the side of his coffee cup with his thumb and still staring at the tabletop absently. "I went upstairs to Colby's room," he said. "The poor guy was hot and damp. I don't think he'd been changed in hours. So I got him out of the crib and called for Kendra one last time, hoping that she was just outside or something. But even then I knew. I knew she wasn't going to answer me. So I took Colby all around the house to search for Kendra, but she wasn't anywhere inside or out and her car wasn't in the garage—"

Candice interrupted him, "You didn't notice her car was missing when you pulled in?"

Tristan shook his head. "Since the driveway's kind of narrow and I'm always the first one to leave in the morning and the last one home at night, she always takes the garage and I park in the driveway."

Candice nodded before getting back to what he'd said earlier. "You were saying that you did a cursory search for Kendra and didn't find her. Did you see anything else unusual—besides both the front door and the back door being unlocked?"

Tristan shook his head, and his expression was so sad that it tugged at me. "No," he said. "I mean, the house was just like it always was—neat and clean. Kendra's a neat freak. She likes everything in its place."

I jumped in again, asking, "And you're sure there was nothing out on the kitchen counter in the way of food preparation?" My radar kept pinging that there was a clue there.

"No," he said, eyeing me curiously, "but there was an empty jar of peanut butter and a small plate in the sink. I figured that was left over from Colby's snack time. He loves peanut butter crackers."

"What time is snack time?" I asked, hoping to narrow the time window.

Tristan sighed and ran a hand over his hair again. "He has two snack times a day. One at around ten a.m.

and one at two p.m. It's hard to say which one was in the sink because right after his snack he's usually a little sleepy, so Kendra puts him down for a short nap at eleven and then again at three."

"And since you found Colby in his crib, it's hard to say which nap time he'd been put down for," Candice pointed out.

"But it does narrow the window a little," I said. "What time would Colby get up from his afternoon nap?"

"Usually around four," Tristan told me.

I turned to Candice. "So because Tristan found Colby still in his crib, we can assume that Kendra went missing sometime between eleven a.m. and four p.m."

"Five hours is a big window," Candice said, but didn't comment on it further. Instead, she changed topics. "Tristan, after you searched the house, what'd you do next?"

"I called the police."

Candice cocked her head. "Did you call around to any of her friends first or maybe the neighbors?"

"No. When I found Colby wet, alone, and looking like he'd been crying for hours, I was positive something bad had happened to my wife. Kendra just wouldn't *ever* do something like go off and leave him like that. Plus, with both the front door and the back door being open and unlocked, and her car being gone, it all added up to something bad."

"What'd the police say?" Candice asked next.

"They didn't say much," he said gruffly. "Mostly they looked around and tried to convince me that she was probably out running an errand, or maybe she was taking a break at a friend's house and she'd be back in a few hours. That's when I called my attorney and asked her to speak to them. I couldn't get the police to even take photos or dust for prints or anything until Chelsea—that's my attorney—showed up."

My brow lifted and I saw the surprised look on Candice's face too. "You called your attorney to get the cops to take you seriously?"

Tristan nodded. "I've known Chelsea since high school. We even went to prom together, and she's a really good friend of ours. She knows Kendra wouldn't go off and leave Colby willingly. She came here, made a few calls, and got someone to finally send two detectives over. They took my statement and gave us the song and dance about needing to wait twenty-four hours before we could file a missing-person's report, but Chelsea kept hammering at them, and eventually, after we'd called all of Kendra's relatives and friends and found out that no one had seen her, the cops finally decided to get serious and an hour later CSI showed up, but from what Chelsea tells me, no unknown prints have been found."

Candice's face was now a blank, but I could feel her energy buzzing. "That's why our contact at the police station said you had lawyered up."

Tristan blinked. "I didn't 'lawyer up,'" he snapped defensively. "I called a really good friend of mine who just happens to be an attorney, and she helped me get the police to take Kendra's disappearance seriously."

Candice cocked her head. "Let me ask you straight up, Tristan," she said. "Have you retained Chelsea as your lawyer?"

Tristan's face flushed bright crimson. "Yeah. But only because the police have made it pretty clear they think I might've had something to do with Kendra's disappearance. It was Chelsea's idea even. She said that if we didn't find Kendra soon, the police might start to look at me suspiciously, and Chelsea also told me that she could keep the focus off me and on the effort to find my wife if I retained her."

"When did the police start to think you had something to do with Kendra's disappearance?" Candice asked next. "And I'm only asking because it seems weird that a guy who pushes to get two detectives over here to look for any evidence of foul play would so quickly become the person of interest in the investigation."

"I think that tide turned the minute they finished talking to Kendra's parents," he said, and I caught a hint of something in the ether that wasn't apparent in Tristan's body language. He didn't much care for the Woodyards. At all. I could see the discord swirling around in his energy. The fact that he was working to hide it was what was interesting to me. "They're so worried about her that they're having a hard time believing I don't know where she is."

"Ah," Candice said in that way that suggested she didn't quite believe he was telling her everything. "I have a personal question to ask you," she said next, "and I hope you don't mind, but were you and Kendra getting along okay?"

Tristan didn't seem surprised that she'd asked that. "We were," he said.

I picked up on the lie right away. I decided to call him on it. "You're sure?" I asked.

He didn't reply verbally. He simply nodded. Interesting.

"No arguments or fights that might've caused Kendra to take a break from her married life for a little while?" Candice said, picking up on the fact that I'd pressed Tristan on the issue.

He shook his head, and I knew he was concealing

something, but I also could see his determination to keep us from knowing what. I made a small motion with my hand for Candice to drop it before he stopped talking to us altogether, and she moved on.

"This next question, Tristan, is even more invasive, and I'm so sorry to have to ask you this, but in your relationship with Kendra, did things ever get . . . heated?"

He cut her a sharp look. "Heated?" he repeated, his tone holding an edge.

Candice pretended not to notice how her question had affected him. "Yeah, you know, was there ever a time when you two maybe had an argument and things escalated a little too far?" She asked that like they were just enjoying a nice chat over coffee.

Tristan's gaze dropped to his hands. "No." My radar, however, said otherwise.

"You're lying," I told him bluntly. I couldn't help the accusatory tone. He wasn't doing himself any favors by lying to us, and if he had also lied to the police when they asked him this same question—as I had no doubt they already had—they would find a way to use it against him even if he'd had nothing to do with his wife's disappearance.

Tristan glared at me. "No, I'm not."

Liar, liar, pants on fire . . . , the familiar phrase sang in my mind. "Yes," I said evenly. "You are."

He continued to look stonily at me for a beat, and then his eyes cut back to Candice. "You know, you never answered my question, Candice."

"What question was that, Tristan?"

"Who hired you to look into my wife's case?"

"No one," she confessed, keeping her voice even and cool.

Tristan's face registered both his surprise and alarm,

and his defensiveness only got worse. "Then what the hell are you two doing here?"

I knew we were pushing him, and I may have believed he was innocent of foul play right up until he'd started lying to us. "It was my idea," I told him. "We saw Kendra's story on the news, and as I've worked as a consultant on quite a few missing-persons cases for the FBI, I thought Candice and I could be useful to the investigation."

"Right now we're just getting a preliminary feel for the case," Candice said quickly. "But I believe we might be able to contribute to the investigation, and, if you'd like to hire us, I can assure you that our rates are quite reasonable."

I felt my insides tighten. I didn't like pushing our services on other people—it felt weird. And Candice's offer hung awkwardly in the air until Tristan shook his head slowly back and forth and added a sort of laugh, but it held no real mirth. "I think you two should go."

Candice and I both sat there for a beat, maybe hoping he'd change his mind.

"Now," he added, his tone flinty.

Candice stood, and with a bit of effort, so did I. Setting the frozen peas to the side, I said, "Thank you, Tristan. And I'm so sorry for what's happening to you and your family right now."

He only gave me a stony look, and with that we left him.

As we were making out way down the drive, I could tell Candice was silently beating herself up for her final statement to Tristan. I was about to comfort her and tell her not to worry about it when I happened to catch sight of a truck parked at the Morenos' neighbor's house. On the side of the vehicle were the words "Russ's Pest Control." To the side of the truck was a big guy in gray wellies tugging on a hose that extended from the truck to the front lawn.

I grinned. The universe was watching out for me again. "I'll be right back," I told Candice, and limped over to the guy in the wellies. After introducing myself and discovering that he was Russ, I told him about my scorpion problem.

"I'd be happy to take care of that for you, ma'am," he said with a warm smile, handing over his card. One thing about the people in Austin—they sure are a friendly lot.

"Awesome! I'll call you in the next day or so," I promised.

Once we were back in Candice's car, she turned to me, curious. "Bugs?"

"Scorpions," I replied with a shudder as I fished out my phone to plug Russ's contact information into my contacts list.

"Blach," Candice said, adding a shudder of her own. "Where'd you see one of those?"

I rolled up my sleeve and pointed to the little purple dot on my arm. "Right there!"

"Yikes," she said as she started the car. "Please tell me one didn't land on you in our new offices."

"Naw, he's a squatter at the new house, and I'm gonna have Russell over there evict his creepy little ass—"

"Careful," Candice warned, "or you'll need to take a second job just to pay the swear jar."

"Terisk." I said, and stuck out my tongue at her. (Mature done skipped me by.)

She laughed before changing the subject. "Okay, so what'd you get from Tristan?"

I rolled my window down a little. It was turning into a lovely warm day. "He's a tough nut to crack. I mean, my first impression was that he's an innocent player in all of this, but then he started lying about when things may have gotten heated between him and his wife, and now I don't know what to think."

"I already dug through his public records," Candice said. "The only thing on Tristan's record is a DUI about nine years ago. He hasn't had so much as a traffic ticket since then."

"You're sure? No record of domestic violence or any other kind of assault?"

Candice shook her head. "Nope. Since the DUI he's been clean as a whistle."

"Well, that fits with what I found in the house," I said. "I mean, the energy in the kitchen was pretty neutral. If Kendra and Tristan fought, they either didn't argue often or they argued in another room of the house."

Candice tapped her lip thoughtfully. "Well, that makes sense if you've got a little kid around, doesn't it? I'm assuming Colby would have been present a lot at mealtime. Maybe if they argued or fought, they did it only when their son wasn't within hearing distance—like in their bedroom, for instance."

"That makes sense. But Tristan was definitely lying about a time when he and Kendra got into it and things escalated. I know he's done something physical to his wife that he regrets very much. The question in front of us is: How long ago?"

Candice nodded and added, "If it was in the past few days, then that's a very bad sign."

"Yep. But if it was years ago and she never reported it and he's worked to control his anger issues, then it's not such a big deal."

"Do you think that's the case, Abs?"

I sighed. "I want to say yes, but I wish we could've gotten a feel for the energy in the rest of the house."

"And what about that part where Tristan said he called his attorney when he couldn't get the police to take his wife's disappearance seriously?" Candice said.

"It sheds a whole new light on the fact that he lawyered up, doesn't it?" I agreed. "Maybe now that he knows we know about his attorney, we should just go meet her and see if she's the woman who came to my office."

But Candice seemed reluctant. "I don't know," she said. "I mean, the woman who came to see you worked pretty hard to conceal her identity. If we just show up at Gagliano's office and she is the mysterious Ms. Smith, seeing us might totally freak her out."

"Agreed, but right now don't you think it's the fastest way to identify if Tristan really did murder his wife? If we have that as an advantage, Candice, then we can focus on helping the police make a case against him and hopefully find Kendra's remains and give her parents some closure."

Candice eyed the dashboard clock. "Okay," she said at last. "But let's not simply show up at the office, Abs. If someone there remembers that we asked to meet with Tristan's attorney and we're later connected to solving the case by the press, they could connect the dots and think she's the one who leaked it about her client."

"I'll go along with whatever you want to do," I assured her.

Candice lifted her smart phone out of her purse and tapped at the screen for a bit before setting the phone down and typing an address into the car's GPS. We then drove north away from the city for a good fifteen minutes, exiting just inside the neighboring city of Round Rock. Candice followed the directions until she pulled to a stop in front of a six-story office building with blue-tinted windows and gray slate walls. On the signage I could see in big white print that we'd come to a stop in front of the law offices of Turner, Kramer, and Marr. Candice picked up her cell again, scanned the street, then made a call. It was quickly clear to me that she was attempting to connect with Tristan's lawyer.

After inquiring at the switchboard, Candice was patched through. "Ms. Gagliano?" she said in a voice that didn't sound like Candice at all. "My name is Mercedes Roosevelt, and I may be able to help with the location of Kendra Moreno. Can we meet?" There was a pause, then, "I know I should go to the police, but I really don't want to. You see, I've had encounters with them before, and it didn't go so well for me. I'd really rather not get involved in an official way, if you know what I mean."

I crossed my fingers and a moment later Candice smiled and said, "Great. I'm sitting inside the restaurant right across from your office." I looked to my right. We were parked in front of said restaurant. "I've got long black hair and I'm dressed in a purple sweatshirt and jeans." (For the record, my short-blond-haired friend was wearing an ivory-colored leather jacket and dark blue dress slacks.) After another slight pause, Candice said, "And, in case I'm able to spot you first, ma'am, what're you wearing?"

I eyed the office, squinting at the windows as if I could peer inside and see Chelsea Gagliano.

"A black suit?" Candice repeated, and I pulled my attention back to her. "Well, that should be easy enough to spot." Candice rolled her eyes and I smiled. "All right, see you in ten minutes."

After Candice hung up the phone, we waited and watched the front of the office building across the street. "Shouldn't we move?" I asked nervously as the minutes ticked by.

"Why would we want to move? She'll have to walk right by our car to go inside and we'll get a really good look at her when she does."

"Yeah, but she might see us."

"So?"

"If it is the mysterious woman who came to my office, she'll recognize me at least."

Candice shrugged. "So what if she does, Abby? Out here in the open no one's going to connect us to her. And if Moreno's attorney is the lady in question, and if she does spot us, then all she'll likely conclude is that we're working the case, which is what she wanted from us anyway."

I weighed that and decided that Candice was right. A few minutes later a trim woman with chin-length ash brown hair, wearing a gorgeous black suit and patent leather pumps, came out of the building and began to walk briskly in our direction. I felt my heartbeat quicken, but only because I'm not very good at all this sneaky spy stuff.

As she paused at the curb to wait for an opening in traffic, I said, "It's not her, Candice."

"Hold on," my partner replied. "She's not close enough to tell for sure, Abs."

"She is for me," I insisted. Her energy was different. So was her posture. This woman carried herself with such an air of confidence that it was easy to tell the difference between her and the woman who'd come to see me a few days before.

Still, I sat very still as Chelsea Gagliano crossed the

road and passed directly in front of our car with only a cursory glance in our direction. Her focus was on the restaurant and meeting Mercedes Roosevelt. As she passed through the door, Candice turned the ignition and shifted into drive. "You're right," she agreed. "That's not her."

We drove for all of two stoplights before either of us spoke. I was the first to break the silence. "It could have been another attorney from that same office," I said. "Someone assisting Chelsea with Tristan's representation."

Candice nodded. "Yep. And if that's the case, then we can't risk walking into that law firm and exposing her."

I sighed and my stomach grumbled. It was close to lunchtime, and all I could think about was what a bummer it was that we'd just left a perfectly good restaurant. Candice eyed me slyly. "You're like that plant from that play *Little Shop of Horrors*," she said.

I laughed and balled my hands into fists, pumping them up and down as I dropped my voice a few octaves and sang, "Feed me, Seymour!"

Candice didn't even consult with me on where to eat. She merely parked in front of a quaint-looking bar and grill and we went in. "Eat something healthy for a change, will you?" she asked while she looked over her menu.

I hid an eye roll and hunted for something fried. I come from a long line of junk-food lovers, and luckily for the Coopers and the Kirschners (Mommy dearest's side of the family), we all seem to live long, happy, high-metabolism lives without the nuisance of heart disease, obesity, or high cholesterol. I was banking on that double dose of good-luck genes to carry me through every salty, greasy, delicious meal, as I fully expect to depart this world holding tightly to a Coney dog and a basket of chili cheese fries.

After weathering Candice's withering look of disapproval when I ordered the fish and chips, I asked her what she thought we should focus on next for Kendra's case.

Candice drummed her fingers on the table for a moment while she thought that through. "We'll have to continue to keep an eye on Tristan and Bailey, but I'd still like to expand the suspect pool by researching Kendra a little more thoroughly. Maybe there's something in her associations that we can focus on, some hidden clue on her Facebook page that'll lead us to Kendra's body and a suspect."

"I wish I could narrow down where she is," I said, frustrated by all the obstacles in this case.

Candice sat up and leaned her elbows on the table. "What'd you get when you focused on her remains again?"

"That she's buried in the woods somewhere."

"How do you know she's specifically in the woods?"

I thought back to the first impressions I'd written on my diagram when I'd focused on her remains. "Well, for one thing, I picked up a strong, earthy dirt smell, and I think I remember sensing a lot of plant life all around her. The surrounding area feels dense with it, in fact, and there's a dampness to the air there that you don't get with places that are out in the open."

Candice was looking at me as if she was wondering how I could pick all that out of the ether.

"It's a gift," I told her with a wink.

She gave me a lopsided smile. "Any landmarks nearby?"

"No, not really. Wherever she is, it's not densely pop-ulated. There may be a few nondescript structures nearby, though."

"Nondescript structures?" she repeated. "Like what?"

I rubbed the welt on my forehead. The Excedrin I'd taken after my trip into the elevator was starting to wear off. "Not sure. Could be houses or it could be small shops or something like that. There's nothing around her, Candice, that feels significant enough for my radar to pick up and identify. I know because since I first hit on her remains, I've tried several times to home in on her location. The best that I can do is tell you I think she's east of downtown, but where and how far, I couldn't say."

Candice played with her straw. "There's a lot of greenbelt in east Austin."

"There's a lot of greenbelt everywhere in Austin," I said. We lived in a city known for its surrounding acres of greenbelt.

"Needle in a haystack," Candice muttered just as our food arrived. "Beyond frustrating to have so many clues and not be able to put them together."

"Now you know why I eat so much comfort food," I told her, popping a fry into my mouth.

Her expression clearly said that she thought that was no excuse.

Chapter Eight

I got home later that day feeling dispirited and like Candice and I were really spinning our wheels and going nowhere. We'd made attempts all the rest of that afternoon to contact Kendra's friends, but either the word was out about us or Kendra's friends weren't very friendly. We couldn't get a single person to e-mail or call us back.

After tossing the ball around in the backyard with the pups for half an hour, I did feel better. Nothing perks you up like a little pup time. As I was setting down their dinner, the doorbell rang.

I wasn't expecting anybody, so I approached the front entrance warily and checked the peephole before opening the door. Truth be told, when I saw who was out there, I almost pretended I wasn't home. After thinking on it for a few seconds, though, I finally gave in. "Dave," I said levelly to the dusty guy on my front porch.

He gave me a little two-finger salute. "Abs. How's the arm?"

"Fine."

"Good, good," he said. I could see he was lugging a big duffel bag, but I'd be danged if I was gonna ask him about it. "Mind if I come in?"

I did mind. Dave was sort of the last person I wanted to deal with at the moment, especially after such a long and fruitless day. He seemed to read my hesitation because he added, "It won't take long. I promise."

I stepped reluctantly to the side and let him in, and the moment he was through the door both Eggy and Tuttle left their dinners to come racing out to greet him. The traitors.

Moving into the kitchen, Dave set his big duffel on the table and unzipped it.

I eased myself into a chair and put my feet up, wondering how long before I could kick Dave out and head upstairs for a hot bath.

My handyman began removing items from the duffel—a piece of tile, a stained piece of wood, a block of granite, etcetera—and set them carefully and methodically in front of me.

Before he'd gotten them all lined up on the table, I clamped a hand on his arm. "Hold on," I said, knowing full well what he was up to. "I can't do this tonight, Dave. I've had a really long day, and the last thing I want to do is sort through home decor."

Dave patted the hand clamped firmly to his forearm and offered me his most winning smile. "Oh, I figured with all the wedding stuff and your other work that you were avoiding me for a reason," he said. "Which is why I've made it super easy for you, Abs. In fact, if you'll unhinge your hand from my arm, I promise you'll really only have to make one decision and be done with it."

"*One* decision?"

"Yep."

I narrowed my eyes at him but let go and sat back with crossed arms. "Okay," I said cautiously. "Color me curious."

Dave laid out all the rest of the items from his duffel, and I began to notice that he'd brought only one of each sample. Taking a seat, he said, "I've known you a long time, right?"

"Four years," I affirmed, although, with Dave, it sometimes felt like a lot longer.

"And I've worked on a few of your houses in that time, right?"

"Five . . . and counting."

"Right," he said. "And I think I know your taste pretty well by now. So what I did was make all the selections for you, keeping both your taste and Dutch's taste in mind. If you like the look, then all you have to do is say yes and my guys will get busy ordering and installing all of it first thing in the morning."

I leaned forward. Dave suddenly had my full attention.

Encouraged, Dave began telling me about the samples. "See, I know you guys like your floors dark, but not too dark, so I picked this sample because it'll give the floors a grounded feeling without showing every speck of dust." Dave then held up a hardwood floor sample that was a rich chocolate and exactly the color I would have chosen.

I nodded to encourage him to continue.

"And I also know that you both like your horizontal surfaces above the floors light, so for the bath and kitchen granite, I thought this would suit both of you. It's mostly white with some tans and a speck of blue-gray here and there, and then it's got these little threads of red running in patches all over. I tried to bring a sample big enough where you could see all that and—"

"I love it," I said, cutting him off before he took up my entire night talking about the granite.

Dave smiled like he'd just scored ten yards in the fourth quarter. And I wanted to scowl at him, but the truth was that the granite sample he'd just shown me was absolutely gorgeous and I loved it instantly. "Knew you'd like it," he said, moving that to the side.

For the next hour and a half Dave took me slowly and methodically through every single choice, from cabinets to countertops to backsplash to molding to bathroom tile and everything in between. I had to hand it to him, because most of what he showed me was exactly my taste, and even those selections where I would have gone lighter or softer, I could see that Dave had picked the sample as a compromise between my taste and Dutch's.

"That does it," he said at last, after showing me the photos of the lighting fixtures he'd selected for the outside of the house. "So what do you say?"

I grinned at him and reached for his hand. "I sometimes forget what a good friend you are, Dave. Sorry about that."

My handyman actually blushed. "So that's a yes?"

I laughed. "It's a yes and an invitation."

"An invitation? To what?"

"Dinner," I said. "I want you to stay for dinner."

Dave grinned too. "Thought you'd never ask."

Since Dutch was still stuck at the office, I had to "cook" dinner. And by "cook" I mean dial the phone and order a pizza. Still, it was a delicious pie—when I cook I go all out—and by the time Dave left around nine, we were both in a pretty good doughy-cheesy food coma. I was on my way up the stairs when the front door opened and in came my hunka man.

"Hey, cowboy!" I said, happy he was home. But then I happened to see his face and I knew it'd been a tough day.

"Mmrrph," he mumbled, heading straight to the kitchen.

I followed him. "I made dinner!" I sang, hoping my good cheer would help bring him out of the grumps.

"Mmrrph," he muttered again, twisting the cap off a fresh bottle of scotch. Dutch went for the hard stuff only when his day was *really* bad.

"It's pizza!" I told him, my voice heavy on the enthusiasm. He didn't even reply; he merely poured two fingers of amber liquid into a glass and downed it in one gulp. Uh-oh.

"I'll just warm it up for you," I said helpfully, moving to get him a plate and put a couple of slices into the microwave.

"I'm not hungry," he grumbled, pouring another two fingers into the glass before taking it—and the bottle—out to the living room.

I hit the button on the microwave, waited for the cheese to get good and gooey, then brought the plate back to the living room. Holding it in front of my sweetie, I said, "I'm guessing your last meal was around noon, right?"

Dutch was sitting sullenly on the couch, his drink in one hand and the remote in the other. "We didn't have time for lunch," he said moodily.

Since I'd seen Dutch scarf down only a slice of toast that morning, I knew that at least some of his current mood could be attributed to low blood sugar.

I put the pizza on the coffee table and sat down next to him. "No breaks in the mall-bombing case?"

"Nope."

I waited for him to elaborate, but his eyes were staring hard at the TV. ESPN was running football highlights. After a stretch of silence during which Dutch just sipped his drink and stared listlessly at the TV, I got up and brought him back a napkin, hoping he'd get the hint.

I set it on his knee and vowed not to say another word about it. The last thing I wanted to be was one of those nagging women who treat their mates like children.

Five more minutes passed and Dutch poured himself another two fingers of scotch.

My finger started to tap the top of my knee.

Ten more minutes passed; all the while Dutch stared at the TV and just sipped away at his drink.

I played with the tassel on one of the throw pillows, ignoring the pizza, on which the cheese had now recongealed.

Siiiip, went Dutch.

I took an interest in the curtains. Had I picked out curtains with Dave?

Siiiip.

No. We'd picked out blinds. That's right. Shutters actually, which would give the windows a great modern feel.

Siiiip.

What color were the shutters again? Oh, yeah, they were dark like the floors. They'd go really well with the granite in the kitchen too.

Siiiip.

I wondered if I should tell Dutch about wrapping up the house decor with Dave? (*Siiip.*) Yes. Yes, I should.

That'd help lighten the mood maybe. Ease his mind that we'd be moving into the new home soon. (*Siiiip.*) And wouldn't he be happy to hear that?

Plastering a sweet smile onto my face, I turned to tell him all about it just as he was raising the glass to his lips again. *"Will you please eat something?"*

Dutch jumped, spilling his drink, and then he cut me a look that could cool five-alarm chili. "Abs," he said, his voice even and hard. "I'll eat when I'm hungry."

I snatched the drink out of his hand, spilling much of the rest of it on the couch. "You want this back, you'll eat a piece of that pizza!"

I knew Dutch well, and I'd seen him drink a little too much on an empty stomach before, only to wake up with a killer hangover the next morning and indigestion for several days after that.

His brow furrowed angrily, and instead of reaching for the pizza, he grabbed the bottle of scotch and took a sip right from it, glaring at me the whole time.

"Nice," I told him.

"What's with you, anyway?" he grumbled.

"It's not me," I said in a raised voice as I slammed the glass on top of the coffee table. "It's *you*."

"I'm a grown man, Edgar. If I want to have a couple drinks, I can have a couple drinks."

I rolled my eyes. "Of course you can, you idiot. And I will even be your personal bartender this evening if you want. But you know how you are the day after you drink on an empty stomach. You're hungover, irritable, and suffering from indigestion for days afterward. How're you going to be able to focus at work tomorrow, Dutch, feeling like shih tzu?"

It took a few seconds, but the angry, defensive glint

in Dutch's midnight blues softened, and at last he inhaled deeply and let it out slowly. Then, without a word, he set down the bottle of scotch and reached for the plate of pizza.

I turned my attention to the TV and let him eat in silence. He polished off all three pieces . . . surprise, surprise.

Around ten I felt a hand gently stroke the back of my head. "Sorry, Edgar," he said softly.

I shifted on the sofa and cuddled up close to him. "I'm sorry you had a bad day, cowboy."

"Thanks, dollface."

"You guys are really having no luck solving your case?"

"Nope," he said, rubbing his eyes. "Everywhere we turn, we keep coming up empty. And I'll admit that today I came very close to breaking down and calling you for help."

I turned in surprise to look at him and found his expression riddled with guilt. I smoothed down a lock of his blond hair and said, "Sweetie, this isn't a case that I'm going to solve. My crew is practically forbidding me to get involved."

Dutch pulled his own head back in surprise. "Why's that?" I could see some worry in his eyes again.

I laughed it off. "Oh, probably because there's a danger of my leading you in the wrong direction. You know how the ether is always subject to interpretation."

"Huh," he said. "I hadn't thought of that."

"Yeah, well, it could happen, you know. Anyway, I've already sensed that you guys will be the ones to solve the case without my help, so even though it seems like you've hit a roadblock and aren't making progress, try not to get too frustrated. You'll solve it. I know it."

Dutch squeezed me to him and kissed the top of my head. We sat in comfortable silence until I thought of something. "I'm guessing you haven't had time to meet with Cat in the past day or two, huh?"

His heavy sigh told me even before the words were out of his mouth. "No. But that didn't stop her from leaving me eight hundred messages."

I couldn't help but smile. "Well, you should do what I did," I said. "Make an appointment with her for some-time when you know you'll be free, and tackle all the big decisions at once."

Dutch pulled away to look curiously down at me. "You met with Dave?"

I grinned smugly up at him. "I did. And I picked out everything from floors to crown molding."

"You're kidding."

"Nope. I'm done, cowboy. And our house should be ready in about three to four weeks! If the guys work hard, we can move in right before the wedding."

Dutch reached for the scotch again. "I knew I should've had you toss the coin."

The next week passed without a single lead in the Ken-dra Moreno case. I didn't know who was more anxious about it—me or Candice. At least I didn't know until I arrived at my office for a ten a.m. appointment with a client and found my partner hunched over her computer with several discarded cardboard coffee cups littering her desktop.

"Hey, Cassidy," I said cordially from the doorway. (Okay, so I said it more carefully than cordially, but only because she had a bit of a crazy look going on.)

"Mellobby," Candice grunted. I almost heard a "hello" and my name in there, but I wasn't certain.

Not knowing what to say to that, I continued to hover in her doorway, and without even taking her eyes off her computer screen, Candice blindly grabbed for one of the cardboard coffee cups, slugged down the contents like it was a shot of tequila, and went back to peering at her computer screen.

"How's it going?" I asked, still trying to feel out how nervous I should be about finding her in such a state. It looked very much like she'd slept at her desk—if she'd slept at all, which, given the copious amounts of caffeine she'd obviously ingested and the disheveled cast to her appearance, I seriously doubted.

"Mmph," she said.

Walking slowly and carefully . . . the way you'd move around an ornery tiger, let's say . . . I eased into her office and sat in the seat opposite her. "Candice?"

"Mmph?"

I waited for her to lift her eyes. She didn't. Taking a deep breath, I lifted my cane, extending it slowly forward over the top of her desk, and with a quick poke I shut the lid of her laptop. "Hey!" she yelled.

"Honey," I said evenly, keeping my cane firmly on the top of her computer. "What's going on here?"

Candice's eyes darted around the room, kinda like a wild animal looking for the nearest exit. "What?"

"How many cups of coffee have you had?"

Candice blinked. Then she seemed to take in the top of her desk. "A few."

"I count seven." Leaning over to hook her wastepaper basket with my cane, I pulled it closer. "Make that nine."

"I like coffee."

"Honey, Juan Valdez doesn't like coffee that much."

Candice rubbed her face. "I was working on something. I needed to stay awake."

"How long have you been here?"

Candice sighed and leaned back in her chair. I could see that her hands were shaking from all the caffeine. "I don't know. Since sometime last night."

I reached out and pulled her laptop close. Swiveling it around, I opened the lid and took a peek. "This is a spreadsheet."

"Yep," Candice said quietly.

"How many names are on here?" I asked. The spreadsheet had rows and columns of names, but why they were listed or who they were was nothing I could quickly make sense of.

"About sixty. Maybe seventy," she said, giving me no more detail than that.

I cocked my head. "Wanna tell me what this means? Or would you rather continue to keep me in suspense?"

Candice got up and stretched. "I've been putting together a spreadsheet of Kendra's friends and acquaintances and cross-referencing them with Bailey's friends and acquaintances," she explained. "If we assume Tristan isn't our murderer—but let me be clear: no one's off the table here—and he is telling the truth about coming home and finding his wife missing, then we also have to assume the unlocked and partially open front door indicates that someone came to visit Kendra between the hours of eleven a.m. and four p.m. It's light enough outside at four o'clock to see whoever's outside on the front step; therefore, Kendra *must* have trusted whomever she let in the door. If there were no signs of struggle, I'm going to further assume that she was attacked pretty quick, maybe when her back was turned to lead the killer into her house. Maybe he pounced then and over-powered her right away. By drugging her with something in a syringe or hitting her hard enough in the lower back to cause some sort of paralysis, he would have been able to drag her or carry her out the back door in about a minute to a minute and a half."

I stared in surprise at my partner. She'd obviously been thinking this through quite thoroughly.

"Now," she went on in a voice loud enough to cause me to jump, "at the Moreno residence, I remember seeing a set of key hooks, and there was only one set on the hooks there," Candice said, her movements animated and jittery. "I think the killer simply lifted Kendra up, slung her over his shoulder, and carried her out the back door, taking her keys and her car as he went. He then took her to a remote location, raped her, beat her, and smothered her; then he buried her in the woods somewhere—probably not very deep . . . what, maybe two or three feet if he was in a hurry?"

I had personal experience with hurried woodland grave digging, but I held back revealing that particular top secret and allowed Candice to continue her rant. "So say it takes the killer half an hour to get to any one of the six nearby greenbelts, then find a secluded spot—we're talking another fifteen minutes or so—park the car, get her out, do all that terrible business to her, then bury her . . . He could have been finished with the whole thing in, what? Two, three hours tops?"

Candice wasn't really asking me these questions; she was just rattling them off and figuring them out on her own. But so far I'd kept my radar attuned to what she was saying, and for the most part I found that what was in the ether wasn't much different from what Candice was saying.

"See, this is where Tristan's alibi gets him into trouble," Candice said, suddenly changing tack entirely. "According to the police report, he—"

"How'd you get a copy of the police report?"

Candice waved an impatient hand my way. "Brice got it for me through some connection he had. Anyway, Moreno told the police that he headed out to see a client of his in Dallas, but the client couldn't confirm it because the client had canceled. Tristan says that he forgot his cell phone at home and didn't notice he didn't have it on him until he was too far away to go back without being super late for his meeting with the client. So there's no way to track his whereabouts that afternoon. He didn't use the GPS in his Lexus, and with no cell phone in the car, there was nothing to provide a record of pings on the drive. Sure, he could have gone to Dallas, or he could have invented the story just for the purpose of laying the groundwork for reasonable doubt should it come to that.

"But, I'm getting ahead of myself," Candice said, whipping around to pace back the other way. "Back to the list. Since you picked up a guilty vibe off Bailey," she said, "I thought I'd organize a spreadsheet of people both girls have in common. Those names on the list are people connected to both girls according to Facebook, Twitter, Google Plus, Pinterest, Foursquare, and LinkedIn, which were all the active social sites I could find accounts for in both Bailey's and Kendra's names."

"Whoa," I said taking in the long list again. "I'm seriously impressed, honey."

She scowled. "Don't be. In fact, I'm starting to really regret all that effort."

"Why?"

Candice stopped pacing and sat back down with a tired sigh. In an instant it was like all that high energy seemed to seep right out of her. "Because now we've got at least sixty potential suspects, Abs—not including Tristan, whose alibi I just don't."

I squinted at her. "Don't what?"

"Buy. Who's ali-bi I just don't buy."

I stared at her wondering what the heck to say to *that*.

"It was more clever in my head."

I looked away. Most of what she was saying would probably have been far more clever eight cups of coffee and sixteen hours ago.

"The point is, Abs, that there's no way we can possibly work our way through that list in less than a month. In fact, it might take us two or more."

I frowned. I could see what Candice was getting at. By opening up the suspect pool to anything bigger than a half dozen people, she'd effectively made our little two-man team completely undermanned.

"Is there maybe a way to break this list down and prioritize it?" I asked. "You know, into subgroups of close friends, not-so-close friends, acquaintances, work associates . . . stuff like that?"

"I've already done that," Candice said, reaching over me to wiggle her finger over the mouse pad. A moment later I was looking at another spreadsheet with about a dozen names. "These are girls Kendra and Bailey went to school with." As I started to read the list of names, Candice hit the button again and yet another spreadsheet popped onto the screen. "And these are professional contacts from—"

"Hold on," I said, interrupting her. "Can you go back for a sec?"

Candice moved the spreadsheet back to the previous page and I looked for the name on the list that had jumped out at me. "Her," I said, pointing to the name I swore I recognized. "Hold on," I added, getting up and limping quickly into my office, where I grabbed my appointment book and brought it back to Candice's desk. Flipping through the pages, I found what I was looking for and held up the book for her to see. "Jamie Gregory. She came in for a reading August sixth, the day I came back to work."

"You think it's the same girl?" Candice asked, swiveling the computer toward her to stare at the screen again. "Oh, man, Abs! If that is the same girl, then we may have just hit some pay dirt! Do you think you can call her, see if she'll talk to us?"

But I wasn't really listening to her. I was trying to recall Jamie and her reading with me. I remembered my first day back and the butterflies that'd been in my stomach, which were always there whenever I took any time off from doing readings.

But intuition isn't one of those things that fades from nonuse, which was proved to me again when I came back to my private practice on August sixth and had three terrific sessions in a row.

Glancing at my appointment book, I could see that Jamie had been my third client that day. Three out of four I knew had been awesome readings, but my fourth client had been a bit of a dud. Wouldn't you know that was the only person I could recall with any real clarity? Of the other three, I only remembered the feeling of nailing the details so well that each one had gasped and stared at me wide-eyed. But those three faces tended to blend together in my memory, and for the life of me I couldn't recall what Jamie looked like or what I'd said to her.

"Do you remember her?" Candice asked, obviously reading my expression.

"No," I said, but then I thought of something and sucked in a breath. "Come with me," I told her, turning on my heel again and heading back to my office.

Candice followed and sat down in the chair in front of my desk while I eased into mine and opened up my laptop.

Not long ago I'd finally upgraded to digitally recording all of my sessions. After the session was over and the client paid, I e-mailed them the WAV file of the reading and kept a copy for myself, just in case the person lost it or it failed to download it. I kept all these readings on my hard drive, and after doing a short search I came up with Jamie's session. Pumping up the volume, I pressed play and turned the computer a little so that Candice could hear the whole thing.

"Okay, Jamie, the very first thing I'm getting from the ether around you is that your love life is smack-dab in the middle of a transition. I feel like within the past two months you may have split up with someone you really, really loved, but it just wasn't working out. Is that right?"

"Yes! Oh, my God! Abby, you're good! My ex-boyfriend and I split up in June."

I closed my eyes as the memory of the reading began to come back to me. I could now recall Jamie's face. She'd been a petite little thing, with a round face and freckles giving her the appearance of someone younger than she was. "And that relationship had been very much on-again, off-again before you guys made the permanent split in June, correct?" my recorded voice continued.

"Yes."

"Well, I'm feeling like I need to tell you, Jamie, that this time, the split is permanent. You two aren't getting back together."

"Oh," she'd said, and even now I could detect the disappointment in her voice.

"You were hoping I'd say something different, weren't you?"

"No," she lied. "No. I'm good with it. He's a great guy, but I don't want to get back with him."

I opened my eyes and looked at Candice meaningfully, and she nodded. She'd heard the note of disappointment too. "Well," my voice said from the computer, "I'm glad you're not disappointed, because splitting up was the right move for both of you. Did you know he's moving away?"

There was the sound of a gasp on the recording. "He is?"

"Yes. He's moving to New York. And the move will be quite sudden. I think he's following a job offer or a transfer. Either one will be very advantageous to his career. And Jamie, he won't be coming back."

I smiled and rolled my eyes a little at my own voice coming through the computer. I never openly fought clients' insistence that they were over a past love even when the ether spoke otherwise, but it was just like me to keep drilling the demise of the relationship into them. I always felt it was better to know there was no hope of getting back together with someone, because it was often the only way for them to be open to receiving an even better relationship down the road.

"Now, what's interesting about your energy, Jamie, is that I see you taking this man's move quite hard. I feel it might upset you in ways you hadn't anticipated, and while I can understand that, I want to tell you that the longer you spend thinking about what could have been, the longer you'll delay getting on with your life. I feel like you'll want to shut the door on romance for a while, and I can tell you that your decision to do that would only cause you more sadness. Denying yourself the joy of a new relationship just because you don't want to be disappointed again is absolutely the wrong move for you. Does that make sense?"

"I . . . I guess," she'd said.

"Good. Now, my advice to you is to start dating again. But don't date with any expectations about finding the right guy. Just have fun. Enjoy broadening your social circle. Go out there and kiss a few frogs, and if one of them turns into a prince, awesome. If you just date frogs for a while, then have a great time. And before long, don't be surprised if someone who hadn't been on your social radar at all begins to work his way into your life in a very important way. This man's emergence is unexpected, Jamie. I feel like he's a very good guy, but he's got a lot of stuff on his own plate right now. And many of those loose threads need to be wrapped up before anything can start between the two of you, but I feel like, by the time next spring or summer comes around, you two might become a little bit more than just friends. And the energy around your future relationship with this man feels so good. In fact, it feels better than good; it feels great. You both have a lot of love to give, and when the time is right, I think this would be a great match."

At this point I must have felt satisfied with the topic, because I'd moved on to other things. "How's the house hunting coming?"

Jamie gasped again and started laughing. "You are blowing my mind, Abby. I've been shopping for a condo for the past two months, but I haven't been able to find one I really like that I can also afford."

You could hear my own laughter through the computer. "Two months? Well, no wonder you're not finding anything, Jamie. You should be looking at houses, not condos."

"A house? Really? I was thinking that was going to be too much for me to handle."

I smiled when I found myself shaking my head as I listened. More and more of the reading was coming back to me. I knew I'd very likely shaken my head at her then too. "No, it won't be too much for you, Jamie. You'll find something small, no more than two bedrooms, but they're a nice size and the house feels warm and inviting. Look at single-story, two-bedroom homes and you'll be on the right track. Oh, and with the spacious backyard your home will come with, you're finally gonna get that dog you've been thinking about."

There was yet another little gasp on the recording. "Really?" she'd asked me, her voice high and squeaky. "I've been thinking about getting a dog for a while. You know, to take my mind off the breakup, and I've been volunteering down at Austin Pets Alive on the weekends. There's this adorable little King Charles mix that I'm just in love with."

"Oh, that dog is totally yours," I'd told her. "I'm surprised you've resisted scooping him up for this long, actually. Call your Realtor this afternoon and tell her that you want to skip the condos. You'd rather look at ranch-style homes, especially anything in a bold color like red or yellow. I feel like the house that's made for you will come in a very bright color."

"Really?" she'd said, a bit of skepticism in her voice. "That wouldn't be something I'd normally go for."

"Humor me," I'd told her dryly.

Candice laughed and quickly tried to stifle it, but I knew that she was thinking that I could be a little smug about telling my clients what they needed to do.

Abruptly, I'd switched topics again. "Say, do you know a girlfriend who's launching her own business? Something online maybe?"

There was a slight pause, then, "You know, I do have two girlfriends who're going into business with each other—"

Whatever Jamie had been about to say after that I couldn't know, because I'd run right over her with the rest of my impressions. "Two girlfriends? Oh, well, that won't work. Listen, you tell the girl who's got the brown hair to just do this thing on her own, okay? Tell her that I know she may think the girl with the blond hair is a friend, but I'm here to tell you, she's not. And this brunette should stay away from her. Seriously. It feels like their association with each other means nothing but trouble for the brunette. And I'm not sure why . . ."

My gaze snapped back to Candice, who was already eyeing me keenly as she mouthed, "Kendra and Bailey?"

I nodded vigorously, while on the recording Jamie said, "Oh, you don't have to tell me. *I* know the blonde's not a friend. But I haven't figured out how to tell the brunette."

"Be blunt," I'd told her. "And tell her. It's important."

Candice and I listened to the rest of the reading, but there was nothing more about the blonde and the brunette, which I was convinced was a reference to Kendra and Bailey. Once the tape was finished, I closed the lid of the laptop and asked Candice, "What do you want to do?"

"Do you have Jamie's address on file?"

I opened my laptop again and did a quick search. "All I have is her e-mail."

Candice got up and moved to the hall. "I'll get it," she said over her shoulder.

A minute or two later she was back. "I have an address at an apartment that's about a year old, and a new address on Forty-second Street near Duval."

I smiled. "Looks like someone just bought her first home." I recognized the cross streets as part of a cute residential neighborhood on Austin's central east side.

"She could be renting," Candice pointed out.

"Yes, she could be. But she isn't." Sometimes I just *know* I'm right. Those are the times I may also try other people's patience.

Candice held up her wrist to check the time. "She's probably at work right now."

"And I have a client in ten minutes!" I gasped, suddenly realizing I was late getting my reading room ready.

"Is that your only one?"

I shook my head, getting up from my desk to hobble quickly into the next room. "I have a full list of six clients today all back-to-back except for the half-hour lunch in between." I grabbed a pack of matches and began to light candles.

Candice didn't say anything, and I looked up to see her brow raised. "Six?" she repeated. "That's pretty impressive, Sundance."

I grinned. "Word must be spreading."

Candice nodded. "What time will you be through?" she asked next.

"Four. Want to pick this up then?"

Candice offered me a sly look. "Methinks you'll be hungry after your sessions. We can grab a quick happy-hour snack and give Jamie until five thirty to get home from work."

"You don't want to just call her at home?" I asked. "I'm sure I can get her phone number off her release form." I made all my clients sign release forms listing their names, e-mail addresses, and phone numbers just in case.

"No," Candice said. "I find that catching your subject a little off guard helps get the truth out of them, and showing up unannounced at their house usually puts them exactly in that slightly nervous, very talkative state that I like."

I shrugged. "Okay. I'll be done at four, and I should be ready to go by four fifteen or so."

Candice yawned. "Great. I'm gonna head home and catch some Zs. I'll pick you up downstairs at four fifteen."

"Deal," I told her, already turning back to the candles. I heard the front door close not too long after that, and within a few minutes after that my first client had arrived.

The day with my clients passed quickly. Despite the fact that I've been doing this for almost a decade, it's still rare to hit every reading out of the park. Still, that's always what I go for. I give every single client my all because they pay me well and because I want them to have a good experience. It puts a lot of pressure on my shoulders to deliver an accurate and authentic reading, but it also forces me to remember that I'm providing a service, not a favor. I want every client to feel like a million bucks when they leave, but some people are just never satisfied, and that's a hard thing to accept.

My last client of the day was like this. I'd provided her with what I thought were some really good hits, but she failed to see them as such, only grunting a little here and there when I asked if what I was saying was making sense to her.

At the end, when I turned it over to her for questions, she asked me why I hadn't said anything about her bakery in France.

I did this mental *Say what now?* and asked what she meant by that.

"It's my dream to open a bakery in France."

Thinking maybe I'd missed something important, I scanned the woman's energy again. Nope. No bakery. In France or otherwise. "Do you bake?" I asked her, nearly regretting it the moment it came out of my mouth.

"A little," she said, dropping her eyes to the floor.

Her answer gave me pause, but only because . . . well, where do you go with *that*? "I'm sorry," I said, "I'm not sure I understand this. You only bake a little and you want to open a bakery in a country famous for its bakers?"

Her frown deepened. "Well, I'd take lessons," she snapped. "I mean, if Julia Child can move to France and become a successful cook, why can't I do the same?"

Because you have no savings, don't speak French, and don't even know how to bake, you fool! is what I *thought*. What I *said* was, "Ah. Well, if that's your dream, then lessons are a terrific place to start!"

Luckily, by then we were short on time, and the session ended just a minute or two later. Relieved to see her out the door, I blew out all the candles, powered down my computer (ignoring the red blinking light on my phone that indicated I had voice mail), and locked up my office, vowing to return calls first thing in the morning.

I made it downstairs and to the parking garage by four ten and allowed myself a nice cleansing sigh. It'd been an intense but mostly good day. And my hips didn't even hurt that much, which was a great sign given all the sitting I'd done.

While I waited for Candice to swing by and pick me up, I rolled my shoulders and rocked my head from side to side, listening with satisfaction to the pops as my neck cracked. I closed my eyes to work out the final kink and heard a car roll up. Had to be Candice. Giving my head a final good roll, I opened my eyes to see that a black SUV with smoked-out windows had stopped right in front of me.

I felt a jolt of alarm, especially when the rear door opened and out stepped a virtual ogre of a man. Bald-headed, with a round face, spare chins, and small ears that stuck out away from his head, he came right up, grabbed me around the waist, and began to lift me toward the car.

I screamed and brought my cane down on his head as hard as I could. He uttered a guttural sound and squeezed me around the waist tighter. The way he held me put pressure on my pelvis, and I screamed again, but this time in agony. I brought my cane down again and again and heard a loud crack as I watched it break in two—the lower half skittering across the pavement.

With a grunt the ogre practically threw me into the SUV, climbed in after me more quickly than his size should have allowed, and slammed the door.

"GO!" he shouted to the driver, and the car took off. Before I could even right myself, I realized I'd just been

kidnapped and looming over me was one angry brute with several welts the size of plums rising on his bald ugly head. Welts I'd put there.

"I am so fecked," I whispered, officially scared down to my toes.

Wouldn't you know it—Shrek actually nodded, right before reaching out to grab me again. A moment later my world went dark.

Chapter Nine

I don't know if I was relieved or even more ticked off by the hood being rudely shoved over my head. My abduction was happening so fast that I was having a hard time even making sense of it. One minute I was closing my eyes and bracing myself for what I thought was some serious manhandling, and the next my eyes were open and I couldn't see a thing. My hands were quickly bound up too, but they'd been tied in front of me and not very tightly.

I was then hauled off the floor and propped up in one of the seats. My abductor then strapped me in with the seat belt. Of course, his courtesy stopped there and he gave me a rough shake of the shoulders and ordered me to sit still.

I detected a British accent. Figured. He looked like a beefy English rugby player.

We drove for what felt like a very long while. Of course, if you've ever spent time with a hood over your head, even five minutes can be an eternity. The hood was hot, and it was hard to get enough air—especially given the panicked cadence to my breathing.

I'd tried asking questions at first, and that was met with stony silence. Then I tried to remember the turns, right and left and how far apart. Maybe I could get to my cell and make an emergency call?

But I had no idea where my purse had ended up, or even if it'd made it into the SUV. In those first panicked moments, I only remembered whacking Shrek, not if I'd thought to keep my purse with me.

Also, I tried to avoid thinking too far ahead to when the SUV stopped. They tell you if you're attacked to never, ever, *ever* get into the vehicle to be driven to a second location, because it's likely to be somewhere remote with no one around to hear you scream.

That thought petrified me, and it was hard to think through it. Plus, I knew that Shrek wasn't alone—someone was driving the SUV, which meant I officially had at least two abductors.

But why had I been abducted in the first place? Was this a random kidnapping? And then I thought about another abduction and my blood ran cold. Could it be that Shrek was the same man who'd taken Kendra? And then a detail came to me, blooming in my mind like a firework; the ogre had been wearing a blue blazer, white shirt, and black dress slacks. I closed my eyes to concentrate, and sure enough, the image was clear in my memory. He'd been dressed more for a business meeting than for a kidnapping.

Which meant he was likely a professional. Hired by someone else to grab me. That thought made my cold blood turn to ice.

If this is the first time you've read about me, you

might be surprised to learn that I've made a few enemies over the years. Why, just a few months before, I'd
made a whole host of very powerful enemies when I'd
been recruited by the CIA for a top secret mission
abroad. And a few of the very powerful people I'd en-
countered on the mission had actually been killed.

Was this payback for my participation in that mission?

Or did it have to do with my current work with the
FBI?

Or was I right and this was somehow connected to
Kendra?

All three scenarios weren't likely to end well, but the
more I could figure out before my hood came off and I
met my true abductor, the better.

I thought about trying to talk to the guy next to me
and fish for details, but I had a feeling Shrek wasn't going to utter one more word, and he certainly wasn't going to give me any details about who'd hired him. So I
did the only thing left to me. I calmed my butt down and
turned on my radar.

I got a series of impressions, most of them confusing.
I could feel the anger from the ogre filling the small
space in the backseat. I knew he seriously wanted to
throttle me, but he was holding back, and for that I was
quite relieved.

The energy coming off the driver was even weirder; he
felt super nervous. Like he'd never abducted anyone before and he couldn't wait to get to our destination so his
part in this could be finished. And judging by a slight
shift in his energy, I had a feeling we weren't far from
reaching the journey's end.

I then tried to figure out whom they were taking me
to, because by now I was convinced we were going to

meet someone, and as I checked on that, I felt positive that I'd recognize the organizer of this little soiree. That of course gave me no comfort. I've met some pretty big assholes (the no-swearing rule doesn't count if you've just been abducted) in my crime-fighting career.

Anyway, the best that I could hope for was to talk my way out of trouble, or look for an opportunity to escape. Both would require full use of my radar, which would then require me to remain calm. I'm not so good with calm, but I did my best to breathe slow and easy and wait for their next move.

It came sooner than expected. Pretty much at that exact moment I could feel the car make a sharp left turn. We went up some sort of fairly steep incline and paused, and I distinctly heard the sound of a parking-ticket machine buzzing off a ticket. There was another pause; then we zoomed forward, up another steep ramp, making another sharp left. This pattern repeated for several more turns.

I counted the turns, expecting to head to the roof, where there would be the least number of cars and witnesses. By my count there were at least five stories, and sure enough the light beyond my hood brightened slightly as we came out into daylight again. We were definitely on the roof.

The SUV halted just a few seconds later, and I heard the sound of a gearshift being put into park before the engine was cut. I then felt hands at the seat-belt buckle by my hip, and reflexively I struck out with my bound hands. It was like punching a brick wall, and I'm pretty sure I hurt my wrists more than I hurt my abductor.

Once the seat belt was off, I was yanked roughly to the side and pulled out of the car. Of course I fought for all I was worth, but the ogre just hoisted me up in the air and tossed me onto his shoulder. The indignity of it got to me more than the discomfort of being thrown caveman-style over his shoulder.

My head bobbled and I yelled, but I knew the hood was muffling the sound. Plus, we were at least five or six stories up—who was gonna hear me?

The daylight through the hood dimmed again, and cool air wrapped itself around me. I suspected we'd just entered a building. The walls felt close, and I guessed that we were walking down a long hallway. We stopped rather abruptly again, and I heard three loud knocks. Shrek was probably knocking on a door to allow us entrance. It took a few moments, but then I heard the sound of the door being opened, and the ogre was in motion again. And then I heard someone say, "A hood? Really, Hugo, is that necessary?"

I was then eased down to the floor and the hood was yanked off my disheveled head. I took one look at the person who'd called Shrek "Hugo" and lunged forward, yelling, *"I'm gonna kill you!"*

But unfortunately, it was a scene right out of the elevator again. My hips gave out and I fell ineffectually and pathetically to the floor.

I sat there for a good couple rounds of huffing and puffing, so angry I could scream (again) and ignoring the hand that was outstretched to me by my big, beefy abductor. "Go to hell, you son of a bitch!" I snapped, slapping his hand away. (Trust me, the situation called for a little potty mouth.)

"Abby," I heard the criminal mastermind say with more than a hint of disapproval.

I blew out a breath as much in anger as to puff away the hair in my face and turned my narrowed eyes on the person now sitting calmly in a leather chair across the room. "You too, Cat," I snapped. "You can go to hell too!"

"Is that any way to treat your sister?"

Holding up my bound hands, I yelled, *"Is this?"*

Cat's perfectly glossed lips turned down in a frown. "Hugo," she said to her hired thug. "Really?"

Without a word Hugo undid the bindings, lifted me gently off the floor, and moved me over to a chair next to a large conference table. I glared hard at him until he stepped back, his chest puffed out and his hands clasped behind his back.

The whole thing was so crazy that I could hardly believe it. "Would you mind explaining why *on earth* you had me abducted?" I snarled. I couldn't imagine that my own sister would do something so insane.

But then I happened to take a good long look at the conference table itself, and I saw that on it were all sorts of party favors, candles, flower arrangements, confections, ribbons, and even several small plates of food. "Hold on," I said, waving my hand at the table. "You had me abducted over wedding crap? *Are you seriously kidding me?"*

Cat studied me, the frown still prominent on her features. "You left me no choice," she began. "I've been calling you and calling you and you never return my voice mails."

I glared hard at her, but I couldn't escape the fact that she sorta had a point. "My phone's broken," I growled.

Cat raised a skeptical eyebrow. "Hugo?" she said, and before I knew it he was rooting around in my purse—which he'd obviously brought with him—and out came my cell phone.

"Hey!" I yelled when he walked it over to Cat.

But both of them ignored me. Cat tapped at the

screen and smiled triumphantly when her own voice echoed through the speaker, begging me to give her just a half hour to go over a few things that only the bride could decide. It was a voice mail I hadn't even bothered to listen to. I'd just let that one and several others pile up. "Seems like your iPhone is working again," she taunted, waving it at me.

"Oh, if you think for *one minute* that not returning your calls justifies my being manhandled and groped by your hired thug—!"

"I didn't manhandle or grope you!" Hugo protested.

I turned to him with all the anger and irritation I had in me—which was considerable. *"You broke my cane!"*

His eyes narrowed menacingly and he rubbed the top of his forehead, where three good-sized welts were still prominent. "I'll break something else in a minute," he warned.

"Will you two please?!" Cat snapped. Then she pointed to the door and said, "Hugo, go stand over there. I'll deal with you later." Reluctantly he moved over to the door and took up an at-ease position.

Cat then pocketed my cell and turned to me. "Now—," she began, but whatever she'd been about to say next was cut off by a tremendous crash as Candice kicked the door in and came barreling into the room with a gun in one hand, a Taser in the other, and a deadly look on her face.

"Nobody move!" she shouted.

Everyone ignored her.

Cat screamed and dove for cover. I fell over again and crawled under the table, and Hugo . . . well, he did something seriously stupid. He jumped Candice.

She had him down and out—as in knocked out—in the span of about three seconds. I doubted he even knew what hit him.

Once the dust had settled, I crawled back out and held up my hands when Candice swiveled, pointing her weapons at me. "Don't shoot!"

"Sorry," Candice said, pocketing the Taser but keeping the gun handy. "Who else is in here?" she asked commandingly.

"My sister," I told her, pointing across the room to Cat's empty chair. She was probably cowering behind it.

Candice's jaw dropped. "This guy kidnapped you and your sister?" she asked, giving a good kick to Hugo's hip, which I was pretty sure would leave a bruise to go with the welts on his head and the lovely red mark the Taser had left on his neck.

I grabbed the table and hoisted myself up. "No. *Cat* hired Shrek over there to kidnap me."

Candice stared hard at me, as if she couldn't figure out what I meant by that. Then she took in the table covered in wedding paraphernalia. A moment later she started to laugh. It began as a chuckle that turned into a hearty chuckle, then a deep guffaw that made her eyes leak.

I wasn't quite there yet. I'd probably find it amusing later. Much, *much* later.

Pocketing her gun, Candice said, "Okay, Cat, come on out. I promise not to shoot you."

Cat stood up slowly, with her arms raised above her head and wide, frightened eyes. She eyed Hugo's still slightly twitching form on the floor and audibly gulped. "Maybe bringing you here like this wasn't such a great idea," she admitted.

I crossed my arms. "Gee, Cat, *you think*?"

My attitude set Cat off again. "Well, what did you want me to do, Abby? I mean, your wedding is *in a month*! How am I supposed to pull everything together by then if I don't have your input?"

"Dutch has wedding detail," I told her. "He's the one making the wedding decisions."

"He lost the coin toss?" Candice guessed.

I smiled. "Can you believe he actually thought he had a chance?"

"Well, he isn't returning my calls either!" Cat snapped. "Wedding invitations should have gone out a month ago and I have yet to receive your guest list!"

Crap on a cracker. She had me there. I'd totally forgotten to send the invite list to her.

". . . you two haven't even been out to the venue yet!" my sister continued, throwing up her arms in frustration. "Do you know how many calls I've been getting from them? 'When are the bride and groom going to tour the grounds?' they keep saying! I can't continue to promise them that you'll be there soon! I mean, do you have *any* idea how hard it was to book that place? Do you know how many hoops I had to jump through?"

I felt a pang of guilt. Cat had booked this place called Plantation Hill for our ceremony and reception, which was this beautiful historic mansion on a hill overlooking Lake Travis, and the pictures I'd seen were incredibly charming and lovely. Dutch and I had been meaning to get out to take the tour—a requirement of every bride and groom, according to Cat—but we'd both been so busy that it'd slipped through the cracks in our schedules.

I shook my head; I'd have to find time very soon, before my sister's head exploded, because she was still ranting. "And we have to settle on the menu by *today*!" she shouted. "And the band, by *today*! And the—"

"She's got a point, Abs," Candice said to me, cutting off the rest of Cat's rant. "I mean, I know Dutch and Brice are still working that bombing case, and as this stuff really does need to be decided, I guess that means it's up to you."

I put my hands on my hips and stared in shock at my partner. "You're *siding* with her?"

"Why shouldn't she?" Cat demanded. "You're impossible, you know that, Abby? It's like you don't even want to get married!"

That sorta kicked me in the gut. "*Of course* I want to get married!" I did. I really, really did!

Cat took her chair again, visibly calmer now that Candice was on her side. "Then why haven't you helped to finalize the plans? We could've had all of this worked out months ago, and instead, you've been avoiding me like the plague. I think there might be something going on in your subconscious, Abby. I think that maybe you really *don't* want to settle down, and this is your way of throwing a big monkey wrench into things."

I shook my head vehemently. There was nothing I wanted more than to tie the knot with Dutch. But at the same time, there was nothing I wanted less than a big fancy wedding. Why I hadn't suggested eloping at the start was beyond me, and now I realized that my poor sister had really done a ton of work on a project that I'd pretty much completely thumbed my nose at. "Okay," I said, moving carefully along the table and taking a seat in the chair again. "You're right, Cat. I have been avoiding all this, and you've worked your butt off on my behalf. I'm really sorry that I haven't said thank you."

Cat looked taken aback. "You mean it?" she asked.

"I do," I assured her, scrutinizing the small plates of food covered with silver plate warmers. Something smelled deliciously familiar. Sniffing at the air, I lifted one of the warmers and actually squealed with delight.

On a small plate was a miniature hot dog in an equally small bun, covered in Detroit-style Coney Island chili and mustard. "No *way*!"

Cat grinned. "Those were Dutch's idea," she said. "He wanted to have them created for an appetizer, and I had to bribe a cook up in Michigan to give me the recipe for Detroit-style Coney Island chili just so I could have the caterer prepare a sample for you. I'm not sure how many of your wedding guests will choose that over the mushroom quiche or the petite baguettes, but your fiancé insisted."

Searching for a fork and knife, I found a set of plastic utensils and dove in. My eyes rolled up into the top of my head and for a few seconds I was in serious heaven. All the wonderful flavors of my hometown favorite came flooding back, and it was several seconds before I could focus on my sister again. "You rock," I said to her.

Cat grinned.

Hugo began to moan and move around while I was sampling entrées. "Where'd you pick him up, anyway?" Candice asked my sister while watching the big thug warily.

Cat considered Hugo with obvious disappointment. "My board of directors hired him," she said. Then she looked around. "In fact, they hired him and another man. Where is he anyway?"

"Probably still slumped over the steering wheel," Candice said with a knowing wink. "I rolled up in our parking garage just as Abby and this dynamic duo were speeding away. When I saw her broken cane on the pavement, I gave chase. I was just about to call Dutch to bring in the cavalry when the SUV these idiots were in turned into this building and headed up the ramp. I think I pulled up behind the SUV two seconds after Abs was hauled away inside, and I left the driver in the front seat of his car taking a nice nap, if you get my drift."

Cat paled. "You didn't kill him, did you?"

Candice laughed. "No, Cat, I just knocked him out. He should be coming to very soon."

But I wasn't concerned with him or his partner at the moment. "Hold on," I said, getting my sister's attention. "Cat, your company hired these guys to kidnap me?" I couldn't fathom why her board of directors would go along with that.

Cat laughed. "No," she said. "Hugo and his partner are my bodyguards."

I stopped stuffing my face and pointed my radar straight at Cat. "*Why* exactly do you need a bodyguard?"

Cat waved her hand like it was no big deal. "Oh, just a silly couple of letters that have been coming into my office the past few months. Really, it's nothing to worry about."

Candice and I exchanged glances. Hugo moaned again. "What'd the letters say, Cat?" Candice asked calmly.

"Nothing important," my sister insisted, avoiding the question.

"Humor us," I told her.

Cat sighed like we were making a big deal out of nothing. "The letters were from some lunatic who's been threatening to kidnap me," she explained calmly. "That's actually where I got the idea to grab you and pull you in here."

Candice and I exchanged another look. "How many

letters are we talking about, Cat?" I asked when my radar suggested we needed to take this seriously.

"Well, three letters and a few e-mails. And a suspicious package, which we turned over to the FBI, but that turned out to be nothing too scary. Just some rope and duct tape, you know, probably meant to scare me. The FBI recommended getting a bodyguard, just to be safe."

"Why would someone be targeting you?" I asked next.

Cat shrugged. "Wright Marketing had a *very* good year last year," she said, "and I made it onto the Forbes list. That always brings with it a certain kind of unwanted attention." Cat is CEO and founder of a *huge* marketing company and her personal worth is somewhere in the gajillions.

"And you didn't think to *tell* me about all this?" I asked, flabbergasted.

"Oh, Abby," my sister said. "It's not like it's a valid threat. I mean, who sends a package with rope and duct tape before they actually attempt to kidnap you?"

I could think of plenty of nut jobs who'd raise their hands in answer to that question, and I turned to Candice expectantly. She was already tapping the screen of her phone before putting it to her ear. I knew exactly whom she'd be calling and was a little angry at my sister for not telling me about the threat, as Dutch and his best friend and business partner, Milo, were the perfect men to handle security detail. They owned a security company, after all, which Milo ran and Dutch consulted on.

A moment after putting the phone to her ear, Candice said, "Hey, Milo. Listen, we've got a situation here with Abby's sister . . ." There was a pause; then Candice burst out laughing at something Milo had said, but one look at Cat's narrowed eyes caused her to squash it and get to the point. "It seems Cat's received some threatening letters and the security detail her company hired isn't working out so well."

"What the bloody 'ell hit me?" Hugo mumbled, sitting up and looking around dully.

"Can you get one of your guys assigned to her, stat?" Candice asked Milo; then she seemed to catch the worry in my eyes. "Actually, let's get a team assigned to her. Tonight."

Candice and I left my sister in the company of four highly skilled men, each with arms like tree trunks, and all of whom were packing heat. Two of Milo's guys helped Hugo and his partner back to their hotel rooms and made sure the men had enough cash for their troubles and the plane ride home. Of course, Cat had to fork over a little extra to them—hazard pay for the afternoon with me, but for the most part the time spent with her had been a success. I'd finalized many of the wedding decisions and pinkie swore to Cat that Dutch and I would pay a visit to the wedding venue very, very soon.

I was leaving only a few of the very last-minute decisions to Dutch but promised Cat that if he couldn't break free from his investigation by the end of the week, then I would step up to the plate and finalize everything else.

And that put Cat and me back on good terms. Especially once I had her promise that she wouldn't try anything so crazy as to kidnap me ever again. Well, that and Cat brought out a series of gorgeous hand-carved canes for me right before I left. "I know you're working to walk without one, honey, but I thought we could have one of these on hand as a backup, just in case," she'd whispered kindly.

I selected a white walking stick with a silver spiral handle, which was actually quite elegant and probably wicked expensive. "Ooo," Cat said, eyeing my choice. "That's exactly the one I would've gone with. I ordered it from Comoy's of London. And if you have to use it at the ceremony, I think it'll blend in with your gown and no one will even notice. Take it home with you tonight and test it out. If you like it, its yours."

Sometimes, my sister can be just wonderful—the best sister ever. Other times, she can drive me completely crazy . . . but that's family for you.

Candice offered to take me home and I accepted. "How you doin'?" she asked when I'd fallen silent.

"I'm okay," I said, staring out the window with an unsettled feeling in the pit of my stomach.

"You worried about Cat?"

I rubbed my arms. I had a sudden chill. "Partly."

"Partly?"

"Partly I'm worried about her and partly I can't shake this feeling like something's going to go wrong at the wedding."

Candice chuckled. "Well, it wouldn't be a wedding if something didn't go wrong, Sundance."

I sighed. "Yeah, I guess."

"And Cat's in the best of hands," she assured me. "Milo says he sent us his top guys in Austin, and he's got another team assigned to her in Boston. She'll be protected at all times."

The truth was that I wasn't that worried about Cat. I'd done a thorough check of the ether around her, and I could see some threatening communication, but there didn't appear to be any follow-through.

Still, I thought it pretty smart to surround her with big, beefy men who could keep her out of trouble and talk her out of harebrained ideas like kidnapping her sister, unlike Shrek and his ass for a partner. (Swearing doesn't count if you can turn it into a pun.)

Even though I knew Cat would now be safe, I couldn't shake the disquieting feeling that had taken root and was twisting me up inside. I felt edgy and nervous without knowing why. "Is it too late to stop by Jamie's?" I asked, needing a distraction.

Candice glanced at the clock on the dashboard. "It's after eight," she said. "We'd be pushing it, but I'm up for it if you are."

"I'm game." I was too wound up to go home.

"Cool."

We found our way to Jamie's house, which wasn't too far away, as it happened, and pulled to a stop in front of a terra-cotta orange home with bright white trim. "Not quite red or yellow, but a nice in-between," Candice commented as we got out of her Porsche.

I will admit that the minute I spotted the color, I'd smirked smugly just a bit. It's nice to be right.

As we approached the house, we could see in through the front window, and it appeared that Jamie was still in the unpacking stage. Candice rang the bell and I grinned again when an excited yippy bark answered.

The porch light came on and Candice winked at me, then turned toward the door so that Jamie could clearly see who was on her front step. The door opened slowly and a young, bright-faced woman with freckles looked at us with curiosity. "Yes?"

"Jamie?" I said, taking the lead.

She focused on me. "Oh, my God! Abby Cooper?"

I flashed her a smile. "You remember!"

Jamie opened the door wider. "Well, of course I remember! What're you doing here, though? Did you sense that I'd just bought this place?"

"Sort of. This is my business partner, Candice Fusco. She and I work private investigations together. Can we come in and talk to you for a few minutes?"

Several more yippy barks pulled our attention down, and Jamie blushed while she reached for her dog. "I adopted him the day after I came to see you," she admitted, stepping back to allow us to come inside. "His name's Gismo."

I held up my fingers so Gismo could take a sniff and he gave my hand an enthusiastic lick. "He's adorable!"

Jamie waved us into her cluttered living room, blushing again when she had to swipe away packing paper and bubble wrap so that we could all take a seat.

"How cute is this place?" I said to Jamie, looking around the small but cozy living room with approval.

"Oh, Abby, I can't thank you enough for telling me to buy a house over a condo. You know, I sorta fought the idea for a few weeks after my reading, but then I had this sudden urge to call my Realtor and tell her that I was open to a single-family home. She sent me the link to this listing, like, five minutes later, and the second I saw it I could just picture myself living here! Plus, it'd been on the market for a while, so I got it for a great price!"

Candice sat back on the sofa next to me and crossed her legs leisurely. "It really is charming," she said sweetly. "And you and Bailey should share moving supplies, now that you're moving in and she's moving out."

Jamie's face turned quizzical. "Bailey?" she said. "You mean Bailey Colquitt?"

Candice nodded. "Abby and I went to visit with her last week."

Jamie's brow furrowed. "You did?" she said, turning her attention back to me. "Did you do a reading for her too?"

I shook my head. "Not exactly. Candice and I are looking into Kendra Moreno's disappearance."

Jamie bit her lip. "Oh, God," she whispered. "I didn't even think of that. Abby, do you know when she'll come back home?"

I hesitated, not knowing what to say to that, and Jamie seemed to read into the prolonged pause. Her face drained of color. "Oh, God!" she repeated. "You know what's happened to her!"

I held up my hand. "I'm not certain, Jamie. I have a feeling, and I could be wrong."

Jamie hugged Gismo to her chest. "But she's . . . alive, right?" Again, I didn't answer her, and Jamie's eyes began to water. "Oh, no!" she whispered. "Oh, no, no, no, no!"

I got up and went to sit next to her, wrapping my arm around her shoulders as she dissolved into a puddle of tears. "Why?" she cried. "Why Kendra? She's such a good person!"

I looked up at Candice, and her face held such sympathy. I knew this case was tugging at her insides just as much as it was tugging at mine. When Jamie had settled down a little, I brought her a tissue and started to question her. "Jamie," I began, "do you know of anyone who might want to harm Kendra?"

Jamie shook her head and dabbed at her eyes. "No," she said hoarsely. "Not Kendra. She didn't have an enemy in the world!"

I glanced at Candice again and noticed the skeptical look in her eyes. "Jamie?" I said next. "Do you remember the part during your session where I talked about two women that you knew, one brunette and one blonde, who maybe should be kept away from each other?"

Jamie gasped a little. "Oh, my God! I totally forgot about that! But yeah, I do remember it! You were talking about Kendra and Bailey, weren't you?"

"Yes, I think I was," I agreed. "But, Jamie, I still don't have much of a context for the insight. I mean, there's a limit to what I can see. Now that we have some hindsight, can you tell us why I might've hit on the fact that Bailey wasn't the friend Kendra thought she was?"

Jamie's face seemed to register something, and she looked up at me with alarm. "You don't think . . . ?"

She didn't finish her thought, and I decided to wait her out. I wasn't going to feed her my impressions. I wanted her to tell me.

Jamie bit her lip again. "Kendra and Bailey have been best friends since high school," she said. "They did everything together, and you could never say that they didn't genuinely like each other. None of that frenemy stuff you see with other girls. They were tight."

"But something changed," I prompted when Jamie paused again.

She looked down at Gismo, curled up in her lap. "Yeah," she said. "Something did change. Kendra met Tristan her senior year of college."

"And Bailey got jealous that Kendra wasn't spending so much time with her, right?" Candice guessed.

But Jamie shook her head. "No," she said softly, still not raising her eyes. "Bailey fell in love with Tristan too."

My breath caught. I hadn't picked up on that at all. "Was it mutual?"

Jamie shook her head, but it was halfhearted. "No," she said. "I mean, at least, I don't think so. Not at first at least. Kendra's just this really good person. She's so sweet that you can't help falling for her, you know? She's the kindest person alive, I think."

Jamie's voice hitched as she thought on what she'd just said, and she began to cry again. Finally she looked at me and said, "You're positive she's really dead, Abby?"

"No, Jamie, I'm not," I lied. "Until we find Kendra, there's always hope."

Jamie swallowed hard and continued. "Anyway, Kendra wasn't the beauty queen that Bailey was, and I think it got to Bailey that such a good-looking guy like Tristan picked Kendra over her. She would try to flirt with Tristan, but never in front of Kendra. We all saw it, but none of us said anything because Tristan seemed to be so devoted to Kendra. Then I found Tristan and Bailey making out the night of his bachelor party."

That confession surprised me a little. "Did you say anything to Kendra about it?" I asked.

Jamie's lower lip began to tremble. "No," she whispered. "Tristan had his bachelor party at his best friend's house, and Bailey talked me into going over there to crash the party. The guy I was seeing at the time was going to be there, and I think I agreed because I was starting to get pretty insecure about our relationship, and I wanted to make sure the guys weren't doing anything crazy with some strippers or anything.

"Anyway, we got there pretty late, and Tristan was already pretty drunk. The guys didn't want us to be there, 'cause they did have two strippers and they knew we'd report back to Kendra, so they wouldn't let us inside, but Bailey, she insisted that we sit in the car and watch to make sure nothing too wild went on. She kept telling me we needed to have Kendra's back.

"Then we saw Tristan come out of the house alone—probably to get some fresh air, and Bailey told me she was going to go talk to him to make sure he was okay, and while she did that, I did something stupid."

Jamie paused, and I said, "What, honey? What'd you do?"

"I snuck around back and watched the guys through the big bay window. Like I said, I was really insecure about my relationship with my boyfriend, and I thought the guys might be up to no good with the strippers inside the house, but all I saw was most of the guys involved in a poker game and even the strippers were sitting around looking bored.

"When I came back to the front of the house to tell Bailey that we should go, I found her and Tristan over by the garage making out, and I was so pissed off that I left her there and went home.

"I felt bad about leaving her there, so about an hour later I went back to the bachelor party, but she was already gone. I called and called her, but that night she never picked up. The next morning I went to her house and saw a cab drop her off at her front door. She was still wearing the clothes she'd had on the night before, and sticking out of her purse was her bra. I knocked on her door after she'd gone inside, and when she answered I apologized for leaving her at the party, but then I confronted her about what she'd been doing with Tristan, and she swore up and down that she'd made this big mistake and that she was really, really sorry, and that nothing like that would ever happen again."

"You believed her," I said, more statement than question.

"Yes," Jamie said. "Especially when I saw the way

Tristan flat-out refused to look at Bailey from that point forward, and he even broke down and cried in the middle of his wedding vows. I thought he might've been really sorry that he hooked up with Bailey, and you could see that he loved Kendra so much! So I never said a word to anybody about it. Maybe that was the wrong thing to do, but I really wanted Kendra and Tristan to work out."

I sat back in my seat and considered Jamie. "Do you think that Tristan would ever hurt Kendra?" I asked bluntly.

Jamie shook her head. "No!" she said. "Tristan's this really great guy! I couldn't see him hurting anyone."

"Okay," I said, "then how about Bailey? Do you think she's capable of hurting Kendra? Or hiring someone to hurt Kendra?"

Jamie's eyes returned to her lap. "I don't know, Abby," she said. "Bailey can be sweet when she wants to be, but if you've got something she wants, she'll find a way to get it. All these years since the wedding I've kept my eye on Bailey when Tristan's around, and you can see that she still has a thing for him. So could she have hurt Kendra to get her out of the way? I may be a bad person for thinking this, but yeah, maybe."

"Were you ever suspicious that Bailey and Tristan got together after the wedding?" Candice asked.

"I don't know," Jamie said softly, and I picked up something in the ether around her. Something that suggested she was holding back.

"What?" I asked. "What is it that you're not saying?"

Jamie sighed. "A couple of weeks ago, right when work was really crazy and I was in the middle of going through all the mortgage stuff, trying to buy this place, Kendra left me a voice mail. She said that she'd had a long talk with Bailey and that she was thinking about leaving Tristan and she really needed my advice." Jamie paused again and began crying in earnest once more. "I . . . I . . . never returned her call, Abby. My life was just filled with stress and pressure back then, and I didn't want to get involved and add one more thing to my plate. I mean, I just didn't think I had the energy or the time."

"You think Kendra found out about the night of Tristan's bachelor party?"

Jamie wiped her eyes, but the tears of guilt continued to flow. "Yeah," she said in a choked whisper. "I mean, why else would Kendra even consider leaving Tristan? He's a great guy, works his butt off so they can afford to live in that house, and he loves her and Colby like crazy. The only reason I could think of that she might want to leave him was because she found out about Bailey and him together that night. So when she turned up missing, I figured that she really had found out about Tristan cheating on her, and she just sort of bolted. I've been thinking all she needs is a little time to sort things out, and she'll come back. I mean, she'd never permanently turn her back on her son."

"That's why you haven't been overly worried about her disappearance," I said. Jamie nodded and her eyes welled up again.

"I thought she was off on a mini-vacation, just trying to clear her head a little."

The room fell silent while we all considered what she'd said; then Candice asked, "Jamie, did you know that Bailey is getting divorced?"

My brow rose. We didn't know that for sure; it was just something I'd picked up in the ether. "She is?" Jamie asked.

Candice nodded like it was a known fact. "She's moving out of her house. She's leaving her husband."

Jamie sniffled loudly. "Well, that's not much of a surprise. Chase Colquitt is a total douchebag."

I couldn't help it; I snickered but quickly covered it by clearing my throat. "How long have Bailey and Chase been together?" I asked.

Jamie thought for a moment. "Not long. Bailey met Chase about a month after Kendra and Tristan got married. The two got serious real quick. They were married in the same year they first got together."

"That's fast," Candice said.

Jamie nodded. "I know it sounds weird, but I always felt like Chase was the rebound guy for Bailey after she hooked up with Tristan."

"Rebound guy?" I asked. "But I thought they only hooked up that one night."

Jamie stroked her pup's ears. "As far as I know that's true," she said. "But like I said, it was pretty obvious to me that Bailey was in love with Tristan. It's still obvious, actually. Every time I talk to her, she winds the conversation back to Tristan. It's like she's obsessed with him, which was one of the reasons why I stopped talking to her. It was always Tristan, Tristan, Tristan."

I turned my gaze to Candice, who was looking back at me with a raised brow. Could Jamie have just provided us with a motive for Kendra's abduction and murder? Candice stood up, making a point to note the time. "We should get out of your hair."

I got up too. "Thanks so much for letting us talk to you, Jamie."

"Sure," she said as she set her pooch on the floor and walked us to the door. "And if you have any more questions about Kendra, please just call or come by. I can't imagine what her parents must be going through. Or little Colby."

Jamie began to well up again, and after giving her a brief supportive hug, we left her in peace.

Chapter Ten

The next morning Dutch and I had an argument. It was one of those fights that starts off being about one thing and turns into a squabble about every little issue that's been bugging you both for the past four years.

By the end of it, I was storming (aka hobbling with emphasis) out of the house, suggesting he go . . . er . . . *make love* to himself. (Swearing doesn't count when you're having a big blowup with your fiancé.)

The moment I slammed the door behind me was the instant I realized my car was still at the office.

"Son of a . . . !" I growled. Rummaging around in my purse yielded another unpleasant surprise: My phone was missing. I muttered a few more choice expletives (swearing doesn't count when you're furious with your fiancé and you can't find your phone) and puffed out a couple of big breaths, knowing I'd have to go back inside and hunt for my cell. As I mentally went back through the previous evening, trying to find a moment when I could last remember seeing my phone, the memory of Cat waving it triumphantly came back to me.

Had she returned it? I tapped my new cane on the step a few times. No. No, she hadn't. "Frick, feck, frog!" I groused, turning reluctantly around to go back into the house. Dutch was gathering up a few files before he headed to the office, and I caught him looking up at me when I came back in, but I lifted my chin, averted my eyes from him, and headed straight to the house phone in the kitchen. Picking it up, I was about to dial when I realized I had no idea what Candice's number was. Whenever I needed to call her I just looked her name up in my iPhone's contacts list.

"Goddammit!" I growled, slamming the phone back down on the charger. (Swearing doesn't count when you're furious, just had a fight with your fiancé, forgot that your car's not in the driveway, realize your sister's stolen your phone, and can't remember your best friend's number.)

Dutch pretended to ignore me and continued to mess with his files.

I glared hard at him. The *last* thing I wanted to do was ask him for a favor, but unless I wanted to miss my appointments for the day and irritate five new clients, I'd need his phone to call Candice. You'd think that was a no-brainer, but I still thought about it for a good two minutes before I cleared my throat and said, "Dutch?"

"I'm late for work, Abby," he replied evenly.

I could feel my brow lower to the danger zone, but I kept my own voice calm and collected. "I need your phone to look up Candice's number."

"Where's your phone?"

I took a deep (deeeeeeeeeeep) cleansing breath and

let it out nice and slow (slooooooooow) before answering him. "Cat has it."

Dutch stopped messing with his files and lifted steely eyes to me. We had ourselves a little staring contest for a few beats before he walked over to the dining room table and picked up the box with my wedding present, or as I liked to call it, "argument subject zero," as it'd been the thing that'd started our fight in the first place.

Laying the box on the counter in front of me, Dutch said, "You can have Candice's number if you promise to take your gun to the shooting range to practice."

"I promise," I said quickly. The next time I was at the shooting range, I'd take the stupid gun. Of course, the next time I intended to visit a shooting range was going to be one minute past *never*.

Dutch was onto me, however. Holding up a finger, he said, "And you have to promise to visit the shooting range sometime in the next seven days."

I narrowed my eyes at him. "Why wait for the shooting range when I have a perfectly good target standing right here in front of me?"

"I'm serious, Abby," he growled.

"So. Am. I."

Dutch scoffed at me. "You probably haven't even gotten bullets for it yet." He didn't know Candice had loaded it, and I didn't feel like telling him.

"I can still hit you over the head with it," I countered. The man was well onto my last nerve.

But Dutch wasn't backing down. He held up his phone and wiggled it with emphasis. "Do we have a deal?"

I glared at him for all I was worth, but he only stood there with raised eyebrows and that stupid wiggling phone. *"Fine!"* I snapped, swiping for his phone, but he lifted it out of my reach and moved to the table. Writing down Candice's number on a legal pad, he dropped the pen when he was done, grabbed his files, and walked out without a backward glance.

I think that hurt most of all.

Candice got an earful when she picked me up a half hour later. I think if she'd known that she was going to get said earful, she would've left me at home. "Why're you two still arguing about this?" she asked when I'd run out of substitute expletives and was searching for one I could use to cheat without her demanding a quarter.

"Because he just won't drop it!" I yelled.

"Seems like it's important to him that you get comfortable with his wedding present," she said reasonably. "So why not do him this one little favor, and take it to the range for one round of practice? I mean, it can't be as bad as arguing with Dutch over it and ruining both your days, can it?"

I turned toward the window and stared out at the passing scenery for a while. Why did Candice always have to be so fecking reasonable?

"It's the principle of the thing," I said after a moment.

"What principle would that be?"

I turned back to her. "The principle is that you don't give your new bride a *gun* for a wedding present!"

But Candice only shrugged. "You know, Abs, you can't be sure that you won't need that gun someday. I mean, *really* need it. It's not just that it might come in handy. It's that it could *save your life*. And if you ask me, that's the best wedding present Dutch could ever give you."

I turned myself back to the window and did some really good pouting all the rest of the way to the office.

The moment we parked, I got out of Candice's car without thanking her or looking back. I merely gimped my way to the elevator, got in, punched the button, and rode up alone.

Once I was settled into my office, I managed to hold on to that anger for a whopping ten minutes, but eventually reason returned and I began to realize what an ass I was being. (Swearing here counts, and I socked another quarter into the swear-jar kitty.) I was just about to go apologize to Candice, in fact, when my first client of the morning walked in.

Vowing to make up with Candice after my client, I focused on getting through the session. Luckily, the reading went smoothly, and I managed to land a few really great hits. Buoyed by the energy of having done well, I went in search of my partner, but she wasn't in her office, and I wasn't even sure if she'd come up from the garage. For all I knew, she could've decided to give me some space for the day.

I checked her side of the suite after my next two readings, but if she'd come and gone or hadn't come in at all, I couldn't tell. What's more, I couldn't call her because I'd stupidly left the paper with her number at the house, and I couldn't call Cat because I couldn't remember her number either.

Still, there was one number I did know by heart simply because it ended in the digits 5050. I dialed it, waited out three rings, and heard, "Harrison," on the other end.

"Brice?" I asked.

"Abby?"

"Yeah. Listen, my sister has my phone with all my contacts in it and I need to talk to Candice."

"Isn't she at the office?"

"No, and I can't remember her cell. Can you give me her number, please?"

"Sure," he said, and I heard the sound of a drawer being pulled open. I imagined he was going for his BlackBerry. "You got a pen?"

I wrote the number down and was thanking him when he said, "Say, Abs, I know this is none of my business . . ."

Uh-oh.

". . . but did something happen between you and Agent Rivers today?"

I paused. "Why?"

"Because he's been distracted and biting everybody's head off all morning, and I need him to focus on this bombing case."

Great. Not only had I been exceptionally rude to my best friend, but I was very likely ruining my fiancé's career. "Can you transfer me to his line?" I asked, laying my head down on the desk in defeat.

"That a girl," Brice said, and a second later I was listening to hold music.

When Dutch picked up the line, I said, "Hey."

Dutch answered me with silence.

I sighed and swiveled around in my chair to face the window. "I'm sorry," I said a bit stiffly.

The cold silence on his end continued.

I sighed again, cooling my jets, and softening my voice, I tried again. "Seriously, cowboy, I am really sorry. I know you're just trying to look out for me, and I feel bad that this whole gun thing keeps sparking an argument between us."

"I am," he said at last.

"You are what?"

"Trying to look out for you, Edgar. I need to know

that you can defend yourself. Otherwise, I won't be able to go to work every day and do what I gotta do. And if I'm distracted by thoughts of you in danger without the means to protect yourself, then I leave myself open and vulnerable too."

That hit home. "I get it. I'll go to the range next weekend."

Dutch's skeptical silence returned.

"I swear, cowboy," I insisted. "I really will. And if you'll come with me to give me a few pointers, I'd appreciate it." I threw that last bit in out of desperation. I no more wanted Dutch to come with me than I wanted my highly impatient, curmudgeonly alcoholic father to teach me how to drive again.

Still, it seemed to work because at last the granite tone in his voice cracked and I got a hint of a chuckle. "Deal," he said. "And I'll even spring for the bullets."

I smiled. "No need. Candice already hooked me up."

Once I was sure that he and I were back on good terms, I clicked off and dialed Candice's line. A ringing sound right behind me caused me to jump. Whirling around, I found her standing in front of my desk, arms crossed and a big old grin on her face. "All better?" she asked.

"When did you get back?"

"About five minutes ago."

"How much of my conversation did you hear?"

"Enough," she assured me, that grin getting bigger.

"That apology extends to you too, Cassidy."

"I figured," she said, reaching down next to my desk to retrieve my purse. "Come on. We've got an interview to get to."

I looked at my watch. "But it's my lunch hour!"

"We'll eat on the go," she said, heading out the door.

I was left to grumble and reach for my cane.

I caught up with her at the elevator, and seeing it reminded me of my earlier behavior. I chilled out quick, even allowing her to enter first when the doors opened.

Once we were in her car again, I remembered to ask, "So who're we interviewing?"

"Garrett Velkune. He's an attorney."

That was helpful. "Whose attorney is he?"

"Kendra's."

That was only slightly more helpful. "Her business attorney?"

Candice lowered her shades and gave me a knowing look. "No. He's her divorce attorney."

My mouth fell open. "So she *was* planning on leaving Tristan!"

Candice pushed her shades back into place. "Looks that way. Only, the really weird thing is that the papers for her divorce were filed with the county clerk this morning."

I turned stunned eyes to her and she gave me a sideways grin. "I had a hunch and went fishing down at the county clerk's office. The girls there are super sweet, and one of them said that she'd received the papers just an hour earlier from Kendra's attorney. She didn't put it together that it was the missing girl from TV until I brought it up, and I left her to call the police about it. I figure that since it's lunchtime, we have maybe an hour before the detective assigned to the case follows up on the lead."

My brow furrowed. "But how could Kendra file for divorce this morning when my radar is insisting that she's dead?"

"That's exactly what I want to know," Candice told me. "And why I thought it okay to steal you away from your lunch hour."

"Okay, okay," I conceded. "You're right. But can we maybe grab something to go? I'm starving, and you know my low blood sugar plays havoc with my concentration . . . which I'll need to use with the old radar."

Candice zipped us through a fast-food drive-through, and by the time we made it to Mr. Velkune's office, I'd polished off half my chicken sandwich.

Kendra's attorney worked in a fairly nondescript building, and according to the signage, he hung out his own shingle on the fourth floor. Candice and I rode the elevator up and moved into a completely forgettable hallway with gray Berber carpet and off-white wallpaper mottled with a drab silver-blue print.

We found his office near the end of the hall, and I was prepared for a similar decorative vein inside, but I came up short when Candice and I moved through the door.

The interior of Velkune's suite was a testament to Texas cattle ranching—not something that in any way dominates the ever hip and trendy city of Austin.

Velkune's twin sofas were upholstered in a caramel-marbled leather with silver studs along the trim. A cowhide rug lay over beech-wood floors, and a longhorn skull with absolutely gigantic horns was mounted to the main wall.

A cowboy hat graced the top of a short bookshelf cluttered with rodeo trophies, spurs, a lasso, a cattle prod, and several photos of bull riders and cowboys.

Taking all this in, I eyed Candice nervously, slightly worried that if we didn't watch ourselves, we'd be lassoed and hog-tied.

"Good morning!" said a cheery voice nearby. We turned to see a perky young woman with curly brown hair and a little button nose hurrying to get behind the front desk to welcome us. "Can I help you?"

Candice strode purposely over to her. "We have an emergency appointment with Mr. Velkune. I called about an hour ago?"

Perky trained her gaze to her computer, then back up to Candice. "Ms. Fusco?"

"Yes."

"Please take a seat and I'll let Mr. Velkune know you're here." She indicated the sofa before picking up the phone receiver.

Candice and I both took a seat, though not a very comfortable one. I was a teensy bit overwhelmed by all the "yipee ki yay!"

Ten minutes passed and I began to tap my foot. I had another appointment in forty-five minutes, and it'd take us at least ten of those to get back to our office. Candice seemed anxious about the time too, because she got up and moved to the desk to ask Perky how much longer it might be, as we were on a very tight schedule.

Perky smiled apologetically and lifted the phone to talk to her boss again. After a short exchange, she replaced the receiver and said, "I'm really sorry. He said he'd be out in just a minute. He's running behind because he just got back from his honeymoon."

My brow shot up. "His honeymoon?" I asked. That might explain why Kendra's divorce papers had been filed only that morning. I suddenly wondered if Mr. Velkune knew that Kendra was missing. "Where did he and his wife go?" I asked abruptly. When Perky turned her surprised eyes at me, I added, "I'm getting married next month and I still don't know where we'll be taking our honeymoon." All true, actually.

"Corsica," she told me. "It's one of Mrs. Velkune's favorite places. Her mother's family is from that region, so they go there quite a bit."

I got up and walked casually over to the desk. "Corsica, huh?" I said. "That sounds nice. You say he just got back?"

Perky nodded. "Late last night, so I'm pretty sure he's still a little jet-lagged." Perky then blushed slightly and said, "I think we're all a little jet-lagged, actually. Mr. Velkune gave me some time off too, and I went to California to visit my parents."

Candice and I eyed each other knowingly. "Ah," I said.

At that moment, a very tan, good-looking man in his mid-thirties emerged from an office and flashed us a Texas-sized grin. I noticed his teeth were extra white against the deep tan he'd obviously gotten on his honeymoon. "Hey, there!" he said, hurrying forward to shake our hands and apologize for keeping us. "I've been trying to dig my way out from under a pile of paperwork all morning," he explained in a voice with a notable southern lilt. "I just got back from my honeymoon, and there were a few motions that really needed to be sent over to the courthouse this morning."

"Congratulations," Candice said, walking behind him as he motioned for us to follow him.

"Thanks," he said, holding the door to his private office for us as we entered. The interior here was more of the same decor as out in the lobby, except that, comparatively, I thought he'd held back in the lobby.

Velkune's office was also cluttered with gift baskets and presents, and there was a banner still on the wall that read, "Congratulations Garrett and Seely!"

"Now, what can I do for you two ladies?" he asked when we were all seated.

Candice crossed her legs to hide the fact that she was switching on her iPhone's recording device. Anything

Mr. Velkune told us in confidence about his client wouldn't be admissible in court, but I knew that Candice liked to record all her interviews and type them up into notes for later. "We're here about Kendra Moreno," she told him.

Velkune cocked his head and furrowed his brow. "Kendra?" he said. "I just filed those docs this morning. Are you the opposing counsel for Mr. Moreno?"

Candice shook her head. "No, Mr. Velkune, I'm afraid it's a little more complicated than that. Did you know that Kendra Moreno is missing?"

Velkune's face drained of color and he sucked in a breath. "Missing?" he said. "When?"

"Almost two weeks," Candice told him.

He blinked and wiped his chin. "Oh, God," he said. "I've been out of the country. No one told me."

"We suspected as much when you filed her divorce papers this morning," Candice told him.

"Are you the police?" he asked abruptly, looking Candice up and down like he expected to see a badge somewhere.

"No," Candice told him, but she dug in her purse and pulled out her PI badge. "I'm a private investigator looking into Kendra's disappearance."

"Do the police even know?" he asked next. I could see the shock on his face. The news really seemed to rattle him.

"Yes," Candice assured him. "And I expect they'll be contacting you shortly, but as I'm also investigating her disappearance, I thought we might talk a little before-hand."

Velkune eyed the phone, and I knew he was thinking of calling the police himself. Candice must've caught that too, because she said, "Please, Mr. Velkune? The more people we have looking for Kendra, the faster we might find her."

He nodded—a bit reluctantly, I thought—and said, "What do you want to know?"

"When was the last time you saw Kendra?"

Velkune stood and began to pace the floor. "The morning of my wedding day. The twenty-eighth, to be exact. I was wrapping up some last-minute details here before going over to the church to get ready, and Kendra came into the office looking for me. She said she'd completely forgotten about my wedding, but she begged me for a little time because she felt she was coming apart at the seams. She told me that she was actually afraid for her life."

Candice twisted in her chair to look at him while he paced back and forth. "Afraid for her life?"

Velkune ran a shaking hand through his hair. "Yeah," he said, stopping to stare into space. "She was terrified."

"Of her husband?"

"She didn't come right out and say so, but it was pretty obvious things at home had become untenable. She'd flirted with the idea of leaving her husband a few months before, and I'd counseled her to take her time and make certain that's what she wanted before she went through with filing paperwork. I mean, the couple had a son together, and it's tough on a little kid to get shuffled back and forth between two parents. I know because I've been there myself. Anyway, I suggested counseling, but Kendra seemed reluctant."

"Do you know if their relationship was physically abusive?" Candice asked next.

"I honestly couldn't tell you," he said. "She never confessed that to me in so many words, and I found it difficult to know what was going on in her home."

"So that last day, Kendra came by and . . ." Candice let the rest of her sentence hang.

Velkune shook his head sadly. "We talked for about half an hour, and she said she was done with her marriage. It was over. She'd made up her mind and she was leaving her husband. She looked so upset that I agreed to file the papers for her as soon as possible. I told her that I'd do it the minute I was back from my honeymoon."

"Did that calm her down?" Candice asked.

Velkune shook his head, still staring at the floor with that haunted look on his face. "No," he whispered. "She seemed to get even more upset about having to wait."

"Then what?" Candice asked when Velkune paused.

"I told her that I could recommend someone else for her, but she insisted that she only trusted me, so I told her not to do anything drastic. I asked her if she'd talked to her parents, and she said she hadn't. I thought that she should've done that, you know? Anyway, I told her that it was impossible for me to file anything that day—I had to be at the church—but I promised to put the paperwork in the minute I got back from my honeymoon. I even came in at five a.m. this morning to prepare the motion even though I didn't get home last night until midnight, just to draw up the papers and rush them over to the courthouse the minute they opened."

"Did you recommend she get a restraining order?" Candice asked next.

Velkune went back to his chair and plopped down like he had the weight of the world on his shoulders. He shook his head reluctantly and looked at us with guilt-riddled eyes. "You see, Kendra is a really sweet girl, but she's also quite young and somewhat immature. There'd been no talk of Tristan ever being violent or abusive with her, so I wondered about this sudden urgent need to get the papers filed and this announcement that she was afraid for her life when she'd never suggested that Tristan was in any way physically abusive with her. I'm sorry to admit that I may have suspected this sudden display of emotion wasn't just a way to gain custody of Colby and get out of a marriage that wasn't working for her anymore."

"Her story about being afraid for her life seemed fabricated?" Candice asked.

Velkune sighed. "You have to understand," he said, as if Candice's last question were an accusation. "I was very distracted that day, and maybe I was less patient with her than I should have been. That morning there were things that I absolutely had to attend to before I left on my honeymoon, and I didn't have the time for an upset client who burst into my office and announced that she suddenly wanted a divorce. I sat with her as long as I could to talk some patience into her, and still ended up being a little late to my wedding because of it. If my wife found out that I'd come here and met with a client on my wedding day, she'd kill me." He then lifted his eyes to us, and they were clearly pained. "Do you think I'm partly to blame?" he asked in a breathy whisper.

That caught us both off guard, and neither of us answered him.

"I should've told her to get a restraining order," he said, staring back down at his desk. "I should have insisted that she to go to her parents if she was scared."

"You couldn't have known what would happen to her," Candice told him kindly.

But he just stared forlornly at the floor. After a bit he asked, "Do you or the police have any leads?"

"The police seem to be very interested in Kendra's husband," Candice said. "And the press has already made up its mind that he's responsible. But no arrests have been made and there's no sign of Kendra or her car."

Velkune looked up. "Her car's missing too?"

"It is," she told him.

He seemed to brighten. "Well, then maybe she left on her own."

"But her purse, wallet, credit cards, cash, and cell phone were left behind."

Velkune seemed to think of something. "Is the little boy accounted for?"

"Yes, he's fine," she answered. "We've spoken to Mr. Moreno and he says that on the day of his wife's disappearance, he found Colby in his crib, the front door of the house unlocked and slightly ajar and the back door wide-open with no sign of his wife anywhere on the premises. There was also no sign of a struggle or forced entry, and Kendra hasn't been seen or heard from since the twenty-eighth."

Velkune seemed to take all that in. "That doesn't sound good," he said at last.

"Nope," Candice agreed. "The official status for Kendra is still a missing person. Without a body or direct evidence of foul play, that's how she's likely to remain."

"I really should call the police," Velkune said, reaching for the phone. "They need to know what Kendra told me."

Even before he lifted the handle, there was an urgent knock on his door and Perky opened it without waiting for an answer. "Mr. Velkune?" she said. "I'm so sorry to interrupt, but the police are here and they want to talk to you right away."

Candice and I both stood. "That's our cue," she said,

pocketing her phone before reaching out to shake Velkune's hand. "Thank you so much for your cooperation, sir." She then handed him her business card. "If there's anything else you can think of to share with us, please don't hesitate to call that number."

Candice and I left him and followed Perky out the door and into the reception area. Standing there were two plainclothes detectives: a man and a woman both wearing that hard cop face I often saw on my fiancé.

Candice smiled politely as she passed, but they merely looked at her with that same hard expression. I made sure to wave at them as we left and comment loudly on the beautiful weather. What can I say? Cranky people bring out my sarcastic side.

Once we were in the car again, Candice said, "What was your take?"

I fished out the other half of my sandwich from the bag before answering. "Velkune's telling the truth."

Candice seemed irritated by the revelation that Kendra had been afraid of her husband. "Did you get that vibe from him?" she asked. "Tristan, I mean."

"Are you asking if—when we sat down with Tristan and had coffee—I felt then that he'd murdered his wife? No. No, I didn't get that vibe, but then, he's kind of difficult to read. There's the weird alibi about forgetting his cell phone and missing the message from his client about the cancellation. It means he could have actually gotten the message and realized his opportunity to establish some reasonable doubt surrounding his whereabouts that day. So he either headed up to Dallas or he only pretended he did, and instead he abducted his wife from their home, murdered her, buried her remains in the woods, and stashed her car someplace. Either way, it's a window of at least six and a half hours where his whereabouts can't be confirmed."

Candice frowned and stared out the windshield for several moments. I could practically see the gears in her head turning and turning. "I don't buy it," she said at last.

"Buy what?" I asked, peeling the wrapper away from my sandwich.

"The alibi. I think we need to keep looking at him as a major suspect, especially in light of what Jamie told us about Tristan and Bailey, which would mean that in order to fit the clues you pulled out of the ether, Bailey was in on Kendra's murder."

I set my sandwich down on the bag in my lap. "Yeah, except that if I'm being honest here, I don't know that I figure Blondie for a murderer."

Candice looked at me sideways. "I was afraid you were gonna say something like that."

"Well, do *you* think she did it? I mean, okay, Tristan's alibi is crazy flimsy, and we know that things between him and Kendra were bad enough for her to want to file for divorce, but I just can't see Bailey going along with murder. She's not smart enough not to crack if someone questions her about it, and the idea that she might have hired someone on her own doesn't sit with me too well either."

"Still," Candice insisted, "we can't rule her out. You said yourself that she's hiding something."

I closed my eyes and thought about our suspect pool with only two people in it. It didn't seem big enough. "Fine," I said as Candice started the car and pulled out of the parking slot. "Let's keep our eye on Tristan, but let's also consider looking at other people for the crime too. If we keep the focus too narrow, we may miss something that points us in the right direction."

"Like a neighbor or another acquaintance?"

"Or a lover," I said; then I realized what'd just come out of my mouth and I stared at Candice in surprise.

"A lover?" she asked me. "You think Kendra had a lover?"

"No. I mean, yes. I mean, I didn't think she had one until it came out of my mouth, and now that it's been said I can feel some weight to it in the ether."

"What does all that mean?"

I chewed on a bit of sandwich for a minute, trying to think of a way to explain. "Sometimes my intuition sneaks up on me, and I say something without thinking, and the moment I hear myself say it, I get another feeling of truth that attaches to it. In this case, by saying the words 'Kendra had a lover,' I can intuitively sense that I'm speaking the truth."

Candice lowered her sunglasses with one finger to peer at me over the rim. "Innnnteresting," she said.

"Very."

"If it is in fact true—and knowing how freakishly accurate you are, it is—then it gives Tristan a motive if he knew about it too."

"It also may give someone else a motive," I countered. "What if her lover wanted to end things and was afraid that Kendra might make that process difficult? I mean, I did also say when we were talking through my diagram that Kendra was hiding a secret. I think the secret she may have been hiding was that she was having an affair."

Candice seemed to ponder that for a moment. "Okay," she said at last. "We'll expand the list. You get through the rest of your readings while I do some digging, and we'll regroup at five to talk about it."

I almost told her okay, but then I remembered a previous appointment. "Oh, wait," I said. "I can't. Sorry. I've gotta meet with the exterminator tonight."

"No worries," Candice said. "We can regroup tomorrow morning. And, Abs?"

"Yeah?"

"Get your phone back, okay?"

I slapped my forehead. I'd almost forgotten.

I got my sister's number from Dutch, who was kind enough to e-mail it to me, and called Cat from the office, making arrangements to meet her at the new house later that evening so she could return my cell. Only after I hung up with her did I realize I'd just done the most stupid thing ever by giving her our new address.

I wondered if Dutch would go for putting in a security gate at our front entrance.

The other downside was that I didn't really want to have Cat come to me, as it was easier to leave if I went to her, but I had the exterminator to meet and the pups to feed and I knew that Dutch would be late again so he probably wouldn't be able to help out with any of that.

The rest of my readings from that day went well, and at four thirty on the dot I packed up my stuff and headed out the door. Candice was still in her office when I left, her nose hovering over her computer as she searched her spreadsheet for more possible suspects.

Before making my way to the new house, I swung by our rental to feed the pups and let them out. They looked at me with sad puppy eyes when I headed to the door again, and I had to vow to give them each an extra belly rub that night.

I got to the new house only just a little late and found Russ in his van happily reading a book. He was so engrossed, in fact, that he didn't see me pull up, and he jumped when I tapped on his window. "Sorry!" he said, rolling down his window. I noticed that his front seat was littered with Jim Butcher novels.

"No, I'm the one who's sorry," I told him. "I was late and my sister has my cell, so there was no way to call you. Want to come in?"

Russ set his book aside and got out of his truck carrying a clipboard and a small canister of something I guessed (hoped) was lethal to scorpions.

We got inside and I was surprised at the progress Dave had made in the past several days since I'd been there. Already the wood flooring had been laid and several rooms had a fresh coat of paint gleaming softly in the late afternoon light. "Nice place," Russ said when he entered.

"Thanks," I replied, my gaze trying to take in all the new changes. "I think we'll be very happy here." Russ nodded and seemed to be waiting for me to say something else. "So!" I said, setting aside my purse. "The construction crew has had quite a few scorpion stings, and I got one myself just last week, so we'll need you to kill them all. Quickly."

I shifted uncomfortably, thinking about the dozens of scorpions likely crawling all through the house.

Russ chuckled. "Scorpions are actually pretty hard to kill," he said.

That took me by surprise. "Wait, I thought you said you could kill them for us."

The exterminator threaded the canister through a loop in his belt and attached a small pump and a hose. "I can," he assured me. "I've got some pretty strong pesticide that'll take out most of them."

"Only *most* of them?" I asked, feeling less confident by the second.

Russ chuckled. "Don't worry," he said confidently. "Scorpions like to eat. And they like to eat bugs. I'll add an extra pesticide today to take out all the other bugs the scorpions like to eat. Any critters that survive the first wave will evacuate the area and go in search of more food elsewhere."

"How far away will they go and how soon?" I asked.

Russ winked at me. "They'll be out of your house within a few days, but until your grass comes in, you'll definitely want to watch where you step in the backyard."

I gulped. "What about my puppies?" I asked. "We have two dachshunds who'll be moving in with us in the next few weeks."

Russ moved to a wall and began to spray the baseboard. "Well, the liquid I'm using is completely safe for pets, but you'll still want to watch your dogs in the backyard until your grass comes in and the construction stops. Scorpions like dry, dark spaces and they also like to crawl along packed earth, so as long as you keep your dogs in the yard and out in the open, they should be just fine."

"Okay," I said, still nervous about our chances to rid the house of creepy crawlies.

After a bit of silence, during which I watched Russ spray the walls, he said, "Are you friends with the Morenos?"

I shook my head a little. My mind had been in a completely different place. "I'm sorry?"

"I saw you come out of the Morenos' house the other day. Remember? When you came to get my card?"

"Oh! Yeah . . . sorry, I remember now. And no, we're not really friends with the Morenos per se. My partner and I were there to see if we could help with the investigation."

Russ stopped spraying to look at me curiously. "Investigation? What investigation?"

"Mrs. Moreno's gone missing," I said, a little surprised he didn't know. The story had been all over the news before the bombing at the mall in College Station took it over.

"She's *missing*?" Russ gasped. "For how long?"

"About two weeks now. Didn't you see the story on the news?"

Russ shook his head. "I work a lot and either read or watch movies in my off time. I almost never catch regular TV."

"Ah," I said. Then it occurred to me that he seemed to know the Morenos. "Are they clients of yours?" I asked. "The Morenos, I mean."

"Yeah," he said, still staring at me with a rather incredulous look. "She's *really* missing? Like, no one's seen or heard from her at all?"

"She is, and no one has seen or heard from her since late last month."

Russ shifted on his feet, and I could tell he was thinking of something that made him uncomfortable.

"You know," I said casually, "I *am* investigating the case, Russ. If there's something you know, or maybe that you saw that seemed suspicious, it might be the clue we need to help find Mrs. Moreno and bring her home."

"Are you a cop?" he asked me, and I could see he was only curious.

"No. I'm not. I'm a professional psychic, and my partner is a licensed PI."

"You're a psychic?" he said, his brows shooting up. "That's so cool!"

I had a feeling we were about to get off track here, so I gently eased the conversation back. "On cases like these it can come in handy. Now, do you maybe know something that could be relevant to Kendra's disappearance?"

Russ turned back to the wall, and I had the distinct impression that I'd made him a little uncomfortable. "I don't like to gossip about my customers."

"I can totally respect that. But the fact that no one has seen or heard from Kendra since last month is a bad sign, Russ. If she's in trouble, she might really need your help."

Russ stopped spraying and seemed to consider the wall for a long moment. "Well," he said at last, "it's funny you should say that she's been missing for about two weeks, because I saw something about two weeks ago when I was at the Crawleys'."

"The whom?"

"The Morenos' neighbors," Russ explained. "I've got pretty much everybody on that block."

"Okay, so what did you see?"

Russ turned to face me, his expression anxious. "Everybody on that block is on a different schedule. I don't know what it is with that neighborhood, but every time I try to schedule my clients there for the same day to make it easier on me, they all call and move their appointments around, so I'm usually out there at least six times a month, if not more."

I found myself nodding, encouraging him to go on and get to the relevant part.

"Anyway," he continued, "I'm on that street a lot, so I see stuff. And one thing I've noticed is that lately there's been this guy hanging out at the Morenos' house. He's always there on a weekday around eleven thirty in the morning, and I've never seen his car. I first noticed him a couple months ago because he came walking down the street with his head down, like he didn't want me to get a good look at his face. I see a lot of sneaking around in my line of work, and you kinda develop a sense of knowing when people are up to no good."

I could feel my heart start to race, but I knew I had to play it cool or I'd spook Russ. Digging through my purse for a notepad and pen, I asked, "Any chance this guy hanging out at the Morenos' could have been Kendra's husband?"

Russ shook his head. "No. I've met Mr. Moreno a couple of times. It wasn't him."

"If he came on foot, do you think he could be one of the neighbors, maybe coming over to borrow some sugar or something?"

Russ frowned. "I know most of the people on that street but not everybody, so yeah, it's possible."

"Can you describe what this man looked like?"

Russ scratched his head. "He's white, and both times I saw him in the same kind of clothes: jeans, T-shirt, ball cap, and sunglasses."

"What color hair?" I asked, scribbling the description furiously as I pressed for more details.

Russ tugged on his mustache. "Brown, maybe?"

"Could you describe his face?"

"I never got a good look at him," he told me. "Like I said, when he walks he keeps his head down, and his ball cap hides his face."

Crap. That wasn't much of a description. "How tall?"

Russ shrugged. "Maybe six feet or a little shorter, but at least five-ten."

"Was his build thin, medium, or heavyset?"

"Medium build," Russ told me. "Probably between one seventy-five and one hundred ninety pounds."

"How old?"

Russ shrugged again. "I'd guess early to mid-thirties."

I looked over the description now written in my note-pad and realized that my friendly neighborhood exterminator had just described one-quarter of the Austin male population. Still, he had also confirmed that a man other than Mr. Moreno was in the area of Kendra's house around the time of her disappearance.

"You know what's funny, though," Russ said suddenly.

"What?"

"Well, the last time I saw this guy, he didn't go to the back door like he usually does. He went right to the front and rang the bell."

My breath caught. "Russ, this is really important. Do you happen to know the exact date of the last time you saw him?"

Russ got out his smart phone and began tapping the screen. "It looks like I was at the Crawleys' on Friday, the twenty-eighth of September, around eleven thirty in the morning."

I was tingling with excitement—Russ the exterminator had just given us a brand-new suspect and a possible time for when Kendra was abducted. Still, who was this mysterious stranger in the ball cap?

Just as I was rooting around in my purse for my cell to call Candice, and remembering that Cat still had my phone, the front door opened, and in bounded my sister, loaded down with a huge binder labeled "Abby's Wedding" and trailing two beefy-looking bodyguards also loaded down with bags of wedding stuff.

"Hello!" Cat sang, seeing me in the living room. "Now, Abby, I know I promised to go to Dutch for the rest of the wedding decisions, but he's not returning my calls and I simply *have* to get your opinion on a few things."

I turned to Russ, who was blinking rapidly, trying to take in the flurry of movement coming into the house. "My sister is planning my wedding and I'm probably going to be tied up for the next hour. Can you handle the rest of this yourself?"

"You're getting married?" he asked.

"Next month," I said, watching my sister look for a place to set down her binder.

"Congratulations!" Russ said happily, offering me a big smile.

I had to admit that I liked the exterminator, and I made a mental note to recommend him in the future. I also made a mental note to tell Candice that we'd have to alert the police about what Russ had seen the morning Kendra went missing. Everything fit the timeline now that we knew what time Colby went down for his first nap, and why there'd been no apparent signs of struggle. Whomever this mysterious stranger was, he'd been someone Kendra trusted enough to let him into her home. I suspected he was also the man she'd been having the affair with. He definitely could have murdered her if she'd either wanted to end the affair or threatened him in some way if he was the one who wanted to call it off.

But then I had another chilling thought: If Tristan had suspected his wife's affair and he'd pretended to go to Dallas to meet his client, when in fact he'd really spied on her and waited until her lover left to catch her unawares and murder her, knowing that if anyone began to really dig into her life, they might discover this lover, then he could shift the blame away from himself.

From my impressions of Tristan, I didn't quite know if he was capable of such clever deception, but I realized that we'd still have to keep him in the suspect pool even in light of this new evidence.

And that was the last clear thought I had that early evening, because in the next second Cat handed me my phone and said, "Your vet called. Eggy and Tuttle are due to get their shots. I made the appointment for this Saturday and put it in your calendar." I looked at her a little stunned. She . . . what? "You're welcome," she said when I didn't comment. "Oh, and the guest list is taken care of, so no need to worry about getting that to me, but we still have some stuff to go over, so let's get to it! I've got a few selections for your 'something blue' to look at, and we'll need to think about your 'something old,' but I've got some ideas for that too . . ." and on she went, bulldozing her way through my night the way she often does with my life. And she wonders why I work to avoid her . . .

Chapter Eleven

Candice called me the next morning right before I was about to jump in the shower. "Turn on the news," she said by way of hello.

Moody as my sleep-deprived self was, I managed to flip on the TV without any snark. The newscaster was commenting on live footage of Tristan Moreno being taken away in handcuffs by a whole squad of police while his mother-in-law held protectively to a little boy I assumed must be Colby. "Aw, crap," I muttered.

"I guess they talked to Velkune," Candice said.

"Yeah, well, the police may have it wrong," I told her. Then I quickly explained what my exterminator had seen on the day Kendra went missing.

Candice was quiet through it all, and when I was done, she said, "You know, I really dropped the ball on that one. I saw him the day you got his number and didn't even think to question him. We'll also need to eliminate him as a suspect."

That took me aback. "You think Russ could have abducted Kendra?"

"I think anybody could have done it," Candice replied. "And consider this, Abs: He's a familiar fixture on that street and the Morenos are his regular customers. If he had knocked on Kendra's door, she probably would have let him in, no problem."

I took that in and played it against my intuition, which came back with a surprising feeling, and then I remembered how nervous he'd been when I'd begun questioning him, and how he didn't seem to want to talk to the police so much. "Yeah," I told her. "Look into his background, Candice. We've got to look at everyone."

I then told her my other theory about Tristan, that he could have known about his wife's affair, pretended to go to Dallas, spied on her, seen the exterminator in the neighborhood to act as a witness to the stranger approaching her door, then murdered his wife the moment her lover left. "That is of course assuming that Russ really did see a man in a baseball cap enter Kendra's home that day."

"Absolutely true," Candice said. "So let me start with Russ the bug man. I'll look into his background a little. Give me his number and I'll meet you at the office in an hour, okay?"

I flipped through my contacts list and found Russ's number, reciting it for Candice before hurrying through my morning routine to get to the office in time to meet up with her before my first reading.

Eggy and Tuttle gave me the guilts again. I'd forgotten to give them their belly rubs the night before, so I vowed to play fetch and give two belly rubs each if they'd simply quit with the sad eyes. They just cocked their heads at me, which I took for, "We'll think about it."

I got to the office and found Candice listening to her voice mail. She had a weird look on her face: kind of excited, kind of surprised, kind of troubled. Odd combo, I know.

When she hung up I asked, "What's up?"

"That was Tristan Moreno. He wants to hire us."

My jaw fell open. "From jail?"

"No, his lawyer got him out on bail half an hour ago."

"That was a fast bail hearing," I said, eyeing my watch.

"It was," Candice agreed. "His lawyer's good and she's got some weight to throw around to get him out so fast."

I nodded. "I didn't see that coming," I confessed.

"That he'd be out so soon?"

"No, that he'd want to ever talk to us again, let alone hire us. Kind of makes me wonder if he isn't innocent after all."

"Too soon to tell," Candice replied before checking the time. "He wants to meet at ten. Are you free?"

"Yeah. I have an appointment at nine; then the rest of my morning is clear until one."

"Perfect," she said. "Let's use the conference room on the first floor."

The office building we rent space in has a very nice community conference room located just off the main entrance. Candice and I would sometimes go there after a hard day and just sit and chat. No one else ever seemed to use it, and the chairs were super comfy.

While Candice called Tristan to confirm the appointment, I went into my suite to set down my purse and get ready for my reading.

My client was twenty minutes late. For the record, it seriously ticks me off when clients don't show up on

time without calling to let me know they're running behind. It didn't seem to bug my client, though. She arrived wearing lots of designer labels and an "I'm better
than you" attitude, avoiding even hinting at an apology.
I gritted my teeth and got right to her reading, making
sure to talk fast so I could get in everything I saw in her
energy. No surprise, much of what I discussed had to do
with her relationships—both personal and professional—which were all a hot mess. The woman was a
train wreck in a pretty, designer-label package.

When I was done, I turned it over to her for questions, but at that point we had exactly five minutes left
and she got in only two of her questions before I stood
up and thanked her for coming. "But I didn't get through
my list," she protested as I pocketed her payment,
walked to the door, and held it open for her.

"Well, then, maybe you should think about getting to
your appointments on time from now on," I told her not
so sweetly.

She glared at me and stalked out. "I'll e-mail you the
recording of your reading!" I called to her backside.

"Don't bother!" she yelled back.

I shut the door and sighed. I hated losing a client, but
her kind I could afford to let go.

I then grabbed a protein bar from my desk drawer
(okay, so it was a Snickers, but peanuts count as protein,
right?) and reached for a notebook and a bottled water
to take down to the conference room. Just as I was shutting off my desk lamp, Candice appeared in the doorway. "Ready?"

"I am. And just to clarify, would you prefer my psychic guns be blazing for today's chitchat?"

Candice grinned. "Give him all you got, Sundance."

When we arrived in the lobby, we saw Tristan was

already there, waiting for us. His demeanor was anxious, and I could well understand why.

Candice greeted him and led him into the conference room, where she took her seat at the head of the rectangular table and indicated that I should sit on her right. Tristan sat two chairs down on Candice's left. "Thanks for taking the meeting," he said.

I studied him under the glare of the fluorescent bulbs above us. He appeared haggard, and the dark circles under his eyes indicated that he hadn't gotten much sleep in probably several days.

"I was surprised to get your call," Candice told him. "After our last chat, I figured you didn't want anything to do with us."

Tristan put his elbows on the table and held his head in his hands. "This is all so crazy," he said, his voice muffled slightly. He then lifted his chin and looked at us like a lost little kid who just wanted to go home. "I need some help to figure this thing out."

"Okay," Candice said, still playing it coy.

Tristan seemed to get that he needed to arrive at the point of the meeting pretty quick. "I want to hire you," he said. "I want you two to find out what happened to my wife."

Candice tapped her lip with her pen. "Mr. Moreno," she said, "you should know that Abby and I are *very* good at our jobs. We're quite confident that we'll find out *exactly* what happened to your wife." She paused then, allowing the words to sink in, and when Tristan didn't flinch she added, "Still want to hire us?"

"Yes," he said, and it was odd, but I thought I saw a hint of relief in his eyes.

Candice then set her cell phone in the middle of the table. As she clicked the record button on her app, her eyes lifted briefly to Tristan to see if he would object, but he merely nodded his assent. She then opened a folder and took out two copies of our standard contract, which outlined our methods, set expectations, and, in bold print, listed our hourly rates. "If the terms are agreeable," she said, "please sign both copies—one for us, one for you. Oh, and we'll need a three-thousand-dollar retainer up front."

Tristan took the contracts, read them over, signed both copies, and handed one of them back to Candice. He then pulled his checkbook from his jacket pocket and wrote out a check. Tearing it off, he also handed that to Candice, who tucked the signed agreement and the check back into her folder.

She then turned to me, as if to check how I was doing. I gave her a thumbs-up, and she sat back in her chair and motioned with her hand for me to take the lead.

I was a little caught off guard but tried not to let it show. "Mr. Moreno . . . ," I began.

"Please call me Tristan," he said.

"Tristan," I corrected, "as you know, I'm a professional psychic. My job on these kinds of cases is to look for clues that might be either overlooked by other investigators or completely out of their purview. Instead of waiting for the clues to come in through conventional methods of tips and a lot of CSI stuff, I send my intuitive feelers out into the ether and try to isolate the clues that will lead us to Kendra. Most law enforcement units work backward from the crime scene. I try to work forward from where I can sense the victim is right now."

"I'm not sure if I believe in what you claim to be able to do, Abby," he said, "but I'm willing to keep an open mind if it'll help bring Kendra home."

I actually appreciated his honesty. "Okay," I said, deciding to get the tough questions out of the way first. "Let me get right to the biggest question in front of us: Tristan, on September twenty-eighth, did you physically cause harm to your wife?"

Tristan shook his head vehemently and said, "No. No way would I *ever* hurt Kendra."

My lie detector went off loud and clear. I turned to my partner, and she read my expression. She nodded for me to continue, and subtly I saw her put her hand inside her purse—where her gun was readily accessible.

I was going to push Tristan and call him out on the lie, and if this guy really did kill his wife, things could get dicey pretty fast, but we had to know the truth.

Turning back to Tristan, I said, "See, that's what I have a problem with, Tristan. I know you're lying. I have a special talent for detecting mistruths. And right there I can tell that you just lied to me. You did hurt your wife, didn't you?"

Tristan's expression turned slightly panicked, and his eyes darted to Candice. She stared at him with hard resolve. "I should mention, Tristan, that I am licensed to carry a concealed weapon." Her own gaze traveled pointedly to the hand inside her purse, and he actually gasped.

Finally he swallowed hard and took a couple of deep breaths. "Is there some kind of confidentiality agreement between PIs and their clients?" he asked.

Candice motioned again to the signed contract on the table in front of him. "Yes," she said. "It's on the second page toward the bottom. Anything you tell us will be held in the strictest confidence unless you lie to us again; then all bets are off."

Tristan lifted the top page of the agreement and scanned the area toward the bottom of the second page before answering. "Okay," he said. "You're right. I did hurt Kendra."

Beside me, Candice sucked in a small breath. I didn't think she'd expected him to admit it so quickly.

"That morning we had an argument. It was an old argument, though, and Kendra was really pushing my buttons. All I wanted to do was get out of there before I lost it. But she kept trying to block me at the top of the stairs. She just didn't get that you can't push people like me."

People like him? I wondered what that meant.

"Anyway, I sort of shoved her out of the way and left. I might've hurt her—I don't know. I just had to get out of there. That's why I forgot my phone that morning, and also why I didn't go back for it."

So far Tristan was telling us the truth, but he'd also revealed several other things that needed to be followed up on. "What was this 'old argument' about?" I asked.

Tristan sighed. "We'd been having problems," he began. "They started about six months ago when I was working late, catching up on the books. My wife came to the office and chewed me out."

"What for?" Candice asked.

Tristan licked his lips and stared at the tabletop.

"She found out that you cheated," I said before he could answer. I'd seen the familiar triangle in my mind's eye.

"I didn't cheat!" he snapped, and Candice and I both raised our brows at his outburst. Tristan seemed to catch himself, because he held up both hands in a sort of surrender motion and said, "I'm sorry, I'm sorry! This whole thing has me really on edge and I haven't slept in so long."

Candice and I said nothing; we both simply waited him out. After he took a few deep breaths, he continued. "Kendra thought I had cheated. But I hadn't. She heard that I'd slept with someone at my bachelor party, but she wouldn't tell me who told her that. I swore up and down that I didn't cheat on her. That I wouldn't do that to her ever, but she didn't believe me. She said that she was taking Colby and moving back in with her parents."

"And then?" I pressed when Tristan paused again.

"And then I grabbed her," he said softly, his face flushing with shame. "I grabbed her by the arms, shook her really hard, and shoved her into a wall."

I tensed and I could also feel Candice's posture stiffen too. Like her, I didn't cotton to any man laying a hand on a woman . . . ever. Still, I did register Tristan's expression. He was so filled with remorse and shame that his head was drooping and his eyes were shut tight against the memory.

"My dad was an alcoholic," he whispered. "He used to hit my mom and all three of us kids on a regular basis, and one day, when I was about ten, my mom . . . she just left us. She left us with him and ran away with another guy to California. I didn't see her again until my high school graduation.

"So I carried a lot of anger around inside me, and I had a temper as a kid. My high school football coach sorta took me under his wing and helped me deal with it, and in college I worked really hard to control it. I thought I had it licked too, you know? But that night when Kendra came to the office and said she was leaving me . . . I don't know what happened. I just snapped."

Tristan's lower lip began to quiver and his eyes leaked a few tears. I will admit that I felt more than a little sympathy for him—I'd had an alcoholic father and an abusive mother as a kid too. I more than understood what kind of rage could build up inside a person with a background like that—but because I had also worked hard to control and cope with the emotion, I'd never snapped and lost total control. I wondered if it was maybe a little harder for Tristan to control his rage and those violent outbursts. If, by his own admission, he'd hurt his wife twice, it was reasonable to consider that he might have caused her harm yet a third and final time.

Still, I tried to reserve my judgment until I'd heard him out. "It was all a lie," Tristan continued mournfully. "I *never* cheated on Kendra. I just wanted her to listen to me—to hear me out. Talk it through. That night I just panicked and I grabbed her and shook her. I never, ever meant to hurt her. I just wanted her to listen to me. I wanted her to stay."

"But she didn't leave you back then," I said, thinking that if Kendra had gone to her parents' house that night, surely they would have mentioned the incident to the police.

Tristan shook his head. "No," he said. "She didn't. I broke down when I realized that I'd hurt her and I begged her not to leave me. I told her I'd get help and also told her that I'd take a lie detector test to prove to her that I didn't cheat on her if she'd accept it. The next day I entered anger management therapy, but Kendra never mentioned the cheating thing again, so I thought she believed me."

"Was Kendra hurt?" Candice asked.

Tristan's face flushed with shame again. "She had a few bruises. And I apologized over and over and over, but how can you ever be sorry enough for doing something like that to the woman you love?"

"Did she forgive you, Tristan?" I asked.

At first he nodded, but then he shook his head. "Yes? No?" he said. "At first, she seemed to. When I went into therapy, I thought it helped. She was really supportive and she said she was proud of me for going. But things were never the same between us. I felt her moving away from me, you know? We still lived under the same roof, but it was like she was only going through the motions with me. She wouldn't let me touch her—we hadn't been intimate for months—and I kept going to my therapy hoping that someday she'd trust me again, but I also had this really bad feeling that she was going to leave me again, and that morning . . ."

Tristan's voice trailed off as he became overcome with emotion. We gave him a moment to collect himself, and at last he said, "That morning I thought that she was pushing my buttons on purpose. I felt like she was testing me to see if I'd snap again. She wouldn't let me down the stairs, and she kept pushing me and pushing me and I could feel myself getting madder and madder."

Tristan was silent again for a long moment before he added, "I failed the test. I shoved her out of the way and ran out of the house. I came home later that day expecting her and Colby to be gone—but it was only Kendra who was missing."

"And you're certain that Kendra didn't just leave the house to get away from you—like your mom did to you and your siblings?" Candice asked boldly.

Tristan's face crumbled with her words, and I felt another small wave of empathy for him. It was a long time before he could speak again. "That was mean," he said in a hoarse whisper.

"Yes," Candice agreed, "but we need to know the truth, Tristan. We can't help you if you're holding out on us."

He nodded. "Kendra wasn't my mother, Candice. All Kendra ever wanted to be was a mom, and she was the best mom in the world. She loved Colby more than anything. She might have left me, but she would *never* have left him."

"Do the police know you're in anger management, or about the argument you had that morning with her?" Candice asked next.

"No," Tristan said. "At least not yet. But when they find out, it's just gonna give them even more reasons to accuse me of foul play."

"You said that you didn't cheat on Kendra," I said, trying to get back to something I'd noticed in the ether when he explained about that night at his office.

"I swear to God, I didn't!"

I gave him a half smile. "I believe you."

He appeared a little taken aback. "You do?"

"Yes. Like I said, I can see a lie a mile away. But here's the thing, Tristan. Someone also told us you cheated on your wife."

"Who?" he demanded.

"Jamie Gregory," Candice said. "She said she saw you making out with Bailey Colquitt the night of your bachelor party."

Tristan pulled his chin back and stared at us as if he couldn't believe what we'd just told him. "Seriously?"

"Seriously," Candice and I said in unison.

Tristan shook his head slowly back and forth. "It wasn't like that. Bailey cornered me outside the party when I was drunk off my ass. I barely remember it, except that she kissed me and tried to talk me into sleeping with her, and I pushed her away and went back inside. I'm not interested in that girl at all."

Candice turned to me as if to ask if I thought Tristan was telling the truth. I nodded. "He's not lying."

Candice drummed her fingers on the table before

asking, "What do *you* think happened to Kendra, Tristan?"

At this Kendra's husband seemed to lose it again. His eyes watered, his lower lip trembled, and his nose began to run. "I don't know," he said, his voice so hoarse it was no louder than a whisper. "But I think someone came into our home and hurt her, because my wife wouldn't leave our baby boy in the house alone. And if she could have come back for him, she would have by now."

"Did Kendra have any enemies?" I asked.

"Kendra didn't have an enemy in the world," he said. When I stared doubtfully at him, he insisted, "I swear, there's no one I know who would want to hurt her. She's the sweetest, kindest person you've ever met. She'd give you the shirt off her back if you asked. Everybody who knows her loves her."

But someone out there didn't love Kendra. Someone out there hated her enough to kill her.

I wondered if Tristan knew about the man in the ball cap coming over to the house. "We can accept that you were faithful, Tristan," I said, speaking slowly so that I could tread carefully here. "But did you ever suspect Kendra might've had an affair? Maybe to get back at you for the rumors or something?"

Tristan's eyes dropped to the table again. "I want to say no, that Kendra would never, ever cheat on me, but in the past couple of months something changed. I couldn't put my finger on it, but it was like the thought of being intimate with me repulsed her. She tensed up every time I touched her—and it wasn't the way you tense when you think someone may hurt you; this was different. It was like I made her skin crawl. And I don't know if she was seeing another guy or not. Maybe in the back of my mind I suspected, but I just wanted her to forgive me and stay with me, so I never mentioned it. I just left her alone, gave her as much space as I could, and hoped she'd come back to me."

And then he lifted his gaze and seemed to catch something unspoken between Candice and me because he said, "Why? Do you guys know she was seeing another guy?"

Candice looked at me in a way that said she wanted to take the lead now. "We don't know, Tristan," she told him. "But we had heard from a witness that a white male between five feet eleven inches and six feet tall, wearing a baseball cap, was seen entering your home around eleven thirty the morning your wife went missing. Someone who had been seen near your house on a few other occasions, actually."

Tristan's jaw fell open and he looked like he'd been kicked in the gut. "Do they know who this guy is?"

"No."

"Did they describe his car?"

"He came on foot," my partner told him.

Tristan blinked several times and appeared dumbfounded. I could see he was thinking hard to identify who might've come to his home that morning.

"Does the man's description sound familiar to you?" I asked.

Tristan shook his head. "No. None of our guy friends live in the neighborhood, and Kendra never mentioned anyone coming over to the house." And then he seemed to think of something. "Our house is pretty close to the bus stop near the park," he said. "And it's only a half mile to the metro station too."

"That's good to know," Candice told him, making a note in her binder. "Still, we might want to keep our focus to your specific neighborhood as these types of affairs are often closer than you think."

Tristan swallowed hard and his shoulders sagged. I could tell he was trying to think through his list of neighbors, wondering if any of them might have been having an affair with his wife.

"Tristan, I have a request," I said when an idea suddenly hit me.

"Okay," he said, his voice flat and defeated.

"I'd like to go to your home again and walk around."

"Why?" he asked, more curious than defensive.

"Sometimes I can get a pretty good feel for the residual energy left over after a violent act."

Tristan blanched. "You mean, you'd be able to tell what might've happened to my wife in the house that day she went missing?"

"Yes."

"Would you also be able to sense the argument I had with my wife at the top of the stairs?"

"If it was a heated argument, then yes." I could see the hesitation and anxiety forming in his eyes, so I added, "Tristan, if something violent did happen to your wife later that day, and you weren't the cause of it, I might be able to actually detect the difference between your energy and the perpetrator's. That would go a long way with us," I said, pointing back and forth between Candice and me. "Right now we want to believe you, but until I can feel out your home, there's still some room for doubt as you no doubt can understand."

Tristan seemed to consider my request for a moment. Finally he got up and said, "Let's go."

Chapter Twelve

Tristan parked his car in the drive behind the house and we pulled up behind him. Out front there was at least one news crew, but they'd let us enter the drive without blocking us or trying to take our picture, which was a relief. Still, we moved into the house quickly to get out from under prying eyes.

After unlocking the back door, Tristan held it open for us and we moved inside, coming into the familiar cozy kitchen. I set my purse down and looked at Tristan, who motioned with a wave of his arm that I was free to go anywhere I wanted. Leaning heavily on my cane, I moved past the kitchen into a hall with a bathroom off to the right and the dining room on the left. I paused at each spot but couldn't pick up much other than the normal steady energy that fills most houses.

I continued down the hall, hearing Candice's heels clicking in time with my cane. We moved into the living room, which was decorated in a light turquoise blue with pale yellow accents.

The living room was nestled off to my right, and to my left were the stairs. Directly opposite the main staircase was the front door, but the door was up two steps from the living room.

I moved to the living room first, holding out my free arm to act as an antenna for any residual energy there. I felt something near the sofa, which was positioned with its back to the front door. Moving to the spot directly behind the couch, I closed my eyes and focused. At the edge of my energy I could feel that something violent had taken place right behind where I stood. I opened my eyes and followed the thread away from the sofa and up the two steps to the front door, and in that eight-foot span between the door and the back of the couch, I knew exactly where Kendra had been attacked.

I glanced over at Candice and found both her and Tristan watching me closely. "She was attacked here and she fell or was pushed down to the floor over there," I said, pointing to the area behind the sofa.

Tristan's lips pressed together, and I found it hard to look at him. There appeared to be genuine pain in those eyes.

Turning my back to the door, I extended my arm out again, feeling around the ether, but I found it cumbersome to get a true feel for the little space while holding on to my cane. Setting the walking stick aside, I extended both arms out, closed my eyes, and let the energy settle around me. At first I had to sort through a lot of impressions of badges and lab coats (police and crime techs) and worked to go back just a teensy bit further.

And then I felt her; I felt Kendra's energy. I could almost see her right after opening the door to her attacker, then moving away from him down the steps to lead him into the living room. She'd seemed surprised but not unhappy to see her visitor. And then, quite suddenly, there was a terrible, acutely sharp pain that went up and down my spine, and for an instant I couldn't feel my limbs—my whole body felt paralyzed, which caused me to lose my balance, and that sent me stumbling forward. My legs simply gave out, and I let go a small, frightened squeak as I started to pitch forward down the stairs. My arms were slow to move; in fact, in that second I didn't feel like I could move them either, and just as my body was about to slam hard into the wood floor, I was grabbed by firm hands and held a mere foot off the ground. "You okay?" Tristan asked, and I realized he'd lunged forward to catch me and was now holding me in his arms.

"I'm . . . I'm . . . fine!" I said, a little breathless. I kept thinking about how bad that fall could've been. But then I was overcome by a small wave of dizziness. We hadn't eaten lunch yet, and my blood sugar was dropping fast. "Okay, maybe I don't feel so good after all," I said when my forehead broke out in a cold sweat and I started to feel a touch queasy too.

"I'll get some water," Candice said from behind Tristan, and her heels clicked quickly out of the room.

Tristan shifted his hold to turn me around toward him and lift me all the way into his arms. "You look really pale. Maybe you better come sit down."

I was about to insist that if he'd just hand me my cane I could walk to the sofa but was stopped when we both heard the sound of the front door lock being turned, and a second later it grated as it was pushed opened. Craning my neck to look behind me, I could see Kendra's mother standing there in stunned surprise, holding a large canvas bag in her hands.

For a split second, no one moved or spoke. We all just stared at one another in shock until Mrs. Woodyard snapped, "What's going on here?"

Tristan replied tersely, "What're you doing entering my house without permission, Nancy?"

"I came to get some things for Colby," she replied, looking at us with obvious suspicion.

Tristan set me down next to the banister, and I smoothed out my clothing and felt my cheeks grow hot. I was embarrassed even though the whole thing was quite innocent.

"What is this?" Mrs. Woodyard demanded, pointing back and forth between Tristan and me.

Her son-in-law didn't answer her. Instead he stepped forward to block me from her view and said, "Where's Colby?"

"He's with his grandfather," she told him, setting her hands on her hips. "And I demand to know what's going on here, Tristan! Why did you have another woman in your arms?"

"She fell," he said, leaning around the door to pick up my cane and hand it to me.

Mrs. Woodyard's hands came off her hips and she crossed her arms. "Sure she did. What did you do to my daughter, Tristan?" she asked, her voice cold and mean.

"Nothing, Nancy," he told her levelly.

Mrs. Woodyard leaned out to stare hard at me, and in her gaze I saw pure hate. "Was it you? Did *you* have something to do with her disappearance?"

I shook my head vigorously. "No! Of course not! I came to your house and tried to offer you my help, remember?"

Those hate-filled eyes narrowed to slits. "Help?" she scoffed. "I think you came into my home with the intent to throw the investigation off track! I think you might've had a reason to point the police in a different direction away from the obvious person responsible!"

"Stop it, Nancy!" Tristan commanded, pulling her attention back to him. "Go home, get my son, and bring him back here. The police are finished questioning me for now, and I want Colby to come home."

But Nancy Woodyard only glared at her son-in-law. "No."

Tristan's spine stiffened. "No?"

"I'm keeping him."

"Like hell you are," he growled, taking a step toward her, and although his back was to me, I had a feeling the look on his face was angry enough to scare Mrs. Woodyard, because she took a step back and put her hands up defensively.

Tristan stopped his advance. I saw him work to lower his shoulders, and then he said very firmly, "I want Colby back, Nancy. He's *my* son and you have no right to keep him. If you won't bring him here, then I'll come get him."

Mrs. Woodyard made a noise that sounded like a half growl, half snarl. "Don't you dare set foot on my property, Tristan Moreno! I'm calling the police and my lawyer. You'll get Colby back when hell freezes over!"

With that she turned and pulled the door closed hard behind her.

"What just happened?" I heard behind me. I turned and saw Candice standing there with a glass of ice water and a protein bar.

"Nothing good," I admitted.

Tristan stood staring at the door for a full half minute. He then turned with a determined look on his face and pulled his phone out of his back pocket. "Would you two excuse me? I have to call my lawyer."

Candice looked from me to Tristan as if waiting for one of us to explain, but I waved her back toward the kitchen to give Tristan some privacy. "We should go," I said.

"What happened in there?" she asked me, setting down the water and following me to the door.

"Mrs. Woodyard showed up."

When I didn't elaborate, Candice said, "And?"

"I was a little dizzy, and Tristan picked me up to take me over to the couch. Unfortunately at that exact moment Kendra's mom came through the door and saw us."

"Uh-oh," she said, following me closely as I moved with gimpy haste toward the car. I wanted to get out of there because I had a feeling that the longer I stayed, the worse I was going to make things. "What happened then?" Candice asked.

"Thinly veiled accusations and threats from both parties."

"What kind of threats?" she pressed, clicking the button on her key fob to unlock the Porsche.

"She's going to try to take custody of Colby; he's going to go over there and get his son if he has to."

Candice's eyebrows rose high on her forehead, but she didn't say anything else. She and I got into the car, strapped in, and began to exit the drive.

The moment we hit the street, I felt my mouth go dry. Standing in the middle of the road was Mrs. Woodyard, flapping her yap to a reporter as she pointed angrily at the house. Then she spotted us and the finger moved to Candice's car. I saw a television camera swivel in our direction and I panicked. "Jesus! Hit it, Candice!"

Candice did, and in the next three seconds we'd sped all the way down the street. "I'm wondering if that just made us look guilty," Candice said, glancing nervously in her rearview mirror.

"I'm pretty sure we're already there," I muttered.

My partner sighed as she turned the corner heading back toward the main road. "Were you able to pick up anything in the house at least, Abs?"

"I was," I said. "There was a lot of residual energy near the door. That's what made me go down, actually. It wasn't my hips as much as it was what happened to Kendra."

"Was it like what you'd picked up before? That she got hit in the base of her spine?"

"It was exactly that, but thinking back on it, when I stood near the front door, I felt an acute sharp pain, and then my legs simply went numb."

"So we're back to the theory that she was stabbed in the back?"

I took a deep breath as I thought about that. It hadn't felt like a stab wound. I'd been stabbed before (yet another story), and as the knife had entered my flesh I remembered the searing hot feel of it. This hadn't felt like that—it'd felt sharper, more acute in a way. "I don't think her killer used a knife," I said. And then I mentioned something else that had bugged me about our knife-in-the-back theory, even more than the lack of blood at the scene. "The other thing I can't figure out, Candice, is even if the killer had struck Kendra in the back with something that caused her to become paralyzed, say, from the waist down, she could still have screamed her head off. We know that Russ was outside at the Crawleys' house right across the street—why didn't he hear her?"

"He could have been the killer," Candice said, eyeing me over the rim of her sunglasses.

I rubbed my temples. "Okay, so assuming he wasn't the killer, and this account from him of a man in a baseball cap entering her home is true—again, why didn't Russ hear her? Even if the killer struck her unconscious, she should've been able to get out at least one cry for help, right?"

Candice seemed to think on that. "What about my earlier theory that she was given some sort of injection with something that paralyzed her completely?"

Something about what Candice had just said rang a bell for me. "Yeah," I said, nodding, remembering how my whole body had gone numb on the steps in the Morenos' home. For Kendra to have been taken out like that so quickly—before she could even scream—something had to have completely incapacitated her, head to toe. "What kind of a drug would that be?" I asked. Were there even drugs that worked that quickly?

Candice shrugged. "Don't know, Sundance, but I have a doctor friend who's an anesthesiologist. I'll call her when I get a free minute and maybe she'll be able to point me in the right direction."

We were both quiet for a few seconds, until Candice asked, "Were you able to clear Tristan from the man who attacked Kendra?"

"You mean did I pick up another man's energy?"

"Yeah."

I shook my head. "I didn't have enough time to analyze it," I told her. "All I know is that whoever was at her door surprised Kendra, but not in a bad way. Her energy felt receptive to whoever came to her door."

"Would she have been receptive to Tristan after their fight?"

"I don't know. His account was that she was pushing his buttons—and maybe she was. Maybe she liked this other guy better and was looking for a valid excuse to leave her husband."

"Gives more credence to Velkune's account that she came to see him and was afraid of her husband, right?"

"It does," I said. Still, I had my doubts about pegging Tristan as the killer. Maybe it was because when I'd fallen from those two steps, he'd lunged to help me, and while he held me in his arms, he'd been very gentle. Nothing in his energy spoke of trying to fake some genuine concern for me. I just didn't buy him as the man who had beaten, raped, and murdered his wife in cold blood.

I said as much to Candice, and she sighed. "This case has way more questions than answers. I mean, we don't know what caused Kendra to go down so fast without letting out even one scream, or who this mysterious man in the ball cap is, or where her remains are buried, and for that matter, where the hell is her car?"

"Underwater," I said.

"What?"

I sat bolt upright. That answer, like the one about her lover, had come out of my mouth without my thinking about it. "It's underwater!" I said, focusing my attention on the car.

"You're sure?"

"Yes!" I said, aiming my radar straight at Kendra's car and holding on tight while I sorted through the intuitive clues.

Candice pulled into a Target parking lot. Turning to me, she said, "Can you find the car?"

I closed my eyes. "I think it's east of a main highway."

"Mopac? Three-sixty? One-eighty-three? I-thirty-five?" Candice rattled off most of Austin's major thoroughfares in rapid-fire succession.

I squeezed my eyes shut even tighter, waiting for the ether to give up its clues. And that's when I saw a double-decker bus in my mind's eye.

"Crap," I said, trying to push the image out of my head so that I could figure out which highway we needed to focus on.

"What's crap?"

I growled with irritation. The bus just kept appearing in my mind's eye. "I'm trying to figure out which highway, but all I keep seeing is a double-decker bus."

"A what?"

"Double-decker bus," I said meekly.

"Is that a clue?"

My eyes snapped open. "It must be!"

"About the highway we need to find?"

I concentrated on the red bus, which I could see so clearly in my mind. It moved down the road and stopped at the foot of a lake. "No," I said. "It's a clue to where the car is. It's a clue to a lake. The car is in a lake and there must be a bus depot or something to do with double-decker buses and the lake. The association is too strong for me to ignore."

Candice pulled out her iPhone and began to poke at the screen. I could see her trying several searches, until suddenly she gasped and swiveled the phone to me. "Decker Lake!" she exclaimed before I could even read it.

"Yes! That's it! I know that's it!"

Candice set her phone aside and pulled back on the gearshift. "The lake is just east of Highway one-eighty-three," she told me. "About ten minutes from here."

I tapped my fingers on my knees the whole way there. I was so anxious to see if I was right that I couldn't hold still. As we came up to the lake, however, I could see

Candice's mood shift from excited to frustrated in an instant. "It's huge," she said, eyeing the large body of water.

But I now had a clear bead on Kendra's car. It was drawing me like a beacon. "That way," I said, motioning to the right.

Candice cast me a surprised look, but she didn't hesitate to pull the car to the right and follow the road around the east side of the lake, while I sat forward and scanned both the ether and the area. "Keep going," I said when Candice began to slow down.

She pressed the gas again, and the road got bumpy. We passed a campground and an abandoned bait shop, and the road got worse as we went along. I knew Candice was gripping the wheel and gritting her teeth—her Porsche clearly wasn't made for terrain like this—but she kept going until I suddenly yelled, "Stop!"

For a few seconds we both just sat there and gazed out the windows. The area we were in was a bit off the lake, which was just visible through the trees. I checked my radar and had the feeling I needed to get out of the car and take a look around.

I did, and Candice got out too. Coming over to stand next to me, she seemed to be waiting for me to say something. "Her car is somewhere nearby," I said. I could *feel* its presence. I limped over to the left side of the road and poked with my cane at the underbrush for any sign that a car had been hidden there or had been pushed through the vegetation on its way into the lake. Nothing but thick foliage stared back at me.

"Maybe it's up the road a bit more," Candice suggested.

I shook my head. I knew it wasn't.

Easing back down the road, I kept my eyes peeled,

and about ten feet away from Candice's Porsche, I shouted, "Yes!"

Candice hurried to my side, and I lifted my cane to point down the short slope at the barely visible tread marks, which had flattened the grass and foliage. "See that?" I said, waving my cane at a slight arch between several trees. "The car went in through there."

I made to follow the tracks when Candice caught my arm. "Hang on," she said. "We don't want to disturb the crime scene."

I moved back to the road. "Right. Still, shouldn't we make sure that Kendra's car did go into the lake through here before we call in the cavalry?"

Candice nodded and moved to her own car. Opening the trunk, she pulled out a pair of leather work boots. "I keep these on hand just in case," she said, slipping out of her heels.

After tucking in her pant cuffs, she moved to the far side of the tracks and began walking parallel to them, keeping her eyes trained on the ground. I saw her ease into the underbrush and all but disappear from view.

"Candice?" I called after not hearing from her for a bit.

"I'm here!" she replied. And then she was back in my line of sight and I breathed a sigh of relief.

"What'd you find?" I asked.

She moved back up the slope next to me before answering. "It's hard to see, but I did manage to glimpse the car," she said.

My eyes widened. *"I was right?"* I mean, I knew I could be, but it was still kind of freaky that nothing but my intuition had led us straight to Kendra's car.

"You seem surprised," she said, grinning at me while she pulled her phone from her jacket.

"Hey, even we psychic types get surprised when we take a shot in the dark and it finds the mark."

Candice nodded again and held up a finger. "Hey, handsome," she said into the phone.

My brow rose. I hadn't counted on her calling Brice first.

"I'm with Abby out by Decker Lake on the east side, and I think we might have a bit of a situation on our hands . . ."

I let Candice talk to Brice without interrupting, but I could already tell he wasn't going to rush out with a bunch of agents to dredge the lake. When she hung up, she looked frustrated. "Dammit," she grumbled.

"He wants you to call APD, doesn't he?"

"Yeah. He's knee-deep in the mall bombing case and he can't spare any guys. Plus, he did point out that it's not exactly his jurisdiction."

"It isn't his jurisdiction *yet*," I said wistfully. "It'd be so much easier if the FBI got involved."

"It would," Candice agreed as she tapped the screen on her phone again. She then placed it to her ear and said, "Yes, hello, dispatch? Can you please connect me to the homicide unit?"

Several hours later, Candice and I stood behind yellow "crime scene, do not cross" tape, watching a tow truck ease Kendra's wet car up to the road by a long cable. Hordes of police, CSIs, and homicide detectives swarmed the scene, along with the first of what was likely to be several TV news crews.

The hour was growing late and I was once again light-headed with hunger—no surprise there. I wanted to leave, but we'd been specifically told to wait right where we stood because the detectives had more questions for us—no surprise there either.

At last the lead detective on the case, Jan LenDale, came toward us, motioning for another suit to follow her. "Here we go," I muttered as they approached. I watched their faces closely. There wasn't a hint of warmth in either of their expressions. I felt myself brace for what was to come.

"Ladies," LenDale said when she'd stopped in front of us. "This is my boss, Captain Ramirez."

Candice and I both nodded to the middle-aged man in front of us with a moody and highly skeptical look on his face. "Which one of you is supposed to be psychic?" he asked.

Apparently he wasn't so fond of formalities. "Me. I'm Abby Cooper and I'm a professional intuitive."

He studied me for a minute, the skepticism in his eyes increasing.

I tried not to squirm.

"So . . . what?" he finally asked. "You had a vision about where to find Kendra Moreno or something?"

I tamped down the irritation his derisive tone sparked and simply pointed to the dripping car moving slowly up the incline. "In a manner of speaking."

"Right," he said, adopting a mocking smile.

"It might help you to know that Abby is on the FBI payroll," Candice said evenly.

That got Captain Attitude's attention. "She's a fed?"

"I'm a consultant to the bureau's cold-case squad here in Austin," I said, digging through my purse for my ID.

I had just located it when we heard, "Captain! Detective LenDale! Over here!"

All four of our heads snapped in the direction of

Kendra's car, where one of the CSIs was standing next to the now open trunk.

Captain Attitude turned back to us. "Stay put."

I had the urge to salute smartly, but Candice must have noticed I was close to making a wisecrack because she squeezed my arm and said, "We wouldn't dream of leaving, sir."

LenDale and Ramirez trotted away, and when they reached the trunk they both peered inside as the CSI who'd called them over pointed to something. "Do you think Kendra's body is in there?" Candice asked me.

I shook my head. "No. Her body's somewhere else." The feeling that she had been buried out in the woods in a shallow grave was as strong as ever, so if there was something of interest in the trunk of that car, it wasn't Kendra's body.

We watched LenDale and Captain Attitude question the CSI for a bit; then all three looked our way, and I could tell they were about to come back to us when a car came barreling down the road, plowing through the crime scene tape before braking hard. Out of the door flew Mrs. Woodyard. *"Did you find her?!"* she yelled frantically. *"Did you find my baby?!"*

Everybody seemed completely caught off guard by her sudden appearance, and two patrol officers moved fast to try to restrain her, but she somehow managed to dodge them and dashed forward toward the still-leaking car. *"Kendra!"* she cried, her voice ragged and choked.

Detective LenDale managed to catch her before she could get to the car, and Mrs. Woodyard collapsed in her arms, wailing and flailing about.

As much as I didn't like the woman, my heart went out to her in that moment. The car was the clincher. It was one ominous sign too many that Kendra was no longer alive, and I knew that her mother was finally accepting that something truly terrible had happened to her daughter.

Captain Ramirez helped his detective support Mrs. Woodyard, and all Candice and I could do was watch as the poor woman sobbed and shrieked and flailed her fists in agony.

Once they'd calmed her down, they began to lead her away from the car, and that put us in her direct line of sight. This was unfortunate, because the distraught woman took one look at me, caught her breath, and planted her feet hard. Then she lifted a trembling arm to point straight at me as she asked the captain something. He glanced in our direction before replying.

Suddenly, Mrs. Woodyard's demeanor changed completely. She went from grieving mother to angry accuser, and I could hear snatches of what she was saying to the captain and the detective.

"Uh-oh," said Candice. "Why do I think this isn't gonna end well for us today?"

"Because it never ends well for us," I grumbled.

Sure enough, LenDale called to a patrolman, who took over supporting Mrs. Woodyard, freeing the detective to come back over to us. Stopping directly in front of me, she said, "Were you at Tristan Moreno's home this morning?"

"Yes." I had no reason to lie.

LenDale's expression was mostly unreadable, but I still had the distinct impression she was seriously ticked that I hadn't mentioned that minor detail.

"We'll need you to come down to the department and answer a few questions, Ms. Cooper," she said, lifting up the crime scene tape and waving me forward.

"I'll come too," Candice said when I hesitated.

"No," LenDale replied, her tone icy. "Just Ms. Cooper."

Great.

"Really?" Candice asked, adopting an oh-so-friendly smile. "But I was at the house with Abby this morning too, Detective. And I've been investigating this case right along with her. So if there's something you want to ask her, I'm sure I can corroborate her answers."

"And her alibi?" LenDale asked snidely.

"If need be," Candice told her, dropping the whole friendly shtick.

"Fine," LenDale said, motioning to her sedan parked on the far side of the crime scene. "Stick to the perimeter and get in that blue sedan."

"We'll take my car," Candice insisted, pulling me away from the tape and over to her car. "And we'll meet you there, Detective."

LenDale glared hard at us as we began to walk away, and I saw her motion again to another patrolman to come over to her. "She's gonna have us tailed to the station," I said.

"Yep," Candice said without looking back.

"This just got bad, didn't it?"

Candice grunted. "I'm pretty sure we bypassed bad, Sundance, and wound up smack-dab in the middle of shih tzu."

Chapter Thirteen

Candice and I were separated the minute LenDale got to the station. I had a feeling that might happen, and I had to suffer through a laundry list of questions and slightly veiled accusations by LenDale and another detective, whose only contribution to the discussion seemed to be a rather constant nodding of his head every time LenDale spoke.

I had a serious grudge against him because the rat bastard had discreetly taken my cane on the pretense that it was in the way. What a flight risk I must have seemed with it. I badly wanted to leave, but they'd read me my rights and that'd rattled me a little. I didn't think I was under arrest yet, but I wasn't quite sure. The fact that Candice hadn't burst into the room and announced that we were leaving also confused me. Was she under arrest?

Until I heard from her I thought it best to just answer all the questions put to me and hope that my answers would finally satisfy these clowns and we'd both get to go free.

But so far, my cooperative attitude had gotten me nowhere. "Help me understand this," LenDale said, pretending to look back through her notes. "You say you had a vision about where Kendra's car was dumped, but you don't have any visions about who might've locked her in the trunk and drowned her, do you?"

Bobblehead nodded, and I rolled my eyes and sighed. We'd been at this for three hours already, and I was tired, and so hungry I could've eaten my own cooking. Also I had to pee something awful.

"We all know she wasn't in the trunk, Detective," I replied tersely. They wanted to test me? Okay. Bring it.

Bobblehead stopped nodding. Score one for the psychic.

"Excuse me?" LenDale asked, lowering her reading glasses to peer at me.

"You didn't find Kendra in the trunk or anywhere else in the car. You're bluffing. And the reason you're bluffing is because you've come to the most obvious and easiest of conclusions, that Tristan has murdered his wife because he might've been interested in me. But you're so far off base that while you're coming up with lamebrain theories, Kendra's real killer is somewhere out there living free from worry that you idiots will ever figure any of this shit out." (Swearing doesn't count when you're being interrogated by the police.)

"So why don't you help us figure all this out?" LenDale asked, leaning forward like she couldn't wait to hear everything I had to say. "I mean, you psychics know all, right?"

LenDale's big mistake was denying me food. I'd asked if they could bring me something from the vending machine about two hours before, but she'd said no and had hammered away at me until my blood sugar was well into the downright-snappish-and-rude zone. "Oh, we psychics *do* know all," I said, flashing her a mocking grin. "For starters, I know that you're currently having an affair with your captain—who's married, I might add. Shame on you, Detective."

Bobblehead sputtered and ducked his chin to cough into his hand. I turned my focus on him. "You're one to snicker. Does the department know about how you pulled some strings to get a buddy of yours out of some deep trouble recently? I'm guessing it had something to do with alcohol. A DUI, right?"

Bobblehead's shocked expression told me I'd hit it on the head and it also opened up his energy nice and wide for me to sift through. "Ah, I see that you also recently faked a back injury in order to take some paid time off. There's a connection between that lie and the buddy you helped out of a DUI, isn't there?" Bobblehead's mouth fell open and he uttered a slight squeaking sound. "Hold on," I said, grinning triumphantly when he didn't seem to be able to answer me. "Was he a back doctor? I mean, he was a chiropractor, right? That gives a whole new meaning to you scratching his back, and he scratches yours, right, Detective? But I believe it also gives a whole new meaning to the word *fraud*, right, Detective?"

LenDale gasped loudly, and her suspicious eyes turned to Bobblehead, whose complexion had gone so red that it was almost magenta. "Oh, so shocking, isn't it, Detective LenDale?" I scoffed. "But not half as shocking as the fact that you knew your captain was married, with three young kids, and you still pursued an affair with him. I wonder what his wife must think of you? I wonder if you'll be called in to the deposition for their divorce proceedings. I wonder if he'll have a penny left once her lawyers get through with the two of you!"

Both LenDale and Bobblehead just stared at me with big, horrified eyes, utterly speechless.

"Yeah," I said, sitting back and crossing my arms. "I'm done with you two. I told you that Candice and I had learned from the Morenos' exterminator that he'd seen a stranger go into Kendra's house the morning she disappeared. I've given you the exterminator's name and his contact information, but you two boneheads have yet to make that call. Instead you're wasting my time and yours."

LenDale cleared her throat and nervously glanced several times at the mirror against the wall to my left. Her energy suggested that I'd seriously rattled her, but she somehow managed to collect herself enough to say, "I still don't understand how you knew where Kendra's car was dumped. Or why you think we didn't find her body in it. I know you didn't see inside that trunk. How do you know what we found? Seriously, Ms. Cooper, if you didn't have something to do with Kendra's murder, how do you know all these things?"

"Because," I said, placing both of my hands flat on the table and leaning forward so that she could really hear me, *"I'm fecking psychic, you stupid—"*

At that moment there was a hard knock on the door and it opened abruptly. "Excuse the interruption," said a familiar voice. My eyes snapped over to the door as in walked Special Agent in Charge Brice Harrison: my boss, Candice's fiancé, and at that moment, my all-around hero. "Abby," he said to me, cool as a cucumber.

"Hold on!" said Bobblehead. "You can't just barge in here!"

Brice flashed his badge, and I thought it the shiniest, most glorious thing I'd ever seen. "I'd like to know why you're questioning my profiler."

"This doesn't concern you guys," LenDale said after squinting hard at Brice's badge.

"Oh, but it does," Harrison told her, holding out his hand to me.

I got up and leaned heavily on the table on my way over to him but was immediately thwarted by LenDale, who stood up too and tried to intercept me. Harrison stepped forward to block her from blocking me, and that's when Bobblehead made the most unfortunate mistake of putting a hand on Brice's shoulder.

In a move too fast for me to really follow, Bobblehead had his head mashed against the wall and his arm twisted behind his back. LenDale moved her hand to her gun, and into the room came Captain Ramirez. "Hey!" he shouted at all of us.

Harrison tugged up slightly on Bobblehead's arm and let him go. Stepping back, he reached out for my hand and helped me to him. "We're leaving, unless you idiots want to do something stupid like charge her," he said to Ramirez, who only glared at him. "I thought so," Harrison added. "And let this be a warning to you, Captain Ramirez. If you *ever* haul in either one of my profilers again without my permission, I'll bring a rain of shit down on you so fast, you won't know what hit you. Clear?"

"We're clear, Harrison. Now get the hell out."

As we were leaving, I couldn't help it. I turned back to Ramirez, and wiggling my finger back and forth between him and LenDale, I said, "Your wife knows about the two of you. Expect the divorce papers on your desk by the end of the month."

Harrison squeezed my hand and pulled me along.

"Sorry," I said when we moved through the door. To my delight, my cane was propped right up against the wall next to the door. I grabbed it and realized Brice was chuckling softly.

"Don't worry about it, Abby," he said, letting go of my arm so I had better balance with the cane. "Come on. Candice is back at your place, and if we don't get you home in the next twenty minutes, I'm pretty sure she and Dutch are gonna show up, waving a bunch of six-shooters and making threats that'll get me in trouble with Gaston."

"Candice isn't here?" I asked as we got to the elevator and Brice pressed the DOWN button.

"Naw. She left after fielding questions from some lamebrain detective for a couple of hours. She tried to find out which room you were in, but no one would let her back here, so she called me and told me what was going on. I beat it down here to spring you before they did something stupid like file charges." Ah, that explained why she hadn't come to my rescue earlier.

"Dutch didn't come with you?" I asked next as we moved into the elevator. I was a little surprised and honestly just a teeny bit hurt that he hadn't come with Harrison.

"I ordered him not to," he said, that amused grin back on his face. "If he'd seen what they were putting you through, he'd have hit someone for sure."

I laughed myself. "Yeah. You're probably right about that."

Once we'd made it to Harrison's car, he opened the passenger door for me and helped me into his SUV, which was at a tough angle for my weak hips. "Can we stop at a drive-through?" I asked when he got in.

"I'll do you one better," he said. "Candice had Dutch order pizza. The delivery guy should be at your house with it any minute."

"God bless you three," I said, laying my head back against the seat.

We got home and I could smell the delicious pie from the sidewalk. I think I broke the gimp record for getting up the stairs and into the house.

Dutch greeted me with a big hug and a plate of cheesy goodness. Did I have the best fiancé on the planet or what? "You okay?" he asked, kissing my forehead before placing the plate in my hands.

I took a bite, chewed, and swallowed before answering. "I am now."

While I ate, I filled everybody in on my interrogation, even the part about revealing LenDale's and Bobblehead's secrets. "That's sure to win them over," Dutch muttered, but there was an amused grin on his face all the same.

"Trust me," I told him. "At that point there was no winning. Thanks to Mrs. Woodyard and her uncanny crappy timing, they think I had something to do with Kendra's disappearance."

"I think they were just fishing," Candice said. "I let my interrogation go on only as long as it took me to figure out that the only things they'd found in Kendra's trunk were a roll of duct tape and her headband."

"So where's the body?" Dutch asked me.

I shrugged. "That's the sixty-four-thousand-dollar question, cowboy."

"You know," said Candice, thoughtfully, "there is another suspect the police are looking at."

"You mean besides we fools?" I asked.

Candice grinned. "Yeah, can you believe it?"

"No," I said truthfully.

"Who is it?" Brice asked, reaching for another slice of pizza.

"It's a neighbor," Candice said. "I overheard one of the other detectives tell the captain that there's a registered sex offender in Kendra's neighborhood and that she'd told her dad she was a little nervous being around him."

"There's a registered sex offender living in *that* neighborhood?" I asked. The Morenos lived in one of the pricier parts of town, and their house, although it wasn't huge, still had to appraise for between six and eight hundred thousand.

"There's a registered sex offender living in every neighborhood," Dutch said, leaning in to kiss me on the cheek again. He was being super affectionate tonight. I wondered why until I remembered it was Wednesday. Hump day. As in—the freebie I always tossed him in the middle of the week.

"The registered offender in that hood is a guy who got caught with the family's underage babysitter a few years ago," Candice told us. "At least that's what the detective said to the captain before they caught me eavesdropping and shut up about it."

"Have you looked this sex offender up yet?" I asked.

"Not yet," Candice said, stretching and stifling a yawn. It was almost nine and it'd been a long day for us. "I was gonna dig up his profile and take a run over to his house tomorrow. You in?"

"I am," I said. I had no clients scheduled for the next few days, as I'd purposely set some time aside in my calendar to devote to the case. "I'm free the whole day."

"Perfect." Candice got to her feet and stretched tiredly. "I'll pick you up at nine. Brice? You ready?"

He eyed his half-empty beer like he wanted to stay awhile, but Dutch got up and began to gather the plates. Subtle.

With a bit of throat clearing, Brice finally got the hint and hastened to follow Candice out the door. The moment the door shut, Dutch wrapped me in his arms and said, "Have I told you lately how much I love you?"

I smiled. "You always seem to love me so much more on Wednesdays."

"No," he said, dipping his chin to kiss me sweetly. "I love you the same as all the other days; I just get to show you how much on Wednesdays."

I laughed. "Sure, sure. Okay, hot stuff, you may carry me off to bed."

"Thought you'd never ask," he said, sweeping me into his arms to run me up the stairs. I'd share more of what happened next, but we'd lose the PG-13 rating for sure . . . ahem.

The next morning before Candice came to pick me up, I had the misfortune of catching a glimpse of the news, which featured footage of Candice's bright yellow Porsche and the two of us zipping out of Tristan's driveway, before cutting away to the image of Candice's car in the background while Kendra's silver Toyota Camry was being hauled out of the lake. Then, after another cutaway, the footage moved to Mrs. Woodyard giving an interview to a host of reporters. "I am now convinced that my son-in-law had something to do with my daughter's disappearance," she said. "And I believe this because I've recently learned that Tristan is having an affair with a woman claiming to be psychic who came to my home and tried to convince us that she knows where Kendra is."

"I did not!" I shouted at the TV. Eggy and Tuttle came trotting over to me and wagged their tails nervously, wanting to make sure I was okay. I sat down on the couch, picked them up, and turned up the volume a little.

"This woman is the most unscrupulous character I've ever met," she said, that familiar mean glint in her eye. "She tried to distract us by telling my husband—who has terminal cancer—that he would soon get into a drug trial which would cure him. To prove that she's nothing but a fraud, we called his doctor, and he assured us that there is no such clinical trial available for my husband."

I snarled. "*Which* doctor did you call?" I shouted at her image. "Because the doctor I saw him receiving the call from is a female, you hateful bi—"

"Abs?" I heard from just outside the front door as Candice knocked and opened it to smile at me from the front step.

I muted the TV and pointed furiously at the screen. "Have you gotten a load of this shih tzu?!" (Morning ray of sunshine . . . I am not.)

"Whoa!" Candice said, rushing into the living room to take the remote out of my hand and turn the sound back on. ". . . believe that Tristan and his lover kidnapped my daughter and have done something unspeakable to her," Mrs. Woodyard was saying. "And why the police haven't arrested these two yet is simply beyond me!"

"Did she say your name?" Candice asked.

"Not yet. But it's only a matter of time before one of the reporters digs it up and I become public enemy number one."

"Why aren't the police shutting her down?" Candice asked next, and I knew she was asking it rhetorically.

In the background I could see poor Mr. Woodyard looking frail, a little jaundiced, and miserable. I'd be miserable too if I were married to that wife of his. Oh, yeah, I'd also be miserable if my daughter were missing and I had cancer too. Just then I saw Mr. Woodyard lift his cell phone and answer it while his wife took questions from the reporters.

I felt an intuitive need to keep my focus on Mr. Woodyard, and as he took the call I saw his eyes bulge and his face grow even paler before it seemed to lift with relief. For an instant I wondered if the call was from someone claiming to have found Kendra, but then I clearly saw his lips mouth, "A drug trial? Really?"

A moment later he was excitedly trying to get his wife's attention, but she was still too wrapped up with the reporters. "Mmm-hmm," I said smugly, pointing at him. "I told you so!"

"Told who what?" Candice asked.

I took the remote from her and clicked the TV off, knowing the minute the reporters got wind of Mr. Woodyard being entered into that drug trial, they'd back off me. At least that's what I hoped would happen. "I'll explain in the car," I told her, reaching for my cane. "Let's go see this sex offender."

"We're stopping by Tristan's first," Candice said. "I want to get to him before the news crews show up."

"Okay. Tristan, then the sex offender."

"Then we're heading to Jamie's," Candice said, allowing me first out the door.

"Why her?"

"I keep thinking about Kendra filing for divorce after finding out that Tristan cheated on her. I'm wondering if Jamie held that part back."

"What part?" I asked, waiting for her to unlock the door of her car.

"The part where she told Kendra that he and Bailey had hooked up."

Personally, I hadn't detected that Jamie was holding anything back when we'd interviewed her, but I'd missed stuff before. It'd be good to check it out.

We arrived at Tristan's too late to avoid the news crews, who followed our car up the drive and even boldly swarmed around us as we got out. "Are you the woman having an affair with Tristan Moreno?" one of the reporters asked Candice. Apparently no one wanted to think the gimpy girl with the cane could enjoy a little roll in the hay. If only they'd peeked in my bedroom window the night before.

Candice caught my eye and moved away from the car, drawing the pack with her to give me time to make it to the stairs and begin the climb up. I'm not sure what she told them, but it kept them busy until I reached the landing and knocked. Tristan answered, looking disheveled and even more stressed-out than he had the last time I'd seen him. "Come in," he said, almost curtly, before seeing the pack below and yelling at them to get off his property, as they were currently trespassing. "I'm calling my lawyer and filing suit against all you parasites!" he shouted, the muscles in his neck straining and his face flushing with anger.

He seemed to be coming unglued. "Hey," I whispered softly. "It's okay, buddy. They're backing off. See?"

Candice hurried away from the reporters and climbed the stairs, looking like she'd almost enjoyed that. "What'd you tell them?" I asked.

Candice laughed. "I told them to ask Mr. Woodyard how soon his drug trial was starting, assuring them that your sixth sense had confirmed he was scheduled to begin one very, very soon."

"Do you think they'll bite?"

"Oh, they'll all check it out," she assured me. "I mean, they rolled their eyes and kept pelting me with questions, but they're competitive enough with each other to look into it."

"Damn leeches," Tristan said, moving into the house so that we could follow him.

We went into his kitchen and sat at his table again. "How're you holding up?" Candice asked him.

Tristan shook his head. "Not good." Looking at me, he said, "Kendra's mom won't give Colby back, and now she's got to start this crap about you and I having . . ."

He left the rest unsaid, and it made me realize that Tristan really wouldn't cheat on Kendra. The very idea made him cringe. Still, that didn't mean he didn't kill her when he discovered her having an affair on him. If that was in fact what had happened.

"Your mother-in-law has no right to keep your son," Candice said gently. "You've alerted your attorney?"

"Yes," Tristan said. "She's putting pressure on the police to assist me getting Colby back, but they haven't exactly been racing to help me out."

"He'll come back home," I told him, seeing it in the ether. "Within the next few days, in fact. You'll get your son back no later than Saturday or Sunday."

"You're sure?" he asked me, and there was such vulnerability in his eyes.

"Positive," I assured him. Some things just felt solid in their absoluteness, and Colby's return was one of those things.

"Can I ask you a few questions?" Candice said.

Tristan focused on her. "Sure."

"Did Kendra ever mention a creepy neighbor or the fact that she didn't like living in a neighborhood with a sex offender?"

Tristan blinked. "You mean Dr. Snyder?"

Candice and I both sat forward. Doctor? "Yes," Candice said after giving me a sideways glance.

Tristan seemed to think on it for a minute before answering. "When we first moved in, Kendra signed up for some identity-theft-alert thing that also sent out warnings about registered sex offenders in the area, and that's how we learned that one was living just a few houses away.

"Kendra didn't make a really big deal about it, but I knew she was scared living so close to him, so I checked into it. I mean, I didn't want my wife home alone if there was a psycho around, you know?"

I held my breath, wondering when it would hit Tristan what he'd just said. His face flushed a second later and he looked at the tabletop. "Shit," he said.

"What'd you find out?" Candice asked, trying to pull him back on track.

"I had a buddy—who knows how to look up criminal records—check out the case. It turns out that Snyder had some sort of fling with the seventeen-year-old who babysat his kids. My buddy said that Snyder claimed in court that he didn't know she was only seventeen, but I don't think that held up. I mean, he's a doctor, right? He should know, if the girl's still in high school, there's a pretty good chance she's underage, right?"

Candice and I both nodded.

"Anyway, I told Kendra the story, that he'd done something stupid with the babysitter and he lost his medical license over it and his wife had left him, and he even did a couple of months in jail for it. We both thought he'd been punished pretty good for doing something so stupid, and I think that finding out about the case had eased her mind a little. Snyder wasn't a violent rapist, just a doctor who probably had a God complex and thought he was untouchable or something."

Candice held her phone as Tristan talked, and I knew she was recording the conversation again. "What kind of doctor was he?" she asked.

Tristan shrugged. "Don't know."

"If he lost his practice, what does he do now?" I asked.

"Don't know that either," Tristan said. "He pretty much keeps to himself."

I wondered if the good doctor had any knowledge about paralytic drugs—or maybe had a particular familiarity with them. It'd be good to know if he was perhaps an anesthesiologist. Losing his license meant nothing—you could easily order any kind of drug off the Internet these days.

"What about your exterminator?" Candice asked next. "Do you know Russ?"

Tristan nodded. "I know him," he said. "He seems like a nice guy. Likes to read Jim Butcher novels."

"How do you know that?" I asked, curious that Tristan had pulled that little fact out of the air.

"He's my favorite author too," Tristan replied.

Candice said, "I checked into his background. He seems pretty on the level, no criminal record whatsoever. The only thing that's odd about him is how low under the radar he flies."

I eyed my partner curiously. "He flies low under the radar?" This was new information to me, and I gathered that Candice had probably woken up early to do a little research on the bug man. "Why is that suspicious?"

"Well, it is and it isn't," she said. "Russ is a guy who knows a lot about bugs and what kills them. Every day, he works with poisons that affect their central nervous systems—paralyzing them and their ability to move. He's also got to be familiar with the effect of those poisons on humans so that he can handle those liquids and powders safely—or not, depending upon what his intentions are."

I got the hidden meaning in that little speech, and it did send a tiny chill down my spine.

"Also," Candice continued, "Russ is in his midthirties, with almost no credit to speak of. From what I can tell, his business makes him a really decent living, but he owns no car other than his pest-control truck and no property. He rents an apartment, where he's lived for eleven years, and doesn't have a single credit card. He's got no family, he's unmarried, and he lives alone. It's a little weird."

"I still don't get why that in particular is odd," I said.

"Abs," Candice told me, "the guy's got to be cracking six figures by now. Why doesn't he spend some of that cash?"

I shrugged. "Maybe he's happy living the simple life."

Candice nodded, but I could tell she still didn't trust Russ's profile or the fact that he had access to paralytic poisons, and maybe, just maybe, I was being a little defensive because I'd liked Russ and also maybe my simple below-the-radar lifestyle had been a lot like his before I'd met Dutch.

"Do you think he had something to do with Kendra's disappearance?" Tristan asked—a bit too quickly, I thought. "I mean, if he came to our door, Kendra would have definitely let him in. He's been our bug guy for years, and she knew and trusted him."

"We don't know anything definitive yet," Candice cautioned him. "All we know is that Russ was in the area at the time he claims a man in a baseball cap entered your home on the twenty-eighth. He didn't see anything and he didn't hear anything after that."

Tristan's face twisted in emotion. I could tell that not knowing what'd happened to his wife was killing him almost as much as being without her.

Candice eyed the table and began to trace a circle with her finger. I knew that whatever she was going to ask him next was probably going to be a touchy subject, so I turned up the volume on my radar and watched the ether carefully.

"Did you know that your wife had filed for divorce, Tristan?"

He sighed wearily. It was clear the subject really hurt him. "I had no idea until the police told me about the papers being filed the other day and filled me in on what her divorce attorney said she said to him the morning she went missing. I mean, I'd be lying if I said I was surprised that she'd gone and done that after our fight at the top of the stairs. I deserved it too. I deserved to lose her, but it still hurt like hell to hear that she was really planning on leaving me."

Candice glanced my way, and I nodded. He was telling the truth. He hadn't known she'd been to her attorney's office and was planning to file papers. Just then Tristan's phone rang and after looking at it he said, "Sorry, this is my attorney." We let him take the call, which was brief. When he hung up he said, "Chelsea needs me to meet her at the police station to sign a complaint against my in-laws for not letting me have Colby back. Can we pick this up later?"

Candice tapped her own phone and tucked it away. "Of course," she said to him. "We'll be in touch."

We left Tristan and got back in the car, nearly taking out a reporter who didn't get out of the way fast enough. "Tristan's right," Candice said casually. "They're a bunch of leeches."

I pulled my hand away from my eyes when no loud thump met my ears and focused on ducking low in my seat. "If this Dr. Snyder lives on the street, how're we going to talk to him without the leeches catching on?"

Candice cast a glance at my cane and frowned. "I knew the day would come when I'd have to carry you piggyback," she said. Without further explanation, she made a hard right at the end of the street.

"Why am I very worried about that statement?"

"Relax. You'll be fine. It's my back I'm worried about."

Candice made several more turns, some right, some left, and pretty soon I was lost. "Where the heck are we?"

Candice pointed to the GPS screen on her dash. "We're on the block right behind the Morenos' place," she said. "See that?"

I squinted. "Yeah?"

"That's a park. We're gonna pull the car over to that curb near the playground and hoof it into Snyder's back-yard."

I picked my eyes up to scan the park as we entered the area in question. The place was nicely manicured except near the fence that backed up to the row of houses Candice was indicating. Along that particular fence line it was like a thick jungle of weeds, grass, and underbrush. "You can't be serious," I said, although I knew Candice definitely was.

She didn't answer me. Instead she parked and went right around to the trunk to collect her trusty boots. After this was over, I was definitely hiding them so she'd never get another stupid idea like this again.

Once she had her boots on, she came around to me and opened the door. "Come on."

"Can't I just stay here?"

"Nope. I'll need you when I question him."

"How do you know he's even home?"

"We won't know until we knock on his back door."

I sighed heavily and got out, but when Candice motioned for me to hop onto her back, I simply turned and began to gimp my way straight over to that fence. She came up next to me and held gently to my elbow as I struggled to pick my feet up enough to make headway without falling face-first into the underbrush. "Of all the . . . ," I grunted, feeling myself working up a sweat.

"It's the only way," Candice said, pulling up on my elbow when my cane got tangled around some grass.

We reached the fence and I had to pause to catch my breath. Also, I was stalling because I had no idea how I'd make it over the top. "I miss Nora," I said, referring to a dear friend who'd once pitched both Candice and me over a ten-foot-tall fence in Las Vegas. Nora was crazy strong.

Candice grinned. "I miss her too," she said. "You should invite her and Detective Brosseau to your wedding."

I gripped the top of the fence and pulled my hips up to sort of hang my torso over it before pulling my bottom half slightly (totally) inelegantly over the top and landing with a bit of a thud on my butt in the backyard of Dr. Snyder. Who was actually home. And on his back porch staring at us like he couldn't believe two crazy fools like us would walk through that brush and hop the fence into his backyard.

"Morning!" Candice said to him as she too clambered over the fence, albeit a bit more elegantly. (Confession, a water buffalo would have clambered over the fence more elegantly . . .)

"Can I help you?" he asked in that way that said, "I wonder if I should get my gun."

I reached up and took Candice's outstretched hand, glaring hard at her for good measure. "Are you Dr. Snyder?" she asked while helping me up.

He squinted at us. "Yeah?" he said, answering her with a question mark. Candice moved closer to him and he held up his hand. "Hold on," he said. "Are you two reporters?"

I leaned hard on my cane and walked up to Candice, letting her do all the talking. "No, no!" she assured him. "My name is Candice Fusco and this is my associate, Abigail Cooper."

"You look like reporters," he insisted.

Candice dug through her purse and pulled out her PI badge. He frowned and waved us forward. Once he'd inspected it—thoroughly—he said, "This about the missing woman?"

"It is," Candice said, and she seemed to spot something on the table next to Snyder because she pointed to it and said, "You a Horns fan?"

"Isn't everybody?" Snyder asked with a crooked smile while he reached for the item that had been blocked from my sight by a laptop. The second he put the orange ball cap with the UT longhorn logo on his head, I understood why Candice had asked.

"Hook 'em horns," Candice said. "Anyway, since you ask, yes, we've been hired by your neighbor Mr. Moreno to try to figure out what happened to his wife, Kendra, and since we know you're one of the neighbors, we were hoping maybe you saw or heard something out of the ordinary on the day she disappeared."

Snyder cast her a mocking look. "You mean, did I, the only registered sex offender on this street, see anything unusual the day she disappeared, right?"

Candice didn't reply; she merely gave one slight nod and waited for him to elaborate.

He sighed. "I was home, working all day," he said. "I didn't see nothin' and I didn't hear nothin'."

"What is it that you do exactly?" Candice asked him.

Dr. Snyder seemed to bristle. "I work for WebMD," he said tersely.

Candice was holding her phone in her hand with the display away from Snyder, but I could see that her recording app was on. I thought she'd comment further, but she didn't. She just stood there looking at him expectantly.

The intervening silence went on and Snyder seemed to grow impatient. "It's the same thing I told the police," he said. "And if they get a warrant to search my house, they'll see all the e-mails I sent from my home computer on that day, which were a lot."

"You've already checked?" Candice asked him. I knew she was thinking that he was offering up his alibi pretty quick, like he had a reason to have it handy.

"Once you get into the system, you learn to make sure your ass is covered when something bad goes down."

Well, that was interesting.

"Did you ever speak to Kendra?" I asked, homing in on his energy, which I found shifty and untrustworthy.

"Once or twice," he said.

"And the day she went missing," I pressed, "did you speak to her that day?"

Snyder's lips compressed, and I knew he was close to telling us to go to hell. "Yeah," he said. "That morning I passed her while I was walking my dog. Colby really likes Ziggy."

It was then that I noticed the sleeping old Labradoodle lying in the sun on Snyder's porch.

"When did you learn that Kendra was missing?" Candice asked next. So far my lie detector hadn't gone off, but that didn't mean that Snyder was telling us the whole truth; he might have just stuck with those parts that wouldn't give him away if he was the killer.

Snyder snorted derisively, and I was positive that he was about to tell us off when from the side of his yard the gate opened and in walked a woman in a skimpy negligee. "Yoo-hoo, David!" she called as she turned to close the gate leading directly into the yard to the right of Snyder's. "I'm here, honey. Oh, I thought that husband of mine was never gonna—"

The rest of the woman's sentence hung in the air as she finally realized that the good doctor had company on his back porch. Her face flushed the color of beets and she crossed her arms over herself, trying to hide the skimpy negligee. "Oh, Lord!" she cried, and turned back around to the gate, but not before I caught sight of the rather large diamond ring on her left hand. In another second she was back on the other side of the fence and out of our view.

Candice pointed to the house next door. "She part of your alibi too, Dr. Snyder?"

Snyder glared hard at Candice for all he was worth before tugging on the brim of his ball cap, getting up, and whistling to his dog. Without a backward glance, he opened the screen and stepped into his house. "You have ten seconds to get off my property," he said to us before sliding the glass door closed.

Candice turned to me. "Well, that went well."

We made it back to the car and discussed Snyder at length. "He's a doctor with knowledge about drugs," Candice said, ticking off the list of suspicious things associated with him on her fingers. "He works from home. He wears a ball cap, *and* he's having an affair with at least one of his neighbors."

I nodded. "If he was also having an affair with Kendra, and she found out about the next-door neighbor, that could be what I caught in the ether about another woman being involved but indirectly."

"Exactly," Candice said, pointing at me like I'd just put the final nail in Snyder's coffin. "I like him for the killer. You?"

I wasn't sure. "Stuff fits," I said, "but then it doesn't. I mean, Candice, he's been in the system before and he had to know that the police were going to look into him at some point. Why risk it? And what could have possibly made him so angry? I mean, everything I got from the energy during Kendra's murder points to rage. What could she have possibly known that would have set him off so much?"

Candice tapped the steering wheel with her fingers. "It doesn't all have to fit perfectly, you know, Abby." I could tell she was starting to grow weary of this case with all these unanswered questions leading to ever more questions.

"See, that's where you're wrong," I told her. "I think it does have to make sense, because if we can't explain these things, then we may be focusing in on the wrong guy."

Candice sighed. "Fine. On my list of things to do when I get a free minute will be to look very carefully into Snyder's background, and I'll also check out his neighbor's wife while I'm at it."

"Good," I said, giving her a pat on the arm. "I know there's something we're still missing here, and I won't feel comfortable pointing the finger at anybody until we figure out what that is."

We were silent the rest of the way to where Jamie worked. I remembered from her reading that Jamie was a hairstylist at a place called the Black Orchid on South Congress Avenue. When we walked in, I self-consciously smoothed out my hair. I was really overdue for a new do. After inquiring with the receptionist, we found out that not only did they take walk-ins, but Jamie would be free in the next hour or so. Candice told the girl that we'd take the one-o'clock slot, and at first I thought Candice was only booking the appointment to justify taking up Jamie's time, but when she had the receptionist take down my name, I suddenly realized I'd been hood-winked.

I shot my partner an evil look, and in response she lifted up one of my locks and said, "Oh, please. We're practically having a hair emergency here."

She must have felt a little bad, though, because as we were leaving she looped her arm through mine and said, "How about if I let you pick where we'll have lunch?"

That perked me up. There was a new hot-dog place I wanted to try as I continued my pursuit to find the Texas equivalent of the Detroit-style Coney dog. So far I'd struck out at every hot-dog place I'd tried, but that hadn't deterred me from the quest. With only a small sigh Candice agreed and we were soon happily seated at an adorable joint where I ordered the Coney dog, a side of chili fries, and a mambo Coke.

Candice ordered the shrimp salad and an iced tea.

I frowned and adopted a mocking grin. "Eating like that's gonna kill you."

Her mouth quirked at the edges. "Talk to me in ten years when you're being wheeled in for bypass and my heart's as smart as a fifth grader."

"Ha, ha!" I said. "Good one."

We ate our meal and went over the case, mindful of the hour and getting back to the salon in time for my appointment. Mostly we just complained that so many leads didn't seem to lead us anywhere but round and round in circles. I felt the truth was staring us in the face if only we could arrange all the little bits of information we'd gotten in a way that pointed definitively to Kendra's killer. It seemed that when we focused on any one of our suspects—Tristan, Russ, Dr. Snyder, Bailey—we could find enough there to suggest that he—or she—had either murdered Kendra or arranged for her murder. There was also the possibility that we hadn't yet identified the real killer, and that was the one thing that kept niggling away at me. I knew I was missing something obvious—but what? What hadn't I seen yet that I needed to?

A bit later we arrived back at the salon, and Jamie appeared quite surprised to see us, but not in a bad way. "Can you do something with this?" Candice asked, again lifting up one of my locks until I slapped her hand away.

Jamie giggled and assured both of us that she could work a miracle, and within about ten seconds she and

Candice had me wrapped in a smock with my butt in a chair. Jamie moved off to gather some foils and bleach for highlights, and the minute she came back she asked, "How're you two coming along with the investigation?"

"Not great," Candice admitted, sitting in the empty seat next to me. "Kendra's mom is now convinced that Abby and Tristan are having some kind of relationship."

Jamie paused as she combed out my hair. "You're kidding!"

Candice filled her in on what'd happened the day before and then casually segued into asking Jamie more about what she'd seen the night of Tristan's bachelor party. "The reason I ask," Candice said, "is because we heard you told Kendra that Tristan had cheated."

Jamie stopped brushing bleach on the section of my hair she was about to wrap in a foil and just stared at Candice. "Who told you that?"

"Tristan," Candice said, which wasn't *exactly* a lie, but it sort of wasn't the truth either.

Jamie shook her head vigorously. "I didn't!" she said. "And Tristan never knew I'd seen him making out with Bailey! How could he possibly think I'd tell Kendra that?"

"He seemed to think his wife told him you'd confessed to seeing him with Bailey on the night of the bachelor party," Candice said.

I began to tap my foot nervously. I wished Candice hadn't chosen to ask Jamie about all this during the highlighting period . . . or the cutting period . . . or the blow-drying period. Then I realized there wasn't much period left after all that and maybe I should just cross my fingers and hope for the best.

Jamie blinked a few times, and I knew her mind must be a tumble of thoughts. "No one knew I'd seen Tristan and Bailey together except Bailey," she said. "And I can't see Bailey telling anybody else who might've told Kendra. I mean, Bailey begged me to keep it a secret, and I did. I never told anyone. Well, except you two, but that's only because Kendra's missing and all."

"Do you think Bailey told Kendra?" Candice asked, and I wondered why I hadn't thought of that.

Jamie's brow furrowed even more. "Why would Bailey do that?" she said; then she seemed to put the pieces together. Still, she shook her head. "No. If Bailey told Kendra that she'd hooked up with Tristan, then she would have ruined both her friendship with Kendra and any chance she would've had with Tristan if he and Kendra split up. He'd never forgive Bailey for telling his wife that they'd hooked up right before the wedding."

"Did someone else maybe see Tristan and Bailey making out?" I asked.

Jamie shook her head. "Not that I could see. But who knows what happened after I left? Maybe one of the other guys saw them together and let it spill, or told one of their girlfriends and she eventually told Kendra. I don't really hang with that crowd anymore, so I couldn't tell you who's been saying what anymore."

We all fell silent then for a few seconds before I asked, "Jamie? Did you know that Kendra was having an affair?"

Jamie dropped the bleach brush right on her shoe. "Dammit!" she swore. I could see in the mirror that she was wearing beautiful suede boots, both of which were now splattered with white goop. "I just bought these!" she grumbled, grabbing some paper towels and trying to mop up the mess. "Excuse me, I'll be right back," she added when all she managed to do was smear the goop even more into her shoes.

The poor girl then dashed to the back and Candice and I were left to stare at each other in puzzlement. "I guess she didn't know," I said.

"We don't even know," Candice reminded me. "I mean, all we have is the word of the exterminator, who says he saw a guy in jeans and a ball cap go up her driveway a couple of times. That's hardly evidence of an affair."

"True," I said with a sigh, swiveling back around as Jamie came back.

"Sorry," she said, blushing slightly. "You just really surprised me with that one. Kendra's the last person on earth I'd ever expect to cheat on her husband."

We asked Jamie a few more questions about Kendra, digging for any clue we could think of, but Jamie and Kendra hadn't been as close as they once were and she had little more to give us.

After a while we all lapsed back into silence again, and an hour and a half later, after my hair was cut, highlighted, and fluffy, she seemed relieved to see the back end of us.

"You look great," Candice said as we exited.

"Thanks!" I told her, running my hand through my fresh do. Dutch was gonna wish it was still Wednesday. "Are we off to Bailey's?"

"Yeah. She's not too far from here."

"You okay?" I asked. Candice didn't look right.

"Fine," she said, holding her stomach. "Just a little indigestion."

We rode to Bailey's and rang the bell. It was answered by a good-looking guy with light brown hair and somewhat elfin features. He was striking in a way that caught you off guard and sort of took your breath away. "Yeah?" he asked, staring hard at our chests.

Also, he was clearly an asshole. (Swearing doesn't count when an asshole is ogling your boobs.)

"Is Bailey here?" Candice asked, ignoring the fact that he was watching her cleavage like he expected it to perform a circus act.

"That bitch moved out," he said.

Let's add "dickhead" to his list of characteristics while we're at it.

Candice pushed a smile to her lips and bent sideways, trying to make eye contact. Dickhead kept his eyes trained on her boobs. "Do you know where we can find her?" she asked next.

He shook his head slightly. "Nope. Try her cell. Maybe she'll pick up."

"Could you give us her number?" I asked.

His sleazy gaze shifted over to me, and I had the urge to cross my arms over my chest, but then I realized that wasn't going to get us far. Instead I tugged my blouse open a little and bent ever so slightly forward.

"Got a pen?" he asked, staring hard.

Candice whipped out her phone and tapped the screen. "Go for it."

He rattled off the number; then, without so much as a good-bye, he wiped his nose with his hand, turned, and went back inside to shut the door in our faces.

"Can you believe Bailey left *him*?" I asked loudly.

Candice chuckled. "Come on, Sundance," she sang, turning her back to the door to head down the walk.

We called Bailey from the car and convinced her to meet us at Starbucks. She arrived later than she said she would, but at least she showed up. "We met your husband," I said by way of a greeting. "*Great* guy."

Bailey smirked as she took her seat. "He's a dickhead and an asshole."

I smiled huge. "Our sentiments exactly."

Candice stirred her second cup of tea and got right to the grilling. "Bailey, we know that you and Tristan had some sort of . . . incident the night of his bachelor party."

Bailey nearly choked on her latte. "*Who* told you that?" she demanded, but then she immediately caught herself and tried to pull it back. "I mean . . . that's just a rumor that a former friend of mine made up, but it's not true. I swear."

Liar, liar, pants on fire . . . , went my crew.

"So you didn't try to have your way with Tristan when he was drunk as a skunk the night before he got married?" Candice pressed.

Bailey's fingers curled around her cup. "No."

My lie detector went off again, and I tapped Candice's foot under the table to let her know.

"Okay," she said easily, making like she really believed Bailey. "Sorry to ask, but we have to follow every lead, even if it's just a rumor." Bailey didn't say anything, so Candice continued with, "Your husband tells us you've moved out."

"Yes. I left him. I'm staying with a friend for a few days before I move back home to Dallas."

"Did you know that Kendra was leaving her husband too?" I asked.

Bailey flushed again. "I did." That familiar wave of guilty energy came back into her ether. "In fact, I might've had something to do with it."

Candice and I both sat forward. "You did?" we both said.

Bailey took another sip of her drink. "Kendra told me she was thinking of leaving Tristan, and I gave her the number to my divorce attorney."

"Garrett Velkune?" Candice asked.

Bailey nodded. "Garrett's great. He's not like most of these attorneys who just want your money. He sits down with you and really asks you if you're sure, and if you're not sure, then he tells you what to do to protect yourself until you are."

"Protect yourself?" I asked, thinking she meant physically.

"Your assets," she explained. "He advises you about what'll happen when you file, how it's likely that your liquid assets will be frozen, so if you want to pull out some money from any joint accounts, then you better do it before you file."

"He said that?" Candice asked, her face troubled. "Attorneys aren't supposed to advise their clients to do that."

"He doesn't say that *exactly*," Bailey amended, already backpedaling. "But he implies it, because he knows that we women have to protect ourselves."

"How much does he suggest you put aside?" I asked.

"As much as we can get away with. I said as much to Kendra before I sent her to Garrett, and I know he told her the same thing."

Candice's eyes flashed to me for a second before she asked, "Do you know if Kendra took the advice?"

Bailey shrugged. "She'd have been a fool not to."

"Bailey?" I said next. "Can I ask you one last time what the fight between you and Kendra was about?"

Bailey looked away. "Stupid girl stuff," she said evasively.

Frustrated by her constant dodge of that question, I opened my radar wide and searched for the truth. What came back to me made me gasp. "It *was* you!" I said, pointing my finger at her. "You told Kendra Tristan had cheated on her!"

Bailey's jaw fell open, and she stared at me with a stunned expression. Then her face flushed with shame, and I managed to pull even more detail out of the ether. "But," I said, my tone now accusing, "true friend that you are, Bailey, you didn't tell Kendra *who* Tristan had cheated on her with; you just told her that you knew he had." I remembered Tristan telling us that his wife reacted to a touch from him like it'd repulsed her, and I suspected I knew why. "I think you told her that on the night of his bachelor party you and Jamie had gone over to the party to spy on the boys, and that you'd seen the strippers there, and maybe you suggested that you'd seen Tristan having sex with one of the girls. Does that sound about right to you, Bailey? That's why she called Jamie and told her she was thinking of leaving Tristan but she wanted to talk to her. She'd wanted to know if there really were strippers at the party."

Bailey stared at me with such shock and anger, but I could also see the terrible regret in her eyes. I'd nailed it. I'd nailed exactly what she'd told Kendra.

I continued my accusations. "It was your story that sent Kendra storming over to Tristan's office that night, and when he lost his temper with her, you were the one who tried to get her to leave him, plaguing her with doubt, sending her to see Velkune. You wanted Kendra to leave so that you could move in on Tristan, comfort the heartbroken divorcé, am I right, Bailey? But Kendra began to see through you, didn't she? Maybe she poked holes in the story by talking to some of the other guys at the bachelor party? Maybe she began to doubt your story, realized you were the one who had tried to get him into bed, and that's what your falling-out was about!"

Bailey's eyes welled up and waves of guilt poured off

her. "I never thought she'd actually go off and just leave Colby alone in the house like that!" she said defensively. "But, I mean, that should show you what kind of a person she is! She just took off and left her little boy in his crib without a backward glance!"

It was my turn to stare at her in shock. "You think she's still alive, don't you?" Bailey's brow furrowed. "You think she left that house on her own. You have no idea about what's really happened to her, do you?"

"She took off," she said, swiping her tears away with shaking fingers. "I know it. She took my advice, grabbed some cash from the bank so that Tristan couldn't trace where she went, and she's getting even with me by pulling this stunt!"

I shook my head. I was dumbstruck at the ocean of denial this stupid girl had created.

"She's alive!" Bailey insisted, hitting the table with the flat of her hand. "She is! I can feel it. She'll show up soon, and then y'all will see that she's not the sweet little angel everybody thinks she is." Obviously, Bailey hadn't seen the news about the discovery of Kendra's car in Decker Lake.

"You disgust me," I told her, and I was about to tell her exactly how much when my radar gave a quick warning and my head snapped to the door just as Bailey's soon-to-be-ex appeared in the doorway. "Uh-oh," I said the minute his eyes locked onto the back of his wife's head. Chase then charged right toward us. "Look out!" I yelled, pushing myself to my feet.

Bailey, who had her back to her approaching husband, appeared startled but remained seated, staring at me in confused alarm. Meanwhile Candice came out of her seat so fast her chair shot back and hit the wall. Still, she was hampered by a group of patrons at another table, which prevented her from getting to Bailey's husband before he could get to his wife.

Grabbing Bailey by the hair, he pulled her violently backward, causing her to fall hard onto the floor. Her legs kicked up and pushed the table directly into Candice, who was shoved back against the wall and nearly went down herself. I reacted reflexively, grabbing my coffee before it was knocked off the table and throwing the hot liquid directly into the man's face. He yelled and stumbled back, but not before I took my cane to his head. This time, the cane held strong and I gave Chase three good wallops before he too fell to the floor, where one of the male baristas tackled him and put him into a choke hold.

Around us there was a kind of pandemonium as customers and employees scattered for the exits, toppling tables and chairs and coffee as they dashed out of the place. I heard someone yell to call the police, but I was still too amped up on adrenaline to focus. Instead, as Bailey's husband struggled to get free of the barista's choke hold, I edged forward and gave him a hard crack across his shins. "You move and I'll break your damn legs!" I shouted, hovering over him with my cane raised. I was so angry that I seriously wanted him to give me another excuse.

"What the hell, Chase?" Bailey shouted as Candice helped her to her feet. She was covered in coffee stains from her own drink and maybe a few others littering the floor.

"You bitch!" he replied. "You drained my savings account!"

Bailey stood there shaking from head to toe. "It was *our* savings account, you son of a bitch!"

"*Who* put all the money into that account, you whore?" he demanded. "It sure as hell wasn't *you*!"

"Most of that was from our wedding, you asshole!" Bailey shot back, and I could see this was gonna be one bitter divorce.

Strobe lights on the wall pulled my attention away from the shouting match and over to the parking lot, where no less than three patrol cars had slammed to a stop. Six cops bolted out of their vehicles, their guns drawn, and they approached the Starbucks warily but in a hurry.

I lowered my cane and stepped closer to Bailey and Candice. As the first cop came into the building, all three of us pointed to Chase and yelled, "He did it!"

Chapter Fourteen

It took the cops about two hours to take all the witnesses' statements and finally release us from the scene. As Candice and I pulled out of the lot, we could see Chase sitting in the back of a squad car yelling at a cop in the front seat. "I hope he gets Tased," I said, glaring at him as we passed.

"Oh, I think that's a given," Candice told me.

It was then that I noticed she was grimacing. "You okay?"

"Fine," she said. "Just a touch of indigestion."

"Still?"

"I'll get some Tums when we're done for the day."

"Aren't we done for the day?"

"No."

I waited, but Candice didn't elaborate. "You gonna fill me in or should I just turn on my radar and . . ."

"We're going to see Velkune," Candice told me.

"Why?"

"I'm following through on a hunch."

I blinked. Usually I was the one with the hunches.

We arrived at Garrett's office and headed inside, rushing a little because it was just a minute or two before five now and we didn't want to miss him. We found his perky secretary packing up and looking like she was just about to leave. "Oh!" she said when we came through the door, a look of annoyance flashing briefly across her face. "Can I help you?"

"Sorry for the last-minute intrusion," Candice said, "but by any chance is Mr. Velkune available to see us for a few quick questions about Kendra Moreno?"

The girl's eyelids fluttered as she took in Candice's request. "Actually, I believe he and his wife were just about to leave," she said.

At that moment we heard a woman's amused laughter waft down the hallway and we all turned to see Garrett Velkune and a woman holding his arm come down the corridor. I was a little taken aback by Mrs. Velkune because she was a bit of a mismatch. Dressed smartly in a beautiful chocolate suede jacket with a cream silk blouse, paisley scarf, black leggings, and riding boots, she looked incredibly well put together. Especially when I took in the Chanel leather handbag and elegant jewelry, I figured her outfit alone cost at least ten grand. But although her hair was cut and styled in soft ash blond waves, it couldn't hide a most unattractive face. Mrs. Velkune had puffy round cheeks, a weak chin, small beady eyes, and an unfortunate underbite. The poor woman looked like a Pekinese.

Still, Velkune was looking at her like he'd never seen anyone so beautiful, and that moved me. Most guys as good-looking as Velkune would've gone for a model type like Bailey, but he'd obviously fallen in love with Mrs. Velkune the person, and I gave him big props for it.

When Velkune and his wife saw us, they both were brought up short. "Hi," he said awkwardly. "Are you two here to see me?"

"Yes," Candice said before stepping forward to extend her hand to Mrs. Velkune. "I'm Candice Fusco, a private investigator working on the Kendra Moreno case," she explained.

Mrs. Velkune eased her arm from around her husband's and shook Candice's hand. "Oh, that poor girl," she said. "I know Garrett's been so torn up over her disappearance. I've been following the story on the news, and I can't imagine what her poor family must be going through! I hope you're helping the police make a case against the husband?"

My eyes flashed to Garrett, who seemed surprised by his wife's statement. Candice, however, handled it with ease. "We're just following the truth wherever it leads us. We all want to know what happened to Kendra."

Mrs. Velkune nodded like she and Candice were totally on the same page. "I can wait out here, Garrett," she said, moving over to take a seat. "You help these women and we'll go to dinner when you're done."

For a moment Velkune seemed reluctant, but in a flash that was gone and he pushed a smile to his face and invited us into his office. "How can I help you?" he said when we'd all gotten comfortable around his desk.

As usual, after subtly turning on the recording app on her phone, Candice took the lead. "Mr. Velkune, we just met with Bailey Colquitt and she said that she is also represented by you."

He nodded. "Yes, I've been retained by Mrs. Colquitt."

"She told us that even before she filed for divorce, you had advised her to take out as much money from any joint accounts she shared with her husband as she could get away with."

Velkune's face flushed and he laughed nervously. "She told you that?" he said, shifting in his seat. "I think she may have misinterpreted what I said. As I remember it, I asked her to start *saving* as much cash as she could before she officially moved forward with divorce proceedings. And I might have suggested that she keep that cash in a safe place so that she would have it handy when she moved out of the home she shared with her husband. I knew she'd need some money for living expenses and the like."

"And your retainer, right?" Candice pressed.

Again, Velkune blushed. "Yes. I do require a retainer to begin divorce proceedings."

"How much?" she asked him.

"It varies, but usually I ask for twenty thousand up front."

My brow shot up. Twenty grand? Man, divorce was expensive.

"Were you aware that Bailey drained one of the Colquitts' joint savings accounts?"

Velkune's eyes widened, but my radar pinged. "No," he said. "I had no idea."

I tugged on my earlobe and I saw that Candice caught the move. Velkune was lying. He knew all about what Bailey had done.

Candice then told him about what'd happened at the Starbucks. "That's terrible!" he said. "I'll call Mrs. Colquitt as soon as we're finished and check on her."

"When we left her, she was shaken but unhurt," Candice assured him. "Still, that incident got me thinking about something else Bailey said when we sat down with her."

"What's that?" he asked.

"She said that you had given the same sort of advice to Kendra before she filed."

Velkune flushed red for a third time and cleared his throat. "Ms. Fusco, can I speak frankly?"

"Of course."

"When clients come to me suggesting that they might be in some sort of physical danger from their spouse and talk to me about the necessity of moving out of the family home, I do on those rare occasions suggest that they have access to any resource they can use to see them through the many months or years it may take to get divorced. While frowned upon by many courts, in making that kind of a suggestion, I have done nothing legally, ethically, or morally wrong."

Candice sat back in her chair and studied Velkune for a minute before commenting. "Yes, Mr. Velkune, I know you haven't done anything illegal, and I'm on your side, I swear, but what worries me is that Kendra might have taken your advice and drained one of the joint savings or checking accounts, and that could have triggered a violent reaction from her husband just like what nearly happened today between Bailey and Chase Colquitt. And if he in fact isn't responsible for his wife's disappearance, the minute a prosecutor figures out what you told Kendra to do, he'll have even more evidence to send Tristan away for murder. What you advised Kendra to do really complicates things. Do you see where I'm going with this?"

Garrett leaned his elbows on the desk and ran his hands through his hair. "Do you think that's what happened?" he asked. "Do you think that Kendra drained one of their accounts and Tristan reacted violently when he found out?"

"I don't know," Candice told him. "But we have to research every possible scenario. And when you said that Kendra came here the very morning she went missing, I'm quite positive that you were one of the very last people to see her alive. Did she come here with your retainer and can you think of anything that might help us figure out what she was thinking or planning to do next?"

Velkune sat back in his chair again. "Yes," he said, "that morning she did have some cash on her. It wasn't nearly enough for my full retainer, but it was enough to get us started. To be honest, she was in such a state of distress that I didn't press her on it."

"What was the state of distress about again?" Candice prompted.

"Well, she was of course worried for herself physically, but I believe her biggest fear was that she and her son would be separated. She had a sort of premonition and she felt strongly that Tristan would end up with Colby."

"So she was worried about custody?" Candice asked.

"Yes. She was intent on leaving her husband and the home, but she was very worried about what people would think by her doing that. She knew they'd talk and gossip and speculate, and she was concerned about how that might affect what people thought of her long term." Velkune then sighed and shook his head sadly back and forth. "She appeared to me to be very worried about everything, Ms. Fusco. I know I should have taken her fears more seriously, or given her more time that morning, but I had a wedding to get to. Still, I know I should have advised her to go to her parents' house or the police, but when she came here she had worked herself up into hysterics, and I wasn't sure how much of what she was saying was fact or fabrication. I'd be lying if I didn't tell you that her visit to my office that morning left me confused and upset. I didn't quite know what to think."

I listened with an intuitive ear to everything that Velkune had said and found that it all rang true. But I still wasn't convinced that Tristan was responsible, and none of it told us who the man in the baseball cap was.

Candice looked at me then and said, "Anything you want to ask?"

At first I almost said no, but then I thought back to that mysterious woman who had come to my office and first presented the case to me. I had a sudden desperate need to find her and attempt to convince her to tell us who had abducted and killed Kendra. She alone knew who was responsible, and while I could understand her situation and need to protect the attorney-client privilege, I wanted to find a way around that, a loophole that would allow her to hint at who'd done it so that we could bring Kendra home and never again allow this man to tear another family apart. "Mr. Velkune," I said, "can you tell me a little about the attorney-client privilege as it relates to keeping the secrets of someone you know to be guilty of a felony?"

Velkune pulled his head back and seemed confused by the change of topic. "I'm not sure I understand your question, Ms. Cooper."

I didn't want to reveal anything about the woman who'd come to see me. If I was going to protect her and her career, then I had to make sure I didn't even hint that we'd been visited by this female attorney. I decided to speak in hypotheticals. "Say you've been retained by someone you know has committed murder," I began. "But the police don't know that your client's done anything wrong, and you suspect that your client may do something violent in the future or even repeat that same crime again. Do you have the ability to break privilege and go to the police if you suspect the public at large is in danger?"

Velkune scratched his five-o'clock shadow. "That's tricky," he said. "You'd have to be more than just suspicious that the person was a threat to the public. And you'd need to have some sort of proof to back up and justify breaking the privilege, like a psychiatrist's analysis, or a letter from your client making threatening statements. Something concrete. It couldn't be subjective."

I frowned. That's what I was afraid of. "So if I was an attorney, and someone came to me, retained me, and said that they'd murdered someone but gave no concrete evidence of the crime and I had nothing factual to show the authorities, there'd be nothing I could do to alert the police to investigate the crime?"

Velkune shook his head. "Right," he said. "That'd definitely get you disbarred."

"Okay," I said, trying to word my next question just right. "What if you mentioned it to a friend, like, what if the attorney told someone they trusted and that friend went to the police. What would happen then?"

Velkune appeared amused by my hypothetical attempts to get around privilege. "That would still get the attorney disbarred and would definitely send the whole case into mistrial if it ever got out. I know it seems unbalanced and unfair, but our laws were created to protect the few innocent people caught up in the system. To protect the innocent you've also got to protect the guilty by extending everyone the same ironclad attorney-client privilege. Lawyers must be bound by that oath—to keep their clients' secrets and reveal them to no one—in order for the system to work. Otherwise, clients would never be able to trust their attorneys, and then they couldn't be assured the best defense." Velkune then subtly checked his watch and I knew he was anxious to get out of there and go to dinner with his new bride, so I stood up and thanked him for his time.

We passed Mrs. Velkune in the lobby and she wished us a good evening. "They're an odd couple," I said when we were outside and safely out of earshot.

"You aren't kidding," Candice said, holding her stomach again. The poor girl needed to get her butt to the drugstore soon. "I looked Velkune up after our first meeting, and the *Austin American-Statesmen* did a story on him and the missus after they announced their engagement. According to the paper, she comes from big oil money and he comes from a broken home. They met at some rodeo charity event where he says she wouldn't give him the time of day, but he swears it was love at first sight."

"I'm sure it was," I said with a wink.

Candice bumped me with her elbow. "Yeah, I'm pretty sure that's what everybody else thought too, but from what I read in the article, he seriously adores her. He says that she motivated him to change his life and he got out of riding steers and put himself through college, then law school. He sent her e-mails throughout the years he was in school, telling her how meeting her had redirected his life, and they struck up a correspondence, but she still refused to date him until he graduated from UT law school. The rest is history."

"Huh," I said, setting aside my skepticism as we got to the car. "So true love does exist?"

Candice grinned. "Aren't we both living proof?"

She had me there.

Around eleven o'clock that night I got a call from Candice. "You will never get to pick the restaurant again," she moaned. She sounded terrible.

I gasped. "You okay?"

"No, Sundance," she growled. "I'm seriously *not* okay."

Poor Candice had been sick since shortly after getting home, and it hadn't let up. I knew that Dutch was working late—he'd left me a message on my voice mail—and that probably meant that Brice would be working late too. "Have you heard from Brice?"

"He's still at the office," she confirmed.

"You should call him, sweetie," I said, already moving toward the closet to grab my coat and purse.

"No," she said weakly. "He's busy, and I look like hell."

"I'm on my way," I told her.

When I got to Candice's condo, I very nearly called an ambulance. She was so pale, she was gray, and she could barely hold her head up. She also insisted I just let her die in peace next to the commode. I called Brice immediately and told him in no uncertain terms to get his butt home. I'd never seen Candice looking so bad. I wasn't sure if I should call 911 or not, but I certainly couldn't help her with my stupid bum hips.

Both Brice and Dutch were at the door within ten minutes, and when Brice took one look at Candice, he threw a blanket around her, picked her up, and headed toward the door. Dutch and I followed them to the hospital and stayed with Brice until the nurse came out to tell us that Candice was suffering from food poisoning and that her kidney function wasn't so hot. They wanted to keep her overnight for observation. I felt a small wave of relief and knew she'd be okay. I said as much to Brice, but I also knew he'd worry about her until they released her.

Dutch and I drove home around one a.m., both of us weary to the bone.

The next morning, the minute I woke up I called Brice. He said that he'd just gotten home with Candice, and for now, she was resting comfortably. I promised to check in with them later and headed downstairs.

"Did you do something to your hair?" Dutch asked, handing me a steaming cup of joe after I filled him in about Candice's condition.

I ran a hand through my hair self-consciously. "It was Candice's idea."

"I like it," he said, an amused grin on his face.

I looked closely at him and saw the dark circles under his eyes. I wondered if he'd slept at all. "When was your last day off?" I asked.

He seemed surprised by my question. "Don't know. Maybe a couple weeks ago?"

I frowned. "You need to take a day."

Dutch gave me a lopsided smile. "As it happens, Gaston called while you were still in bed, and he agrees with you. He's giving me and Brice the morning off."

"Wow," I said flatly. "The whole morning? What *will* you do with all that time?"

"Tell me about your case," he said, not so subtly changing the subject.

I took a big sip from my mug. "It's nothing but dead ends. Everything leads to nowhere. I've never worked a case like it."

Dutch chuckled. "You mean you've never worked a case that you couldn't crack."

"True," I agreed. "And this one feels so elusive, you know?"

"How so?"

"There's no one in the suspect pool that feels good to me for the crime."

"No one?"

I shook my head. "Nope. And I feel like we've looked at just about everyone connected to Kendra that had any kind of motive to kill her."

"What if there was no motive?" Dutch asked. "Other than just to kill her, I mean. What if she was abducted and killed by some random psychopath?"

I weighed that against my radar and shook my head. "No," I said. "I really think she was killed by someone close to her. Someone she trusted enough to let into her home. I was in her house and I felt the energy, Dutch. She opened the door to her killer and turned her back to lead him inside. With her son in the house, she wouldn't have done that unless she felt safe."

"And you don't think the husband did it, right?"

"I can't tell. I want to say no, but he had too many motives and an anger-management issue, not to mention a terrifically flimsy alibi that anybody could poke holes in."

"What motives?" he asked.

I began to tick them off on my right hand. "Kendra was going to leave him, she'd just taken money out of their accounts, she could also very well have been having an affair with someone else . . ."

"So why aren't you sure it was him?" Dutch asked me. "I mean, all of that sounds like a prosecutor's dream."

I sighed. "There's this mysterious man in a baseball cap that we can't identify."

"What man?"

"The neighborhood exterminator saw a man who wasn't Tristan Moreno going into Kendra's home the morning she went missing. He also said that he'd seen that same man on a few other occasions."

"And he had no idea who the guy was?"

"No. And there was no car associated with this guy either—he always came on foot."

"Reasonable doubt," Dutch said, and I nodded. He'd just pointed out the one thing that was still really bugging Candice and me: The man in the ball cap created reasonable doubt for any of the accused unless we could definitively identify him.

"What other leads are you working?"

I filled Dutch in on the ones we'd covered, from Bailey to the creepy neighbor, and everybody in between. "You need to find out who the guy in the hat is," Dutch said.

"There you go, stating the obvious," I said dryly.

Dutch gave me a smart look and pulled out his cell phone. He tapped at it a few times, then put it to his ear. He then got up, squeezed my shoulder, and walked out of the kitchen without explanation.

I sighed heavily and got up to see about making some breakfast. No sooner had I pulled out the egg carton than Eggy and Tuttle appeared at my feet. Eggy got his name from his serious devotion to the incredible, edible egg.

I made a Spanish omelet for me and two little cheese omelets for Eggy and Tuttle. We had all started eating in companionable silence when Dutch came back into the kitchen. "What's cooking?" he asked.

"My breakfast," I told him smartly. I make a mean omelet but manage to overcook (i.e., set on fire) just about everything else.

"No breakfast for me?"

I eyed the fridge and the stove meaningfully. "Knock yourself out."

"Ah," Dutch said, selecting a fork from the drawer and coming to sit next to me at the table. "Is that how it is?"

I took a huge bite of the omelet and shoved it into my mouth. "Mmm-hmmm," I told him.

"I see," he said. "Even though I just scored you a major lead on your case?"

I raised one eyebrow skeptically. Sure he had a lead. And pigs were probably flying around our roofline right now.

Dutch raised his fork in the air like he expected me to scoot my plate right underneath it so he could have all the rest of it. "Another woman has gone missing," Dutch said.

My eyes widened, and I swallowed the big bite of food. "Who?"

"Donna King. Missing since yesterday. The police are working the scene right now, and so far, they've found some blood and signs of a struggle but no evidence of a weapon or a body."

"Why do they think it's the same person who abducted Kendra?"

Dutch stopped eyeing my omelet and looked at me. "King lives on the other side of Decker Lake from where Kendra's car was found, and King's car is also missing. The clincher for you, however, is that a neighbor remembers seeing a guy with a ball cap walking up the road close to her home around eight o'clock last night."

I gasped. "Was anybody else besides King there at her house at the time?"

"No. She lived alone. Her paralegal went to her house when she didn't show up this morning."

I dropped my fork. "Her *paralegal*?"

Dutch's expression turned curious. "Yeah. King's an attorney."

I pushed the rest of my omelet at Dutch and got up from the table, making sure to give him a big old smooch and a hug before I hobbled upstairs to shower and change.

Dutch and I arrived at King's house just as the CSI techs were finishing up. There weren't any cops in suits around when Dutch flashed his FBI badge at the patrol officer guarding the scene. "Where's everybody at?" he asked the beat cop.

"They've wrapped it up for now," the cop told him. "CSI's almost done too, from what I hear."

"Mind if we go in and take a look?"

"As long as you don't take all day, it's no skin off my back," the cop said with a shrug.

I loved it when Dutch made my life easy. As we moved to the door, I pointed to Dutch's badge. "You gotta score me one of those, cowboy."

"You get into enough trouble as is," he told me, stopping to put on a pair of rubber gloves and blue booties before helping me into a pair of the same. Once our hands and feet were properly covered, we went inside. I walked just behind him as we made our way through the large wood door with a beautiful knocker. Donna's home was stately and elegant and impeccably neat, except for one wall, which was a hot mess. Near the front door was a side table lying on its side and marked with little numbered evidence tags. Small bits of glass and pottery littered the floor, and I could only guess that the larger shards had been put into evidence bags already. A planter down the hall had been overturned, and dirt and leaves were strewn about as if someone had been dragged backward and had clawed at anything that might have given them a hold.

In fact, as I opened up my radar, that's exactly what I pictured; Donna being dragged backward down the hall, knowing she was going to die and fighting for all she was worth.

We followed the debris, moving past the staircase and stepping carefully to the far side of the hall. As we moved beyond the stairs, a large living room opened up, decorated in shades of soft tans and whites. Numbered tags marked where the sofa had been pulled away from its normal spot, evident by the leg indentations in the plush carpet. Pillows were missing from the sofa, but large paper bags set to the side seemed to carry their shape. Toward the edge of the couch was a spatter of blood, and two techs were working to cut out the carpet that contained the droplets.

My radar was also picking up the violence that had taken place here. Donna had fought her attacker, and I felt strongly that she'd angered him by either striking him or saying something that had caused him to lose his temper and hit her hard enough to draw blood.

My attention moved away from the techs to two beautiful windowed doors that opened up to the backyard. One of those doors was open. The doors were ornately decorated in glass and iron, but I could hardly admire them, because the energy of Donna's struggle was building inside me and drawing me to the backyard. "Can we go out there?" I whispered.

Dutch nodded and carefully maneuvered me past the techs—who hardly looked up as we edged by them.

At the door I paused to take off the booties and happened to look down at the frame of the closed door. There was a bloody handprint there that I knew belonged to Donna by its angle and the way the blood smeared toward the edge. She'd grabbed hold here but was yanked free.

In the backyard another tech was carefully scanning the backyard with a metal detector, while yet another one bagged clumps of grass. Dutch pointed and I looked up, seeing the garage door open and the bay empty. Donna's car was gone.

Beyond the backyard was nothing but woodland. Donna's house backed up to the greenbelt that surrounded Decker Lake, and her closest neighbors were fifty feet away, with high fencing blocking anything that might've taken place here the night before.

My eye, however, kept going back to those woods, and I thought about the intuitive hit I'd gotten surrounding Kendra's remains. "He wouldn't bury her in Donna's backyard, would he?" I said to myself. Even as I spoke the words, I knew they were true. What better way to keep his attorney from going to the police than by putting Kendra's body close enough to cast the hint of suspicion on her. He could probably even claim that she'd been in on the murder, and then I wondered something else—had she? Had she been the woman I'd seen in the ether who had some sort of power over the murderer? Maybe the killer had lost his romantic interest in her and had grown tired of her as a loose thread. He could have killed her to keep her silent.

But then, if she was in on the murder, why had she come to me in the first place?

But wait—was it really her? Was Donna King really the mysterious Ms. Smith?

I went back to the door, shoved the booties on again and gimped inside. Gazing around the living room, I looked for anything that could tell me what Donna had looked like. On a side table to the far right I found a set of pictures and headed over to them for closer inspection. I picked Donna out from a group photo right away. Now that I had her image in front of me, I could recognize her chin and jawline from when she'd come to my office in her wig, hat, and sunglasses. She'd been far prettier than I'd originally guessed, with big brown eyes and wavy black hair. She'd been a stunning woman, but her image was now flat and one-dimensional to my eye, telling me with certainty that she too was dead.

"That answers that question," I muttered, moving back to the door, doing the bootie dance again and quickly growing tired of hauling the things off and on with my aching hips. Once I stepped out to the yard again, I hedged a bit closer to the woods, scanning them for any hint of Kendra.

The sky had been overcast all morning, and a slight drizzle began to fall. The air smelled like wet dirt, and I remembered again the scents that had fluttered under my nose when I was first trying to find Kendra's remains in the ether.

My head swiveled to the left-hand side of the yard. The energy of Kendra's remains was faint, but it was there. I just knew it. My intuition then bumped into something else and I realized that Donna King was also somewhere in those woods.

I looked for Dutch; he was over by the garage, talking to yet another CSI guy. "Hey," I called to him.

Dutch came over and announced, "They're scanning

the lake for her car, and they're hoping if they find it that they'll also find a body this time."

"They won't," I told him. Then I pointed to the woods. "She's in there. And Kendra's body is nearby too."

Dutch seemed surprised, but he didn't question me; one of the many things I loved about him was that he absolutely trusted my radar. "Stay here," he said as he moved off toward the foliage, squinting at the vegetation at the edge of the yard. Dutch then moved over to the garage again and I saw him walk right to a shovel hanging from a peg. He turned to the CSI tech while pointing to the shovel, and they exchanged a few words before Dutch came back to me. "The shovel has fresh dirt on it," he said.

I frowned and looked back toward the woods. "That rat bastard."

Dutch then motioned for us to go back inside and we stopped at the rear door to once again don the booties before carefully wending our way through the house to the front door. There we found the same beat cop standing at the door. "Hey, buddy," Dutch said in his most friendly voice. "I noticed some bent vegetation on the left side of the house and a shovel in the garage with fresh dirt on it. Did anyone bring in the cadaver dogs yet?"

"No," the cop said, already reaching for his phone. "Which side of the yard?" he asked Dutch as he held the phone to his ear.

"The left. I think your intruder might have taken her back there."

The cop nodded, then began to talk into the phone. "Yeah, we got a situation here," he said. "Can you tell Captain Ramirez we may need some cadaver dogs down here?"

Dutch moved me back into the hallway out of the cop's earshot and said, "Did you get anything else?"

I pulled him along to the back again, over to the table with King's picture on it. Pointing to the frame, I said, "That's her on the left."

"You're positive she's . . . ?"

"Yeah," I said bitterly. "She's dead."

"You wanna take a tour around the house to see if you pick up anything else?"

I studied Donna's photo a bit longer, feeling the knot of anger and frustration form in my stomach. If only I could have figured out some clue to her identity and reached her before this happened. I should have been looking for her. It was a serious lapse in judgment to focus on Kendra without considering how much danger the woman who'd come into my office might be in. And then I had it. "Dutch!" I said, whirling around. "I know how to find out who did this!"

"How?"

"Donna came to me just a few days after Kendra went missing, but she was in disguise when we met and she gave me a false name. She admitted to being a lawyer and said that one of her clients was responsible for murdering Kendra, but she had to protect his identity; otherwise, she could be disbarred. I think she was killed by this client of hers who also killed Kendra, and I think the reason he killed her was that he suspected she was super nervous about protecting him, and maybe she was ready to break the attorney-client privilege and go to the authorities. All the police have to do is go through Donna's records and figure out who retained her right before she came to see me, and they'll be able to narrow down who killed her!"

Dutch took out his phone and made a call. While he

was talking to whoever his source was, I moved back to
the front door, carefully sidestepping the debris again. I
stopped in the foyer and studied the scene. The overturned side table kept pulling my attention, and I walked
to the front door and studied it, finding it covered in
black fingerprint powder. Outside, the patrol officer
looked up at me as I played with the door and I nodded
at him before imagining Donna opening the door and
seeing someone there who surprised her, then turning
quickly around and being hit or pushed from behind,
which sent her crashing into the table. No. That wasn't
right. I stood there with my free arm outstretched and
my eyes closed and really *felt* the energy in that hallway.
I had a sudden sharp buzzing sensation in my lower
back, and my legs went weak, forcing me to lean heavily
on my cane. The sensation was identical to the one I'd
felt at Kendra's, but now I had a much clearer impression of what'd happened.

My eyes snapped open and I suddenly realized how
the two women had been overpowered so quickly. I
couldn't wait to tell Dutch, but then something else that'd
been niggling around in my mind bubbled to the surface.
Something about this crime scene bugged me, and it was
that Donna knew that the guy who killed Kendra was
dangerous, so why'd she open the door to him?

"Hey," said Dutch from right behind me, and I startled, letting out a squeal of surprise. The beat cop
looked at me like I was a little weird, and, embarrassed,
I rounded on Dutch.

"Dude! Don't sneak up on the cripple!"

"Sorry," he said, pointing to his feet. "It's the booties.
They squash your footsteps. What'd you pick up?"

"I think Donna and Kendra were both Tased," I said,
moving to the door again.

"Tased?"

"Yeah," I said, distracted as I leaned forward to look through the peephole. "They were hit with a Taser from behind directly in their lower backs, and it rendered them almost completely helpless, at least for as long as it took their killer to secure them."

I couldn't see a thing out the peephole. It was blurry, like something was smudging the view.

"Makes sense," my fiancé said. "Didn't you know that if you hit someone in the lower back with a stun gun it'll paralyze them for at least ten to fifteen minutes?"

I stepped back to open the door again. "No, Sherlock, I didn't know that." Sometimes it irritated me that Dutch was so friggin' smart about all things crime fighting.

As I looked at the peephole on the outside of the door, I could see something goopy covering it. I squinted and motioned to Dutch. "Hey," I said. "Come here."

He did and I pointed to the goop. "Looks like Vaseline," he said.

"Now look through the peephole."

He did. "Huh. This guy's smart. If he'd covered the peephole completely, King probably would've thought twice about opening the door, but by making it only look blurry, he knew her curiosity would get the better of her and she'd open up to take a look."

"He's freaky smart, this guy," I muttered. "Cunning even."

Dutch called out to one of the crime scene techs still in the living room, and when she poked her head out to see what was up, he pointed to the door. "Did you guys tag the peephole?"

She squinted at it. "No. Why?"

"You'll want to take a swab and call the lead detective," he said. "It's covered in Vaseline."

With that, he bent down, pulled off the booties, helped me with mine, then took my hand and led me out of the house. "We'll need to go now before they start asking why the FBI is taking such an interest," he whispered as he walked us straight to the car.

"Good thinking," I said. "By the way, who've you been getting all your info from?"

"One of the junior detectives in homicide," Dutch said. "The kid's first day was the day Kendra went missing. I just told him that if he wanted to make a good impression, he needed to be out here when the cadaver dogs arrived, and I also told him about the dirty shovel and that I saw a faint trail, like something had been dragged through the woods from the left side of the yard."

I gave Dutch a pat on the arm. "You're pretty smart yourself, cowboy. How'd you meet this junior detective, anyway?"

"At the gym. The kid's bright and eventually wants to switch to the FBI. I'm giving him a little advice about how to play it."

"Aw! You've got a little protégé!"

"Quit it," Dutch said, but he was grinning all the same.

I asked Dutch to stop by Candice's on our way home, but he got a call from the office that he needed to go in, so he dropped me at the house and I had to drive over myself. Brice answered the door, and he looked worse for wear too. "How is she?" I asked when he let me in.

"Still sleeping." He then eyed me in that way that suggested he was about to ask me a favor.

"Yes," I said to him.

That took him aback. "I haven't asked you anything yet."

"I'm making it easy for you," I told him, pointing to the door. "Go to the office, Brice. I'll stay with her."

He kissed me on the cheek and promised to call in a few hours to see how Candice was doing.

I peeked into her room and saw that she was sleeping, but she still looked awful. While I waited for her to wake up, I picked up the living room and cleaned the dishes in the sink. Candice was a neat freak, and Brice was too, which meant the unusual clutter in their condo was a sign of how sick Candice was and how stressed-out Brice was.

After that, I sat on the couch and channel surfed but soon got bored. Seeing Candice's cell phone gave me an idea. I opened her recording app and within about ten minutes I'd e-mailed myself all the recordings from all of the interviews we'd done. I knew that Candice would be out of the investigation business for at least the next few days, and while I had nothing going on at the office, I wanted to devote all my time to figuring out who'd killed Kendra and Donna.

As if on cue, my own phone rang, and Dutch said that he'd just gotten a call from his little buddy at homicide. They'd found a woman's badly decomposed body in the woods behind Donna's house. "The remains are too old to be King's," he said.

"That's because they're Kendra's," I told him. "Have they figured out a COD?"

"Not yet," he told me. "Like I said, the body's in pretty rough shape. All they can tell for sure is that it's a naked female with brown hair."

I found it hard to swallow after that. "Okay, well, when they find King's body, will you call me?"

"Will do."

My radar binged. "I think she's a bit farther back

than Kendra. They should let the dogs keep looking in the same area but deeper into the woods."

"I'll tell him," Dutch promised. "One thing that bugs me, though, dollface—if the killer buried King in the woods behind her house, why'd he take her car?"

"He's trying to establish a pattern," I said. "He's creating reasonable doubt all over the place. Unless the police find a definitive connection between Kendra and Donna, they may start to think there's some local Decker Lake serial killer out there randomly selecting women to attack in their homes."

"I told my homicide buddy about your theory that they needed to check King's clients."

"What'd he say?"

"He says that since that's probably gonna require a lot of sifting through paperwork that it'll likely fall to him anyway, so he's going to request the assignment as soon as he gets back to the station. The tricky thing is getting King's office to give up the records."

"Why would that be tricky?" I asked.

"Because privilege may still apply. If King had a partner at her firm, I doubt we'll get the files released without a court order, and that could take time."

"Well, that sucks," I grumbled.

"Yeah, but you're still working the case, so it ain't all bad."

My man. So good to me!

"Any closer to figuring out which of your suspects it is?" he asked next.

I sat back on the couch and sighed. "No. But I just sent myself all the interview tapes we've done on this case. Maybe going back through them will help me figure out a clue that'll point me in the right direction."

Dutch switched topics then. "How's your partner in crime?"

"Resting comfortably. How're you two holding up?"

Dutch lowered his voice to barely a whisper. "I'm worried about Brice. The guy looks dead on his feet."

"Yeah, well, it shocks me that the two of you are still standing," I told him. "Is there any way you guys can get a little time off for good behavior?"

"It's got to be Gaston's idea, cupcake, and he's so determined to keep this case out of the hands of Homeland Security that he'll drive us into the ground if he has to."

I frowned. Why was Gaston so territorial suddenly? "Well, at least make sure you're eating when you're supposed to, okay? No more skipping meals and showing up at home thirsty for a bottle of scotch."

"Still want to be my bartender?" he asked me smoothly.

"I just want you home, cowboy. I really miss you."

"This can't last forever," he promised. "Listen, maybe I can get off on time tonight and you and me can order in and watch a movie or something together. How's that sound?"

"Pretty damn good," I told him.

I could almost hear the grin in Dutch's voice when he said, "I'm gonna let that quarter to the swear jar go, Edgar, just 'cause I love you."

After I hung up with Dutch, I listened to some of the interviews again, writing notes as I went through the recordings, trying to put this big puzzle together. I still didn't have a good feel for the killer, and that nagging feeling that I was missing something big wouldn't leave me.

Candice slept through the entire afternoon, and only when it started to get dark outside did I hear her call out weakly for Brice.

I went to her room armed with a glass of Gatorade, knowing she'd probably been unable to eat or drink anything since getting home from the hospital about ten hours earlier. "How ya doin', sweetie?" I asked when I sat on her bed.

"Great," she replied, her voice hoarse and croaky. "Never better."

I offered her the Gatorade but she made a face and shook her head. "Not yet."

I smoothed her hair away from her eyes. "Man. You look *bad*, Cassidy."

She gave me a faint smile. "What'd you do all day?"

"Hung out here while Brice went to work."

Candice sank back against her pillows. "Will you stay until he gets home?"

"Duh," I said, stroking her tangled hair away from her eyes. The poor thing!

Candice closed her lids tiredly. "Thanks, Sundance. I owe you."

I waited until she was asleep again. I really wanted to tell her about Donna King, but I refused to talk shop when she was so sick.

Dutch called around six to tell me that he and Brice were calling it a night and Brice would be home in about ten minutes. I waited for him to arrive before leaving, and when he came through the door, I was brought up short. He looked dead on his feet. "How is she?" he asked.

"Probably in better shape than you."

"I'm fine," he said stubbornly, heading to the bedroom to see his fiancée for himself. He was back in a minute, tugging at his tie. "Thanks, Abby," he said dully. "I've got it from here."

I raised a skeptical eyebrow, glanced at the clock, then pointed to the couch. "Sit," I ordered before turning to the kitchen, where I rooted around in the fridge and hauled out a beer and the makings for a sandwich. After taking the beer to Brice, I whipped together two roast beef sandwiches with all the toppings, a side of chips, and another beer—as gourmet a meal as I can make without setting the house on fire. I took the fixings over to Brice, who by now was sitting on the couch staring numbly at the TV. "Eat," I told him after setting down the sandwiches and beer. I then waited until he actually took a bite before I headed out the door.

When I got home, I found Dutch in much the same condition as his boss. He too was staring numbly at the TV, but he'd managed to find his own beer. I moved right to our kitchen, fed the dogs, and threw together a dinner composed of leftover meatloaf and mashed potatoes. I almost opened a can of corn and heated that up, but all the meals I'd "cooked" that day had turned out well, so why push my luck?

After I set down Dutch's dinner in front of him, he pulled his attention from the TV long enough to thank me, but he didn't eat much and by eight o'clock he was snoring on my shoulder. So much for our movie and cuddle time.

I eased Dutch's head onto a pillow, threw an afghan over him, and went into the study to make a call. "Gaston," I heard on the other end of the line.

"It's Abby."

"Abigail," he said warmly, but still I could hear the fatigue in his voice too. "What can I do for you?"

I bit my lip, hesitating before I spoke because I knew, deep in my gut, that this was probably gonna cost me. "You're killing my fiancé and you're killing Brice too."

Gaston was silent for so long, I almost thought he'd hung up. "This is a difficult case, Abigail, one I asked you to help us resolve, but I was told you wanted nothing to do with it."

And there it was. The unspoken ultimatum. Gaston wanted my help, and if he didn't get it, he'd work Brice and Dutch down to two tired nubs. But I could be tricky too, if I wanted. "Sir, there's a reason I was adamant about opting out of the investigation."

"And what reason is that?"

"Because I could see that my involvement was going to somehow cause the case to become muddled. I looked into the ether and I saw you and your team resolving this case successfully, and that you were going to do that without me at your side. It's important for me in times like that to honor what I can see in the ether, and not risk leading you in the wrong direction."

Again the silence stretched out between us while Gaston considered his next move. "You won't help us even identify if this bombing was an isolated incident or the beginnings of something far more sinister?"

Dammit. (Okay, so swearing probably counted here. Put me down for a quarter.) Gaston was feeling around for my input, and I had no idea how much I could give him without mucking it up. But I knew I needed to give him something or he'd continue to push Dutch and Brice to the breaking point. "There will be more," I said, closing my eyes against the vision of that horrible scene at the mall in College Station from the video he'd shown me. "I know you're thinking that this could have been a homegrown terrorist cell at work, but, sir, it doesn't feel like that's the case, and you'll need to keep digging. Stop getting distracted by the theory that this was the work of a terrorist, and start focusing on the fact that someone is trying to make a very large statement here."

"Where do we look?" he asked me, and I seriously wanted to yell at him. The more I looked into this, the more dangerous it became that I'd say something that would delay or throw off the investigation in some way.

"I can't answer that, sir," I told him. "And please don't ask me anything more about it. I promise you that you and your team will be the ones to resolve the case, but I can't be a part of it, and unless you give Brice and Dutch a little time off, you're going to miss something big too."

"Can you just tell me how long before we resolve it?" he asked.

I sighed. Gaston was always pushing. "A few weeks, sir. Two, maybe three at the most."

Gaston was quiet again, and I crossed my fingers, hoping he'd give me what I wanted. "All right, Abigail," he said at last.

"All right what, sir?"

"All right, you've won your fiancé and Agent Harrison some time off. Please let them know that they may take the weekend—but if something important comes up I reserve the right to call them in."

"Got it. And thank you, sir. I really appreciate it."

I didn't know if Gaston was going to call Brice and tell him not to come in, but while I was cleaning up the dishes trying to decide whether to risk a call to tell him, my own phone pinged with an incoming text from Brice. It read:

Gaston just called. Thanks. I owe you one.

"Phew!" I said before going to wake up Dutch, tell him the good news, then get him upstairs to bed. That night he slept like a rock, and I sat up long into the wee hours wishing I could resolve at least one of the cases we were working on.

Chapter Fifteen

The next morning I had an early physical therapy appointment. I left the house without waking Dutch but called him on my way back home. He was just getting up after sleeping nearly fourteen straight hours. "How'd it go?" he asked when I told him where I'd been.

"It went great!" I said, feeling excited about the session for the first time in ages. "I actually took two whole steps without the cane!"

"That's great, dollface!" he said. "You on your way home now?"

"I am, and I'm ready to spend the *whole* day with you! So tell me, what would you like to do today?"

When Dutch didn't immediately reply, I tried to encourage him by suggesting we do something fun. "We should totally go out," I said. "I mean, when was the last time you and I went on an actual date?"

"It has been a while . . ."

"It really has. So how about you pick something you

really want to do with me today, and I get to pick something tomorrow?" Again Dutch seemed to hesitate, so I added, "Come on, cowboy! I'll do anything you want, no questions or complaints. You pick and I'll go along with it." I had visions of a sports bar with a big plate of hot wings and ice-cold beer, or an action flick with a plate of hot wings and an ice-cold beer, or a bowling alley with a plate of hot wings and an ice-cold beer.

"You really up for *anything* I want to do?" he asked.

"Yes!" I said loudly, really getting into the idea of a plate of hot wings and an ice-cold beer.

"Well, if it's anything, I want to take you to the shooting range so you can try out your new gun."

Feck. I'd walked right into that one.

"Hello?" he said when I didn't reply.

"I'm here," I said, trying to find a way out of the giant hole I'd just dug for myself. Finally, though, I figured that an hour at the shooting range with my sweetheart on his day off really wasn't *so* terrible. Especially if we could do the wings and beer afterward. "Okay, cowboy, I'm in."

"Wait . . . ," he said. "You *are*?"

That made me laugh. "Yes, you big goober. I should be home in about fifteen minutes, and I'll change and we'll go to the range." But just then my phone's appointment reminder went off and I turned the display toward me. "Aw, crap!" I said loudly.

"What?"

"Cat had my phone and she answered it when the vet called with a reminder that Eggy and Tuttle are due for their shots. My oh-so-helpful sister scheduled them both for today, and I totally forgot!"

"When's the appointment?"

"In twenty minutes." I'd never make it home in time to grab them and get them to the vet.

"Good thing I'm off today," Dutch said, already whistling for the pooches.

"You don't mind taking them?"

"Not at all," he said. "But when we get back, we're going to that range, Edgar. You're learning to shoot that gun today."

"I promise," I vowed.

Before he hung up, Dutch informed me that he'd had a call from his buddy the detective downtown. "They found King's body late last night."

I knew she was dead, but to hear Dutch confirm it made me catch my breath. "That bastard," I said.

"Looks like you were right on the Taser too, Edgar. They found small burn marks all over King's body, and the preliminary report from the coroner is that she was hog-tied and buried facedown alive."

"Smothered," I whispered into the phone. "That's how Kendra was killed too."

"You're probably right, although with Kendra the moist ground did a number on her remains."

I scrunched up my face in distaste. How were guys able to talk so freely about the graphic details?

"There was one interesting fact that the coroner was able to get from Kendra's body, though."

"What was that?"

"She was pregnant."

I nearly drove my car onto the shoulder. "No way!"

"Way."

"Whose kid is it?" If Kendra was having an affair and she got pregnant, then it likely wasn't Tristan's because he'd admitted they hadn't been intimate for months.

"We won't know that answer for several weeks, if not months, Abs. You know how slow the labs are."

"It's the killer's baby," I said, knowing it with absolute certainty. "And it's why he was so angry at her. He murdered her because he found out she was pregnant."

"You're assuming quite a bit, aren't you, sweetheart?"

Dutch. Ever the voice of reason. Even when it was crazy wrong. "Trust me on this, cowboy. I'm right." Then I switched topics. "Were they able to recover any forensic details at the burial sites?"

"Not much," he said. "The best they have so far is a man's footprint—size eleven."

"So he's tall."

"Most likely around six feet," Dutch said.

That fit Tristan, and from what I remembered of Dr. Snyder, him too—but not Russ, who was by my recollection only about five-nine. Then another person entered my mind, and I considered Chase Colquitt, who was also at least five-eleven. But what motive would he have to kill Kendra? And did he have any connection to Donna King?

"You there?" Dutch asked, and I realized I'd been quiet for a few moments.

"Yeah, I'm here," I said. "Anyway, I don't want to make you and the pups late. I'll head home and change and you can pick me up as soon as you're done."

"It's a date," he replied in that oh-so-sexy baritone he has. I smiled as I hung up the phone. God, I loved that man.

I thought about what Dutch had learned from his detective buddy the whole rest of the way home, and coming into a house that was still and quiet seemed to cement the melancholy mood of the morning. It unsettled me to walk into a familiar place with no other heartbeat than mine. After I'd changed out of my sweats into jeans and a light cotton shirt, I came downstairs and saw the box with my gun in it on the coffee table. "Subtle," I said, heading to the kitchen for a Coke.

While I was waiting for Dutch to get back, I called Candice to see how she was feeling and was surprised when she answered sounding so much like her old self. "Hey," she said. "I hear you've been playing nursemaid and labor advocate."

I grinned. "Guilty as charged. How're you doing?"

"Much better, but Brice hasn't done anything but sleep since he got home last night. Thanks for that, by the way."

"My pleasure," I then filled her in on the latest development in the Kendra Moreno case, telling her about Donna King and how they'd found Taser marks all over her body. "I'm sure that's what I felt when I was at the Morenos' on the steps by the front door. I think he used the stun gun to take her down and incapacitate her."

"That'd be the way to do it," Candice said. "A stun gun to the lower back sends an electrical impulse right into your spinal cord. It'll drop you and leave you paralyzed for a while."

"Yeah, well, hopefully the police will be able to work their way through King's list of recent clients and see who didn't have an alibi for last night." I then told her about Kendra's pregnancy.

"You know what, Abs?" Candice suddenly said.

"What?"

"Do you remember how you said that you suspected this killer had done this type of thing before?"

"Yeah, but we already looked into that and came up empty."

"Not necessarily," she said. "Maybe we didn't plug in the right variables. We didn't know at the time that a Taser was used. I wonder if we look into crimes where someone used a Taser to rape or murder women if we'll come up with anything."

"That'd take waking up your fiancé," I said.

Candice exhaled loudly. "Poor Brice," she said. "Well, he's had fifteen hours of sleep. He needs to wake up for some breakfast sometime."

"Are you in any shape to cook?"

"Toast," she said. "Toast and coffee."

I laughed. "Okay, Cassidy, good luck with that, and call me if you get anything or if you need us to bring you guys some sustenance other than toast and coffee. Dutch and I are headed to the gun range in a few, so if I don't answer it's because I'm dodging bullets."

It was Candice's turn to laugh, and she wished me—and Dutch—luck before hanging up.

While I waited for my fiancé to get home, I leafed through all the notes I'd made while listening to the interviews we'd already conducted. What bugged me was that either my lie detector was off or everyone we'd talked to was telling the truth, because except for a few lies that we'd already exposed, no one's interview triggered my *liar, liar, pants on fire* . . .

While I was pondering all that, my radar gave a ping of warning. "Uh-oh," I said, picking up my head and looking toward the door. "Cat," I muttered. My sister was on her way over, and I couldn't leave because Dutch would kill me if I stuck him with her on his first day off in ages.

I texted Dutch and asked how much longer he was going to be, just as my radar gave another warning ping. He replied that he'd just wrapped it up with the vet and he was on his way back home with the pooches. I knew it'd take him fifteen minutes or so, and I became anxious because I didn't know if he'd make it in time to beat my sister to the door. I didn't tell him that she was on her way; I just told him to hurry.

While I waited, I tried to concentrate on the Moreno case, but I was too jittery. "Focus!" I said to myself, picking up my notes again. There wasn't anything I could do about my sister; if she beat Dutch here, I'd just have to deal with her. My radar gave another urgent ping, and I snapped, "Yes, yes! I know, okay?!"

With irritation, I shuffled through the notes, trying to get back on track. What had I been focusing on before the warning bell had gone off about Cat? Oh, yeah, the fact that everybody we interviewed seemed to be telling the truth. That could be because we hadn't spoken to the killer yet, but something told me that we had interviewed him. "But who's lying?" I asked aloud, looking back through my notes one last time . . . And then I had it. "Holy shit!" I gasped. (Swearing doesn't count when you've just cracked the case.) I wondered how on earth I'd missed it before. With shaking hands, I grabbed my cell and called Candice. "Come on, come on!" I urged as her cell rang and rang. But finally, she answered just as my doorbell rang.

"Brice is calling in the search on any perps with Tasers," she said. "Can I call you back in two minutes?"

"No!" I told her, glaring angrily at the front door. Cat and her stupid timing! The doorbell rang again, and I impatiently got up to open it. I'd give her a piece of my mind the moment after I told Candice my news. "I know who did it!" I said, trying to juggle my cane and the cell and the door at the same time. "Hang on, though," I added as I pulled it open. I'd been so sure that the alarm pinging in my head was to warn me about my sister that I hadn't even considered that the alarm might be for someone else altogether, and as the person standing on my doorstep was revealed, I realized my horrible mistake.

"Abby?" Candice said. "You there?"

Kendra Moreno's killer grinned wickedly at me as I stared at him, my mouth agape and frightened down to my toes. "Hey there," he said casually, his eyes peeking out from under a U.T. ball cap. "Funny catching you here all alone, huh?"

"Abby?" I heard Candice say, more urgently this time.

I began to tremble and felt my knees grow weak. I dropped the phone and took a step back, unable to speak or scream or plead.

The friendly smile vanished, and out from behind the killer's back appeared a long thin rod ending in a forked prong. I shrieked and whirled around, but my hips gave out and I went crashing to the floor.

In the next instant I felt the most god-awful hot sting of an electrical current pulsing up and down my spine. It hurt so much and was so consuming that I couldn't even breathe. I just felt my whole body seize, and the torturous sensation seemed to go on and on.

Finally the current subsided and I was left to weakly draw in oxygen but otherwise lie there completely helpless. In the background I heard the faint sound of Candice's shouts through the phone. Garrett Velkune picked up the cell with a gloved hand and chucked it so hard, it hit the wall, smashing into a thousand pieces.

"So you little bitches figured it out, huh?" he said, leaning down to pull my head up by the hair. "I got a visit from a newbie detective this morning. The runt said he heard that some psychic lady was working the case, and she had a hunch that Donna had been murdered by one of her clients. He said the psychic had told him right where to find Donna's body, along with another woman who'd been missing for a couple of weeks now. He saw my name on Donna's client roster, and he also saw an invitation to my wedding stuck to her fridge. He said he'd already spoken to one of the wedding guests—turns out I was a half hour late to the big event, and he wondered what I'd been doing that'd made me so late to my own wedding."

I tried to scream . . . to move . . . to kick . . . to do *any*-thing, but my body refused to cooperate. I was rocked by spasms that left me utterly helpless and completely vulnerable.

"I knew you and your girlfriend were close to the truth," he hissed, slamming my head down violently into the floor and splitting my lip in the process. "I just needed a little more time to convince my wife to move with me out of the country someplace with no extradition. There're plenty of cozy little islands you can set yourself up on, you know," he said, picking my head up again to glare angrily into my eyes.

Tears leaked down my cheeks and my ears rang with the pain of the head slam. "Puh . . . puh . . . puh . . . ," I stuttered. It was the only sound I could make. I couldn't even get the word "please" out. Not that it mattered. Garrett was way beyond mercy at that point.

With a look of disgust, he pushed my head away and stood up. "You couldn't just let the police go with Tristan, could you?" he snapped, kicking me hard in the leg. I felt nothing, and that terrified me. "Do you know how hard I worked to win Seely over?" he said next. "I *love* my wife, okay? And before I got married, I wanted one last little fling with no strings attached, and who better to have a fling with than a woman who's about to leave her husband?"

Kendra. He'd had an affair with Kendra. I could see it all in the ether around him, how he'd seduced her and slept with her and thought nothing of it until she'd shown up in his office the morning of his wedding and told him that she was pregnant. And he hadn't lied to us in the interviews. He'd been totally honest. The last time he'd seen Kendra, she had been terrified and afraid for her life. And she'd been equally terrified about leaving her son, and her home, and having no one realize what'd happened to her. Velkune could state all those facts clearly because he'd been there, listening to Kendra plead for her life. A plea he'd ignored.

"That little bitch wanted to ruin everything!" he growled. "She waltzes into my office on my wedding day and announces that she's pregnant and she's leaving her husband. She wants me to know she's going to file for child support. She says the kid is mine, and she wants me to be a part of its life. She then tells me that she wants me to leave Seely for *her*! Like I'd ever leave my angel Seely for a whore like that! I knew what she was up to too. If I went through with the wedding I could tell she was going to tell my wife about the kid! Seely would have left me in a hot second!"

Garrett was so angry that he kicked me in the thigh again. I knew the blow was bad, but I still felt nothing. I was close to losing it until I realized I could wiggle my fingers. Dutch was on his way home, and if I could keep Garrett talking, maybe, just maybe, Dutch could get here before it was too late.

Garrett grabbed me by the back of my shirt, lifting my torso completely off the ground. I could see the cattle prod in his right hand and I prayed like I've never prayed before that he wouldn't use it on me again. "Donna was one of Seely's bridesmaids. I knew she'd be at the church all morning helping Seely get ready, and she's got all those woods behind her house to hide a body in. I broke into her garage, borrowed her shovel, and buried that bitch. Then all I had to do was drive Kendra's car around the back side of the lake and let it slip into the water.

"The whole thing would've gone off without a hitch too if I hadn't left the cattle prod at Donna's. When I went back to get it, Donna was there. She came back for a steamer because Seely's dress was wrinkled or some bullshit. She saw me coming out of the woods, dirty, sweaty, carrying the cow prod, and with a fair amount of blood on my shirt. I knew right then that the only way to keep her from talking was to retain her on the spot as my attorney and hope she kept her mouth shut—but she obviously didn't, because she came to see you, didn't she?"

I realized that Velkune had put all my little hypotheticals together, and he'd known that Donna had come to me. That's why he'd killed her. I'd been the one to seal her fate, and that was an awful thing to realize.

I sucked in a ragged breath and closed my eyes. I had to think, and I couldn't do that with the horrible feelings of guilt, fear, and pain all threatening to overwhelm me.

Garrett shook me hard, forcing me to open my eyes and look at him. "I had it all worked out too," he said. "On our honeymoon I talked Seely into moving overseas, but she wanted to come back home for the holidays, and I knew she'd get suspicious if I pushed too hard, so when we got back, I drafted up that motion for Kendra's divorce the second I could. I figured that'd throw the suspicion permanently onto Tristan, but then you and your bitch of a partner had to keep picking away at things, didn't you?" He snarled viciously at me, shaking me one last time before dropping me again. My body landed with a hard thud on the floor. Garrett then stepped over my still-twitching form. He headed toward the kitchen. "Where're your keys?" he demanded.

I wiggled my fingers and managed to move my hand. *"Keys!"* he shouted from the kitchen.

I closed my eyes, and more tears leaked down my cheeks. Candice would send help, but once Garrett found my keys, we'd be out of here in less than a minute. And although it felt like a lifetime, really only about two minutes had passed since Velkune had come into the house. Candice would've called me back before calling the police. Their response time was good, but was it two minutes good?

I heard footsteps approach and I opened my eyes just in time to duck my chin as he kicked me in the back. That one I felt because it just about knocked all the air out of my lungs. *"KEYS!"*

Somehow I managed to whisper, "Up . . . ," and point with one shaking finger toward the stairs. Garrett swore and tore up the steps. My keys weren't up there, however; they were in my purse resting on a hook in the front hall closet. I knew that Garrett would do a quick cursory search of the upstairs looking for my keys, and when he didn't find them, he'd come downstairs and kill me. I also knew why he'd picked me over Candice. Candice lived in a crowded high-rise condo, and Garrett would never catch her alone and isolated. But I was a different story. He could lie in wait on a day like today and easily catch me alone. If he killed me, it would devastate her. Two birds, one stone.

The second he'd bolted up the stairs, I knew what I had to do. I set my sights on the coffee table. My body was still convulsing and shaking violently, but I knew I had only one chance left. If he came down those stairs before I reached my goal, I was dead.

Gritting my teeth, I reached out and clawed at the floor, pulling myself only a few inches as I listened to him stomping around upstairs. Focusing with all my might, I tried again, and this time I was able to pull myself several feet. My heart hammered in my chest when I heard furniture being toppled, and I reached again and again, frantic now to get to the beech-wood box resting peacefully on top of the table.

I heard footfalls on the landing and knew Velkune was about to descend the stairs. I clawed again and got to the table. His footsteps started to descend, and I reached up and pulled at the box. It toppled down on top of me, striking me in the cheek, but I barely winced. The latch flipped up and the box cracked open. Garrett was midway down the stairs.

My hand was now shaking so hard, I could barely wedge it into the opening. "You think you're so smart," he was saying as he reached the last few steps. "Sending me on a wild-goose chase upstairs, huh?"

I curled myself around the box, willing my fingers to clutch the grip of the gun and pull it free. "You ever wonder what it's like to be electrocuted, Abby?" he asked as he reached the landing and began to make his way back over to me with that cattle prod held out in front of him sending little blue currents between the two prongs of the fork.

I tore my eyes away from it and focused on the gun.

"If you get hit with one of these at the base of your neck, they say that you can hear the blood in your brain boil before you die."

I clenched my jaw so tight it hurt and rolled to the side just as he raised the prod to jam it into my neck. The rod went into the floor and three bullets went into Garrett Velkune.

He dropped to his knees and stared at me as if he couldn't believe I'd actually shot him. Then he fell over backward and was still.

I managed to squirm over to the sofa and prop myself up against it so I could lay the gun on my belly, still pointing it feebly at Velkune's body, worried that someone that evil might actually thwart death and get up to attack me again. The sound of sirens finally came to my ears, and just then Dutch burst into the room, gun drawn and looking as shaken as I've ever seen him. His eyes darted about the room, spotting first Velkune, then me, then going back to Velkune.

"What the hell happened?" he shouted, his face pale and frightened as he looked again at me.

I managed to wave the gun a little in Garrett's direction. "He brought a cattle prod to a gun fight," I said, and then I actually laughed. It wasn't a good healthy laugh, more like a "I can't believe I just survived that" laugh. It still felt good, either way.

Dutch holstered his weapon and came forward, and just as he got to me I heard someone else's voice coming up the steps. "Dutch? Your car's parked all caca in the driveway. I could barely get my Mercedes to fit and I didn't want to leave it in the street. Those sirens sound like they might be coming this way. I wonder what all the fuss is about?"

And then my sister's face appeared in the door, and she dropped her wedding binder the moment she took in the scene. It made a loud thud, but not as loud as the shriek that erupted out of her when she saw us. Guess that'll be the last time she drops by unexpectedly.

Meanwhile Dutch bent down and picked me up into

his arms. "Sweet Jesus!" he whispered as he cradled me close. "Candice called me and said you were being attacked. I heard the gunshots from down the street and I thought . . ." He didn't finish his sentence; he just held me close.

When he finally let me go a little, I wiped the moisture from his cheeks and managed a weak smile. "Thanks for the wedding present, cowboy," I told him. "On our anniversary, could you maybe get me a holster?"

I was sent to the hospital along with Garrett Velkune, who, miraculously, had survived the three bullets I'd pumped into him. If there was any justice at all to be found that day, it was in the fact that one of those bullets had permanently paralyzed him from the waist down.

The police began to put together the pieces of the Moreno and King cases, and they took a lot of the confession Garrett had given to me to lead them through the discovery of evidence, because Velkune wasn't talking.

His ever-faithful wife had hired the best defense lawyer money could buy, but I doubted it would get him anything other than maybe a life sentence instead of the chair. That was better in my book. I wanted him to suffer for as long as possible.

DNA on Kendra's fetus came back positive to Velkune, and everyone from his wedding remembered him being late to the big event. Someone at Decker Lake also remembered seeing a guy in a ball cap pass by driving a silver Toyota Camry along the lake road, but then later seeing the same man jogging the other way on that road with no sign of the car. Investigators found a path through the woods behind Donna's house that led to that part of the road, and they knew that was likely the route that Velkune had taken back to Donna's after dumping the car.

If he killed Kendra before dumping the car or after was something I was left to wonder about. My guess was that he'd hauled her to Donna's, probably hiding her in the garage, where he'd hog-tied and gagged her before heading out to dump her car in the lake. He'd then hurried back to finish her off. The reason I thought this was that he was a sick fecker, he enjoyed torturing women, and he'd mentioned to me that he'd gone back to retrieve his cattle prod from the garage, which was when Seely had seen him.

Donna King's car was never found, but I suspected that if the area lake levels dropped low enough during a summer drought, it'd show up. The police didn't really need it anyway. They had Velkune's cattle prod, which perfectly matched the burn marks on her body.

There was also the testimony of three very pretty girls from small towns along the Texas rodeo circuit from several years back who'd been attacked in their homes by a man with a cattle prod. Their statements all described the same thing—a man in a ball cap had knocked on their doors, claimed that his truck had broken down, and he'd asked to use their phones. The moment their backs were turned, he'd zapped them with a cattle prod. He'd then taken them out to the woods, tied them up, and raped them. None of the poor girls had been murdered, thank God, but all of them remember their rapist as looking remarkably like Velkune. DNA from at least one of the rape kits was sure to be a match, I figured.

All in all the DA had a solid case, thanks to the team of Fusco and Cooper, but did they thank us? No. Some minds are just locked up tight, I guess.

Still, we did discover one ally—the newbie detective Dutch had befriended was fast discovering that I was a pretty good resource, and he made a point to send me flowers and a note of appreciation. I showed the card to Candice, who grinned and said, "I guess we found our reliable source at APD."

I smiled too. "Yeah, but I'll miss Purcell."

Candice laughed. She was looking better and better since her bout with the bad shrimp salad.

Over the course of the next week, things really settled down, which I was very grateful for—except for one tiny thing that blew up quite unexpectedly the following Friday. I received a frantic call from my sister—which I actually took for a change—and at her urging flipped on the news. There on the screen lit up like a bonfire was the venue for our nuptials—completely ablaze. Cat was actually crying into the phone, and it took me about an hour to calm her down.

Dutch called me too, right after I hung up with Cat. "Did you hear?" he said.

"I'm watching it right now," I told him.

"It was a grease fire in the kitchen," he told me. "The old place went up like a dried-out Christmas tree. They were lucky no one was hurt."

"So I guess we're back on for an elopement?" I asked hopefully.

Dutch laughed. "I like how your brain works, Edgar."

My phone beeped and I looked at the display. "That's Cat, cowboy; she's pretty upset. Let me call you back."

I hung up with Dutch and clicked over to Cat. "Great news!" she said, and the switch from distraught to happy was so fast in her that it took me a minute to catch up.

"What?" I asked. "What's great news?"

"I found another venue!"

I blinked. "How? I only hung up with you ten minutes ago!"

"Money can make things happen fast, Abby," Cat said. "Anyway, we'll have to move the date up to October thirty-first—"

"Are you crazy?" I said to her. "I can't get married on Halloween!"

"Oh, pish!" she scolded. "Abby, it's just a date on a calendar. We don't have to have a Halloween theme or anything."

But Halloween had never been a good day for me. Bad things always seemed to happen to me at the end of October. "Cat—," I tried, but her bulldozer was in high gear.

"I have to go," she said. "I've got to call the caterer, the band, the flower shop, the photographer, etcetera, etcetera. Thank God those wedding invitations didn't go out yet. I'll have to change the date on those right away to get them out in today's mail."

"Cat—," I tried again, but she'd already hung up.

Well, that confirmed it. I'd felt something very bad was going to happen at my wedding, and the venue burning down and the date being moved to Halloween pretty much counted as "very bad."

The thing of it is, however, that on that morning in late October, I didn't even know the half of it yet.

But that's another story . . .

Turn the page for an excerpt from
Victoria Laurie's next Psychic Eye Mystery,

Deadly Forecast

Coming in July 2013 from
Obsidian Hardcover

The first thing I noticed after regaining consciousness was a splitting headache and how uncomfortable I was. My head throbbed, but more than that, my body felt wrapped in iron. With effort I tried to sit up, and so many realizations sprinted into my brain that it made the ache in my head even more acute.

The ensuing dump of adrenaline quashed much of the headache, but I was hardly relieved. My fingers found the metal cage wrapped around my torso, and also the wires poking out from a device centered over my heart.

I knew exactly what that device was—I'd seen the havoc it could wreak firsthand, and I also knew I had very little time left to live. Feeling a sob bubble up from the center of my chest, I did my best to quell it—I had to think!

But thinking proved nearly impossible. "Oh, God!" I whispered, as tears filled my eyes. Carefully, and I do mean *carefully*, I moved my fingers along the metal, hunting for a way out. It was then that I realized I was wearing a bundle of cloth that made movement even more cumbersome. Lifting my chin, I looked down at myself. I was wrapped in metal and white silk.

Raising my right arm, I saw the ornate lace of the cuff and I could feel the puffy fabric around my arms, but I could also feel that my shoulders were nearly exposed and as I turned my head from side to side, I could see that the wedding dress I'd been wrapped in was about four sizes too big.

This wasn't my wedding dress, though, so why would it fit? I knew who it belonged to, and also who'd dressed me in it and strapped the metal, wires, and timepiece to my chest.

Looking around the room, I was shocked to realize where I was. Lying on a large king-sized four-poster bed with soft linens, romantic lighting, and a painting on the wall of the manor home where I was to be married, I knew this had to be the little cottage my sister had told me about. Dutch and I would have come here after the reception and fallen into this bed together to begin our life together as man and wife, but instead, I was strapped to a bomb that would likely go off before all the wedding guests had arrived.

And then my breath caught again. Had the countdown already begun? How long had I been out? I swallowed hard and summoned the courage to slowly prop myself up on my elbows, searching out the digital numbers and hoping for time.

"Hello, Banes," said a voice, and my gaze snapped to the other side of the room where a figure sat, speaking into a disposable cell phone. "The clock is now ticking. You have two hours."

And then, as if on cue, there was a little beep from the device strapped to my chest and as I looked down, I could see a digital display come to life. Even though it was upside down, I could tell the countdown had begun. I had two hours to live.

My thoughts railed against the reality of it. How could this have happened to me? And how was it that I hadn't seen it coming?

But as I stared in shock at the digital display counting down the seconds I had left to live, I realized the clues had been there all along. I'd simply failed to put them together. I'd been focused in another direction entirely, and it'd never occurred to me that I would end up as the target.

My thoughts darted back to when I knew that fate had turned against me—a mere two weeks earlier—to the day I'd gotten involved and I'd unwittingly altered everything.

I remembered the start of that day well. It'd been a beautiful fall morning, with temps in the low seventies. My fiancé had brought me breakfast in bed. He'd looked so worried as he set the tray of pancakes down next to me. "How're you feeling?"

"I'm fine," I assured him, moving my legs under the covers so he could see they were functioning properly. Two Saturdays ago had been awful. I'd solved the case of a missing woman and in doing so I'd nearly paid with my life. I'd incurred a few injuries, and I'd taken it very easy for a week, doing little more than resting on the couch and catching up on my sleep.

"Any pain?" Dutch asked. He'd been crazy busy with work, and had gotten in late most evenings, so he hadn't seen me improve much over the course of the week.

"No, no real pain," I assured him. "But I am still a little sore from the beating."

Dutch pulled down the comforter to eye my right thigh with concern. It was covered in purple and black bruises. "I'll bring you up an ice pack."

I put a hand on his arm to keep him from leaving me. "Later, cowboy. Right now I just want to look at you."

My fiancé, Dutch Rivers, is about the most gorgeous hunk'a man you've ever seen. He's tall, blond, and muscular, with midnight blue eyes, a firm jaw, and a beautifully straight nose.

He's just as handsome on the inside too. And for whatever reason, he's crazy about me. Which is his only fault, because I'm a handful. Just ask him, and he'll tell you. Heck, just ask *anyone* in my inner circle about how I can be, and they'll ask you how much time you have.

Still, for whatever reason, the Dutch and Abby partnership has always worked, and after three and a half years together, we were about to make it official with a walk down the aisle. "Your physical therapist called," Dutch said, scooting onto the bed to help me eat the pancakes. (And by "help" I mean one bite for me, five bites for him. . . .)

"Ugh. I forgot I had an appointment with her today."

"I told her you were canceling."

I eyed him with surprise. "Why?"

"Are you kidding?"

"No. I can make the appointment, sweetie."

"Edgar," he said, using his pet name for me after famed psychic Edgar Cayce. "There's no way you can go to physical therapy with a leg that looks like that."

You'd think by now Dutch would know better than to tell me what I could and couldn't do. "Oh, please," I said, throwing the covers to the side and easing my legs gingerly out from under them. "It looks way worse than it is. Besides, we're getting married at the end of the month, cowboy. There's no way I'm giving up on the idea of walking down that aisle without my cane."

Several months earlier I'd been in a really bad accident, and my pelvis had been broken in several places. My recovery had been very slow, frustrating, and painful. (But mostly for my friends and family. For me, it'd been that times a hundred.) Still, I was determined to at least gimp my way down that aisle.

Dutch responded to my declaration with a skeptically raised eyebrow.

I glared at him. "Challenge accepted," I said, before carefully planting my feet and standing up. Very slowly I took one small step, mentally crossing my fingers that I wouldn't fall. To my surprise, the step didn't hurt or feel weak; it felt sure and steady. Encouraged, I took another step. Then another. And another. And another. Then one more for good measure.

When I looked behind me, Dutch was sitting straight up and staring at me in shock. "How long have you been able to walk that far without your cane?"

I glanced down at my toes gleefully. I hadn't taken more than three steps on my own since the accident. I'd just doubled my long-distance record. "I haven't been able to do more than three steps until today! Holy freakballs, honey! I can walk!" And then my hip gave out and I fell face-first into the wing chair by the window.

Dutch was at my side in a hot second. "You okay?" he asked, picking me up into his arms.

Embarrassed, I swiped at my hair, which had fallen over my eyes, and tried to play it off. "I meant to do that."

Dutch chuckled. "Of course you did."

"No, really. I did. How else could I get you to sweep me off my feet?"

Dutch leaned forward to give me a kiss, but I stopped him because now that I'd actually walked several steps, I wanted some reassurance. "Honey, do you think I'll really be able to make it down the aisle without the cane?"

"Have you given any thought to an escort?" he asked.

I frowned. I'm not close with my parents, and by that, I mean I don't speak to them and haven't in years, so I'd always planned on walking down the aisle alone at my wedding.

"Abs, I only say that because if you're determined to leave the cane behind, having someone at your side to lean on would help steady you, and if you choose the right guy, he'll protect you from falling if you trip or your hip gives out."

I eyed him with interest. "Who volunteered?"

"Milo, Brice, Dave, and—curiously—Director Gaston."

That got me to smile. "Brice is out," I said right away. "He's Candice's groomsman. And Dave will be so nervous he'll trip over his own two feet and take me down with him. I couldn't walk with Director Gaston, because walking down the aisle with your boss's boss would make *me* so nervous I'd trip for sure."

"So it's Milo?" Dutch asked hopefully.

I frowned again and shook my head. "He's your best man. I can't take him away from you."

"He's willing to do double duty, dollface."

"You five guys have already talked about this, huh?"

"We have."

"Who's your pick?"

"Milo. I trust him to take care of you."

"You really think I should walk with someone?"

Dutch leaned in for his kiss and did his best Humphrey Bogart impression. "I do, I do, I do, sweethot."

In a flash I had the most horrible feeling wash over me in a strange sort of déjà vu. The sensation was so intense that I actually gasped.

Dutch mistook that for desire and gave me a passionate kiss that normally would have started those belly embers burnin', but instead I stiffened and pushed at him.

He pulled away immediately. "What's wrong?"

I gripped his shirt in my hands and stared intensely at him. The intuitive feeling rippling along my energy suggested that some terrible fate awaited my fiancé. And by terrible, I mean deadly. "Something's wrong."

Dutch held very still. After almost four years together he could read me like a book. "A vision?"

I shook my head. "Not exactly." That terrible feeling of something really, really, *really* bad happening to him wouldn't leave. I continued to stare at him, trying to make sense of the psychic vibe surging between us. I couldn't see what would happen to him, but I knew that some new and terrible danger was lurking in the shadows somewhere. And I knew he was defenseless against it. His fate felt so completely fatal that it set my heart racing in a panic. "What is it?" I whispered, trying to isolate the origins of this threat.

"What's what, doll?" he asked me, his eyes searching my face.

My gaze locked with his, and I almost couldn't form the words. "You're in danger, Dutch."

His brows rose. "Me?"

"Yes," I said, cupping his face and feeling a cold shiver take root at the base of my spine. "It's connected to your work."

His expression softened. "Comes with the territory," he said, full of that bravado that makes courageous men say and do stupid things.

Dutch works for the FBI, and although his division is more focused on solving cold cases than active ones, it still means that he has to deal with the occasional dicey situation.

But this wasn't just a dicey situation. This was his murder. And the fact that it felt so close and so definite left me reeling and panic-stricken. "Dutch," I said, my eyes welling with tears. "Please don't go to work today."

He looked down at me in puzzlement. "Edgar, what is it?"

I opened my mouth but couldn't find the words to articulate what I was picking up in the ether. It was like a thousand warning bells going off all around us, and I knew with absolute certainty that before the month was out, my fiancé, the person I loved most in the world, would be dead. I choked on a sob and threw my arms around his neck, clinging to him, and willing him to stay next to me where I could try to keep him safe.

New York Times bestselling author

VICTORIA LAURIE

Deadly Forecast
A Psychic Eye Mystery

It's said to be good luck if it rains on your wedding day, but Abby sees something darker than storm clouds on the horizon. She's just had a disturbing premonition of her fiancé's murder. Her husband-to-be has been assigned to a case involving a series of suicide bombings, and Abby's spirit guides warn her of imminent danger.

FBI agent Dutch Rivers is keeping his cool, but Abby can't quell her anxiety. After another suicide bombing at a local beauty salon, Abby vows to do everything in her power to keep Dutch safe and get him to the altar. But on the morning of the ceremony, she finds herself in a dire situation, with time running out....

"Victoria Laurie's books are intense, compelling, and unforgettable. I always have a hard time putting them down."
—Once Upon a Romance

Available wherever books are sold or at
penguin.com

Facebook.com/TheCrimeSceneBooks

om0112

VICTORIA LAURIE

The Psychic Eye Mysteries

Abby Cooper is a psychic intuitive.
And trying to help the police solve crimes
seems like a good enough idea—but it could
land her in more trouble than even she could
see coming.

AVAILABLE IN THE SERIES

Abby Cooper, Psychic Eye
Better Read Than Dead
A Vision of Murder
Killer Insight
Crime Seen
Death Perception
Doom with a View
A Glimpse of Evil
Vision Impossible
Lethal Outlook

Available wherever books are sold or at
penguin.com

OM0014